THE
HIGHLANDER'S
BARGAIN

D1023967

802-503-1357

Also by Barbara Longley

The Novels of Loch Moigh
True to the Highlander

Love from the Heartland series, set in Perfect, Indiana
Far from Perfect
The Difference a Day Makes
A Change of Heart

390750475626022

THE
HIGHLANDER'S
BARGAIN

A Novel of Loch Moigh

Barbara Longley

Withdrawn/ABCL

 Montlake
Romance

This is a work of fiction. Names, characters, organizations, places, events, and incidents are either products of the author's imagination or are used fictitiously.

Text copyright © 2014 Barbara Longley
All rights reserved.

No part of this book may be reproduced, or stored in a retrieval system, or transmitted in any form or by any means, electronic, mechanical, photocopying, recording, or otherwise, without express written permission of the publisher.

Published by Montlake Romance, Seattle

www.apub.com

Amazon, the Amazon logo, and Montlake Romance are trademarks of Amazon.com, Inc., or its affiliates.

ISBN-13: 9781477823927
ISBN-10: 1477823921

Cover design by becker&mayer! LLC
Illustrated by Dana Ashton France

Library of Congress Control Number: 2014903124

Printed in the United States of America

This book is dedicated to Robert W. Longley.
Thank you, Dad, for igniting the spark of curiosity that
still burns brightly. Thank you for encouraging me to
exercise my imagination. I miss you!

CHAPTER ONE

Scotland, 1426

Robley sat in his uncle's solar, his thoughts drifting like thistle-down in a stiff breeze. His father, uncle and cousin droned on and on about their clan's kine, the condition of this year's crops, the villagers and the needs of their crofters. He placed his elbows on the table and scrubbed his face with both hands, stifling the urge to yawn.

"Something ailing you, lad?" Robley's uncle William, the earl of Fife, asked, his tone slightly exasperated.

Robley straightened, taking his elbows off the table. "Nay, just a bit fatigued."

"Mayhap less time spent in the village inn drinking and carousing and more time sleeping at night would no' be amiss," the earl scolded.

Robley's brow shot up, but he kept his mouth shut. Since the return of their King James to take his rightful place on Scotland's throne, Robley's role in their clan's welfare had been reduced to that of page. He ran errands, carried messages and aided his father in the execution of his duties as seneschal for the MacKintosh holdings.

Robley's future, right down to the kine, the crops and the crofters, offered little in the way of excitement. The drinking and carousing gave him a brief respite from the powerful yearning for adventure plaguing him and filling his dreams.

He sorely missed the days when he had a battle or a tournament to anticipate. He missed the adventures he'd had with his brother and cousin while traipsing across the continent. Malcolm and Liam were settled with families to raise. Peace had its merits, aye, but naught stirred the blood like a war of wits and brawn.

"'Tis long past time you took a wife, my lad." His father placed a hand on Robley's shoulder and gave it a shake. "Your mother and I long to dandle both our sons' bairns on our knees. We wish to see you settled and content." Robert turned to his brother "What say you, William? Shall we cast about for a suitable bride for my lad? Mayhap the ladies can recommend a willing lass with a generous dowry."

Settled? His mouth went dry. He couldn't be much more settled than he was now, and the tedium was killing him. "Ah . . ."

His cousin Malcolm smirked. "Aye, Rob. 'Tis time you married. Have you no' said you wished to find a braw and bonnie lass like my True?"

"There are none like your lady here." He scowled. "Shall I seek the faerie who sent her to you through time, and request she fetch me a bride from the future as well?" Had he given voice to his heart's desire? Was this the source of his restless obsession? Aye, and truth be told, he wanted to find the lass himself. He yearned to see with his own eyes the wonders the future held: airplanes, automobiles and lights that came on by the mere flick of a switch. These were but a few of the marvels True had mentioned. How could he not turn his mind once again to the fantastic tales she told of her life in the twenty-first century? His obsession. He longed to see the future. 'Twould be his last adventure. How he kent this, he could not say, but the certainty had lodged itself firmly in his gut, and he could not free himself of the notion.

Malcolm shrugged. "My wife was sent here to save a life. That we fell in love had naught to do with Giselle's purpose, and I dinna suppose her ilk take well to requests of any kind. 'Tis best to stay as far from the fae as possible, lest you get caught up in their machinations. We mere mortals are naught but pawns to them."

"Aye, keep your distance, Rob." The earl rose from his chair. "You've a responsibility to our clan. One day you will take your father's place as seneschal, as Malcolm will take mine. I remember what it is to be young and restless, but have a care. The well-being of our people rests squarely upon our shoulders." He fixed Robley to the spot with a stern stare. "Come. We've work to do, and the hour grows late."

"I ken well my responsibilities, Uncle." He pushed his chair back and stood, chafing at the scolding. He was a man of four and twenty, and a blooded warrior besides. "If anyone should need me to carry a message or inventory the buttery, I'll be in the lists." His remark garnered sharp looks, but no more reprimands. Striding out of the solar, he contemplated his situation.

He could let his family arrange a marriage for him. Mayhap he'd even come to care for whomever they chose, but would he love her? Would his heart thrill at the sight of her, as Malcolm's did still when his lady wife entered the room? "No' bloody likely."

Jealousy burned a path through him, and the weight of his future settled upon his shoulders like a yoke. One more adventure—was it too much to ask?—and then he'd settle into his predestined role within the clan.

He took the stairs down to the great hall, pausing when he found his cousin's wife there consulting with their cook, Molly. Lady True was already growing large with her second bairn, and another pang of jealousy shot through him. He wanted a family of his own, but not without love. The indignity of the scolding he'd received still stung, along with the restless desire to act. He waited until True sent

Molly on her way before approaching. A plan, such as it was, had germinated in his mind for far too long. The time was at hand to put it into motion. "Good morn, True. How do you fare?"

"I'm fine." She rubbed her belly and studied him in that piercing way she had. Her abilities as a truth-sayer had saved their clan more than once, and now she turned her powers his way. "What troubles you, Robley?"

"There's something I wish to ask. A favor." His resolve firmed. The more he thought about it, the more powerfully the notion took hold. "Do you have a moment to walk about the bailey?" He offered his arm.

"Of course. I always have time for you." She grinned and took his arm. "If it's within my power to help, you know I will, but I sense whatever it is will be met with opposition from our family."

"Aye, which is why we will keep it between ourselves." He led her out the door. Deep into summer, the air was warm, and the sky held fat clouds to offer shade from the hot sun. "Do you recall the time I helped you secure weapons against Malcolm's wishes?"

"Of course I do." She laughed. "And now you plan to use that to leverage a payback?"

"If it will help." He drew a breath, gathering all of his courage and determination. "I wish to visit the future. Nay, that does no' describe what I feel." He shook his head. "It's something I must do, and I canna free myself from the certainty that I'm meant to go there for some reason."

Her brow furrowed as she studied him once again. "It's possible that what you feel is a form of manipulation." Her expression filled with concern. "You know I don't have the power to send you to the future, nor do I have the power to prevent you from trying to get there on your own.

"Madame Giselle sought me out because of the little bit of faerie blood running through my veins. You know how Giselle loves to meddle. Had it not been for her, I would still be living my life in the twenty-first century." She squeezed his forearm. "I sense she might be stirring the pot here, and you can't trust her. Be careful."

"I ken well enough the fae canna be trusted, but . . ." Their clan had ties to the fae, especially Madame Giselle, because Hunter, True and Malcolm's foster son, was her direct descendant. He raked his free hand through his hair, unsure how to put words to what stirred within him. "Giselle cares for you, Hunter and your daughter, aye? When she brought you to us, 'twas for good. Think of the lives you've saved, True. Mayhap her purpose will also be for the good of our clan. Did you no' tell us when we needed help, help would come to us? Was that no' the vow Giselle made to you and Malcolm?"

"Hmm. 'When you need help the most, help shall find you,' is what she said. More like a benediction than a vow, and not necessarily directed at our clan as a whole." She placed her hand protectively over the bairn growing inside her. "I might be all wrong about her having anything to do with your compulsion. Your desire may stem from your own curiosity about my time and nothing more."

"I dinna ken, nor do I care. The future is all I've thought of since you shared with us the truth of your journey here. Are you no' tired of my pestering you for more of your tales?"

"I am, and your relentlessness is the reason I suspect Giselle is behind it. You're not normally obsessive about anything." She shook her head. "And you know when I sense the hidden truths in any given situation, it's wise for all of us to listen—including me. My abilities have never led us astray, have they?"

"Nay, your abilities have saved lives, mine included. Whether 'tis compulsion or no', if Giselle is still to be found in Inverness, I *will* see her. There's naught you can say that will prevent me from doing what I must. The favor I ask is that you help me prepare."

"There's no guarantee Giselle will send you anywhere but out her door." She brought her thumbnail to her mouth, a sure sign she gave serious consideration to his request. "Malcolm is going to kill me for sure this time."

Triumph surged. "Do you still have the paper currency from your time? That and information are all I seek. My cousin canna be angered by a simple exchange of knowledge, can he?"

"Can't he?" Her brow rose. "This is my husband we're talking about. Overbearing, controlling and arrogant to the bone."

He winked at her. "Dinna tell him."

Robley walked toward the edge of the village on his way to the cottage where Madame Giselle was rumored to live while in Inverness. According to the villagers, he'd find her there this very day. Things had fallen into place neatly. Only a fortnight had passed since his conversation with True, and he'd been sent to Inverness to settle a dispute on the earl's behalf. He couldn't help but feel even more certain this was meant to be.

He reached into his sporran to check that the currency and debit card True had given him were safely tucked away. She'd explained about ATMs and instructed him on their use. He could scarce believe her. A metal box would spew money at him when he entered the correct sequence of numbers? He shook his head.

At the very end of the road, a path veered to the right toward the wood. He took it, following the cool, shaded trail through the forest. The evergreen tang of pine and yew filled the air, and the boughs cast dark shadows across the path before him. The farther he went, the more the fine hairs at the back of his neck rose, and his palms grew damp. He put his hand on the hilt of his dagger, scanning the shadows for the source of his unease. A murder of crows took flight above him, their raucous cawing sending his heart racing. He drew his sword and crouched, ready to fight. Shaking his head at his folly, he straightened and slid his claymore back into his scabbard. What good was a man's sword against magic?

As courageous as any knight of the realm, he had no difficulty facing a mortal enemy. Facing the fae, however, was entirely another matter. They were not mortal, nor were they of this natural world. The *Tuatha Dé Danann* held power and sorcery far beyond his ken, and no matter how set his mind or how brave his heart, he could not keep his soul from recoiling at the very thought of being in Madame Giselle's presence.

Wiping the sweat from his brow, he considered turning back. What business did he have consorting with the fae? What if Giselle sent him to the future with no way to return, like she had sent Lady True to the fifteenth century? Why hadn't he considered the possibility? Mayhap because Giselle truly had compelled him to come to her, and it had naught to do with his own free will. His chest tightened, and he stood rooted to the spot. The rasp of his labored breathing filled the unnatural silence.

"Are you lost, lad?" The old crone appeared from out of nowhere. She held a walking stick in one hand and a basket filled with plants in the other.

Robley nearly jumped out of his skin. She hadn't stepped onto the path from the wood. She'd appeared out of thin air, or so it seemed to him. Her appearance hadn't changed one whit since he'd seen her a decade ago whilst attending the fair at Inverness with his kin. *Unnatural and not of this world.* A chill snaked its way down his spine.

Wrinkled face, silver-streaked dark hair and stooped, she could be ancient . . . or ageless. Dark, birdlike eyes assessed him. She canted her head, waiting, and her visage called to mind the crows that had just taken flight.

He wiped his palms against the wool of his plaid. "I wish to speak with you, Madame Giselle, if you've a moment."

"With me?" The wrinkles lining her face deepened with amusement. "Do you wish to know what the future holds in store for you,

Robley of clan MacKintosh? Shall I tell your fortune?" Her eyes narrowed. "'Twill cost you dear."

"I . . . I seek a favor." That she knew his name came as a shock, and fear gripped his very bones. Nay. His father was the earl's brother and seneschal over all the MacKintosh holdings. They were oft in Inverness, sometimes staying for months at a time. The entire village knew who he was. Why wouldn't Giselle? He took a deep, calming breath and let it out slowly. "'Tis no' my fortune or my future I've come to speak with you about."

"Hmm. Is it not?" She turned on the path. "Come. I would hear this favor of yours, but first a cup of tea." She started down the path, leading him farther from the village.

His feet remained fixed in place, while the instinct for self-preservation battled with his compulsion for adventure. He should turn on his heel and run for the safety of the portcullis.

"Come, lad," Giselle called without turning back. "'Tis far too late to turn back now."

She lifted a hand in a slight wave, and his legs moved him forward against his will. Goose bumps skittered like mice along his skin, and the prickle of fear had him uttering prayers beneath his breath as his family's warnings came back to him. No adventure was worth putting his life at risk, and he had no doubt that his life now balanced on the cutting edge of fate's blade. "I've changed my mind," he called out.

Giselle's eerie cackle nearly brought him to his knees. "Shite," he muttered as a fresh sheen of sweat drenched him. He had no choice but to move forward, for his legs were still not abiding by his will. For certes the faerie had her own agenda where he was concerned, and he was no longer certain that it might be for good. How could he have been so naïve?

The path opened to a clearing where a neat cottage stood at the center. Constructed of timber, wattle and daub, the dwelling boasted a newly thatched roof. The toft surrounding the cottage was also tidy, and a few chickens wandered about, pecking the ground, foraging for insects and grain. The sight of the ordinary home eased his panic, and his legs were his own once more. Had he imagined they'd carried him forward of their own volition? Giselle opened the sturdy wooden door and gestured for him to enter.

All manner of herbs hung from the rafters, along with onions, garlic and other vegetables, permeating the interior with savory, earthy smells. A small hearth held a banked fire. Giselle swung a blackened pot hanging from an iron hook over the glowing embers. She stirred the flames back to life and added a square of peat. "Sit."

He obeyed, curiosity and resolve filling him. Taking one of the two chairs by the scarred wooden table, he kept his eye on her as she fetched two earthenware mugs from a row of shelves built into the wall. True had come to no harm from this being, and if Giselle wished him ill, there was naught he could do to stop her. He swallowed against the tightness in his throat. He'd come for a reason, and he meant to see it through.

He turned his attention to the interior of the dwelling. Giselle lived comfortably. The cottage even had a wood-plank floor instead of packed dirt like so many others. Like the yard, the inside was tidy and held a wealth of household goods. A narrow staircase led to a sleeping loft above, and two curtained windows let in the light and fresh air.

Giselle set a mug of fragrant tea in front of him and took her seat. "What is it you want from me?" she asked, a speculative gleam in her eye.

"I wish to visit the future."

"Ha! And you believe I'm the one to send you there? What nonsense! I am but a humble healer is all. I tell fortunes and read palms on occasion to supplement my coffers."

"Nay." He shook his head. "You are so much more. I ken you have the power. You sent Alethia Goodsky through time. Our lady

True told us the tale and revealed enough from the future that I dinna doubt her word. I ken you are one of the ancient ones, *Tuatha Dé Danann*. Faerie. True told us that as well."

"I see. Then you also *ken* 'tis folly for *your* kind to come begging favors from *my* kind." She shrugged her bony shoulders. "There was a time when such was possible, even commonplace, but it is against our laws to meddle in human affairs now."

The need to persuade her flooded his senses. "Yet you did so when you brought True to us. You live amongst my kind, tell fortunes and predict futures. Meddlesome activities by all accounts. What is to prevent you from doing so once more?"

She crossed her arms in front of her and shook her head, her wrinkled face resolute. "Nay. 'Tis impossible."

"I know you needed True to do something for you when you took her through the ages. Is there naught I can do? Can we no' barter for what we both might want?"

Giselle tapped her chin and scrutinized him. "Did she tell you my true identity? Do you know my name?"

"Nay." He frowned. "What has that to do with my request?"

"Everything." She cackled again.

The flesh on his arms and at the back of his neck rose. Her visage shimmered and shifted. A bright blue light shone from her eyes and surrounded her form. A shudder ran down his spine and sent his blood thundering through his veins.

"There is something," she muttered. "Simple really. So simple the task hardly warrants the favor *you* seek in exchange, but . . ."

"Aye?" His ears rang from the pounding of his poor heart. "What is it?"

"I wish you to retrieve something that was taken from me—a silver platter chased with gold. It belongs to me and holds great sentimental value."

"Where might I find this item?"

"In Avalon, the realm of the *Tuatha Dé Danann*. You cannot get there on your own, for it is betwixt this world and the realm of shadow." The shimmer and blue light dissipated, and her appearance became that of an old crone once again. "I must send you there and bring you back."

"If you ken where this thing is, and it's within your realm, why do you no' fetch it for yourself? If you can send me to it and bring me back . . ." He frowned. What was he getting himself into?

She pushed her mug away and rose from her place. "It is of no importance to *me* whether or not you go to the future, mortal. My reasons are not your concern. You grow wearisome and impertinent." She crossed the room to the door and opened it. "Good day to you."

The air grew cold, and once again the blue light formed a halo around Giselle. Fearing he'd let his chance slip away, he pushed his doubts aside. "I'll do it. I'll get your platter for you, if in exchange you'll provide me with the means to visit the future and return when I will it. Do we have a bargain?"

"Done." Her birdlike eyes held a sharp-edged glint.

Her satisfied smile sent another tremor of self-doubt through him. He opened his mouth to rescind the offer just as she raised her hand and formed runes of bright blue in the air. In a trice, all that he knew disappeared, and in its place a thick mist swirled and eddied around him. He didn't move and hardly breathed. Where had she taken him? What if the vapors swirling around him were poisonous? By the Virgin, what had he done? Panic stole his reason, and he waved his arms at the mist in an effort to see beyond the curtain. "Saints preserve me, what sort of hellish place is this?" Giselle's laughter echoed through the mist, just as her voice filled his head.

"It is a void dimension, a place where, with our magic, we create whatever reality we wish for our own comfort and pleasure. Be still, mortal. You will come to no harm. I am placing you exactly where you will find the object you are to fetch. The mist will clear, and your

task will be easier than you ever imagined. Breathe. 'Tis naught but ordinary mist."

He did as he was told, and gradually the swirling curtain thinned. He found himself in a corridor, very much like those he'd find in keeps throughout Scotia. The familiar sight lessened the fear gripping him, but not by much. He flattened himself against the stone wall.

"No one is about. My kin are all at court, and we've no use for guards here. You can cease trying to blend in with the stone against your back."

Giselle's condescending tone sparked his indignation. He was not a wee lad to cower with his back to the wall. Stepping away from the stones at his back, he rested his hand on the hilt of his dagger.

"Your weapons are useless in our realm, human. Move forward. You will come to a door on your left. Go into the chamber, and I will direct you to that which I seek."

He followed her direction, and the door she spoke of loomed before him. He slipped inside to a richly appointed chamber. A thick rug covered the floor beside an opulent bed with the finest velvet curtains. There on the mantelpiece over the hearth, he saw a number of items displayed, including a round silver platter.

"That's it. There on the mantel." Giselle's voice held an edge of excitement. "It's mine, made for me eons ago and given as a wedding gift. Take it quickly. Someone comes."

Footsteps and voices echoed through the corridor, growing louder by the second. He strode to the mantel and snatched the disk, clutching it to his chest. The tugging sensation took hold, and again he was dragged through the gray mist from the realm of the fae. In an instant, Robley returned to Giselle's cottage, the pilfered item still clutched to his chest. He set it on the table. "I've done my part."

"So you have." She turned the platter over and traced her finger reverently over the inlaid gold. "So you have."

"Now for your part—"

"Impatience?" Giselle straightened and raised an eyebrow. "Very well then." She crossed the room and took a large wooden box from the floor, carrying it to the table. She set it down and opened the lid. "Now, I'm sure I put them in here," she muttered while rummaging through the contents. "Ah, here they are." Her eyes lit up, and she lifted a small leather pouch. "Listen carefully." Placing the pouch in his hand, she gestured for him to sit.

He pressed the leather between his hands, trying to ascertain its contents.

"This holds two crystals, tokens for your passage to the future and back. Wherever you choose to depart from will be the very point of your return. Hold fast in your mind the time and place you wish to be, and spin one of the crystals like you would a child's toy."

"A toy?" His brow rose, and he tugged the pouch open to take a look.

"Not now." Giselle covered his hands with hers. "Just listen. When you spin the crystal, you'll see a change in the air above it. Remember—hold fast the time and place you wish to visit, and step into the disturbance. Time travel is not always exact," she warned. "Less so on the journey to than from. You will always return to the exact spot of your departure, but you must also hold the time you mean to return to in your mind. It's crucial, or you may end up in an era not your own."

"I understand." He stood and opened his sporran, dropping the pouch inside. Much had to be done before he began his grand adventure. He wanted one more conversation with True before he left. He needed more details about the Renaissance fair in New York she'd been attending when Giselle had taken her. The fair would be the perfect destination. His appearance would not be so odd in such a place. Aye, it felt right. "My thanks, Madame Giselle."

"Do not thank me yet, lad. You've no idea whether or not the trip will be to your liking." She walked toward the door behind him.

"Good luck to you. May you find whatever it is you seek on your journey."

Floating on a cloud of elation, he took his leave and set his course for Castle Inverness. Tomorrow he'd start out for home. He'd return to Loch Moigh with his fate held securely in a leather pouch within his sporran. Bloody hell! He'd just been to the realm of the fae and lived to tell the tale. How many men could say the like? Fetching the silver disk had been simple, just as Giselle had said.

For certes he'd gotten the better end of the bargain. Hadn't he?

CHAPTER TWO

Erin swiped at the perspiration wrecking her makeup and checked the ground at the base of the cottonwood. She didn't want to get anything on her Renaissance gown during her short break. Scanning the area for anthills, she set down her bowl of "the Queen's Caramel Apples" and settled herself on the grass.

She tugged off her veil and headpiece, tossing them to the ground. Leaning back against the rough bark, Erin closed her eyes against the mother of all headaches. The unseasonably hot day, constant blowing grit and the smell of fried food and stale beer sure didn't help. She massaged her temples, trying to ease the throbbing. If only she could ease her own pain the same way she did for her patients, but no. Her gifts had never worked like that.

No doubt her headache was stress related, exacerbated by the heat and too many layers of heavy brocade and linen. Maybe if she pounded her head against the tree, she'd knock out the pain. Or not. She let out a long sigh, opened her eyes and stared up at the canopy of leaves.

What was she going to do? Erin was almost at the end of her master's program, so close to getting her midwife certification, and her roommate chose *now* to move out of their apartment without notice? "Just my luck."

She couldn't afford the rent on her own, no matter how much she loved her large, old apartment with its oak floors, trim and built-in buffet. Thinking about the daunting task of finding a cheaper place and moving while school was in full swing sent another throb pounding through her skull. Her plate was already too full. Plus, only one more weekend before the Renaissance festival closed, and this little bit of extra income would come to an end. With classes and clinicals, she hardly had any time to pick up nursing shifts. She could give up sleeping . . .

"Screwed. I'm so screwed."

She surveyed the back lot of the fairgrounds. The grassy field held all the RVs, trucks and trailers the seasonal workers brought with them for their weekends working the fair. The scent of manure drifted to her resting place, reminding her of the state of her life. *Crap.*

Well, there wasn't anything she could do about it right this minute. She brought her treat to her lap, dipped an apple slice into the gooey caramel and took a big bite. The tartness coupled with the caramel was so good she swore her mood lifted a few millimeters. Nothing like a bowl filled with something sweet to bring her spirits up. She popped the remaining bit of apple in her mouth and sorted through her options.

Going to her mother for help was out. She and stepdad-number-four were going through another *rough patch*, and no doubt her mother would soon be single and impoverished again herself. She'd be coming to her daughter for help. It was too late to take out a larger student loan for the semester. Did she have anything to pawn? Nope. She'd just have to float some bills and find a new roommate in a big fat hurry.

Dipping another apple slice into the dark-golden sweetness, she caught movement from the corner of her eye and lifted her gaze, squinting a bit. About five yards from where she sat, heat waves shimmered and rose from the dirt like something radiating off a blacktop road, only way more defined and about a yard wide. As she watched, the anomaly grew even stronger. "What the heck?"

She set her snack aside and pushed herself up to investigate. The moment she rose, the undulating waves took on color. Bands of pale pink and green radiated upward. "Huh, a mini aurora borealis right here in the middle of the grass on a bright sunlit day?"

She moved closer, glancing around to see if anyone else had noticed. No one had. All alone and standing an arm's length away, she fought the urge to reach out and see what would happen if she stuck her hand into the mirage. "Probably not a good idea," she muttered, mesmerized by the dancing light show.

Something changed. A form appeared behind the shimmer. A man? Erin gasped a second before the impact sent her flying. Flat on her back with the wind knocked out of her, she found herself pinned beneath him. She stared into the bluest eyes she'd ever seen. Her mouth went dry, and her heart pummeled her rib cage. Frightened out of her wits, she blinked a few times, hoping he'd disappear and everything would go back to normal. It didn't.

Impossible! Men didn't just fall out of the air. She struggled to regain her breath, and for a moment, he looked as dazed as she felt. "Wha—?" Stunned, all she could do was stare and gasp for breath. "What just happened?" She shoved at his chest. He didn't budge.

"'Tis fortuitous indeed that you are here. I've just come through time."

He grinned, revealing deadly gorgeous dimples on either side of his sexy mouth, a mouth that was only part of the best-looking, totally masculine face she'd ever seen. Tawny blond hair hung to his shoulders, and slightly darker stubble covered his cheeks, chin and throat. He wore a billowing saffron shirt, and an earth-tone muted plaid kilt draped across his chest and over one shoulder. Supporting his weight on his elbows, he stared down at her, his gaze roaming her face. "What year is it, lass?"

Again with the wicked-dimpled grin, stealing her ability to think straight. "Through time?" She struggled to get out from under him. "That's impossible."

"Aye. From the past. What year is it?"

She pushed against his rock-hard chest. His scent, all male, slightly smoky and tinged with an outdoorsy freshness, filled her senses. His heavy weight pressing against her so intimately disturbed her, stirred her up in ways she didn't want. He could be some kind of a con. She should *not* be reacting to a complete stranger like this, especially a stranger who appeared out of thin air. She *should* be calling for help, not getting turned on. She pushed again. "Get off me!"

"Will you abandon me if I do?"

"Absolutely."

"You saw, lass. The doorway through time. You saw, aye?" For a second, she glimpsed a flash of anguish play across his face.

She *had* seen. He'd appeared out of the shimmering, waving aurora borealis thing and slammed right into her. "Not possible," she muttered again, her heart clogging her throat. She tried to force it back where it belonged. "Please get off me."

He canted his head, peering into her eyes with an intensity that stole her breath. "You were there in the very spot at the very moment I came through. 'Twas meant to be. Our meeting like this canna be simply by chance."

"Sure it can." Her heart continued to pound away in her chest, and now spots danced before her eyes. Great. Was she going to faint? *Don't you dare. Breathe!* She sucked in a huge breath and glared at him. "Move, or I'm going to start screaming. You don't want that, do you? Security will haul your butt away so fast you won't know what hit you."

He rolled off, sat up and scrubbed his hands over his face. "My apologies. 'Twas you who put yourself in place to break my fall. Traveling through time is no' an easy task. For certes, I feared I would be torn asunder. I'm no' yet myself. I need a few moments." He searched her face again, his eyes lingering on her mouth and coming back to her eyes. "Will you stay and hear my plea?"

His perusal brought a fresh rush of heat to her face. "Your *plea*? Now that you don't have me pinned to the ground I might," she huffed. "This ought to be good." Her headache forgotten, she scooted a short distance away and sat facing him. Once again she scanned the area for someone she could call out to if she needed help. A couple of men dressed in hose and tunics with swords hanging from their waists were walking toward a trailer nearby. She recognized them.

One was a part of her reenactment group, though she didn't know him well. They'd come running if she shouted. Good, because this whole situation filled her with a mixed bag of anxiety and curiosity. The curiosity proved more powerful. She couldn't walk away without first hearing what the good-looking guy with the heavy Scottish brogue had to say.

Besides, she *had* been standing exactly where he came through, and maybe meeting him wasn't accidental. As far-fetched as his claim of time travel seemed, could he be telling the truth? Now that she was past the shock, she focused all of her energy to get a read on him.

She'd always had the ability to pick up on things about people, mostly physical impressions, and her gifts served her well in the health-care industry. She knew what her patients needed without them having to tell her, even the babies still in the womb. Nothing felt "off" about the man beside her. She didn't sense any darkness within him, only a lively intellect and robust health. He wasn't attempting to conceal anything from her. That fact came through loud and clear.

The alleged time traveler leaped to his feet and offered her a hand. She ignored the proffered help and rose on her own. "It's 2010, by the way."

"Perfect. 'Tis exactly the year True left her time for ours." He rubbed his hands together. "And am I in New York? Is this the Sterling Renaissance Festival? Is it August?"

"Nope. Not even close. You're in Shakopee, Minnesota, and it's almost October." Something flickered across his face—a shot of confusion followed by a fear chaser?

"Shock-o-pee?" His brow creased. "Minnesota, you say?" His hand came up to swipe at the lower half of his face. "'Tis Lady True's realm."

Lady True? "Not where your ticket was supposed to take you, eh?"

"Ticket?" His mouth turned down.

"OK, you said you came here through time, and if I hadn't seen what I just saw with my own eyes . . ." She threw her braid back over her shoulder before reaching for her veil and headpiece. She put them back on and wondered how much time she had left before her break ended. "I'll bite. When are you from?"

"The year of our Lord 1426."

Shock arced along her nerve endings. *So not possible.* Was it? She took in the draped, not pleated, rustic wool he wore, the leather sporran fastened to his belt next to a sheathed dagger, and the broadsword hanging down his back. He stood about five foot nine or ten, and not an inch of him was wasted. Ripped. The man might not be overly tall, but he certainly was a powerhouse.

Glancing at the soft leather boots he wore, she could almost believe he'd walked out of the fifteenth century in them. Still, it had nothing to do with her, and she had enough to deal with on her own without getting drawn in by this man and any pleas he might make.

"Well, beam me up, hot Scotty" she muttered, pulling her iPhone from her pocket. She checked the time. "My break is over. Enjoy your visit." She snatched up her unfinished treat and started for her next post as lady-in-waiting to this year's Renaissance queen.

"Wait. My name is Robley of clan MacKintosh, and I need a guide." He came around in front of her and reached into his sporran, pulling out an impressive wad of good old American cash. "And I'll need a place to lay my head. I'll gladly pay whatever you ask in exchange for your help. All I ask is a bit of floor space and aid in navigating my way 'round. I'll no' be any trouble." He placed his free hand over his chest. "I give you my word as a knight of the Scottish realm."

"If you're truly from the past, how is it you have a fistful of modern money?"

"'Twas given to me by one who was sent back to my time in much the same way that I've come to yours. She has no use for it now." He kept his hand over his heart, imploring her with an earnest look.

OK, it did stand to reason. If a person could move forward through time, they could also go back. Was he really a knight? Her heart pinballed around in her chest. Could he be the answer to her financial woes, the answer to her prayers? No. Her prayers were never answered. Every inch of ground she'd ever gained had been earned through her own blood, sweat and tears. Too many tears. Still, she couldn't ignore the serendipitous way they'd collided into each other—or the wad of modern-day bills he flashed in her face.

"How long do you plan to stay?" She narrowed her eyes at him. "Wait. It's crazy to even consider something like this. You're a stranger. For all I know, you could be a time-traveling serial killer." Again she focused on him, and again she detected nothing mental or physical to be concerned about, but that didn't necessarily mean he wasn't dangerous.

A flash of desperation passed through his eyes. Desperation she knew on an up close and personal basis, and something inside her softened. How would it feel to travel through centuries, ending up in a place and time where you didn't know a soul or a thing about how the world worked? What kind of balls did you have to have to do something so utterly insane? Now *that* she could respect.

"A fortnight, mayhap a month. No more." He leveled a pleading stare her way. "I swear I'd never harm you. We MacKintosh men cherish and revere our women."

"Yeah?" She snorted. "Well I'm not a MacKintosh woman though, am I?"

"I dinna ken." His mouth quirked up, as if he sensed he'd won her over. "By what name are you called?"

"Erin. Erin Durie, and I really do have to get back to work." She lengthened her stride, dropping her unfinished treat into a trash bin as they passed.

"Ha! Just as I thought. We were fated to meet. Though you're from a mere Lowland clan, while *I'm* a Highlander, you're still a Scot."

"*Mere* Lowland clan?" She snorted. "Hardly. I'm an American girl through and through." She glanced at him and shook her head, her mind filled mostly with the temporary solution to her current pressing financial problems. "I can't believe I'm going to do this." His face lit up, and her breath caught. "Don't get your hopes up, buddy. All I'm going to suggest is that you spend the rest of the day with me, and we'll see how I feel by the end of my shift."

"Fair enough." He bowed. "I am at your service, my lady."

She couldn't help smiling at his courtly gesture. "If everything goes OK, I'll agree to be your guide. We can figure out the fee later." At least their arrangement would buy her some time to find a new roommate. She'd put something up on a few of the bulletin boards at school right away. Of course, she didn't mention she had a furnished spare room where he could stay. Bringing this total stranger into her home was a very bad idea. Best find him a motel nearby.

"We have a bargain." He put the money back in his sporran. "There's more currency where this came from. Lady True gave me her debit card."

Who was this Lady True he kept mentioning? A girlfriend? She hoped not. What? No. She'd sworn to remain forever unattached, focusing instead on her career. Still, she was human, and he was hot. She bit her lip, and her stomach flipped. *Keep your hands to yourself, Durie.* No messing around with the sexy Scot. She stifled the regret before it took hold.

Casual sex had never worked for her. She felt too much, sensed too much, and it always led to heartache. Besides, hadn't she learned anything growing up her mother's daughter? Good old Mom went through loser men like most people went through paper towels. Her mom and dad had split by the time Erin turned three, and she had long ago been sadly disabused of the whole notion of "happily ever after." She could be a guide for a month without allowing herself to become emotionally or physically involved. Robley of clan MacKintosh would be a means to an end, nothing more.

They came to the main drag of the fairgrounds, with all its false-fronted shops, food vendors and hordes of fairgoers. She glanced at Robley. His eyes widened as he took in the sight of all the performances that were underway: jugglers, musicians and dancers. A magician's show on the stage across the square drew his attention. A collective "ooh" went up from the crowd as the performer stuck a sword through the coffin-sized box holding his lovely assistant.

All of the food booths had long lines, and people walked around with grilled turkey legs and ears of roasted corn. Flush-faced parents pushed fussy children in strollers. Little girls waving beribboned wands and wearing cone-shaped satin hats darted here and there, while little boys with wooden swords and shields gave chase. With so many people teeming around, it was impossible to walk a straight line.

She kept them moving, wending their way through the milling crowd. The parade of nobles would begin any minute, and she had to hurry to the starting point. Robley blocked a man from running into her and hovered protectively near her side as they walked, touching a soft spot in her heart. *Don't even think like that!* "So, who is this Lady True you keep mentioning? Is she your girlfriend or something?" *Gah! None of your business, Durie.*

"Nay. Lady True is—"

"Forget it for now. Stick close." They'd reached the assembled reenactors, and it was not a conversation she wanted others to hear.

Anne, this year's elected queen, glared at her. "You're late."

Once again she couldn't believe she'd been aced out of the role of queen by her nemesis. Dammit. She wanted to be queen. Just once she'd hoped things would go her way, but no. She'd worked her way up from alewife to nobility through the Society for the Preservation of Medieval and Renaissance History. Plus, she'd been a member longer than Anne. The only difference between them was that, unlike Anne, Erin wasn't sleeping her way through all the unattached voting males. "Sorry. I ran into a friend." She gestured toward Robley. "Robley's joining us today."

Anne's brow rose. She did a once-over, starting at his broad shoulders, traveling down to his leather boots and all the way back up to his handsome face. She placed her hand in their king's hand, smiling at Robley all the while. "Well, hello there, and welcome to my court."

"*Your* court?" Erin snorted and rolled her eyes. "Don't forget this is just make-believe."

"Besides that, I'm right next to you." Michael, the man Anne had been dating for the past three months, grumbled, straightening his crown.

"Whatever." Anne shrugged as the trumpets heralded the beginning of their march.

Erin took up her place behind the queen, motioning for her time traveler to join them. He came to stand beside her, crooked his elbow and looped her arm through his, setting her hand on his forearm. His well-defined muscles shifted beneath her palm, and her stomach did a somersault or three.

He leaned close. "What are we doing, lass?"

"We're about to parade through the fairgrounds. It's all part of the show, part of what people here pay to see."

"Humph. The villagers must pay to enter your fair?" His brow creased.

"Villagers?" She laughed. "I'll explain later. Just try to look noble."

"I am the nephew of the earl of Fife and a knight." He straightened, lifting his strong chin a notch. "I've no need to *appear* so. Nobility runs through my veins."

"Which adds up to a whole lot of *who cares* here," she whispered. His scowl made her laugh. "You really have no idea, do you?"

"None whatsoever." He winked at her. "'Tis why I need you to guide me."

Again her breath hitched. She turned away, hiding the way he affected her. Best to immerse herself in her role as they passed through the spectators. Oh boy, was this guy tempting. Thank goodness he'd only be around for a month at the most. She could handle a month, especially as busy as she was. Somehow, she'd have to carve out some time to show him the sights, expose him to the marvels of her century. It would be fun to see how he reacted.

When had she decided she believed he really was from the past? Ah, well. She had no reason to doubt him, and she had witnessed his arrival. She had always been curious and open to the possibilities, and having the abilities she had, she'd suspected there was way more to this world than met the eye. Now she had proof.

"You have a lovely smile, my lady." Robley placed his hand over hers and gave it a brief squeeze. "I swear, your beauty alone is reason enough for my journey to your time."

Gah! Her insides fluttered, and her knees wobbled a bit. That had never happened before. Never. Her cheeks heated. "It's really hot out, don't you think? That wool you're wearing must be unbearable." She stared out at the crowd and pursed her lips. The low rumble of his chuckle went right through her, setting off a slew of physical sensations she'd be better off ignoring.

"You are unaccustomed to receiving compliments, I think. 'Tis hardly credible. Are the men of your time so dense? Do they no' fall at your feet?"

"Jeez, lay it on a little thicker, why don't you?"

This time he laughed out loud, drawing Anne's attention— drawing the attention of every female within range. She'd known Robley all of thirty minutes. How could she possibly be jealous? Yet she was. Erin inched closer to his side and glared at the women whose appreciative looks lingered a bit too long on his very fine form.

Stop it! She searched the crowd for something to distract her, all the while trying to keep her knees from buckling. "We're going to have to stop at Target after the fair. You can't walk around dressed like that while you're here."

Yep. Robley of clan MacKintosh was dangerous, all right, and she'd have to gather up all her defenses if this arrangement was going to work.

CHAPTER THREE

Robley covered Erin's hand where it rested on his forearm, anchoring himself to the enchanting lass into whom he'd fallen. They hadn't met by chance, he was certain. As they made their slow promenade through the throng of twenty-first-century villagers, he took it all in. So many booths with wares to sell: works of art, crockery, windows forming pictures out of bits of colored glass, jewelry, clothing of all sorts, scented oils and soaps, toys and leather goods. And the smells! Delicious and overwhelming all at once.

Never in his life had he seen so many people gathered in one place—not even in London or Paris! He reveled at the sights, sounds and smells, and tremors of excitement shook him to the core. He'd made it. This was the future, and he could hardly wait to explore.

Still, doubt niggled at him. How had he come to Lady True's realm in Minnesota? He'd intended to arrive at the same fair in New York where she'd been working when Giselle sent her back to their century. So that he'd have a place to stay, True had given him directions and the key to the apartment where she lived while attending Juilliard. He'd followed Giselle's instructions perfectly, fixing New

York and the month of August in his mind. Surely the faerie had interfered and manipulated him into something not yet clear.

Trepidation and uncertainty tightened around his chest like chain mail a size too small. Was he merely a puppet, or did his arrival in Minnesota have more to do with time travel being far from exact? Giselle had warned him. Had he held Minnesota, True's homeland, in the recesses of his mind while entering the disturbance?

He glanced at Erin, wondering how she fit in with all of this. His heart leaped at the sight of her. By the Virgin, he'd never before encountered such a breathtaking beauty, and he'd fallen right into her arms. Recalling her shocked expression as they lay entwined like lovers brought a smile to his face—and sent heat coursing through him. It had to mean something. Was she his destiny? Had Giselle sent him to her? Erin's eyes, the greenest he'd ever seen and flecked with a rich brown, had held him spellbound from the first moment he'd beheld them. For certes, 'tis why he'd forgotten his manners altogether and kept her trapped beneath him. That and the feel of her feminine softness cushioning him. How could he not linger once he'd glimpsed her luscious lips and that wealth of thick, honey-colored hair she wore bound in a long braid? Lord, he longed to undo that braid and run his fingers through her silken tresses. He was but a man after all, with a man's lusty appetites.

Studying her out of the corner of his eye, he prayed fervently that she was indeed meant for him. She glanced at him and smiled, and his heart tumbled over itself. Was this what Malcolm had gone on about? Was this the thrill his cousin felt whenever he laid eyes on his lady wife?

"We're almost to the end of the parade," she whispered. "Then I'm supposed to roam through the fairgrounds and make myself available to talk with our guests. I'm done for the day in a couple of hours."

"Aye?" Transfixed, all he wanted to do was gaze upon her like a besotted fool. They'd come to a set of gates bordered by a tower to one side and cottages with windows facing the crowd on the other.

Roughly clad villeins lined the catwalk. One of them grinned lewdly and pointed. "Oy, what have we here, lads?"

A corpulent man with filthy hands and face leaned over the railing and called to them, "Ah, such lovely flowers! I might have to pluck one for meself."

"I've dibs on the queen. You may have her lady-in-waiting," another coarsely dressed lout shouted. "Such sweet fruit. She's ripe for plucking, aye?" He waggled his bushy eyebrows, staring insolently Erin's way.

Robley tensed and put himself before his lady, shielding her from their vile speech and impertinent gestures. "How dare you speak thus to your betters," he called out. "You will cease your harassment at once or suffer the consequences."

Widening his stance, he glared at the miscreants. His warning only egged them on, making them bolder still, and they continued to make rude gestures and hurl unsavory comments their way. "Stand back, my lady." He reached for his claymore, and all eyes turned to him. Erin stopped him from drawing his sword.

"It's all part of the show, Robley," she whispered as she leaned close. "Relax."

"Show? I dinna ken what you mean, lass." He kept his eyes fixed on the catwalk, lest the ruffians attempt anything more severe than words.

"It's all make-believe, a pageant. Including those guys. I know them. We belong to the same club." She tugged on his arm. "Come on. The parade is over. Let's go. I'll show you around and explain how things work."

He sent one more scowl toward the louts and let his lady lead him away. Confused and disoriented, he had difficulty grasping what had just transpired, especially once the clapping ensued. "Force of habit prevails," he muttered. "'Tis ingrained in me to protect those who cannot defend themselves. A gently bred lady should no' be subjected to the insults and rudeness of such rabble."

"You think I can't defend myself?" She laughed. "Oh, Robley, you have a lot to learn about the twenty-first century."

"Without a doubt." He glanced back at the catwalk, still angry that their party had been subjected to such an outrage.

"Come on. I'll take you to the jousting arena. That should be a kick."

"A kick?" He frowned. "I swear, your speech is passing strange. Even more so than Lady True's used to be."

"Ha! It's the other way around, sir knight. You're the foreigner here. It's your speech that is *passing strange*."

"Ah, I take your meaning." He nodded. "'Tis true. I dinna exactly fit in, do I?"

"Not even a little bit," she said, grinning at him. "Tell me about this Lady True you keep mentioning." Erin looped her arm through his again, steering him in the direction she wished him to go.

Warmth spread through his chest, and once again he covered her wee hand with his, marveling at the feel of her soft skin next to his callused palm. "Alethia Goodsky was sent to us from your time. We call her True for many reasons, one being she is a truth-sayer. She has the ability to discern whether or no' a person speaks truly, and occasionally she has visions of the future. Her gifts have saved our clan more than once. The faerie who sent her to us—"

"Whoa. Hold up." She stopped walking and gaped at him wide-eyed. "Faerie?"

"Och, aye, one of the ancient ones, the *Tuatha Dé Danann*." He nudged her into motion again. "Madame Giselle poses as a fortune-teller at fairs like this one." He nodded to the surrounding area. "She stole Alethia from your time and sent her to ours so that she might save the life of a young orphaned lad who needed her special kind of help. He has the blood of the fae running through his veins, as does she. 'Tis why she has *the gift*. True is wed to my cousin Malcolm now. They have a daughter and another bairn on the way. Plus, they've adopted Hunter, the lad whose life she saved. The lad is also gifted."

A stunned expression suffused Erin's lovely features, and she brought her hand up to press against her mouth.

"What is it, lass? What troubles you?"

She shook her head and averted her gaze. "Nothing. It's just . . . well, it's all kind of difficult to believe."

"I speak naught but the truth." He suspected there was more to her reaction than that, but he let it go. "We found Lady True all alone and fast asleep by the side of the road. I believe my cousin fell in love with her that very moment." He smiled. "Believe you me, she led him on a merry chase. Malcolm did his best to keep her safe and by his side, but she wouldn't have it. 'Twas quite entertaining."

"For you." She bumped her shoulder against his. "Probably not so much for him."

"To be sure." He chuckled. "Malcolm's beleaguered heart nearly faltered more than once. Our True has a propensity for placing herself in harm's way, but only to protect those she loves." They'd come to a circle of fairgoers oohing and aahing as they watched something going on in the center. The familiar metallic ring of sword upon sword came to him. "Another show?"

"Yep. Sword fighting. It's very popular."

"I would see this exhibition, if you dinna mind stopping."

"By all means."

The crowd let them through easily enough once they saw how they were garbed. Robley watched the two knights. The rush he always got at the possibility of engaging in swordplay raced through his veins. Their form was sloppy and their technique poor by his standards.

"You call this swordplay?" he shouted. The two knights glanced his way. He thrust out his chest in challenge. "I call it child's play." The two stopped their mock battle, the glint in their eyes unmistakable.

"Think you to challenge *us*, both blooded knights?" the one wearing a black tunic under his chain mail shouted back, strutting toward him. His crest was embroidered in gold thread upon his breast.

"Aye, and both at once." Robley drew his claymore, striding forward to meet him. "You two fight like squires, no' blooded knights," he threw out. "Unless by blooded you mean easily defeated. I've no' yet spent time in the lists this day. 'Twill provide me with a bit of sport, nothing more." He flexed his shoulders, rotated his neck and sent his sword turning in a series of arcs to warm up. "Do ye accept the challenge, lads?"

His opponents watched his movements, their expressions eager. He took up a battle-ready stance. "Come then. I vow to disarm you both."

They both lunged for him at once, their swords swinging wildly. Robley blocked one blow, then the other. He planted his foot in the center of the black knight's chest and sent him flying, pivoting to engage the single opponent coming at him. Bringing the edge of his claymore against the other man's blade, he circled it, waited for his opponent's wrist to assume just the right position, pivoted and applied pressure. The knight's sword flew from his hand. The spectators applauded and cheered. The lad bowed slightly, retrieved his weapon and backed away.

Robley turned to face the more skilled, larger knight. "Have at me, *squire*."

The knight in black laughed. "Squire is it? I shall reduce you to mincemeat before the hour is done." He circled him in a boastful stride, looking Robley over with a scornful smirk.

"Come then. Dinna waste my time." Robley stood his ground, looking bored. Letting loose a battle cry, the man came at him.

Robley blocked his blows and worked him back with several well-placed strikes. Gleefully, he settled in for some much-needed physical exertion. "I am called Robley," he said in an even tone, making a point of showing that his breathing hadn't yet deepened. "By what name are you known, *squire?*" Steel on steel rang out, and the crowd widened the circle to accommodate them.

"My name is Mark. Mark Pilon."

"Ah, a Norman. I've fought side by side with Normans against the *Sassenach* many a time. We are allies."

"True enough." Mark began a series of offensive moves, taking Robley by surprise for an instant, before he retaliated with his own tried-and-true tactics. Shutting out everything else, he set himself to his task, to the battle of wits and brawn. His muscles were warm and loosened, and he drew a long, slow breath, savoring the activity.

Swordplay, hand-to-hand combat, jousting and hunting had always been his favorite pursuits. He thrived on action and exertion. The sense of accomplishment following a good bout never failed to bring him contentment. Aye, physical activities, including a tumble or two with one of the village widows, were all that had kept him sane this past year.

Mark dripped with sweat and breathed heavily, grunting with each blow he parried and with each strike of his sword.

"More time in the lists will build your stamina, lad," Robley taunted. Mark's glance darted toward Erin. Robley scowled. Did she glance back? He couldn't risk finding out. Time to end this, though he was nowhere near expending his strength. Making short work of it, he divested his opponent of his weapon and bowed to the calls of "huzzah" from the spectators as they began to wander off.

Mark sheathed his sword and bent over, placing his hands on his knees for several moments to catch his breath. He straightened and approached. "Man, you have some moves. Where'd you learn to fight like that?"

"My da placed a wooden sword in my hands when I was but three or four winters, and I've been training ever since." He clasped his defeated opponent's proffered forearm briefly. "I fostered under the earl of Seakirk and earned my spurs by the time I turned ten and six."

Mark swiped a sleeve across his brow and turned to Erin, embarrassment at having been soundly thrashed, and longing for her, plain to see.

Jealousy, swift and hot, churned through Robley, until he too looked at the lady. Her eyes met his and fairly glowed with appreciation. Lucky for Mark, or he'd have been forced to continue their mock battle, just to pummel the man into the ground. "I'm from the—"

"He's from Scotland." She came to his side and slipped her arm through his. "Robley is staying for a month. He's on vacation."

"A month? Great. Maybe we can work out together, and you can teach me some of your moves."

"Mayhap we can arrange to meet again for that purpose. 'Tis up to Erin. She's my—"

"Host. I'm hosting him while he's visiting." Erin nodded. "We're distant cousins."

Cousins? Vacation? Robley arched a brow at her, eliciting a blush and a stern look on her part.

"Yeah? Cool." Mark muttered and glanced around. "Did you see where Jerry went?"

"Is he the other knight, the first I disarmed?" Smirking, he slid his claymore back into its scabbard. "He's on yon hill nursing his wounded pride with an ale. I've worked up a powerful thirst as well. Shall we find refreshment, my lady?" He glanced at her and offered his arm. "Would you care for a glass of wine?"

"Wow, you really do stay in character." Mark laughed. "I'll catch you later. Should I call you, Erin?" He shot her a hopeful look. "To get hold of Robley, I mean."

"Sure. I'm in the club directory."

"OK." Mark nodded. "Later then."

As his rival took his leave, Robley wondered what a club directory might be. The only clubs he knew of were those used in battle to bash in a man's skull.

Erin steered him toward a booth with grapes, barley and hops painted on the front. "Don't tell anyone else you're a time traveler. They'll think you're certifiable."

"Humph. I meant only to say I'm from the Scottish Highlands." Did she think him so foolish as to blurt to all and sundry that he'd recently arrived from the distant past? He'd only told her so freely due to the circumstances, and because he wished to gain her trust. How else to explain his sudden appearance?

"Oh." She shrugged as they queued up for refreshments. "Let me order, and give me a ten-dollar bill."

"Are you always so managing a female?"

Her cheeks grew a darker shade of pink. "The word you're looking for is *controlling*, and no. I'm not. I was only trying to help. You said you wanted a guide, someone to help you navigate." She stepped away and gestured toward the counter. "Go for it. I can't drink anything with alcohol anyway. I'm still on duty."

He'd offended her, and the look of hurt he'd glimpsed in her eyes cleaved him in two. He'd have to take more care with her tender feelings in future. Robley studied the placard on the wall behind the serving wench. He told her what he wanted and peeled off the requisite bills from the currency True had given him.

The lass placed two flimsy cups on the counter and handed him a few coins, which he dropped into his sporran. Some of the ale sloshed over the sides when he made the mistake of gripping the cup too firmly. Taking a few gulps, he moved out of the way and walked over to where Erin waited under the shade of a large oak.

"'Tis good ale and so cold." He drank deeply again and sighed. "Quite refreshing." He handed her the other container. "I brought you a lemonade, lass. What is this called?" He tapped the container holding the amber liquid.

"Thank you." She took the refreshment, a pleased expression lighting her face. "It's called a plastic Solo cup. Don't ask what it's made of, because I can't explain it to you." She smiled and took a drink. "So what do you think of our Renaissance festival?"

"'Tis no' so very different from our fairs in appearance, except for the way the villagers are dressed. We also have performers and merchants who sell their wares, but mostly it's a time to gather the clans together to trade surplus crops for needed commodities. Our fairs are about commerce and coming together to celebrate the harvest. We dinna charge anyone to enter." He gestured to the goings on about him. "This is naught but a thespian's arena."

"Trust me, Robley. It's all about commerce here as well. I earn money playing the role of lady-in-waiting. We all earn money playing a role, as do the participants selling their art. It's meant to be fun. Wait until you see a grocery store. We don't really need to come together to sell surplus crops anymore, and maybe that's not such a good thing." She frowned. "There are local farmers' markets though. Come on. There's more to see."

They passed the rest of the afternoon witnessing one wonder after another, and though he wouldn't admit it to Erin, weariness had taken hold. He was ready to be free of the endless sea of humanity and the incessant noise. But oh, the tales he'd tell once he returned home. He'd ridden an elephant and a camel. Erin had captured the images on the strange device she kept in her pocket, and she'd promised to print the pictures for him. True had the same kind of device, which she referred to as a *smartphone*. He wanted a closer look.

"I'm off duty now," Erin said. "Are you sure you don't want to try the bungee cord jump before we leave?"

He glanced at the people dangling and bouncing from the stretchy ropes attached to a tower. As a youth, he'd never been one to swing on a rope out over the loch with the other lads. Doing so made him ill. Just watching the spectacle sent a shudder through him. "I'm certain. If it pleases you, I'm ready to leave."

"All right. We have to go back to the area where we met. I want to change into my street clothes. Then it's off to Target for a few pairs of jeans, T-shirts, sweatshirts, shoes and grooming stuff. That should do for a few weeks. Didn't you say your friend gave you her debit card?"

"Aye, and she said there is quite a bit of money in her account, all she earned working during the summer and her tuition funding for school."

"Great. We'll use it to pay for your stuff, but since it's in a woman's name, I'd better take care of checking out. It'll look suspicious for a man to use a debit card with a woman's name on the front." She headed for the back of the fairgrounds where the club kept a trailer for changing and taking breaks.

"Do I no' have enough currency to make the necessary purchases?"

Her eyes narrowed. "You don't trust me?"

"Och, lass. I do, but I'm a man. I should pay. Tongues will wag if—"

"Seriously?"

Her expression cleared, and her smile precipitated a rush of desire so great he nearly stumbled over his own feet. He wanted to taste that lovely smile, to delve into the sweetness of her enticing mouth. He fought for control. If she had any idea how her nearness affected him, he feared she'd abandon him. He needed to gain her trust, and lusting after her was not the way to do so.

They stopped before a wagon of sorts, not unlike those used by the wandering Romany he'd oft spied on the roads in France. Only this was constructed out of some kind of flimsy metal. Erin disappeared, leaving him to settle his mind and senses. He leaned back against the wagon and closed his eyes. He'd been overwhelmed from the moment he'd stepped foot into the passage between the ages, and he saw no end in sight. 'Twould take some time to adjust.

Erin walked out of the wagon wearing blue trews like the ones he'd seen True wear when she hunted. The fabric fit Erin like hosiery, and she wore naught but a thin, sleeveless chemise on top. Every curve and contour of her form enticed him, and the revealing garments ignited his blood. His mouth went dry, and it was all he could do to refrain from drawing her into his arms and pressing her up against the wagon.

"Let's go," she said, seemingly unaware of the havoc she wreaked upon him.

He'd sprung to life below the belt. Shifting his sporran to hide the tenting plaid, he followed her to a gate set in a fence resembling loose chain mail. Desire scorched him from the inside out. Casting about for something else to capture his attention, he halted, placing his hand over the hilt of his dagger.

Beyond the gate, an endless expanse of wagons in varying shapes, colors and sizes spread out over the field before him, all arranged in neat rows. "Automobiles," he murmured. "Cars, trucks, SUVs. True spoke of them, but I never imagined . . ." He turned to Erin, excitement tensing every muscle. "Do you have one, lass? Will we depart in such a contraption?"

"Yes. We will indeed *depart in such a contraption*." She laughed. "Oh, this should be good."

He gazed out over the spectacle laid out before him. "Aye, it should."

She pulled a set of keys from a bag slung over her shoulder and led him to a small silver-colored car. The front end held numerous dents, and so did the back. Rust spots under each door caught his eye. Compared to the sleek, shiny automobiles on either side, he guessed hers to be quite a bit older and much abused. "Is it safe, lass?"

"Of course. My car got me here, didn't it?" She opened a compartment at the back. "Take off your sword and stow it in here, the dagger too. You can't wear them inside the store."

"Must I?"

"You must. You'll catch on soon enough. People don't walk around carrying an arsenal unless they're police officers."

She waited while he unfastened his claymore. Wrapping the leather belt around the scabbard, he placed it inside the storage space. Next he removed his dagger from the sheath at his waist and tossed it in beside his sword. Naked. Without his weapons he was rendered vulnerable in this strange place. Never had he traveled without them within easy reach.

She closed the compartment and rounded the car to unlock a door. "Get in, and prepare for the ride of your life."

Swinging the opened door wide, he studied the tight space, doubtful he'd be able to fold himself onto the wee seat. Still, he climbed in, and his knees pressed against the front.

"I'm sorry." Erin cast him a sympathetic look. "I should've adjusted the seat before you got in. Reach underneath the front. There's a lever. Pull it up and you can give yourself more leg room."

Robley did as she directed, and the seat slid back. "Better. My thanks."

"Buckle up."

"I beg your pardon?"

"I keep forgetting this is all new to you." Erin leaned over him and pulled a strap across his chest.

He inhaled deeply, taking in the soft, sweet scent unique to her, letting it settle into his soul for all time. "I must be strapped in for this ride? For certes, my head is spinning with all I've seen and experienced this day."

"You could probably use a break." She fastened the strap and studied him. "After Target, I'll take you to a motel near where I live.

Once we get you settled into a room, we'll head to Fat Lorenzo's for pizza."

"A motel?" *Pizza? Target?*

"It's like an inn. You pay to stay there in a private room."

Suddenly overtaken with it all, he didn't even try to grasp anything else she'd said, other than she planned to leave him. What if she never came back? "I canna stay with you, lass?"

Her lips compressed, and her cheeks turned a lovely shade of dusky rose again. "No, I don't think that would be a good idea. You'll be nearby. I'll teach you how to use the phone, and when I'm done with school tomorrow, I'll come by to pick you up. We'll go see a movie. You'd like that, wouldn't you?"

"How would I ken whether or no' I'd *like that*," he groused, wanting nothing more than a meal, rest and quiet after this latest disappointment. He couldn't really blame her. He knew naught of her situation at home. Mayhap her parents would object to bringing a stranger into their dwelling. After all, he was no longer in the Scottish Highlands where hospitality was freely offered to wayfarers. 'Twas not his time or place, and he had no right to expect anything of anyone.

For the first time in his life, he gained a fresh perspective upon the fortunate circumstances of his birth and a new appreciation for his family and clan. The sudden pang of homesickness took him by surprise. He'd been nothing but eager to leave them behind.

Erin started her vehicle, and the rumble had him gripping the front panel with both hands. She started it moving, and he relaxed. The pace was not unlike that of an oxcart, and the sways and bumps as they hit dips in the ground were familiar and not too disturbing. He blew out the breath he hadn't realized he'd been holding and settled back. They followed a line of other vehicles exiting the fair, while people wearing brightly colored tunics directed them with small banners. She stopped the car at a red sign, and Robley gasped.

Cars rushed by at impossible speeds on a roadway made of some kind of smooth stone. "Och, you're no' going to . . ."

She pulled out, turning onto the roadway and sped up. He prayed. Bracing his feet against the floor and his hands against the front, he fought the rising nausea. "Shite! May the saints preserve me. Men are no' meant to travel at so great a speed."

"I'm not even going the speed limit." Erin glanced at him. "You'll be OK."

"I dinna think so." He leaned his head back, which only made it worse.

"Maybe if I put on some tunes to distract you, it'll help." She pushed a button, and the inside of the car filled with blaring sound the likes of which he'd never heard before and never cared to again.

He pressed the same button she had, stopping the discordant cacophony, and shot her a panic-filled look. Fearing he'd disgrace himself by casting up what little he had in his stomach, he clenched his jaw shut.

"Oh crap. You're going to throw up in my car."

A sheen of sweat covered his brow, and his mouth salivated uncontrollably. He nodded.

She pulled off onto a smaller road, stopped the car and undid his seat belt. He fumbled with the door, wishing nothing more than to be free of the deathtrap. "God's blood, how does this confounded thing work?"

"Hold on." Erin hopped out and rushed around the car to his side. She yanked the door open and backed away.

He shot out, headed for the tall grass and heaved until his gut ached. Mortification scalded him. What must she think?

"I'm so sorry." Erin ran her hand up and down his back. "I can't even imagine how weird riding in a car must be for you."

Warmth and comfort spread through him at her touch, and the roiling in his stomach disappeared. How could that be? Mayhap she simply had that effect upon him, and he found her presence calming. She continued to soothe him with her touch, and his mortification receded as well. "'Tis no' your fault." He straightened. "I dinna handle some kinds of motion well. I prefer to ride a horse rather than travel in a wagon or a cart."

"Wait here. I have bottled water in the backseat. It'll be warm, but you can rinse your mouth." She hurried to her car and back. Twisting off the top, she handed him a clear vessel filled with water.

He took it from her, rinsed his mouth and spat into the grass. The day had been full of ups and downs with no respite in between, and he'd simply attended a fair. Was it always thus in the twenty-first century? Were it not for Erin, he'd consider going home this very minute, but something about her drew him. He'd see where it led, at least for a se'nnight. Mayhap he'd regain his enthusiasm after a good rest. "Naught about this adventure is as I expected," he muttered.

She moved close, smoothing her hand up and down his back again, and again the comforting sensation flooded his senses.

"Expectations are tricky little buggers," she murmured. "It's best not to have them at all."

He frowned, scrutinizing her. "Why is that, lass?"

"Well, if you don't have any expectations, you'll never be disappointed."

His breath hitched. "Are you oft disappointed, my lady?"

"Not anymore." She handed him the lid to the container, averting her eyes. "Are you better now? I'll take the back roads where I can. It'll take longer, but I think you'll be able to handle the ride."

"Speaking of roads," he said as he ran his boot over the hard surface, "what is this?"

"Asphalt."

His brow shot up, and he shook his head. "*Ass* fault?"

She glanced at him, and one side of her mouth quirked up. "It's hard to explain."

Lady True used the word *ass* to mean *arse*. He wasn't certain he wanted an explanation. "I'll take your word on the matter."

"Ready to go?"

Following her back to her vehicle, he pondered what he'd learned about her. He'd glimpsed the deeply buried wounds reflected in her eyes. Who had hurt her so badly that she no longer held any expectations for her life? He reached for the dagger always at his waist, finding nothing where it ought to be. She didn't know it yet, but she'd just secured a champion. He wanted nothing more than to protect her from harm and erase the hurt. Mayhap she'd heal in the process, and one day he'd see joy reflected in those lovely eyes. Joy and expectation.

CHAPTER FOUR

Erin stood next to Robley by the side of the frontage road, his discomfort a tangible force. The nausea, stress, fatigue and disorientation he suffered brought a wave of empathy crashing over her. Poor man. Poor sweet, protective and totally unprepared, naïve, fifteenth-century knight. And to think he'd come to the twenty-first century on purpose. What would've happened to him if she hadn't been there when he came through? He might have eventually turned into one of the homeless roaming the streets of Minneapolis, robbed of his cash and his weapons.

How could he possibly have known what to expect? The pace of twenty-first-century life, the culture and societal norms, technology and the sheer numbers of humanity compared to his time must cause all kinds of overload. She ran her hand over his back, knowing her touch would settle him. Another of her gifts—healing touch. Nothing miraculous. She couldn't cure cancer or anything like that, but she could ease pain and physical discomfort. She could calm overwrought nerves.

Did she have faerie blood running through her veins? Is that where she'd inherited her abilities? If so, it had to have come from her dad's side, because her mom was totally oblivious to other people's feelings. Her dad, on the other hand, could charm bark off a tree. Was that because he picked up on what pleased others? Maybe she'd give him a call and ask him a few pointed questions. She turned her attention back to Robley. "Are you feeling better?"

"Aye." He nodded. "Let us continue on our journey, only slower if you please, my lady."

A tiny thread of pleasure wormed its way into her heart. She loved the way he called her his lady, even though she knew it was nothing more than a common way of addressing a woman in his era. Oh boy. She needed to distance herself from him, clamp down on the attraction flowing between them, or she'd suffer the inevitable heartbreak sure to follow. Had she learned nothing growing up with a mother who thought each new lover would be her ticket to happy town? And even if they weren't all losers, the relationships never lasted. Erin had absolutely no interest in setting herself up for that kind of heartache and disappointment.

"I'll do my best to go slower," she said. "We have to take the freeway to cross the river, but then I can follow the back roads. I think I have a plastic bag in the back you can keep with you in case you need to hurl again." He nodded, and once again she was awash in his reactions. This time confusion and frustration.

For some reason, he was way easier for her to read than most people, and her ability with him had grown as the day wore on. She usually had to concentrate to get a sense of what people were feeling. With Robley, the impressions just flowed. She didn't know if that was a good thing or not, but she'd have to remember to shut it out. "The faster we get to Target and get you situated the better."

"Dinna fash. I've been through worse, lass. Let us be off." He gestured forward. "Do all women in your time dress as you do?"

"For the most part." She arched her brow. "Why?" As if she didn't know. She'd learned over the years how to ignore the testosterone-laden vibes coming at her. She'd been bombarded with them during high school and college. Even when they weren't directed her way, they filled the atmosphere like pollen during late spring. With Robley, it was doubly hard, because she found him equally attractive. She couldn't help reacting.

"'Tis disconcerting. Women of my time are much more modestly clad."

"You'll get used to it."

"Humph." He shot her a rueful expression. "I dinna believe I will."

Erin turned her car off of Cedar Avenue and into the motel parking lot. She glanced at Robley. He was ready to drop, and exhaustion fairly pulsed from him. The Super Target experience had been almost as overwhelming and fascinating for him as the Renaissance festival, and she'd had a tough time dragging him out of the store. Her backseat was piled high with bags, some full of nonperishable food so he wouldn't starve before she could get back to him. The rest held clothing and necessities. She pulled into a parking space and cut the engine. "You sure experienced a lot of new stuff today, huh?"

He shifted, nodding. "This is the inn?" he asked in a less-than-impressed tone.

She fought hard to shut out the distressed uncertainty rolling off him. She needed to give the poor guy some privacy, and she didn't need the guilt. "This is it. My place is only a few minutes from here." She grabbed her purse, which held the debit card he'd given her when they'd shopped. "You ready?"

"How much will this cost? Do the innkeepers provide their patrons with hot meals?"

"Um, not this particular inn, no. That's why we bought the groceries." She pointed to the sign. "It's cheap. Let's go. Once you have a room, I'll teach you how to use the phone. You can call me if you need help. We'll unload these bags once we have your key. Ready?"

His jaw clenched. His unhappiness was clear even without her gifts, and she hardened her heart against the onslaught. It would be OK. He was a full-grown man and a knight. He'd be fine. Maybe if she said it enough times, she'd believe it.

"Aye." He opened his door and climbed out. "Where do I go?"

"We need to get you checked in. Follow me." She led him toward the office, each step adding another dollop of guilt to her growing heap. If their situations were reversed, would he dump her at an unfamiliar, seedy place in a foreign land? She shook it off. Even though their day together had been great, and she knew enough about him to know he posed no threat, who in their right mind would open their home to a complete stranger?

Wait. Hadn't she done that with roommates over the past couple years? Sure, she'd been in school with them, but they hadn't been close friends or anything. *Argh!* Why had fate chosen her to break Robley's fall through time? Wasn't her life already complicated enough?

He opened the heavy glass door and held it for her. She heaved a sigh and approached the counter, where a short balding man sat on a tall stool with his nose buried in one of those gossip rag newspapers. A vacuum cleaner hummed from somewhere down the hall, and the dark burgundy carpeting reeked of mildew. "He needs a room." She jerked a thumb toward Robley.

The attendant's eyes widened as he took in Robley's kilt. He fired up his computer. "Name?"

"Robley MacKintosh," she supplied before he could go into his "of clan MacKintosh" routine.

"How many nights, and will he be using Visa, MasterCard, American Express or a Discover card?"

"I dinna ken . . ."

Erin placed her hand on Robley's forearm and spoke to the guy behind the counter. "Do you take cash?"

"Certainly. All I need is a driver's license." The man glanced at Robley. "Or a passport."

Crap, crap, crap. Why hadn't she thought of that? Robley frowned in confusion at her and waited. She averted her gaze. Now what? She could put his room on her credit card, which was close to maxed out, but what if he disappeared back to the past after weeks of charges? She couldn't handle one more iota of debt, nor did she want to take the risk.

Should she try to use Alethia's debit card? But if the attendant asked her for ID, which he might now that they'd cast a cloud of suspicion over Robley's presence, she'd be screwed. They'd both be screwed. The attendant might report the card as stolen, and that source of extra money would disappear. Stymied, she scowled at Robley. "Come on." She turned on her heel and stomped out of the cheap, smelly motel.

"Where are we going now?" he asked. "To another inn?"

"Nope. To my place." She was nearly bowled over by the flood of relief coming her way. His smile nearly blinded her with its brightness, and all the misery he'd carried on the way into the nasty place disappeared. Her insides melted, and relief thrummed through her as well. Oh boy. Not good. "You're going to have to pay me, just like you would if I ran an inn."

"Agreed." His stride quickened, his step much lighter. "Room and board."

"Sure, and when I take you places or we do stuff, we use True's debit card." Her stomach growled, reminding her that they hadn't eaten. "We'll stop at my place. You can change your clothes, and then we'll go for pizza."

"If it pleases you, lass." His eyes, so very impossibly blue, fairly sparkled.

She drove them the short distance to her apartment building, an old, dark brick building with four large apartments on each of the two floors. She lived a few blocks off Cedar Avenue, very close to Lake Nokomis and Minnehaha Parkway. She loved her neighborhood. It was so close to great places to eat, the beach, and the walkway around the lake. She parked in her reserved spot in back and shut off her car, just as a 747 roared overhead low enough to rattle windows. Air traffic over her south Minneapolis home was the only drawback, but she hardly even noticed the noise anymore.

"Bloody hell!" Robley cringed into his seat, his eyes turned to the sky with a look of alarm followed by stunned disbelief. "What the devil is that?"

"Sorry. I should've mentioned the airplanes." She opened her door and climbed out, ducking to peer through the window at him. "We're near the airport here, and we get planes overhead all the time. You'll get used to it."

"Planes? Airport? I dinna believe I will," he grumbled, unfastening his seat belt. Mumbling to himself, he climbed out.

More prayers? She bit the inside of her cheek, trying not to laugh. "I'll bet you're rethinking your whole 'trip to the future' idea about now."

"Nay." He arched an eyebrow and shot her a lopsided grin.

Thump, thump, thump went her treacherous heart. Maybe she could rethink her "no messing around with the sexy Scot" policy while they were at it? *Noooo.* She clamped down on her raging hormones and opened the back door to grab a few bags. But he'd be in the twenty-first century for such a short time, she rationalized. Too short to mess her up. She lifted her gaze to find him staring at her. How could such cool blue eyes look so dang hot? "Grab some bags. I'm starving. The faster you get settled and changed, the sooner we can eat." She moved to her trunk and opened it. "Don't forget your weapons."

He did as he was told, muttering, "Managing female."

"Motel?" she shot back. He laughed, and if she'd had a tail, it would've wagged like crazy at the sound of his sexy laughter raining over her. Once they had everything, she led him into the building to her second-floor apartment. "Here we are." She shifted her load around and unlocked the door. "Home sweet home."

He walked into her apartment, his gaze traveling over everything. "Where is everyone?"

"Everyone?"

"Your family. Do you no' have siblings, uncles and aunts, parents, grandparents?"

"Of course I have a family, but they don't live with me. Most people get their own places once they reach adulthood." She moved into her small kitchen and dropped the bags containing food on the counter. "Come on. I'll give you the tour and show you to your room."

"No wonder you balked at my staying here with you. We are without chaperones."

She snorted. "Yeah, that's it. No chaperones." Bags in hand, she led him to the second bedroom across the hall from hers. "I'll bring the bedding once you're done changing and putting your things away." She stepped back while he entered.

Before she started her master's program, she'd worked as an OB-GYN surgical nurse, making a pretty decent living. She'd been able to furnish her place, including the extra bedroom. She, her stepsister and two half brothers got along well, and Erin liked having a place for them to stay when they were in town. Once she started school, having the extra room had allowed her to take in roommates to help cover the rent.

Robley set his Target bags down and moved around the large, airy room, testing the mattress and opening a drawer of the dresser. "This will do nicely. My thanks. I shall endeavor to be a worthy guest."

"Just put the seat down and clean up after yourself, and I'll be happy."

His brow furrowed. "Seat down?"

"Yep. Before you change into your new clothes, let me show you the bathroom." She stuffed her hands into her front pockets and backed out of his room.

"We have a bathing room in our keep at Loch Moigh, but no' yet in Castle Inverness or at Meikle Geddes, which is where my parents make their home."

"Wow." She opened the door to her bathroom, glad she'd taken the time to clean on Friday. "That's a lot of real estate."

"Real estate?" His gaze roamed around the room, his eyes widening when they lit on the toilet. "Och, you . . . uh . . . you *bathe* in the same room where . . ." Color crept up his neck to fill his cheeks.

She chuckled. "Watch, Robley." Erin took a square of Charmin and dropped it into the toilet. He moved closer.

"There is water inside?"

"Yes. When you're done, you push this lever." She flushed.

"'Tis a wonder, for certes." He continued to watch as the porcelain bowl refilled.

Lifting the seat, she shot him a pointed look. "This gets lifted when you pee. Men in our time *always* put the seat back down when they're done. Got it?"

"Pee. Lift seat. Done. Put seat back down. Got it," he repeated. One side of his mouth quirked up, and a dimple appeared. His eyes filled with humor.

Her heart rate surged. He was onto her. Did fifteenth-century bathrooms have seats? *Garderobes.* That's what they were called back then. Did fifteenth-century women scold their men for leaving the seat up? Could this be any more awkward?

"Moving on, this is the tub and shower for bathing." She turned to the old claw-foot bathtub, which she loved. A shower had been added, with the plastic curtain going all the way around the perimeter. "Here's how it works." She showed him how to adjust the temperature and switch from tub to shower.

"Where does the hot water come from, lass?" His tone was filled with wonder.

"The water heaters are in the basement along with the boiler to heat the building." She patted the radiator against the wall. "This radiates warmth when it's cold outside. I'll take you to the basement at some point, but not now. Aren't you hungry?"

"I am, but no' all that eager to depart once again." He shrugged his broad shoulders. "I fear I've no energy left."

"Oh. Right. I didn't think of that. Sorry." Another dollop of guilt plopped onto her pile. "You've been through a lot in one day. I'll have pizza delivered. We can relax and watch TV while we're waiting." She grinned. "I even have a six-pack in the fridge."

"Six-pack in the fridge," he mumbled. "You do ken I understand but a small portion of what you say, lass. Aye?"

On impulse, she reached for his hand. The contact sent all kinds of exciting fluttery sensations whizzing through her. She tried to ignore them. "Come on." She tugged. "I'll show you what a six-pack in the fridge means." He tugged back.

"I'll join you anon." His face colored up again. "I need to . . . ah . . ."

"Use the bathroom? Toilet, facilities, bathroom or restroom. That's what we call this." She whirled her hand to encompass the room, which grew smaller by the second. *Uncomfortable moment.* She pointed to the roll of toilet paper and released his hand. "For your comfort, convenience and personal cleanliness," she practically chirped. Wow. Charmin ought to hire her to do their ads. "Remember to put the seat back down." Entirely embarrassed, she backpedaled her way into the hall and turned to head for the kitchen. "And close the door!"

Oh no. You did not just say that! She heard his muffled chuckle as he shut the door. Thank goodness the man had a sense of humor. She made her way back to the kitchen and grabbed the refrigerator magnet with the phone number of her favorite pizza delivery place. Moving to the counter, she took the cordless phone from its jack. Once she'd placed the order for an extra-large, thin-crust deluxe combination pizza, she settled herself on the living room couch and turned on the TV.

Thank goodness she hadn't cancelled her cable service yet. She channel surfed, selected an action movie scheduled to begin in fifteen minutes, and ordered it on pay-per-view. Her nerves were all over the place, driving her crazy with a butterfly rampage and self-consciousness. Why did she feel like she was on a first date? She and Robley were not dating. He was her tenant.

It wasn't long before she became super aware of him as he opened and closed drawers in his room. She should get clean sheets and make the bed for him, but just the thought of being in his bedroom together sent her pulse surging again. Later. She'd go make the bed while he watched TV.

Robley strolled into the living room wearing a pair of jeans that emphasized his narrow hips and muscled thighs. His navy-blue V-neck T-shirt stretched across his sculpted pecs, and without the billowing shirt he'd worn earlier, his biceps put on quite a show. It was all she could do to keep from drooling. "Those clothes look good on you."

What an understatement! She'd gone for a casual, indifferent tone, but even she could hear the *Oh-my-I-so-want-to-jump-your-bones* undercurrent. If only she could tear her eyes away from him. She swallowed a few times. He shot her a high-wattage full-on dimpled grin, and her lungs stopped working—and then she drooled.

"Pizza should be here soon," she managed to squeak out before shooting off the couch. "Come and see what a six-pack in the fridge means." She'd love to see *his* six-pack. Surely he had one hidden under that sexy cotton T-shirt.

Her cheeks burned, and her blood sizzled. She hadn't seen him in jeans while they were at Target. Estimating his size, she'd handed him a bunch to try on, instructing him to keep what worked. He'd disappeared into the dressing room and came back out in his kilt with a pile of denim draped over his arm. She opened the refrigerator door, took a step back and bumped right into him. "Argh."

"What vexes you, lass?" He leaned down to whisper in her ear.

"Nothing. I'm not at all vexed." She reached in and grabbed a couple bottles of beer. "A six-pack refers to packaging." She handed him a bottle and twisted the top off of hers. "Six bottles of beer in one carrier, and the fridge is how we keep our food from spoiling." She moved out of the way so he could take a closer look. Gripping the cold bottle, she took a long, fortifying swallow of her Leinenkugel.

He reached in to touch a few things. "'Tis a marvel. Where is the ice that keeps it cold?"

"There isn't any, except for the ice it makes in the freezer. It's all done with electricity and coolant. Freon." She reached over his head to open the freezer. "Check this out."

Straightening, he reached into the freezer compartment and pulled out a bag of frozen peas. "Humph." His brow shot up.

"I don't have to be at school until ten tomorrow morning. I'll show you how to use the range top, oven and microwave before I leave. And the phone. Don't let me forget to show you how to use the phone." Her doorbell buzzed. "Pizza's here." She set her beer on the counter, grabbed her wallet out of her purse and dashed for the door. "Make yourself comfortable. I'll be right back."

Get a grip! Never in her life had she reacted to a man the way she did to Robley of clan MacKintosh. How embarrassing. She was twenty-five years old, not fifteen. She made her way to the front door of her building, paid the pizza guy and started back to her apartment.

Maybe she would jump his bones, get it out of her system, and then she'd calm down. After all, he'd be heading back to his place and time in a short while.

She huffed out a breath. *Sure, 'cause you're such a seductress. Not.* Walking back into her place, she found him watching the action movie she'd chosen. He glanced at her, and then his eyes slid back to the flat screen.

"Television," he said, slightly awed. "True told me all about TV, but I never imagined 'twould be like this."

She set the pizza on the kitchen counter and opened a cupboard to get a couple of plates. "Come and get some pizza." She reached into a drawer for napkins and set them next to the box. The tomato sauce, cheese, sausage and garlic smells made her mouth water. Pulling the top of the cardboard back, she inhaled. "Mmm."

Robley stood before the counter, looking skeptical. "What is this?"

"Other than the bread and cheese, it wouldn't do you any good to hear what's on top. I doubt you've heard of most of the ingredients. Just try it." She lifted four cheesy squares and set them on a plate for him. "Take a few napkins and go sit down. We can eat and watch the movie at the same time."

He took the plate and the napkins she handed him and returned to the couch. Erin helped herself to a plateful of pizza and joined him. She tore a square off and took a bite. His eyes focused on her mouth as she bit off a chunk of the garlicky, gooey goodness. She chewed, swallowed, and still his eyes never left her. Even eating in his proximity turned her on. Jeez. "Go on. Try it. I know you're hungry."

Tentatively, he lifted a piece, sniffed at it and took a small bite. His eyes lit up. He grinned and stuffed the rest of the square into his mouth.

"Told ya." She smiled back. "Beer and pizza, a little slice of heaven here on earth. Just wait until you try ice cream and chocolate."

He shot her a questioning look with his mouth full—so adorable she could hardly stand it.

After they'd consumed more than half the pizza and a couple of beers each, she was stuffed. Robley flopped back and groaned, patting his stomach. "Done?" she asked. He nodded, and she got up, reaching for their plates, empty beer bottles and napkins. "Ordinarily, I'd expect you to help with the cleanup, but everything is so new to you right now. I'd rather you continue watching the movie."

"My thanks for your generous hospitality . . . Erin." His shy glance darted to her and back to the TV. "May I call you by your given name? It suits you, lass."

"Of course, Robley. We all call each other by our given names these days." Full and slightly buzzed from the two beers she'd consumed, she busied herself with putting the leftover pizza away, rinsing out the bottles for recycling and stowing the dishes in the dishwasher. After wiping the counter down, she returned to find Robley sound asleep, still sitting upright with his head leaned back on the couch. Lord, he was gorgeous. Soft, rhythmic snores emanated from him. Her heart turned over, exposing its soft underbelly like a puppy wanting a good scratch. She could stare at him for hours and never get bored.

Two people with 584 years between them in evolutionary terms didn't stand a chance. Besides, he'd be returning to his century soon. She was so close to reaching her career goals. Becoming a midwife was more important to her than anything. Her place was in the present, and his place was in the distant past. No use entertaining any ideas of anything more than a brief, very hot tryst, and she wasn't certain she could handle that. No. She was certain she couldn't. Best let it go. Fantasize like crazy, but don't act on the impulse. Tomorrow she'd lay down some parameters with him, making her position clear.

She headed for the linen closet at the end of the hall and made his bed before returning to wake him. Sitting down on the couch, she reached out and shook his shoulder. "Robley, wake up."

He shifted, taking her into his arms and drawing her close. He nuzzled her neck for a second and started snoring again with his face planted against her bare skin. His soft breaths tickled her senses and did funny things to her insides. Enveloped in his heady masculine scent and pressed against him, she melted into his warmth, more reluctant to move than she cared to admit. She stroked his cheek, stubble and all, and then ran her fingers through his hair. Hmm, who knew it would be so silky-soft?

He stirred, letting out another long sigh, and tightened his arms around her. Oh yeah. Life had never been fair where she was concerned, and Robley of clan MacKintosh was just another hardball thrown her way. It would all end badly, and she'd be in pain, but man—never before had life felt so fine as it led her toward disaster.

"Robley, wake up." She shoved his shoulder again.

His eyes opened to half-mast, sexy and sleepy. He let out a rumbling, purring sound from deep in his chest and hugged her to him. "Have I fallen into your arms once again, *mo cridhe*? Seems we're back where we started." He nuzzled her neck and whispered, "Right where we belong."

Flustered, Erin extricated herself from his embrace and shot off the couch. "It's late, and you're obviously out of your mind with exhaustion. I made your bed, now go lie in it."

CHAPTER FIVE

Robley sipped the coffee Erin had fixed for him. He found he enjoyed the bitter, dark brew, so different from the tea or ale he usually drank. She'd added cream and sugar, making it even better. Fascinated, he took another sip and watched the bowl of porridge rotate inside the microwave.

As promised, she'd taught him how to use all the wonders of her kitchen, including the sink faucets and the cordless phone. He'd taken notes with yet another futuristic marvel: a ballpoint pen. Plus, she'd provided him with a pad of paper. Erin had called it a legal pad. The thin yellow sheets had lines of blue running across and two lines of red running down either side. Wonderful!

The microwave pinged, and he opened the wee door. The rolled oats had cooked in but a few moments. In his time they had to soak the grain overnight and boil it for a good long while before the oats were edible. Mayhap he could figure out a way to cut and flatten the grain once he returned home. His mouth watered at the scent of the butter and brown sugar melted on top. Sugar was a rare treat at home, though they oft used honey to sweeten things.

He snatched a cloth from the counter and lifted the steaming bowl, placing it on the kitchen table where he'd set his spoon in readiness. As instructed by his lady, he moved to fetch the milk she insisted had to be added before he could truly enjoy the oatmeal, as if he hadn't been eating porridge almost his entire life. He poured a bit into the bowl and put the carton back in its place inside the large, cold box. Refrigerator. That's what she'd called it, fridge for short. So much to learn.

Thinking of Erin brought a smile to his face. She'd fussed over him like a mother hen this morn, clearly reluctant to leave him on his own. He knew she'd thought him asleep when she'd stroked his face and ran her fingers through his hair last night, but he always slept lightly. Years of training and numerous nights sleeping out on an open battlefield had schooled him to come to alertness quickly. He'd been well aware and deeply moved by her gentle touch. The way she blushed when he teased her made him chuckle. Aye, she found him attractive. He was off to a good start in wooing her.

Taking his seat, he tucked into his meal, savoring the sweetness of the brown sugar. The telephone rang, and though he'd heard the jarring sound before, he still jumped from his place with his heart in his throat. Snatching it from the stand, he took a moment to recover his breath before bringing it to his ear. "Aye?"

"Robley? It's Mark. Do you have time to do some training today?"

He grinned. "I always have time to spend in the lists."

"You crack me up, man. No need to sound like a medieval knight on a Monday morning."

"I've no other way to sound, lad." He frowned. "How shall I find you?"

"Do you have a rental car?"

"Nay. I've no means for transport."

"OK. I have Erin's address from the club directory. All I have right now is my motorcycle. My car is waiting for new brakes at my uncle's garage." He paused. "You all right with riding on the back of my bike?"

As usual, most of what was said in this age held no meaning. "I've no idea . . ."

"It's a Harley Davidson Breakout," Mark said, as if that should make all the difference in the world.

"Ah," he said, still with no notion what that might be. "'Twill be fine, I'm sure."

"Yeah. We don't have far to go. I train at the Minnesota Fencing Club in Minneapolis. How about I pick you up right after lunch, about one o'clock?"

"I'll be ready." The shorter hand told the hour, and the longer hand counted the minutes, that's what Erin had said. He glanced at the clock, which reminded him of the sundials oft found near kirks, cloisters and in courtyards. Not difficult at all to read. 'Twas half past ten at present.

"Bring your own sword. They have plastic ones to borrow, but yours is wicked. Would you mind showing it to the owner? He's a collector, and I know he'd appreciate taking a look. He keeps a real one in his office."

"All right." He blinked in puzzlement. Why would anyone want a claymore made of the flimsy plastic stuff? And why would he use another's weapon when his had been made specifically for him, for his height, reach, grip and balance? "One o'clock then. I'll await your arrival in front of Erin's building."

"Great. Uh . . . speaking of Erin, is she there?"

"Nay. She left earlier this morn." Yesterday's look of longing upon Mark's face brought a frown to his. "Why do you ask?"

"No reason. Just thought I'd say hello . . . maybe ask her out. Do you think she'd go out with me? Did she say anything about me yesterday?"

Robley's grip on the phone tightened, and a surge of possessiveness had him clenching his jaw. He had no right to her, leastwise no more than Mark. "I dinna ken. Naught was said on her part, but we dinna share such intimacies. We are newly acquainted."

"Sure, but you're her cousin. Ask her if she's interested in me, would you, bro?"

He stifled the growl rising in his throat. "Mayhap. Until later, Mark. I must say farewell for now."

"OK. Later."

He set the phone back in its place and returned to the table. Somehow the fare before him had lost its appeal. Mark belonged to Erin's time, while he did not. Did it matter? Should it matter? Aye, it should and it did. He had a responsibility to his clan, obligations, and expecting Erin to leave her life to join him in the past would be far too presumptuous. Still, what if they were *meant* to be together?

Och, could he even take her back through time with him when he returned? He had but one crystal. Mayhap if they walked into the disturbance simultaneously 'twould work, but what if he lost her along the way? He'd clasp her hands in his, or better yet, hold her tight in his arms. He should have bargained for more than the two tokens. After all, one of the reasons for this journey was to find a lady of his own. Would fate be so cruel as to lead him to her, only to be thwarted when it came time to return? His gut wrenched. "Why did I no' think to ask Giselle what my future held?"

Shaking himself out of his reverie, he focused on more pressing matters. If he meant to train today, he'd need sustenance. He finished his porridge and rinsed the bowl before placing it and the spoon into the contraption that would wash them. Robley grabbed his mug of coffee and headed for the bathing room. A bath, shave and dressing in his new twenty-first-century garments would be his next adventure.

Though he found the jeans somewhat constricting, he had not mistaken Erin's appreciative glances. Her eyes had darkened, and she'd become breathless when she'd spied him in his jeans and T-shirt. Her reaction did much to encourage him. She had not looked upon Mark in the same way. In fact, she'd hardly cast her eyes in the other man's direction at all.

By the time he'd finished his ablutions, it was past eleven o'clock, and Robley prowled around Erin's great room, picking up this item and that to turn over in his hands for inspection. She had entire shelves filled with books, flimsy by his standards, but books nonetheless. A treasure, to be sure. It took months for a monk to copy and bind a book in his time.

He drew one from its place and glanced at the cover. His brow rose nearly to his hairline at the picture of a half-naked man wearing a broad-brimmed hat, jeans and boots. He thumbed through the thin pages. What manner of book did his lady read? Curious, he took the tome with him to the couch and settled himself to read.

Scandalous! His pulse quickened, and he couldn't prevent the erotic images from flooding his mind. He set the book down, but not before taking note of the page number. Why, the man and woman had scarce made each other's acquaintance, and they were already tumbling into bed, doing all sorts of sensual things to each other. Visions of Erin danced through his head, and he imagined holding her. Naked. His jeans grew uncomfortably tight. He picked the book back up to read more.

A few chapters later, he glanced at the clock. He had just enough time to warm some leftover pizza in the microwave for his midday meal before Mark arrived. Taking the book with him, he laid it on the table and propped it open with the salt shaker. He took a plate out of the cabinet and brought it to the fridge to fetch the pizza. Erin had said only a minute or so to warm the leftovers. He put a generous helping onto the plate and set it in the microwave. Again he watched the plate rotate inside. Molly, their cook, would never believe such a thing was possible. He hardly believed it himself. The ping sounded. He moved to the table to eat his pizza . . . and read.

Robley stood outside Erin's building with his claymore strapped to his back over his hooded sweatshirt. He searched the roadway for any sign of Mark. A moment later, a deep rumble commenced from down the road, growing louder as it approached. Robley stared at the sleek, shiny, two-wheeled black-and-silver vehicle and the lone helmeted rider fast approaching.

Wonder of wonders! The rider pulled the beast up beside him, kicked a stand down and shut off the marvelous sound. He pulled the helmet from his head.

Robley's eyes widened in unadulterated admiration. "What is this?"

A cocky grin lit Mark's face. "This is my Harley, or what I like to refer to as my *chick magnet*." He dismounted and joined him in mutual appreciation for the bike.

"Chick magnet? What has this to do with chickens?" He shot him a questioning look. "I dinna take your meaning."

"The ladies love to ride, and Harleys are the gold standard in bikes." Mark chuckled and shook his head. "You act like you've never seen a motorcycle before."

"Humph." Would he become nauseated when they rode? By the saints, he prayed not. Anticipation lit a fire within him. "Let us depart."

"OK. I only have the one helmet." Mark straddled the bike. "Do you want to wear it?"

"Nay."

"Hold on to this." He indicated the metal rack extending up from the back of the second seat. "Climb on. Your feet go here." He pointed again.

Robley climbed on, adjusted his sword and kept his feet on the ground until the Harley moved onto the roadway. The bike vibrated and roared to life as they gathered speed. A wide smile broke free. No nausea, only an exhilarating thrill. "I wish to learn how to operate this vehicle," he shouted over the rumble.

Mark nodded his helmeted head, and excitement thrummed through Robley's veins. Did he possess enough of the modern-day currency to purchase a Harley Davidson? Because he wanted one— by the end of the day if possible.

Far too soon, they pulled up next to a building, and Mark shut off the bike. He set the stand and removed his helmet. "You liked the ride?" he asked as he dismounted.

"Indeed." Reluctantly, Rob climbed off the amazing machine. "In exchange for my tutelage in combat techniques, you will teach me how to drive a Harley?" Truth be told, he would gladly forfeit the time in the lists for another ride. Only this time, he wished to go faster and farther afield. Much faster and farther.

"If you want. After our workout, we'll find an empty parking lot where we can practice. It's not hard. The clutch is the pedal here." He tapped his foot on the part. "The gears and accelerator are on the handlebars, and these are the brakes." He indicated each part as he named it. "Let's go inside. I want you to teach me how to disarm my opponent the way you did with Jerry the other day. He's meeting us here, by the way. I hope that's all right with you."

"For certes, he needs to train as well." He followed Mark through the door to a very large chamber. The wood-plank floor was polished to a high shine and had lines and circles painted upon its surface. Racks and shelving positioned near the wall on one end held all manner of swords and accoutrements. Most of the swords were unlike any he'd seen—smaller, shorter, with narrow, unsharpened blades and blunted tips covered with small plastic circlets. But there were also many resembling his claymore, only made of plastic. A group of individuals wearing padded garments like he wore under his armor were engaged in practice with broadswords. "What do they wear over their faces?" he murmured.

"Ah, it's just protective gear. Come on. There's Connor. He owns the place." Mark took off for the tall, fit man standing to the side and watching over the group practicing. He held a long plastic sword with the flat side of the blade resting upon his shoulder.

"Connor, I want to introduce you to my friend. You won't believe the mad skills he has with that weapon he's carrying. Robley MacKintosh, this is Connor McGladrey."

His stance, assessing stare, the width of his shoulders and the condition of his well-toned muscles took Robley by surprise. He recognized a hardened warrior when he saw one. Connor appeared somewhat older than Robley, perhaps in his late thirties or early forties. His red hair and beard were neatly groomed and threaded with silver. Robley extended his hand. "'Tis glad I am to make your acquaintance." They clasped forearms for a second. Robley gestured to his own claymore. "Do you fancy a new sparring partner?"

"Aye." McGladrey's eyes lit up. "But first I must fetch my sword. Prepare to be soundly trounced, boyo."

Robley laughed. "You have the lilt of the Irish."

"And you've the brogue of a bluidy Scott." He eyed the hilt of Robley's sword intently, his expression inscrutable. "Wait here."

He strode up a short flight of stairs and moved behind a counter to a back room, returning just as quickly. This time he held a real broadsword. "Let us move to where we have room to move." He swaggered off to the center of the indoor lists. Robley and Mark followed.

Robley rotated his neck and shoulders, stretching his muscles in readiness. In Connor McGladrey, he sensed he'd finally found a worthy opponent. He drew his claymore, and they faced off, slightly crouched, loose and battle ready. Robley shifted, first right, then left, taking his weight upon the heels of his feet. He adjusted his grip, balancing his weapon. Everything slid into its proper place.

"Normally, I'd insist you wear protective gear, and we'd use mock weapons," McGladrey informed him as he paced, running his eyes over Rob. "Liability, ye see."

"Och. No need. 'Tis unlikely you'll manage to touch me." He watched Connor, waiting for the first strike, gauging how the other man moved, how he held himself, which side he favored. Wits and brawn. Their swords rose at the same time, crashing together in midair. The force of the first blow reverberated down his arms. They both backed off. Robley grinned.

The dance had begun in earnest. The next clash involved a series of offensive strikes, advances and defensive feints, forward and back. Robley slid his blade along Connor's, pivoting as he applied pressure in a circular motion.

Connor laughed aloud. "I've not defended against that move since . . ." Shock crossed his face for an instant and disappeared just as quickly. Instead of attempting to parry, he'd allowed his blade to glide into the rotation, effectively thwarting Robley's attempt to disarm him. Robley's brow rose, and he bowed his head slightly in respect. Connor was no novice. He faced a true knight of noble blood, judging by the way he carried himself.

Keeping his glare focused upon Rob, Connor initiated a flurry of blows, forcing him back. Robley blocked each swing and shifted into the offensive, gaining ground. They both backed off, circling each other again, swords at the ready, nerves on edge.

"You're quite handy with a claymore, but no' nearly as handy as meself," his opponent boasted.

Robley shrugged, his manner nonchalant. "Come then. Prove it."

Connor advanced, striking hard, high, low, pivot and thrust. Rob jumped back. They parted, stepping around each other warily, looking for openings, seeking weaknesses. Tension pulsed between them. Determination and battle lust washed through him. Predatory instinct took over, and he moved in for the kill, beating Connor back to the very edge of his limits. In a sudden spurt, Connor came back at Robley, just as determined—every bit as skilled.

Robley laughed aloud. "'Tis good to be alive, aye?"

"Aye, that it is, boyo." McGladrey nodded. "That it is."

They continued on for a good while. Robley reveled in the physical exertion, the contest of wills, wit and strength. Equally matched, neither got the upper hand for long; neither gave ground for long. They had an audience. The clanging ring and hiss of steel on steel rent the air, and sweat dripped into his eyes. His muscles were loose, his blood hot, and his lungs worked like a bellows. This is what he lived for. "Had enough, old man?" he taunted.

"Not nearly enough, *laddie*," Connor taunted back, blocking his attack. "But we need to talk, aye? Pax?"

"Pax." Robley backed up and touched the flat of his blade to his forehead in salute. He reached for his scabbard, sliding his claymore home. Mark handed him a small white cloth, and Rob wiped the sweat from his face and the back of his neck while catching his breath. "My thanks."

"That was incredible, man." Mark followed them toward a door marked "Office."

"Mark, will you take my place instructing the class while I have a word with our guest? Jerry has arrived. Have him join you."

"Oh." Mark's face lit up. "Sure." He veered off to take up his role as instructor, his posture a little straighter and his stride a bit longer.

Connor opened the door and waved him in. He placed his sword across a rack hanging from the wall. "What year are you from, Robley of clan MacKintosh?" he asked, sliding behind the desk. He sank into the chair and propped his elbows on the surface. Clasping his hands together, he arched an eyebrow and flashed Robley an arrogant look.

Connor was of noble blood for certes, he thought to himself. "I beg your pardon?" Rob shifted his claymore and took the seat opposite. Heat crept up his neck.

"I know a well-seasoned, blooded warrior when I meet one in the lists, and I'll wager noble blood runs through your veins. Your sword," he said, jutting his chin toward Robley's scabbard. "As sure as I'm sitting here, that blade was made for you centuries ago." Connor leaned back in his chair, regarding him with steady intensity. "When are you from?"

No wonder he'd recognized a worthy opponent in Connor. He should be more shocked than he was, but True had come through time, as had he. There were bound to be others. "And you? When are you from?"

"The year of our Lord 1299." Connor shrugged. "I was an arrogant boyo, full of meself, and the heir to a chiefdom. I was out hunting with a group of my friends when I spied a strange woman. Limned in blue fire she was, tall and slender with hair the color of moonlight. None noticed her but me, and I wanted her for meself. I ordered my fellows to continue on and told them I'd catch up with them later." He grunted.

"Foolishness. I thought to gain her favor or some kind of edge over my fellows, so I followed the faerie. I know that's what she was. She led me all the way to the hills of Tara. The air around her began to ripple and shimmer. She disappeared. The shimmer remained." He paused, his expression turning inward. "I went to have a closer look. The next thing I knew, a stranger was shaking me awake where I lay unconscious in the midst of a field of wheat." He shuddered.

"I've not seen the blue-rimmed being since, though for years I searched. I did my best to find a way home." He shot Robley a pointed look. "That was more than twenty-five years ago." He slid a picture around for him to see. "I'm married now, with a family. I have two fine sons and a daughter. The laddie who found me asleep in his field took me to his home. I helped the family with farming in exchange for lodging and their help. They secured false documents for me, like a birth certificate and passport. Eventually I married their daughter and started this business."

"I'm from the year of our Lord 1426," Robley confessed. He thought better of mentioning his bargain or the crystals. "The same rippling disturbance in the air brought me here. I fell into a lass as I came through. She has taken me in for now."

"Ah." Connor nodded. "You need a job, money. Work here, and I'll pay you in cash until we can get you into the system. My oldest son is off to his first year of college. Though he pitches in as much as he can when he's home, I could use the help now. My other son has no interest, and my daughter is still too young to work here."

"Your daughter wields a sword?" Rob blinked.

"Aye." He barked out a laugh. "Out of the three, she's the most adept with a sword, dagger and bow. Meghan also studies mixed martial arts. She's a natural, a wonder," he said with obvious pride.

"Martial arts?"

"Hand-to-hand combat from the Orient, which is now called Asia, by the way." He straightened. "I'd like to help you the same way the family who took me in helped me. There are ways to secure a false birth certificate, and with that you can get a driver's license and passport." His mouth tightened. "I know you must be missing your kin, but there's no way back, laddie. Believe me, I tried. Best accept your fate and let it go. The sooner you do, the sooner you can begin building a new life in the here and now."

"I dinna ken how I'd manage to find my way back to your establishment each day, but I'd like to take you up on your offer. Would I teach sword fighting?" He'd have to remember to ask Erin about "the system" Connor mentioned.

"Absolutely." Connor stood. "There are buses. We'll figure it all out, but in the meantime, I want you and your lassie to come to dinner. Meet my family, and we'll talk about what must be done. They'll accept your presence without question." He reached for a small rectangle of paper and a pen. "I'm writing my cell phone and landline numbers on the back. Talk it over with . . . What's your lassie's name?"

"Erin Durie."

"Aye?" His eyes widened. "I know Erin. Years ago, my wife and I started a reenactment organization to preserve the history and way of life from my time. Erin has been a member for at least five years now. This is good. She'll be a great help to you." He handed him the bit of paper.

Robley glanced at it before tucking it into his pocket. "It almost seems as if . . ."

"Like your coming here and meeting Erin was meant to be?" Connor's wry grin hit home. "That's exactly how I felt once I'd accepted what happened. I fell in love with my sweet Katherine the moment I laid eyes on her. I was but ten and five, and she but ten and four. I resisted the attraction until I could fight it no more, because I wanted to return home. I'm happy. Content. You will be too." He came around the desk and put his hand on Robley's shoulder for an instant. "Give it time, laddie."

After hearing Connor's tale, Robley didn't have the heart to tell the man he had a way to return and planned only to be in this era or time for a short while. Connor hadn't had a choice in the matter, and he didn't want to upset him. "My thanks. I'd best return to Erin's before she arrives home. I wouldn't want her to believe I've disappeared." Plus, he wanted his first lesson on Mark's Harley.

"Do that. Call me once you've discussed things with Erin. It'll be good for her to know you aren't the only man to fall through time as you did."

"I will." He left Connor in his office and crossed the indoor lists for Mark. The group had dispersed, and Mark was deep in conversation with Jerry.

"Are you ready to go?" Rob asked, nodding a greeting to Jerry. He finally realized they weren't knights, but "reenactors." Pretenders. The concept made him want to shake his head, but he refrained.

"Sure." Mark shrugged. "But we never did get a chance to spar."

"Another time. Connor offered me work. I'll be spending quite a bit of time here."

Jerry's gaze swung from the young lady he had his eye on to Rob. "Wow, that's great. I'd love to take lessons from you."

"Me too, and it makes sense," Mark added, with a thoughtful expression. "You fight like you've done it for real."

"I have done it for real, and for my life." Rob shot him a challenging look.

"Yeah, right," Mark quipped. He and Jerry laughed as they made their way to the door.

"'Tis the truth." Robley pushed the double doors open with some force, relishing the crisp, fresh air greeting him. "Now about that Harley—where might I find one for myself?"

CHAPTER SIX

Erin locked her car door and hurried into her apartment building. Poor Robley. He'd been alone all day and must be bored out of his mind, not to mention baffled by everything that had happened to him in the past twenty-four hours. After a quick shower and a change out of her scrubs, she'd take him out for Thai food and a 3-D movie. She couldn't wait to see how he reacted to both. Hopefully she could find an action flick he'd enjoy, or maybe something animated. Would he go for a kid's movie? She glanced at her watch—almost three thirty. Maybe they could walk around Lake Nokomis before dinner. He was probably used to a lot more activity.

She opened her door . . . and found her apartment empty. Her stomach dropped. Disappointment brought a sudden sting to her eyes. "Robley?" she called, moving through the apartment, knowing full well she wouldn't find him. A quick check of his room confirmed her worst fears. He'd disappeared. Maybe he'd been returned to his own time. She wandered back to the living room. A book lay open and facedown on her coffee table. Drawing closer, she glanced at the title. And the cover. She snatched it up and slammed it shut.

Yikes. What must he think? Had her erotica sent him fleeing back to his own time?

Her apartment door opened. She swung around with the book still in her hands. Robley strode in, all lit up with excitement like a neon light on steroids. His hair was a wild, tangled mess, and the boundless joy and excitement pulsing from him stole her breath. She scowled. "Where have you been?"

He glanced at the book in her hand, met her eyes and flashed her one of those double-dimpled, sexy grins. Her face heated. "This book is not mine." She tossed the paperback onto the couch like it burned her fingers. "I've had a few roommates. One of them must've left it."

"Aye? Well . . . judging by the color blooming upon your cheeks, you *must've* read it." His gaze traveled all over her, pausing at her chest, then sliding to her mouth. He arched an eyebrow and met her eyes again. "Did you no'?"

She cleared her throat, embarrassment gripping her. "Are you really reading it?"

"I am, and you've just lost my place," he complained, picking it up and flipping through the pages. "'Tis . . . *it's* quite . . . instructive. Enlightening. Truly enlightening."

She swallowed her gasp, and more heat suffused her. Only this time, the rise in temperature headed in an altogether different direction. "Where have you been, and what happened to your hair?"

He set the novel back on the coffee table. "Riding a Harley Davidson motorcycle," he said, his tone filled with reverence. "Is there a way to find out how much money is left on True's debit card?"

"Why?" She blinked, her head spinning.

"I want a *Harley*."

His tone when he said the word *Harley* was so little-boy-at-Christmastime, she laughed. "You're kidding, right?"

"Kidding?"

"Surely you jest," she replied, slipping into his mode of speech.

"Nay, er . . . no. Mark taught me how to drive his bike, and I desire one of my own. Now that I have work, I'll need transport to and from."

"Wait. What?" Stunned, she dropped to the couch and stared at him, totally dumbfounded. "I . . . I came home to an empty apartment, and . . . I thought you'd gone back to your century." The sting in her eyes defied explanation. She blinked it away and bit her lower lip. "You've been here one freaking day. Twenty-four hours. One. Day." She shook her head. "Are you telling me you have a . . . a *job*? You spent the day reading erotica, riding a Harley and looking for a *job*?" she managed to squeak out.

"This is my second day, lass, and I did not leave you," he said softly.

"Well, obviously. Not that it matters one way or the other." She shot up from her place and headed for the hall, or the hills, whichever came first. "What's with the modern-day speech all of a sudden?"

"This is a modern-day world. I'm simply trying to fit in."

"'*Tis* a modern-day world. I liked the *'tis*es and the *'twould*s." She stomped down the hallway. "I'm gonna take a shower. I need a few minutes to . . . adjust. Do *not* leave this apartment." The low, sexy rumble of his laughter skipped down her spine, leaving delicious shivers in its wake. She blew out a breath, grabbed her robe from the back of her bedroom door and crossed the hall to the bathroom. "You need to do anything in here before I shower?"

"I'm fine, babe."

Her mouth dropped open, and her eyebrows nearly hit the ceiling. *The book.* He'd gotten that from the book. She might have to pack 'em all up and stow them in the basement. "My name is not *babe*," she called out before slamming the door on another sexy chuckle. Why the heck was she so upset? *Because you thought he needed you, that's why. And clearly he does not.* "It's fine. I'm glad he's independent. This just frees me up to concentrate on school and my own life," she muttered to herself.

She twisted her braid on top of her head, fastening it with a clip, and stripped out of her hospital scrubs. Turning on the water, she waited for the hot to kick in. For all she knew, Robley already had plans for the evening and wouldn't want to go to the movies and dinner with her. She hadn't brought it up.

Erin stepped into the shower and let the hot water ease her tension enough so that she could think. Robley of clan MacKintosh was just one surprise after another. How could he have a job? He didn't have a social security number or ID of any kind. Come to think of it, he was in the United States illegally. Besides that, why would he want a job when he only planned to stay for a month tops? She rinsed quickly, shut off the water and grabbed a towel from the rack. They hadn't discussed money recently. Did he want to work because he feared he didn't have enough to pay for his room and board?

She didn't feel like reapplying her makeup, or going out for that matter. Things were all jumbled inside her, leaving her off-kilter. The disappointment she'd experienced when she thought he was gone for good was a warning. *Don't get attached. Don't think he needs you, and for heaven's sake, don't begin to need him!*

Pregnant women and their babies needed her. Wrapping herself up in her career worked for her, and that had to remain her focus. Erin slipped into her robe and crossed back to her room. She unclipped her hair so that her braid fell down her back. Then she rummaged through her dresser for something to wear.

Dressed in a dark-green Henley and blue jeans, she padded barefoot back to the living room. Robley sat on the couch, her erotic romance novel in front of his face. *Gah!* "How could you have a job, Robley? You're not even in the system."

"Explain the 'system' to me, lass." He set aside the book and patted the couch beside him. "This is no' the first I've heard of it this day."

She shrugged. "It's the way our government keeps track of its citizens. When you're born, you get a birth certificate and a social security number. Then, when you get older, those are the documents you need to hold a job and get a driver's license. You can't just drive a Harley around. You need a license and insurance."

"Insurance?" His brow furrowed.

"It's complicated, like the biggest Ponzi scheme ever, but you have to have it."

"Ponzi scheme?"

Sighing, she sat beside him and put her feet on the coffee table. "That's not important right now."

"Your feet are bare." His gaze fixed on them.

"So? You've never seen bare feet before?"

"Not yours." He slid her a lopsided grin and winked. "They're quite lovely."

Her insides melted. She tucked her feet up on the couch. "The job. Tell me about the job."

"Aye, we need to talk."

Adrenaline shot through her. Heart racing and mouth dry, she nodded. *This is where he tells me he's going to go stay with Mark, Jerry or whomever.*

"You know Connor McGladrey?"

"Sure." She frowned.

"He's from the past, sent here in much the same manner as Lady True, only by accident rather than by design."

"Get out!"

He stood abruptly, hurt and confusion wafting from him. His face clouded. "I meant no offense, but if it pleases you, I'll leave."

"Oh. No. Sorry." She tugged at his sleeve. "Sit back down. 'Get out' is just an expression of surprise. I wasn't telling you to leave." His relief swamped her. She'd done a fairly good job of tuning him out, but when he had such strong reactions, it was impossible.

"That makes no sense at all," he muttered, taking his place again.

"There are a lot of things that make no sense," she agreed. "Like people traveling through time. When is Connor from? How'd he get here? How'd *you* get here, for that matter?"

He shared what Connor had told him, and Erin took it all in, wondering how many people from the past or future might be lurking around her neighborhood. "OK, but you came on purpose, and you plan to go back. Connor is stuck. You're not. How is that possible?"

"I formed a bargain with the same faerie who sent True to us. She gave me two tokens for my passage. One I used to get here; the other is for my return."

Her treacherous heart wrenched at the "for my return" part. "What kind of token?"

"Do you wish to see it? 'Tis a crystal."

She thought about what she knew of Connor and his family. So much made sense about the McGladreys now. It had been Connor and his wife who had started the reenactment group, and she knew he owned the fencing club. He'd managed to carve out a niche for himself in the present. She'd met his children at several club events. Connor made a good living and supported a family. Robley could do the same. He could make a life here—if he wanted.

She shook herself free of the notion. Wouldn't happen. "Yeah, show me this token of yours."

Robley reached into his back pocket and pulled out a small leather pouch. He placed it on her lap. "This is how I'll return to my time, lass."

She tugged the drawstrings open and dumped the crystal into her palm. "Jeez, do you have any idea what this is?"

"A crystal of some sort."

"It's an uncut diamond, and it's huge." Turning it over, she studied the gem resting in her palm. "I took a class in geology when I was in high school. My teacher had one, but his diamond was very small and of poor quality." She held it up between her thumb and a finger. "This has got to be at least ten to fifteen karats. It's worth a fortune." She slid it back into the pouch and handed it to Robley. If he stayed, he'd certainly have a nice little financial cushion to start with, without having to do anything but find a buyer. "You had two of these? Did you tell Connor?"

"Nay. I did no' want to upset him. He's settled, happy, and he has a wife and family. Best no' stir the pot, as True would say."

"I agree." Rubbing both her palms along her jeans, she scrambled to pull all the facts together. "So, I'm guessing Mark took you to play with swords today. You met Connor. He saw you in action and offered you a job. He intends to pay you under the table, and by *under the table* I mean in cash."

"Aye." He slid his arm around her shoulder and squeezed the *steady* right out of her heartbeat. "You are a canny lass."

"And now you're jonesing for a Harley."

He chuckled, giving her another heart-stopping hug. "If by *jonesing* you mean I want one of my own, then aye. I'm jonesing for a Harley."

Lord, he smelled good, and man, did it feel wonderful having his arms around her. He took his arms back, and she felt deprived, achy. She always felt too much, and it had always been her cross to bear.

"Connor wants us to come to dinner soon. He can help me get into the system, with a birth certificate, driver's license and anything else I need."

"Why would you want all of that if you intend to leave after a month?" She shot off the couch, heading for the kitchen. "More than likely it'll take longer than thirty days to pull everything together." She stopped, turning back to throw her hands up in the air. "Who spends upward of ten thousand dollars for a motorcycle they'll only own for a few weeks?"

"Mayhap I'll stay longer."

And there went the floor from under her feet. "I don't feel like going out tonight. Is it all right with you if we stay in?"

"'Twould be delightful to stay in with you tonight, babe."

A little too close to hysteria, she stifled the laugh bubbling up her throat. A fifteenth-century knight was living with her in her apartment, reading erotica and calling her babe. Impossible. Incredible. Mind-altering and heart-threatening, this gorgeous man was turning her life upside down. "I'm going to take you to a Harley Davidson dealer on my day off. We're going to buy you an official black leather Harley jacket complete with a big fat logo embroidered on the front and the back. What do you think of that?"

"Hmm. We'll purchase two. One for each of us."

Happiness tugged at her heart, and she couldn't keep the goofy smile off her face. "If you insist."

"Erin?"

"Yes?"

"When might we go to dinner at Connor's?"

"Wednesday evening would be good. I have the day off, but I have to work a night shift. I don't start until ten though." She walked to the fridge.

"What might a shift be?" he called after her.

"I'm a nurse, a health-care provider, and I'm working toward my midwife certification. That's why I'm in school. Are you hungry?" When he didn't answer, she leaned around the kitchen cabinets to see what he was up to.

Deep in thought, he'd leaned forward with his elbows propped on his knees and his chin resting on his thumbs. Tapping his steepled fingers against his lips, he stared out at nothing, a slight frown on his face. "What's wrong, sir knight?"

"Hmm?" He glanced at her. "No' a thing."

"Are you hungry?"

"Always, babe." He flopped back on the couch and scrubbed his face with both hands.

She let the "babe" thing go. For now. Clearly something was bothering him, and he didn't want to share it with her. Sighing, she rooted around in her freezer for the container of chicken noodle soup she'd made a couple weeks ago. Soup and grilled cheese, perfect for a day like today. The temperature had dropped considerably. Her favorite kind of weather—crisp, cool air and warm sunshine. Rob had worked out today. She'd better make two sandwiches for him.

She set the glass bowl in the microwave to heat the soup and gathered what she needed to make the sandwiches. "Is it all right with you if I put some music on?"

"Um . . ."

"Something easy on the ears this time. I promise."

"If you wish."

She crossed the living room to her iPod dock and scrolled through her library until she found some Celtic music. Selecting the playlist, she hit play, and soft harp and flute music filled the room. "OK?"

"OK." He nodded and picked up the book.

Erin busied herself with dinner preparations and soon had everything ready. She set a plate of grilled cheese sandwiches at the center of the table, followed by two steaming bowls of hearty soup, and a dish of sliced apples. "Come and get it."

Robley slid into his chair and rubbed his hands together. "This smells and looks delicious, Erin. My thanks." He took one of the sandwiches and transferred it to his plate. "That reminds me. I've no' yet paid you for my room and board. Name your price."

A burden lifted from her shoulders. "My rent is roughly a thousand dollars a month. If you pay me half the rent, plus two hundred for food, that comes to seven hundred for the month. Does that sound fair?"

"Aye. That sounds fair enough. Take it from the debit card." He took a bite and chewed thoughtfully. "Do you ken how most women die in my century? And well before their time, I might add."

"The plague?" Had this been what put the *serious* in his body language a while ago?

"Nay." He flashed her a look of such intensity. "Most die—"

"Oh wait. I do know this. We had to take a class on the history of midwifery early in the program. Childbirth is the leading cause of death for women in your era. It's tragic, and I wish there was something I could do about it, but—"

"Do you?" He stilled, scrutinizing her.

"Sure." She shrugged. "But my life is here, and here is where I intend to stay. I've worked so hard to get where I am. I'm so close to finishing my program. I have less than three months to go." She leaned back in her chair and put her spoon down.

"I've been working at Fairview Riverside Hospital since I graduated from nursing school. I'll be able to stay on there as a midwife. It's my dream." Glancing his way, she tried hard to ignore his hopeful expression. Surely he didn't expect her to return with him.

"Your century lacks the technology for one lone practitioner to make a dent. If you want, I can send you back with some books on the subject of childbirth if you think that'll help."

"My thanks. Any knowledge you're willing to share would be greatly appreciated." His brow lowered, he went back to eating. "Mark wanted me to ask you if you're interested in 'going out' with him. I assume that means he wishes to court you."

She nearly choked on the soup she'd just put into her mouth. Clearing her throat, she reached for her napkin and wiped her mouth. Finally composed, she answered, "I'm not interested in going out with Mark. I'm not interested in going out with anybody."

"Why is that, lass?" Rob fixed his blue eyes on her. They were filled with puzzlement. "You're young and beautiful beyond compare. If Mark is any indication, the men of your time find you extremely desirable. Indeed, in any era men would find you irresistible, as do I. Do you no' wish to someday have a husband and bairns of your own?"

"No." She swallowed against the sudden constriction blocking her throat and kept her eyes on the egg noodles floating around in her bowl.

"Tell me why no'."

She shrugged. "There's nothing to tell, really. My mother has had five husbands. I kind of think she's used up her quota and mine. I don't want to go through what she's gone through. Scratch that." She lifted her chin. "I *won't* put myself through that kind of misery."

"To have buried so many husbands surely caused immeasurable grief, but—"

"Buried?" She huffed out a laugh. "None of them are under the ground, sir knight. My mom divorces them, or they divorce her. I've had so many stepdads, I can't keep them straight."

"*All* divorced?"

"All but her current, and it's looking like another split is imminent." His shocked expression went straight through her, and embarrassment churned the soup and sandwich combo in her belly into an uncomfortable glop. Yep. That's the kind of background every woman wants to share with a hunkmeister like Robley.

"Ah."

"Exactly. Ah." She played with her spoon and glanced at him

through her lashes. "So you see why there won't be anything between us other than friendship."

"Humph."

A dimple appeared, and something indefinable put a glint in his eyes, setting all kinds of warning bells chiming in her head—and in her heart.

CHAPTER SEVEN

Robley sat on the couch reading the book in his lap, while darting glances at the clock upon the kitchen wall. Erin would be home soon, and tonight they were going to dinner at the McGladreys'.

"Hello!" Erin burst through the door, a brown sack clutched to her chest and her heavy pack hanging from one shoulder.

Placing his book facedown, Robley rose to meet her. "Good day to you. Here, let me take these for you." He removed her pack from her shoulder and placed it on a chair. "What have you here?" he asked, taking the sack and peeking inside.

"White chocolate chips and macadamia nuts." She took the bag back and set it on the kitchen counter. "Once I wash off the hospital smell, I'm going to make cookies for tonight."

"Cookies?"

"Small, round, sweet treats." She patted his face, stopping his heart. "You're going to love them."

"Might I help with this endeavor?"

"Sure." She glanced at the table by the couch. "Go back to your book while I shower and change." Her eyes sparkled with amusement. "You aren't still reading that same book, are you?"

"Nay. You've quite a collection by some fellow named Louis L'Amour, and I'm reading one of his tomes now. 'Tis quite informative and entertaining. I can hardly credit that a man could write so many books in one lifetime. It takes our monks at least a full year to copy but one."

She'd started down the hall, and he followed. "How was your day at school, lass?"

"Wonderful. I'll tell you all about it after I shower. Would you mind making a pot of coffee?"

"'Twould be my pleasure." He bowed and made his way back to the kitchen to do as his lady bid him, marveling at the sweetness of having Erin walk through the door to greet him. Grinning like a besotted fool, he readied the coffeemaker as she'd taught him and then pushed the brew button. Too restless to read, he wiped the kitchen counter down and wondered what he might do to prepare for the cookie making.

He'd oft spent hours in the kitchen at Loch Moigh and Meikle Geddes. Especially during the long winter months. For certes it was the warmest place to be found in both keeps. The cooks used bowls and wooden paddles to mix their pastries. Mayhap Erin had the like hidden away somewhere in her tiny kitchen.

Opening a cabinet door, he crouched to investigate the contents. He found a set of stacked earthenware bowls and drew them out. She kept another earthenware container next to the oven, and there he found two wooden spoons to his liking. By the time he had assembled everything, she was back.

She wore a pair of jeans and a soft-looking garment that clung to her shapely form. The midnight blue accentuated the color of her hair just so. She pushed up the sleeves and smiled at him. His mouth went dry, and he gestured to the pile of things he'd put together. "I hope these might be of use in this cookie-baking business."

"Perfect." Erin placed her hands on his shoulders and moved him out of her way.

He caught a whiff of her fresh, clean scent and drew her in for a quick embrace. "You smell so good; I vow there can be no treat as sweet as you."

She laughed and set him at arm's length. "You are so full of it."

"Full of what, lass?" He put his hands in his pockets and moved aside as she gathered the foodstuffs she required.

"Never mind. Get the bag I brought in with me." She pointed to the kitchen table. "Do you know anything about halves and quarters?"

"Aye. I ken that when I cleave my enemy in half, he will fall to the ground in two equal pieces, and if a man be drawn and quartered, he will die in—"

"Eww. That's gross!" She smacked his shoulder lightly with the wooden spoon. "I meant measuring cups and spoons. Here's what I'm talking about," she said, pointing to a set of cups, nestled one inside the other, and varying sizes of spoons. "They are labeled. All you have to do is match up the label with what the recipe calls for. Use the straight edge of a knife to skim the top to remove excess."

She thrust one of the bowls at him. "Here. You can put the dry ingredients together, and I'll cream the butter, sugar and eggs." She shot him a wry look. "Do you think a bloodthirsty knight such as yourself might be able to handle such a tame task?"

"Aye, though I might need fortification first. Coffee?"

"I'd love some."

He poured two mugs of the fresh brew and fixed Erin's just the way she liked it, sweet and full of cream. "My lady," he said, handing her the first mug.

She sipped, made appreciative noises and set it down on the counter. "Thank you, Rob. I have trained you well."

"That you have." He leaned in and kissed her forehead. She didn't back away, and his heart soared. He moved to the area where she'd set the dry ingredients and went about measuring, dumping and mixing. "This cooking business is no' so complicated."

Erin turned on the oven and put on an apron that had been hanging on a hook. "Nope. Not at all complicated." She cracked an egg on the edge of her bowl and reached for another. "Do you want to hear what happened today?" She glanced at him, her eyes alight and a shy smile gracing her lovely mouth.

"Absolutely." He nudged her with his hip. "I live to hear of your adventures during clinicals."

"I got to deliver a baby girl today," she said, her tone hushed and awe-filled. "It was so amazing. She didn't even cry when she came out. She was so alert, looking at everything and taking it all in." She sighed. "Everything went perfect, and I'm the one who got to place that baby on her mother's tummy the moment she slid out."

"You truly love what you do, don't you, lass?"

"I do. I'm a very lucky woman to have a vocation I'm passionate about."

"You could do it anywhere, aye?" Like, in his century, serving his clan.

"I suppose I could." She glanced into his bowl. "We're ready to put these together. Look in that far cabinet underneath the silverware drawer. There are a couple of flat cookie sheets. Let's bake these cookies, and then we'll have a little while to relax before we leave." She sipped her coffee again and watched as he combined the dry ingredients with her mixture.

"Thanks for helping, sir knight." She added the white chips and nuts and folded them into the mixture.

"'Twas my pleasure, my lady."

Erin taught him how to drop spoonfuls of the batter onto the flat pans to bake, and the rest of the afternoon they spent baking and cooling the delicious cookies.

She brought out a large plastic container with a lid. "If you keep eating those, you're not going to want dinner," she admonished, loading the cooled treats into the plastic bowl.

"Mmm." He swallowed the sixth or seventh sample and washed it down with a gulp of coffee. "I've no' had the like. I swear, they are bewitched, for I canna seem to stop myself from going for more."

Erin moved the rack of cooling cookies out of his reach and transferred them into her container. "At this rate, we won't have any left to bring to the McGladreys." He reached for another, and she sheltered the bowl against her midriff and turned away. "Stop!"

"I dinna wish to stop." He reached around her with both arms, drew her back against his chest and dropped his chin to her shoulder. "One more. Please?" Truth be told, nothing compared with the sweetness of having Erin in his arms. Laughing, she twisted and turned as he tried to pilfer another cookie. "One more, and I swear 'twill be the last."

"OK. One more, but that's it." She handed him a cookie and looked at the clock. "Shoot. We have to get going. Baking the cookies took longer than I thought."

They hurried to clean up, gathered coats and shoes and got ready to depart. Erin made one more round to ensure that she'd turned off the oven and coffeemaker, and then he escorted her out of the building to her small car.

"Did I tell you about the baby I got to deliver this morning during my clinicals?" Erin's voice practically trilled with excitement.

Robley opened her car door for her before circling the front and climbing into the passenger side himself. "Aye, lass, you did, but I'd love to hear the tale again." He grinned at her as he buckled his seat belt. "Tell me." He took the container of cookies they'd baked and set it on his lap.

She'd been rattling on about her experience all afternoon, and he loved seeing her so happy. He loved that he was the one with whom she shared the events of her day. Warmth spread through his chest, and he reached for her hand to give it a squeeze.

She squeezed back. "I should take you to see the hospital where I work. You could meet some of the midwives I'm training with and see firsthand some of the modern-day medical technologies."

"I'd very much enjoy seeing that."

She pulled onto the roadway and headed for Connor's dwelling. "Don't you think it's kind of spooky how your life, mine and the McGladreys' lives have all kind of intersected? What are the odds that you'd fall into me the way you did, and that I'd be so closely associated with another time traveler?"

"'Tis the way of the faeries, lass. I dinna believe for a moment that any of our meetings could be termed 'coincidental.'"

She sighed. "That makes it all the more spooky."

"Nay. 'Twas meant to be is all. My thanks, by the way, for the lesson in cookie baking earlier." A soft smile lit her face, and he lost his breath.

"Thanks for the help. It was fun."

"I agree. Will you teach me how to cook other things as well? Mayhap once I'm more skilled, you'd let me cook you dinner."

"Oh, I'd love that. I can't even imagine what it would be like to come home after a long day of school and work to find dinner ready and waiting." She glanced at him. "I'd feel so spoiled."

"I'd love to spoil you a bit if you'd let me."

He heard her breath catch, and she turned her concentration back to the road ahead. The rest of their journey, he was able to settle back and stare at her unimpaired. She truly was a delight to look upon, especially so when lit from within with happiness. Would that he could endeavor to keep her thus for all time.

Soon she pulled to the curb in front of the McGladreys' home. Robley surveyed the dwelling and the surrounding toft. About the size of a wealthy merchant's two-storied manor, their home was grand enough he supposed, but hardly comparable to Moigh Hall, Castle Inverness or even Meikle Geddes. He couldn't imagine five or more people living in such close proximity. On the other hand, he quite liked Erin's cozy apartment, which to his thinking was more akin to one grand chamber for a couple who were wed. Mostly he found it adequate because she was there. He'd enjoy it even more if they shared one bed.

He jumped out of the car and raced around to the driver's side to help her out. He handed her the container of cookies and placed his hand at the small of her back, guiding her toward the McGladreys' front door.

"Wow. They have a nice house," Erin whispered. She shifted the container of cookies to one hand and slung her purse strap over her shoulder. "I've met Connor's wife. She's a pediatrician."

"I dinna ken what that means."

"She's a doctor who works with children."

The word *doctor* was not familiar either, but he let it go. "You smell good, lass."

"Like the white chocolate and macadamia nut cookies we spent all afternoon baking?" She shot him a wry grin.

"Mmm. Mayhap a taste before we go inside?" He drew her close, and barely brushing her skin, he nuzzled her neck and inhaled. Heaven. Her sweet, fresh scent filled him, and the velvety soft warmth of her skin heated his blood. She raised her shoulder and shivered, proving he affected her the way she did him.

"You've already eaten a half dozen of these cookies," she said. "I think you've tasted enough."

"I was no' referring to the cookies, love."

"Robley . . ."

"Aye?"

"We talked about this."

"Did we? I recall a conversation regarding your mother, lass, but you are no' your mother." He gazed into her eyes, gauging just how much he could say before she hid behind the wall she'd built around her heart. "I recall hearing about your misguided notion that because of the many stepfathers passing through your life that you and I canna be together. I didna agree with you then, and I dinna agree with you now."

Did she not realize she never pulled away when he touched her? Though she feared getting close, they were becoming so anyway. He understood her fears, but it only made him more determined to prove to her that she could trust him with her heart.

Madame Giselle had sent him to Erin. Of this he was certain. With her skills and knowledge as a midwife, she'd be a treasure to his clan. They were meant for each other, and his determination to win her strengthened tenfold. The task of convincing her to return with him to his century presented a challenge—but MacKintosh men thrived on challenges.

Surely it would take more than a month's time to make her his, and this era held so much to discover and enjoy. Perhaps a year would suffice. After all, when they returned, he could focus upon the very date he'd left, and it would be like no time at all had passed. A full year's time would also provide him with the opportunity to own a Harley, at least for a short while. Aye, he'd stay as long as it took to achieve his goals: win his lady's heart and trust, convince her to return with him to the fifteenth century and own a Harley Davidson.

Grinning, he reached out and used the knocker on the McGladreys' door. A young girl with a smartphone in hand answered. Mayhap she was ten and five or six years old, and she had her father's reddish-gold hair and freckles, but where Connor's eyes were blue, his daughter's eyes were a dark brown. Robley bowed. "You must be Meghan."

"That's right, and you must be the fifteenth-century knight my dad told us about."

"I am. Robley of clan MacKintosh at your service, lass." He gestured toward Erin. "This is my lady, Erin of clan Durie. Our thanks for your hospitality."

Meghan rolled her eyes and opened the door wider, ushering them inside. "My parents are in the kitchen. This way." She led them toward the back of the house.

"Smells good in here," Erin said.

"Mom made her famous pot roast. It's Dad's favorite."

They entered a large, bright kitchen. Connor stood at the counter, knife in hand and a pile of vegetables before him. "Robley, Erin, welcome. This is my wife, Katherine."

"Call me Kathy." A tall, fair lass glanced at them from her place by the stove. "It's good to see you again, Erin, and it's amazing to meet another man from the Middle Ages." She cast him a welcoming smile. "I'm sure this has been quite an adjustment for you. Meghan, take over making the salad for your dad. Connor, would you get our guests something to drink?"

"Of course." Connor handed the knife to his daughter and moved out of the way. "Ale or wine?"

"Ale, if you please." Robley took off his hooded sweatshirt and draped it over the back of a kitchen chair.

"As promised, here's dessert." Erin placed her container of cookies on the counter. "I'd love a glass of wine. Whatever you have handy is fine." Shrugging out of her jacket, she turned to Kathy. "Is there anything I can do to help?"

"Nope. Meg and I have it covered, and the dining room table is already set. I know there are things Connor and Robley need to discuss, and since it involves you, you should be there."

"Follow me." Connor handed them their drinks and beckoned them to follow. He opened a door next to the one leading to their attached garage. "My wife calls this my man cave." Connor switched on an overhead light. "When our children were small, we had this area set up as a playroom, but now that they're mostly grown, it's my space."

They descended into a finished room in their basement. Antique swords of all sizes and styles had been mounted on one wall, and a set of armor stood on a stand in the corner. A large desk sat opposite the armor, with a laptop similar to the one Lady True had shown him.

"Is this the armor you wear when jousting at the Renaissance festivals?" Erin walked over and ran her hand over the shiny metal.

"It is. Because of his skill and they way he goes about his craft, I suspect the blacksmith who makes the reproduction chain mail, armor and weaponry is also from the past, but he won't say for certain." Connor took a seat behind his desk and booted up his computer. "First and foremost, you'll need a birth certificate, Robley. It's best to stick as close to the truth as possible. Have a seat."

Robley twined his fingers through Erin's, pleased beyond measure when she didn't pull free, and led her to the lone leather couch. He drew her down beside him, keeping her hand in his. He set his ale on a small table beside him. "What do you need from me?" "Your date of birth, or as close to it as possible, and the location. Once we have your birth certificate established, we'll work on a passport and green card."

"Green card?"

"You're in this country illegally. A green card is like permission to be here for a specific period of time," Erin told him. "In fact, you don't really exist at all in terms of a paper trail. It's weird to think about."

"I see. I was born in the spring, the tenth day of May, 1402, at Meikle Geddes."

"Huh. I'm older than you." Erin's mouth quirked up.

"Hardly. At present, am I no' six hundred and eight? How old are you?"

"That just blows my mind. You've only been alive for twenty-four years, but you were born so long ago." She laughed. "I'm twenty-five."

"Let's get this done. Dinner will be ready soon." Connor glanced at them. "Father and mother's names, birthdates and places of birth?"

Robley gave him all the information, and Connor entered it into the computer. "With this, we can have a birth certificate and a Scottish passport created. I'll need to take your picture tonight, and then I'll send the information to the man I know who does this sort of thing. It's going to cost you. I can lend you the money against your wages if you wish."

"Nay, er . . . no. I have the funds."

"How?" Connor's brow rose. "Didn't you say you just came through a few days ago?"

"From me." Erin tightened her grip on his hand. "We've already agreed that I'll give him the money, and he'll pay me back once he's earning a regular paycheck."

Robley arched an eyebrow at her.

"Hmm. That reminds me, do you want a fake marriage license and certificate? It would be easier for Rob to become a citizen, if he wishes to remain in the United States, that is."

Erin's face turned a lovely shade of pink. Rob slid his arm around her shoulders. "I like the idea. What say you, lass? Will you do me the honor of becoming my pretend wife?"

"I don't like the idea at all." She shot him a mutinous glare. "All of this is completely illegal, and I'm not sure I want to get messed up in all these false documents."

"It's not Rob's fault he's been displaced," Connor said. "He doesn't exist at all in this century. What we are doing is not the same as stealing someone's identity to engage in criminal behavior. We're simply moving him from his time to ours. Since he's not stealing the birth certificate of anyone living or deceased from our time, it's unlikely anyone will discover the documents are false. The information he's giving is true and not stolen. It's just from a different time." Connor leaned back in his chair and fixed her with a hard stare.

"What do you expect him to do, lassie? He needs to build a life. A man needs to make a living if he wants to support himself. He'll want to support his family should he choose to have one. Would you rather condemn him to a half-life on the fringes of society?"

"Aye, lass," Robley agreed. Erin flashed him another scowl.

"Dinner is ready," Katherine called from the top of the stairs.

"We'll finish later." Connor rose from his place behind the desk. "My wife's pot roast is best when it's consumed right from the oven."

"We'll be along anon. Erin and I have a few things to settle." Robley tightened his grip on her hand. "I want a few words with my wife-to-be."

"Good idea." Connor looked from Rob to Erin and back to him. "Don't be too long."

He waited until Connor closed the door at the top of the stairs before turning to her. "Why did you say you'd lend me the money? I have plenty."

"I know, but you said you didn't want to tell Connor you had a way back. How would you have explained the debit card and cash without making it clear you planned this little holiday to the future? Wouldn't that lead to the logical assumption that you have a way to return?" She shrugged. "It just seemed simpler to say I'm floating you the loan. He doesn't know anything about my personal situation."

"Ah, I take your meaning." He rubbed his chin. "My mistake."

"I don't normally lie, Robley, and I've never broken any laws." She shook her head. "I am not agreeing to a fake marriage. There's no need." She lifted her chin a defiant notch. "I don't really see why you want any of this fake documentation anyway. You'll be leaving soon." She shot off the couch, but not before he glimpsed the hurt in her eyes. "Let's go eat. It's rude to stay down here when we've been invited to dinner."

She clomped up the stairs, wineglass gripped in her hand, and he was left wondering what upset her the most: believing that he would leave her soon, or the deceit involved in creating a false paper trail of his existence? Judging by the way she'd reacted on Monday when she'd thought him gone for good, he chose to believe the former.

He knew her father and stepfathers had let her down, leaving her all too soon, and he understood the source of her anxiety. Recognizing the source provided him with a problem to fix, and fix it he would. Grinning like a fool, he followed her.

Robley ran his hand over the sleeve of his brand-new black leather Harley Davidson jacket and glanced at Erin. She wore hers as well, carrying the jackets they'd walked in with in a bag slung over her arm. He took the bag from her while she handed the man behind the counter True's debit card. Their new jackets were identical, with one orange and one white stripe on the sleeves and the Harley logo on the front and back. He liked that she'd chosen to purchase the identical jacket to his. 'Twas a sign to other men that she belonged to him, like wearing the plaid of his clan.

He could hardly believe he'd already been there three weeks. He'd taken over several classes Connor had been teaching, freeing his friend to get caught up on the paperwork stacked high on his desk. The two of them had begun sparring on a regular basis, and Erin seemed to get on well with Connor and his family. He'd even accompanied Erin to the Renaissance festival the last weekend she'd worked there. Mayhap he'd join the reenactment club. He certainly had much to offer.

He surveyed the store while waiting by the counter as his lady signed the slip of paper the merchant had handed her along with True's debit card. "I want to look at bikes before we leave, babe."

"Of course you do." Erin arched her brow. "Thanks," she told the fellow who had helped them, sliding the pen and the slip of paper toward him.

"My pleasure. The showroom is right next door." He gestured toward a door separating the shop they were in from the chamber housing the motorcycles.

Rob reached for Erin's hand, tugging her close. "Let's go."

She laughed. "All right already. Relax. We have two hours before the movie starts, and you can spend the time looking at all the shiny new motorcycles, but we are not buying one today."

He frowned. "But we could. You said there's enough money in the account, and I'm earning more now."

"Where would you keep it, Rob? Winter is coming, and believe me, you have no idea how cold and snowy it gets here in Minnesota. You couldn't ride it until spring."

She spoke in terms of the future, warming his heart and causing his spirits to soar. He drew her into his arms and kissed her soundly on the lips, backing off right away lest she protest.

"What was that for?" she asked, wide-eyed.

"I'm happy. Are you no' happy, love?" Taking her hand again, he opened the door to the showroom and ushered her through.

"I am." Her expression clouded. "But—"

"No buts today. Behold." He swept his hand out in a semicircle. "My trusty mount awaits."

The corners of her mouth turned up. "I suppose once you get your hands on one of these bad boys you'll never want to leave. In fact, I'll bet you'd give the dang thing a name."

"Hmm." He rubbed his chin, feigning deep thought. "I shall call him Harley. No point in confusing the beast." Erin laughed, and the sweet sound filled him near to bursting with satisfaction. He'd brought a smile to her face, brought laughter to her heart. Surely she cared for him as he cared for her.

Erin had begun to open up to him, sharing stories of her day, giving voice to the things that caused her to worry. Her compassion had no bounds when it came to the women and bairns she worked with during her clinicals, as she called them. Intelligent, compassionate, warm, sensitive and beautiful, Erin held him spellbound, and she had no idea just how amazing he found her.

"It's no' the machines or the technology that keeps me here, love." Again he drew her into his arms, losing himself in the depths of her lovely green eyes, not to mention the feel of her curves against him. "You must know that I—"

"Can I help you folks?"

Erin backed out of his embrace and averted her gaze. He couldn't let her retreat, didn't want to lose the closeness they'd shared all day. Nay. He'd worked too hard to build that closeness over the past three weeks as he slowly chipped away at her defenses and fear. She'd grown accustomed to his affection, allowing him to hold her hand, accepting brief hugs and a chaste kiss from time to time. He reached for her hand again, twining his fingers with hers. "We're just looking."

"All right." The merchant put his hands in his pockets and nodded. "If you need anything or have any questions, I'll be around." He moved off toward another man walking through the showroom.

Robley drew her along beside him. They had time yet for the talk he longed to have with her. For now, he'd be content to spend the day with her hand in his. "What color do you prefer?" He ran his hand over a shiny blue gas tank.

"I like classic black."

"Black would look nice with our matching jackets." They spent an hour looking at the different bikes, hand in hand. Rob found one he really liked, counting the months before spring. Six. He'd have his documents long before then, and he'd insisted on getting the proper license so he could drive a motorcycle of his own. He thought less and less about returning home the more his life in this time took shape. He should be alarmed by the realization, but one look at Erin walking by his side, and all his worries fled.

"Are you ready to head to the mall, Rob?"

"If you're certain we cannot purchase my Harley today, then aye."

"I'm certain. Let's go."

She towed him along, and he feigned reluctance to leave, just to coax another smile from her. "Shall I drive?" He shot her a hopeful look.

"Do you know the way to the Roseville Mall?" She arched her brow.

"Uh, no, but you could direct me. I need more practice. Besides, I don't get nauseated if I'm driving."

"Not this time. Driving around in a parking lot or on city streets isn't the same as driving on the freeway."

"Aye, and how am I to learn if you willna let me practice?"

She unlocked the passenger door. "Not today."

"Fine." He squeezed himself into her wee car and buckled his seat belt.

Fifteen minutes later they were searching for a parking place in a large lot situated in the midst of a huge complex of connected buildings. "This is what you meant by a mall?"

"Yep. It's called a mall because you can remain inside and get to all the stores facing a common open area." She pulled into a spot that had just been vacated. "There's the theater." She pointed. "Not all of the movies are three-dimensional. Some are flat, like you see on my TV, but I thought you'd enjoy seeing something in 3-D."

Holding hands, they wove their way through the other parked vehicles and entered the glass-fronted theater to get in line. "We're also going to buy popcorn." She inhaled. "With lots of butter."

"If it pleases you, babe." He watched for a reaction to his endearment. It never came. She was growing accustomed to him, accustomed to his affection and his touch. Just to prove his point, he placed his hands on her shoulders as they moved slowly forward in line.

She smiled at him over her shoulder. "I was thinking I should take you to the Mall of America next weekend. It's one of the largest malls in the world and quite a tourist attraction. Would you like that?"

He gave her shoulders a squeeze. "If you're with me, aye."

"And then we should visit a few museums, live theater and the airport. Maybe a water park, too."

He blinked. "A park for water?"

"Water rides, like slides and wave pools and stuff."

"Humph."

"I forget." She laughed. "You don't know what any of that is, do you?"

"Nay." They'd reached the head of the line, and Erin purchased their tickets. He followed her to another set of doors leading to the interior of the theater, where they handed over their tickets to a young lad, who gave them two pairs of 3-D glasses in exchange. Erin had told him they'd have to wear the glasses during the movie. He waited in yet another line while Erin purchased a large bucket of buttered popcorn and a soda for them to share.

His mind drifted, thinking about how best to begin the conversation he longed to have with her. How should he go about asking her to return to his century with him? Though staying in her time appealed to him, he couldn't prevent his rising concern for his clan and family. He had obligations, and even if he did remain in the twenty-first century for a year, he was meant to return to his home. Following Erin again, they entered a large great hall with a huge screen in front and row upon row of upholstered seating.

She chose two seats with a railing before them. "I like to put my feet up," she explained, handing him the tub of popcorn. She placed the soda in a holder between their two places and took her jacket off, settling it on the back of her chair. Once she sat down, she reached for the popcorn again. "Get settled."

Slipping out of his jacket, he sat beside her. The scent of the popcorn enticed him. "I would try this popcorn of yours." She handed him a few paper napkins, and he took a handful of the white snack, putting it in his mouth. The buttery, salty taste filled his senses. "Good," he mumbled, reaching for more.

"As good as pizza?"

"Nay, but still good." The lights dimmed, and the screen in front of them came to life.

Erin leaned closer to him. "There will be about twenty minutes of ads and previews before the movie starts. You don't put on your glasses until the screen tells you to."

He nodded and slipped his arm around her. Contentment filled him. It didn't matter what century he found himself in, so long as he had Erin beside him. Longing to hold her in his arms and make sweet love to her swept through him. Once he made his intentions toward her clear, mayhap she'd invite him into her bed. Thoughts of their naked bodies twined together sent heat and lust spiraling through him.

She nudged him and pointed to the screen. "Put your glasses on."

He did, and immediately things jumped off the screen, heading straight for him. Taking the glasses off, he studied them.

"It's OK, Rob. The glasses only make it appear like things on the screen have depth, like they're coming off the screen. They aren't really."

"I ken that, lass. I'm just wondering how it happens?" He slipped them back on as their movie began. At first, everything was fine, but as soon as the action started and the cars and flames shot out at him, nausea overtook him. He tore off the glasses and leaped out of his seat, heading for the dark hallway. He strode out of the theater into the foyer beyond. Leaning against the wall, he closed his eyes against the spinning sensation and the nausea roiling in his gut.

"You OK, Robley?" Erin asked.

He cracked an eye open and shook his head. "It's like I get sometimes with motion. I fear I might vomit."

"I can help." She laid her hands on him, running them up and down his arms from his shoulders to his elbows. "Breathe deep and slow."

The moment she touched him, the dizziness ceased, and a mere second later his stomach stopped churning. The same had happened when she stroked his back after his very first car ride. He frowned. Why had he not noticed before, or at least made the connection between her magical touch and the easing of his nausea? "Erin, the moment you touched me, my discomfort eased. Why is that, love?"

She bit her lip and averted her face, fisting her hands at her sides. Robley placed a finger under her chin, bringing her gaze to his. "Is there something you wish to tell me?"

"I . . . I don't know for sure, but . . ." She swallowed. "I think I might have some of that faerie blood running through my veins," she whispered.

Shock sluiced through him, realization fast on its heels. He was naught but a pawn in some scheme Madame Giselle had foisted upon him, a means to an end, the end being bringing Erin back through time like she had True. What did the faerie know that led her to seek out Erin, and how could he protect her from whatever fate lay in wait for her?

CHAPTER EIGHT

Right there in the Roseville AMC theater, Erin shared her secret. Not since her unstable, less-than-ideal childhood had she ever told another living soul about her abilities, and here she was spilling it to Robley of freaking fifteenth-century clan MacKintosh. "I can tell things about people, like where they hurt, whether or not they're healthy, stuff like that," she stammered.

"When I touch my patients, their pain lets up some, or their nerves calm. Things like nausea or headaches I can handle with no problem. Bigger things, like broken bones or disease"—she shook her head—"not so much. All I can do is ease discomfort a little for the more serious conditions."

She glanced at him, trying to gauge his reaction. When he spoke of True, she'd never detected anything but respect, but still. After a lifetime of hiding who she was, sharing left her vulnerable. Exposed. He gave nothing away. She'd grown more than accustomed to his presence in her life, to the easy closeness that had developed between them. She didn't want that to change, didn't want him to see her differently, and that was bound to happen. Before she'd just been ordinary Erin Durie. Now she was *gifted*. Would he be guarded around her, less accessible?

"Perhaps somewhere in my family tree there's a faerie perching on one of the limbs. Like what you said about True and the boy she saved. I don't know where else I would've come by my abilities. Do you?"

"Humph."

That was it? A grunt? No comment? His intense scrutiny put her more on edge than she already was. She studied the shoelaces of her boots. The lace on the right was coming undone. "So I guess 3-D movies are out. Do you want to see if they'll exchange our tickets? We can see the same movie without the 3-D, or maybe something different."

"If it pleases you, I'd rather go home. There is much we need to discuss."

Her eyes widened. Maybe she preferred his lack of comment on the matter. Discussions about her abilities had never gone well when she was a kid. Her stepdads had never appreciated hearing their livers, hearts and lungs were suffering from all the abuse they heaped on them. Her mom had scoffed at her, insisting she was just being a little smart-ass with an overactive imagination.

Her heart raced, and the inside of her mouth went as dry as soda cracker crumbs. "What is there to discuss? My giftedness doesn't really change anything. You're here for a while, and—"

"Can we have this conversation in private, love?" He drew her into his arms and rested his chin on top of her head. "We can watch a movie at home anytime."

Anytime? Like his month-long vacation wasn't almost up, and he wasn't planning on leaving her soon? Lately, the leaving part obsessed her. Any day he could pop out of her life the same way he'd popped into it. The thought of him leaving sent her into a tailspin. She put her arms around his waist and burrowed into his warmth.

If only she could stay in his arms forever. She sighed. Thoughts like that would only lead to heartbreak. Correction, more heartbreak.

"All right." She stepped away from his warmth. "Let's go get our jackets. Toss your glasses in there." She pointed to a cardboard box set up just inside the door to the theater.

"I'll get our things." He took the 3-D glasses from her hand and dropped both pairs into the box. "Wait here for me."

They left the theater and walked through the parking lot to her car. On the ride home, the silence stretched between them, unsettling her even more. Rob stared out at nothing with a pensive expression on his face.

"What are you thinking about?" she asked. "You're so quiet."

"Hmm." He spared her a glance. "When I came back through time, I fixed New York in my mind. Giselle said focusing on a particular time and place would take me there." He shifted and ran his palms down his denim-clad thighs. "Instead of New York, I ended up in your arms. I'm certain 'twas no accident. Lady True suggested my obsession with the future and the overwhelming desire to come here may have been planted by the faerie."

"Do you regret coming here instead of ending up in New York?" She held her breath.

He scowled at her. "How can you ask such a question? You know I dinna. I think less and less of returning to my time. That should frighten me, but it doesn't." He reached out and lifted her braid in his hand to run his thumb over the end. "I've yet to see your hair free of this braid and flowing about your shoulders, lass. I'd very much like to see that."

His touch caused an internal riot of sensations—all of them sensual. What did he mean when he said he thought less about returning to his time? Did he mean he wanted to stay because of her? Or was he referring to the new life he'd begun, working with Connor and forming friendships with the men in her reenactment club? She flashed him a confused look. "What does seeing my hair down have to do with anything?"

He dropped her hair and went back to staring out the window. "It has naught to do with it."

"Well, that was cryptic," she huffed out. "What's really on your mind?"

He plowed his fingers through his hair and blew out a breath. "Giselle had a reason for sending me to you. I believe I'm to bring you back with me to the past."

OK! Did not see that coming. Now she knew what a knee-jerk reaction felt like, 'cause pretty much everything inside her jerked. "Sorry, Rob. I don't have the kind of balls it would take to leave my time for yours." She gripped the steering wheel with both hands, her eyes wide. "That's not going to happen."

"Nay? That's it? You willna even consider the matter?"

"I'm strictly a twenty-first-century girl." She shook her head. "My life is here. I have goals and plans. Ending up in the fifteenth century does not figure into my future."

"Plans dinna always unfold the way we wish them to, lass. Mayhap fate has another purpose in store for you, a greater one." He shot her a look, his eyes filled with a challenging glint. "Why do you belong to that reenactment club? Surely the past holds some attraction, aye?"

"Yes. It does—as a social outlet, and I love getting dressed up." She lifted her chin. "I may be drawn to some aspects of the past, but I like my HDTV, hot water, central heat, electricity and all the other technological perks that my time has to offer. I like the advances we've made in medicine. I want to work in a hospital where I know I'm backed up by a team of experts if something goes wrong with a delivery."

They reached her apartment building. She pulled into her parking spot and cut the engine. "If I knew I could return, I might consider a visit, but my place and time are here." Slinging her purse over her shoulder, she climbed out and headed for the door.

Robley followed. "Humph."

"I don't know what 'humph' means. You do that a lot. I'm going to start calling you Sir Grunts-a-Lot." More than anything she wanted to ask him to stay with her, but even if he did, it wouldn't last. They'd get tired of each other. Then the fights would start. They'd hurl hurtful words, resentment would grow and all the good feelings would disappear. She'd seen it over and over. *Love never lasts, and neither do relationships.*

What about Connor and Kathy? They'd been together since they were teens, and their love and respect fairly lit up a room. The green serpent of envy coiled in her gut, and she blinked against the hot tears filling her eyes. OK, there were a few exceptions, but she had no reason to believe she'd be one of them. Infidelity was probably an inherited trait, and she'd gotten it from both sides. The only difference between her and good old Mom was that she never let herself get close enough to a man to find out whether or not she could make the good feelings last. Why risk it? The disappointment would pulverize her.

Anxiety laced with sadness gripped her heart. Dragging herself up the stairs to her apartment, memories from her childhood swamped her. It was always the same. Her mother and her latest-and-greatest would start out giddy with love, and Erin would be showered with false affection and presents by the stepdad *du jour*. After a honeymoon period lasting all of six months, maybe a full year, the wear and tear would start to show. Then the angry words would fly through the air like poison darts. During those times, Erin was pretty much ignored by both the adults she should've been able to depend on the most. Who needs it? She opened her door and walked into her apartment.

Before she could even take her jacket off, Robley took her by the shoulders, turned her around and wrapped her up in his arms. "I understand, love."

"What do you understand?" She scowled at him.

"I ken why you dinna allow yourself to have expectations. 'Tis clear as day why you gird your heart with impenetrable armor, but I can see through to the hurt you wish to hide. More than anything, I wish to sweep the pain away and leave naught but joy in its wake."

Before she could respond, his mouth covered hers in a kiss so tender and sweet, her soul took flight. The man could kiss. Her legs went weak, and her breath got hung up in the flutters and flips happening in all her other major organs. Delicious heat spiraled through her as his tongue slid over and around hers. She pressed closer to his fine, muscled chest and circled her arms around his neck to play with the soft hair covering his collar.

She should back away, but she couldn't. Instead, she kissed him back, opening up to him like a flower desperate for sunlight. He *was* the sun, the center of her galaxy, and she had been drawn by his magnetism into his orbit. When had that happened? How would she survive once he left? He pulled back, eliciting a groan of protest from her.

"There are things you need to understand, love." He rested his forehead against hers. "Things I must tell you before we continue down this path."

"Yeah?" She imagined a path all right, a path leading straight to her bedroom, with items of clothing littering the oak floor like bread crumbs along the way. "Like what?"

"MacKintosh men give their hearts but once and for all time. We do no' take our vows lightly. When I take that step, I mean to see it through to the end of my days. There are no divorces, lass. I am no' a fickle man. You can depend upon it—you can depend upon me."

"Oh, Rob." Her eyes stung, and her stupid chin quivered like a five-year-old's. "Don't you think everyone believes that in the beginning? Love starts out all shiny and bright. New lovers behave as if they're on some kind of high, drugged on a magical substance that only *they* have access to. But eventually the high wears off and they come down. Things always turn ugly."

"Nay, lass." He cradled her face in his large hands. "My mother and father still love each other as much as they did when first they wed. Mayhap even more, for they have a lifetime of memories to shore them up during the tough times. The trials they've been through have strengthened their bond, deepened their respect and regard for one another. They've been married nigh on thirty years now. 'Tis the same for my uncle and his lady wife and my cousin and True. Love *does* last. Marriages can be a wellspring of love and respect lasting a lifetime and beyond. They don't have to end in acrimony and bitterness."

He lifted her chin with a finger and brushed his lips across hers. "The marriages of my clan are the lasting kind. 'Twill be the same for us. I swear it by all that I hold dear. Will you accept my love, Erin of clan Durie? For my heart longs to make a home with yours. I burn for you, and I always will."

She swallowed against the tightness in her throat. "Oh, Rob . . . I don't think . . . It's too soon to talk about this stuff. You've only been here a few weeks. We hardly know each other."

"I know you were meant for me." He gripped her shoulders and dragged her back into his arms with bone-crushing force. "No matter how long it takes, I shall convince you of the veracity of my convictions."

"I don't even know what that means," she wailed, burying her face against the bare skin at his throat. She took in his unique, wonderful smell. "I need a dictionary just to talk to you." She placed her palms against his pecs, just as the temperature in her apartment took a sudden nosedive.

Wait. A hot guy kisses you, holds you in his arms and tells you his heart wants to shack up with yours . . . and the temperature drops? Shouldn't it rise? Is this some kind of sign?

A wave of scent followed the sudden change in temperature. "What is that?" She sniffed the air. "It reminds me of the way it smells outside just before a rainstorm hits, only we're inside. Weird." Her brow furrowed, and she scanned her apartment. "Is it natural gas? Maybe there's a leak. We should get out of here."

"Shite. Get behind me, lass."

"Why?"

Rob pivoted and shoved her behind him just as neon-blue light flashed through her living room.

"Human."

What the hell? An otherworldly voice reverberated throughout her apartment, its tone derisive. Erin peeked over Robley's shoulder, and her mouth fell open. Right there in the middle of her ordinary apartment stood a tall, slender man limned in blue light, like the blue flames you'd see at the center of a campfire. Long, white hair fell around his shoulders, and his large, luminous eyes were an impossible shade of pale sky-blue. He glanced at her, and his eyes widened for a second before aiming his glare at Robley. "You have stolen from the high king of the *Tuatha Dé Danann*. The penalty for such a grievous offense is death."

Whoa. Adrenaline pulsed through her, and she ducked back behind Rob's broad back. The being didn't hold any weapons that she could see. Good. Fishing through the junk cluttering the inside of her purse, she searched desperately for the canister of pepper spray she always kept with her. No way was she going to let this thing hurt Robley. No. Way. Her heart pounded away like a kettle drum, making her ears ring. *Where is it?*

"Where is the pensieve, mortal? Return it to me now, and your life might still be spared."

"I know naught of any pensieve, or what a pensieve might be." Rob widened his stance. "How is it you've come after me?"

He wanted to have a conversation with this being? "Shut up," she hissed. He responded by reaching around to encircle her waist, pinning her to his back. She continued her search for the leather-bound canister buried somewhere in her stupid too-big bag, glancing over Rob's shoulder at the being again.

"I followed the trail of your stench from my king's chamber in Avalon to this hovel." The being raised his hands, and blue fire appeared at his fingertips. "Where is the king's pensieve?"

Oh shit! It doesn't need weapons. We're about to be incinerated!

"I was commissioned and sent to Avalon to fetch a silver platter for one of your kind, and once I did the deed, I handed it over to her." Robley let go of her to fold his arms in front of him. "Is that what you are referring to?"

"Who asked this of you? To whom was it given?"

"In human guise she calls herself Madame Giselle. I dinna know her fae name." And now he kent why it had been so important to Giselle that he couldn't call her by her true name. Conniving faerie! "In exchange for my part, I was granted two tokens for travel through time. She said the item belonged to her."

"You were . . . misled."

"Humph. Used like a pawn in her game of chess, you mean."

Finally! Erin pulled the small cylinder out, unsnapped the leather covering the nozzle and gripped it so she could shoot straight. Pushing out from behind Robley, she lunged forward, aimed for the creature's eyes and sprayed for all she was worth.

The combination of pepper and mace came right back at her—and Rob. "Augh!" She dropped the canister and covered her burning eyes and nose.

"What the devil did you do, Erin?" Rob cried. "I canna see!"

"I was trying to protect you," she shot back.

"And then what?" he rasped out.

"I don't know," she snapped. "Maybe run for it?"

Eerie laughter echoed off her walls, and the temperature dropped even lower. "You have thirty of your human days to retrieve the pensieve, mortal. I'll return for it then. If you wish to live, do not fail. This is not your time, nor your place—another of our laws you have broken."

The world around her began to spin at a sickening speed. "Robley," she cried, stretching her arms out in a blind search.

"Here, lass." He pulled her into his arms and held her tight. "I'm here."

Pressure from all sides wracked her, pulling, pushing and pressing into her all at once, threatening to tear her apart. Her head hurt, and her heart climbed into her throat, while her face burned like it was on fire. Tears streamed down her cheeks, and she clung to Rob. Screaming at the top of her lungs, she held on to him for dear life.

After what seemed like forever, she landed on her back with a thud against something hard, and Robley landed on top of her. Struggling to draw breath, she swiped at her eyes and cried, this time not from the spray, but from the horror and the sublime realization that she'd survived the ordeal. "What just happened? What have you done?"

"What have *I* done? What have *you* done? I'm blind. You've blinded me." He rolled away to lie on his back beside her. "Shite! What is it that causes such agony?"

"It's a combination of pepper spray and mace."

"Lay your hands on me, lass. Make the burning stop."

"No."

"No?" His voice came out an incredulous croak.

"That's right. You heard me. No. I'm too *pissed*." She sniffed and wished she had a box of Kleenex to take care of the snotty mess she'd become. A twinge of guilt tugged at her, but it passed just as quickly as it came. The burn would go away eventually, and he wasn't the only one suffering.

"By *pissed*, I take it to mean you are none too pleased with me."

"Exactly. What did you do, Robley?"

"I told you. I made a bargain with a faerie in exchange for the two crystals."

"Yes, but you failed to mention you stole from their high king. What were you thinking?"

"Giselle never told me *whose* chamber I'd entered, and I didn't care to ask. Besides, we'll never know the truth of the matter. They're fae. They live for intrigue and games."

"Great." Erin opened her puffy eyes a slit. They lay in a field of dry grass and wildflowers that had gone to seed. The air held a crisp chill, and the forest behind them wore the brilliant colors of late autumn—gold, crimson and burgundy, interspersed with the deep hue of evergreens. She caught sight of a large, uncut diamond on the ground between them, like the one Robley kept stashed in his back pocket. This must be the place where his journey began. Hadn't he told her the return trip always took the time traveler back to the exact point of their departure? "I don't think we're in Minnesota anymore."

"Nay." Rob swiped his hands over his watering eyes. "We're in Scotland."

"I found the other diamond." She picked up the valuable gem and closed her fist around its cool hardness. She held it out to him. "Here."

"Keep it, lass."

"Do you think it'll get me home?" she asked in a quavering voice. She slid the crystal into her purse, which she'd somehow managed to keep during their tumultuous passage.

He shook his head. "I've already used the magic in the first, but I willna keep you here against your will." He pushed himself up from the ground to loom over her. Blinking and tearing, he peered at her through red, swollen eyes. "Had I kent what the faerie intended, I would no' have drawn you into my arms. 'Twas pure instinct. I apologize, lass."

His tone was flat and filled with pain. She'd hurt him, rejected him, and that cut her deeply. But what did he expect? Did he think she'd just up and leave behind everything she knew, everything she'd struggled so hard to achieve? Unfair. Asking so much of her had been unfair. He offered her a hand, and she took it.

"At least I have the Harley jacket to remember you by." He drew her into a hard hug, releasing her all too quickly. Reaching into his back pocket, he fished out the leather pouch holding the unused diamond. "I'll miss that claymore. 'Twas made for me by a master blacksmith who passed from this world years ago."

Things? He wanted to talk about things while her heart was about to be ripped from her chest? "Rob, I wasn't rejecting you. You do know that, don't you? I . . . of course I care for you. You know I do, but—"

"Then stay. Give us time. Take a chance, and I swear by all that is holy that I'll never let you down. 'Tis all I ask."

"I can't. I *have* to finish school. I have to." She grabbed the edges of his jacket front. "Come back with me. You still want that Harley, right?"

"You heard the faerie." He covered her fists with his large, callused hands. "If I wish to live beyond my four and twenty years, I must find Madame Giselle and grovel at her feet for the return of the bloody pensieve." He grunted. "I suspected the task was far too simple. My parents are right. I am impetuous, impulsive. More frequently than no', I fail to think things through before acting."

"This . . . I guess this is good-bye. Having you with me these past few weeks has been amazing. Really amazing." She could hardly breathe. How would she go on without him? He'd wormed his way into her heart, and losing him would leave her hollow. "I hope you're able to find Giselle and that everything works out for you."

Another reason to go. How could she bear it if she stayed only to lose him? If she left, no matter what really happened, she could pretend that he'd lived on, married and had a family. She could imagine him happy. She held out her hand, and he poured the diamond into her palm. "How does this work?"

"Find a hard spot on the ground and spin the crystal like a top. You'll see the air above it begin to shimmer. Fix in your mind where and when you want to be, and then step into the shimmering air."

"I suppose it'll hurt just as much on the return journey." Sighing, she studied the gem, looking for the magic held within its depths. "I'll miss you, Rob."

"You dinna have to leave, Erin. I dinna want to lose you."

She bit her lip and searched his face for understanding. "I know, but my family . . . it isn't much, but . . . my mom is going to need me soon. I just know it. And there's school. I have a life." Kind of. Mostly she felt as if her real life had begun the day he fell into her. He'd filled her thoughts and her days, and she'd been happier than ever before. She'd miss having him to come home to, miss sharing tidbits of her day, hearing about his and relaxing over dinner or a TV show with her hand in his. "That faerie said time travel is against their laws. Even if I did stay, I'd probably be sent back once he catches up with us."

The muscles along Rob's jaw tightened and twitched. He nodded, turning his gaze toward the tree line behind them. "Best get on with it, babe."

A strangled laugh broke free. "Babe? It cracks me up when you slip that into your fifteenth-century vernacular." She found a hard, bare place on the ground and crouched low. Placing the diamond in the center, she gave it a good spin. Nothing happened. She tried again, and once more nothing changed. "Why isn't it working?"

"Humph." Rob stepped closer. "Mayhap I must be the one to spin the crystal, since the tokens were given to me."

"Do it then." She handed over the diamond.

He took it and looked from the gem into her eyes. "Erin—"

"Don't, Rob. This is already difficult enough. Don't make it worse."

Nodding, he placed the crystal on the ground and sent it spinning. Nothing happened.

Erin went all weak and wobbly inside. Collapsing back onto the grass, she stretched out and stared into the sky. So many emotions swirled through her at once, she could hardly catch hold of a single one. Fear. Panic. Disbelief. The option to return to her own time had been taken from her, and even though she was scared out of her wits, an overwhelming sense of relief came right on the tail of all the other emotions.

Relief?

She'd have to think about that, but not now. Right now she was beyond thought. A crushing weariness pressed her into the ground. "Well," she said to the clear blue sky, "it's been quite a day."

"That it has." Rob lay down beside her and reached for her hand. "I'm sorry, lass. I'm so sorry my actions have interfered with your plans," he rasped out, his voice breaking.

"Not your fault. Not entirely, anyway." She sighed. "I'm having a hard time keeping my eyes open all of a sudden." She twined her fingers with his. "I need a nap."

"Time travel has that effect. We're on MacKintosh land and safe enough for now, and at any rate, I dinna want to return to Loch Moigh until Vespers."

"What does that mean?" She glanced at him.

"Early evening around six, going by your modern clocks. Dressed as we are, I'd rather slip in when it's no' full daylight. Sleep, babe. I'll watch over you."

Exhausted and far too close to hysteria, a giggle burst free. "You think the Harley jackets might raise a few eyebrows?"

"Aye, for certes." He put his strong arms around her, sharing his warmth and strength. "Wheesht now, lass, and dinna fash yourself. Rest."

What choice did she have? She curled into his side, let everything go and did just that.

CHAPTER NINE

He'd been selfish, impulsive, and look where it had landed him—in a month's time, 'twas more than likely he'd be dead, leaving his love alone and stranded in a century and place not her own. What new bargain could he possibly enter into with Giselle that would persuade her to give up what he'd only just handed over? Wracking his brain, he could think of naught.

Guilt tore him apart as he held Erin in his arms and watched her sleep. "I *will* recover the pensieve and keep you safe. I swear it," he whispered. By the saints, he prayed he could make good on his vow.

His remorse was chased in equal measure by a surge of relief, and he sent up a fervent prayer of thanks. The crystal hadn't worked, and more than ever he believed Erin was meant to be with him. If that were true, then it only stood to reason everything else would sort itself out.

All Erin needed was time to adjust before she could accept that his love for her was true. Now they had the time. He'd convince her that lasting love did exist, and once she trusted him, surely she'd agree to stay if given a choice. He ran his knuckles over the delicate curve of her soft cheek, then tucked an errant strand of her honey-colored hair behind her ear.

Her ferocious attempt to protect him from the faerie brought a bittersweet smile to his face. Tenderness and desire welled in his chest, and he drew her closer, cradling her cheek next to his heart. *Mine.* The thought brought a fresh sting to his eyes having naught to do with the horrific pepper spray. He had indeed found his braw, canny lass, and he had no intention of losing her.

The sun neared the western horizon, casting the landscape in long shadows. "Wake up, babe." He shook her gently. "Time to go."

She stretched, yawned and rubbed at her eyes. "More sleep."

"Later. A bed awaits. Up now." Rising from the ground, he too stretched. "Come, love. We dinna want to spend the night out in the open where we are unprotected. I have no weapons to hand. Let us be off while there is still light enough to guide our way."

"All right," she grumbled.

He helped her to her feet. "We shan't take the ferry across the loch. 'Twill draw too much attention. We'll borrow a *curach*."

"A what?"

"Hmm, a boat and paddles. I believe True refers to them as *canoes*."

"Steal one you mean?" She snorted. "I sure wish I'd known you were a thief before I invited you to stay with me."

"I am no' a thief—more like an ill-informed page. I'll send the boat back on the morrow. I'm the earl's nephew, Erin, a noble, and one day I will be seneschal over all the MacKintosh holdings, as is my father. None would begrudge me the use of their *curach*."

His future prospects were assured, and he could well afford a wife and family. Did she no' see? *Huh.* He'd seen his preordained path as a burden less than a month ago, and now he longed to take up that yoke. When had his thinking altered so? The prospect of dying surely played a part—that and the sweet lass standing beside him. He could be content to live out his days as Malcolm's seneschal as long as he had Erin. If only his life would last beyond the thirty days given to him . . .

Robley led Erin along the path he'd traversed most of his life. They came over the rise, and she gasped, tugging him to a standstill.

"Oh, Rob." She stared. "This is . . . this is where you live?"

He surveyed the sight laid before them, trying to see it through her eyes. Their village lined the shore. Curls of smoke rose from the chimneys, sending the scent of burning wood, peat and roasting meat wafting toward them. Their island keep stood proud, with a number of smaller buildings on the outskirts of the bailey wall. Shaggy MacKintosh kine dotted the hills surrounding the village, along with flocks of sheep and horses. The sun threw streaks of bright orange, pink and indigo behind the island, and in the distance, the mountains cast their silhouettes like dark guardians over all the land.

"Aye," he said with pride. "This is our home, the ancestral seat of the MacKintosh clan and the center of a thriving earldom."

"Spectacular," she whispered. "Wow."

"Come. A hot meal and a warm bed are but a short distance away." He continued down the hill, hugging the shadows along the forest bordering the village. He knew where a number of small boats lined the shore, turned upside down with the oars tucked underneath. They hid behind the brush as the blacksmith crossed the road to enter the busy inn. Then they dashed for the shoreline.

Crouching low, they crept to the boats resting on the sand near the water's edge. Rob chose a sturdy skiff and turned it over. He pushed it into the water and fit the oars into place. "Climb in," he whispered. "Sit in the front." Waiting until she settled herself, he looked to the island. Best to head for the trail that ran to the kitchen in back. They could slip in through the servants' entrance and take the back stairs to the living quarters. He hoped to avoid running into anyone but family.

He took his time so as not to draw attention and rowed toward the island in the growing darkness. 'Twas no' so unusual for a boat with one or two of their clansmen to travel between the mainland and the island at this hour—at any hour, for that matter. Two people posed no threat, and 'twas unlikely any of their guards would challenge them. By the time they reached the island, full dark was almost upon them.

Erin hopped to shore and held the bow for him as he stepped out. He pulled the boat onto the shore and scanned the area. Once the borrowed skiff was secure, he turned to Erin. "Ready to meet my family?"

"Not really." Her shoulders slumped, and her voice quavered. "I'm not ready for any of this."

"They'll love you, lass, and you'll have more women seeking your help than you can imagine. We've no' had a midwife or a healer for a number of years. No' since Hunter's granddam passed away." He slipped his arm around her waist and ushered her toward the postern gate leading to the kitchen gardens.

Her shoulders straightened. "I hadn't thought of that." She sent him a small smile. "I can open my own clinic, can't I?"

"That you can. I'll help, and True has some knowledge of healing herbs. I'm certain that between the two of you, you'll keep our clan strong and healthy. A midwife is quite a treasure to any clan, and you have the benefit of training beyond that available in our time. Just think of the good you could do."

"While I'm here, anyway."

His heart plummeted. She was right. Once the faerie caught up with them . . . He shook off the thought. He had thirty days to find a solution. Thirty days to woo and win Erin of clan Durie. He opened the postern gate and ushered her through, steering her along the path toward the back door into their keep. "Our cook will be in the kitchen with her helpers. We need to slip by as quietly as possible. I dinna want to try to explain to the servants where I've been or why I'm dressed as I am. 'Twas midsummer when I left home, and 'tis late autumn now. Best discuss things with my family first."

"OK. I'm right behind you."

They made it past the kitchen and up the stairs, just as Malcolm and Hunter reached the top of the front stairway. His cousin froze, his eyes narrowing at the sight of them in the dimly lit corridor.

"Where the devil have you been?" He glared. "What were you thinking, Rob? Do you have any idea what you've put your parents through?" Malcolm strode toward them as if he hadn't noticed Erin cowering behind him. "If it had no' been for my wife's confession that she kent what you were about, we would still be scouring the countryside for your remains."

"I had intended to return to the same time I left. None were to ken I'd even left." Tension banded his chest. He hated being spoken to as if he were a lad with no sense. It had always been thus with Malcom and his brother Liam. Mayhap because he was the young-est of the three of them, and the three had always been more like beloved brothers than cousins. "We encountered a bit of a compli-cation and—"

"We?" Malcolm scowled.

Rob stepped aside and gently drew Erin forward, tucking her against his side. "Aye. We. This is Erin of clan Durie."

"Just Erin," she stammered, shaking her head. "I really don't have a clan."

His cousin's brow rose as his glance moved over Erin and came back to him. He turned to Hunter. "Go fetch your ma and tell her to come at once to the lady's solar. Dinna say anything about this to any but her, especially no' to your shadow, Tieren."

"He's going to find out, Da. Everyone is." Hunter's gaze fixed upon Erin, a look of intense concentration on his face. Erin sucked in a sudden breath as she returned the stare. Hunter glanced at

Robley, his eyes filled with understanding. "She's gifted—like me, Sky and Ma."

"Go now," Malcolm commanded. Hunter took off like an arrow, and Malcolm turned back to them. "Come. To the solar. My mother and father are there with Sky. I was just on my way there to kiss my wee daughter goodnight. Come."

Rob's heart pounded against his rib cage. His uncle would no' be pleased with him for the worry he'd caused. Mayhap once they learned of the prize he'd brought home with him, all would be forgiven. They'd see his journey to the future was meant to be, like True's coming to them in their hour of need. "Are my parents here?"

Rob reached for Erin's hand as they followed his cousin down the corridor. Hers was cold and shaking. A rush of anger shot through him at Malcolm's harsh reception. Erin was frightened and exhausted as it was, and Malcolm had only made it worse.

"Nay," Malcolm tossed back over his shoulder. "They're at Meikle Geddes, mourning the loss of their youngest son."

The words cleaved through his heart. What had he told Erin? Plans dinna always unfold as we wish. Had things gone the way he'd intended, his absence would hardly have been noticed by the time he returned. "I must send word anon, or travel to Meikle Geddes myself on the morrow."

Erin tightened her grip on his hand. "Not without me."

"Let us discuss the matter with my father first." Malcolm rapped twice on the solar door and entered. "Look who I found skulking about in our halls."

"Oh my!" His aunt Lydia covered her heart, while keeping her other arm protectively around Sky. The two-year-old sat on her granddam's lap with two of her fingers stuck into her mouth and one of the many books True had made for her clasped in her other hand.

Sky dropped the book, and it slid to the floor. She held her arms out to Malcolm. "Da, want up," she said. Malcolm obliged, scooping her into his arms and hugging her to his chest. He kissed her forehead.

"Rob!" His uncle leaped from his place and crossed the room. "We despaired of ever seeing you home and safe again." William gripped his shoulders and gave him a shake. "What became of you, lad?" He held him away, his brow lowering as he took in Rob's garments and the silent woman standing behind him. "Who is this, Rob?"

"Uncle, Aunt, I beg your forgiveness for any worry I may have caused. I will tell the entire tale, but let us wait until True joins us." He slid his arm around Erin's shoulders and brought her to his side again. "This is Erin of clan Durie. She's a midwife and a healer," he said, his words infused with pride. He was proud of her. She'd worked hard to better herself and her circumstances. Compassionate, intelligent, spirited and beautiful inside and out, he could not have found her equal had he searched the entire world over. Still, right now she was overwhelmed and uncertain. "Might we offer our guest something to eat and make ready a chamber for her?"

"Aye." Malcolm handed his daughter back to Lydia, who had begun to rise. "Stay, Mother. I'll see to it."

Once he'd gone, Lydia turned to Erin. "Please, sit." She gestured toward the seat across from her. "Welcome to Moigh Hall."

"Down." Sky squirmed, making her wishes known. Lydia slid the child off her lap. "This is my granddaughter, Sky Elizabeth, and I'm Lydia, Robley's aunt. This is his uncle and my husband, the earl of Fife. Most address him as Laird."

"Nice to meet you." Erin sank into the chair and smiled at the curious toddler studying her with large brown eyes.

Sky picked up the fallen book and dropped it in Erin's lap. "Mine," she said. "Book." she touched it with a chubby finger.

"She's adorable."

"Aye, and she's grown during the months of my absence." Rob went to lean against the wall by the hearth.

"Aye, that she has." Lydia stared at Erin's jacket and blue trews. "We must find you something . . . more appropriate to wear, my dear. I believe we might still have a few gowns here belonging to my daughter, Elaine. They will do nicely."

Erin shrugged out of her jacket. "Thank you."

"This must all be so very strange and intimidating for you. Put your mind at ease, lass," his uncle William said. "You are most welcome."

"True came to us through time as well. 'Tis hard to imagine such a journey," Lydia added. "What wonders you must have seen, Robley!"

How like his aunt and uncle to accept and forgive in an instant. Affection for his kin filled him, warmed him through and through. "Aye, I've ridden an elephant, a camel and a Harley."

Lydia frowned. "What manner of animal is a Harley?"

"'Tis a motorcycle, a mode of transport, no' an animal at all, Aunt. Erin has pictures on her smartphone. Once everyone is here, we'll share them."

Malcolm returned, followed by Beth, the servant who had taken care of True when first she'd arrived. She held a tray in front of her, and the smell of lamb stew elicited a resounding rumble from his stomach.

Beth's eyes widened when they lit on Erin. She curtsied. "Milady, milord, I've brought ye some of Cook's stew. Once ye've done here for the evening, send for me, and I'll show the lady to her chamber." She set the tray on the small table in the corner and backed away, never taking her eyes from Erin.

"Beth, find whatever remains here of Elaine's wardrobe. Our guest will make use of them. See to it that at least one of the gowns is made ready for her to wear on the morrow."

"Aye, milady, right away. I've sent a maid to make ready a guest chamber."

"I trow you will keep this to yourself." Lydia smiled warmly and raised her gaze to Beth's.

"Aye, milady." She curtsied again before leaving.

"We can trust Beth." William took his place beside his wife again. "She's cared well for True since her arrival, and she kens her tale in full."

Lydia reached for Sky, who yawned and laid her head on her granddam's knee. "We'll have to agree upon a plausible story to explain Erin's sudden appearance in our midst—and your sudden reappearance, Rob."

"Come eat something, Erin. You must be hungry." Rob pulled out a chair from the table.

"I am. Thank you." She allowed him to lead her to the table where Beth had placed the tray. "Thank you for everything," she said, turning to his uncle and aunt. "For making me feel welcome, the food and . . ." Her voice trailed off, and she blinked as her eyes filled.

"Think nothing of it. You are most welcome, lass," William told her gruffly. "You've naught to fash about. You are in our care now."

Rob squeezed her shoulders. "A hot meal in your stomach will give you strength."

He took the seat beside her and tore into his stew. "We can say I've returned from a visit with Elaine and her family," he said between mouthfuls. "I met Erin there and persuaded her to return to Moigh Hall with me. The entire clan kens we need a wisewoman and midwife. They'll accept the tale without question."

The door to the solar opened, and a very pregnant True hurried through, her face flushed. Hunter followed, heading straight for Sky. The little girl fussed and held out her arms. Hunter gave her a big hug and kissed her tiny face all over until she giggled.

True's eyes shot to Robley, taking in the leather jacket he still wore, his jeans and twenty-first-century shoes. "Nice jacket." She shook her head. "It figures you'd take to my era like a duck to water. Welcome home, Rob. You gave us quite a scare. I was afraid you wouldn't return to us." Her expression solemn, she turned her gaze to Erin. Their eyes met and held.

"Oh." Erin dropped the bread she'd just dunked into her bowl. Her gaze fixed upon True's belly. She rose from the table and walked to True as if drawn by an invisible tether. "May I?" Her hands hovered over True's belly.

"Of course." True put her arms to her sides. "You have the gift? I felt your energy reaching for me."

Erin nodded. "I can ease pain, and I get impressions about physical well-being. I'm Erin Durie, by the way. I got caught up in Robley's drama with a faerie, and here I am."

"It's nice to meet you, Erin. I'm Alethia Goodsky, or I was anyway. Now I'm Lady True of clan MacKintosh. I got caught up in faerie drama too. I've been here for three years now."

"I'm a midwife, by the way, and before that I was an OB-GYN surgical nurse." Erin placed her hands on True's belly, and a broad smile lit her face. Rob and his family went still, watching and waiting. Once again pride swelled his chest to almost bursting.

"Fraternal twins!" Erin announced. "Both your sons are healthy, quite active and eager to come into the world. Do you know how far along you are? I'm guessing between thirty and thirty-two weeks?" Erin stepped back and rubbed her hands together.

"I told you we were having twins." True smirked at Malcolm. "Yes, I'm around thirty-two weeks, as close as I can tell."

"I never doubted you, *mo cridhe*." Malcolm paled. "I had only *hoped* you might be mistaken."

"It's all right, *mo céile*." True crossed the solar and took his hand in hers. "Everything is going to be fine. I'm not the first woman to give birth to twins, and we have a twenty-first-century midwife with us now." She turned to Erin. "My husband worries he'll lose me to childbirth. When I was pregnant with Sky, he even asked Madame Giselle to send me to my century to give birth."

"Twins do carry a greater risk, and they are often born early," Erin said. "In fact, in another week, I want you confined to the upstairs. No lifting. No climbing stairs or strenuous activity at all."

Malcolm pulled True down to his lap and put his arms around her. "I'll see to it that my wife takes your words to heart, lass."

True rolled her eyes. "I'm fine."

"And we want to keep it that way. Aye?" William shot her a stern look. "You carry the future earl of Fife, good daughter, not to mention you hold my son's heart in your wee hands. You *will* listen to your husband in this."

"All right. Enough. I'll do whatever our new midwife says." She grinned at Erin. "The men in this age are very bossy. You may as well get used to it." She glanced at him. "Can we move on? I want to hear about Robley's adventures, but first, Sky and Hunter need to go to bed."

"Och, Ma! I'm no' a bairn. Tell her I'm no' a bairn, Da." Hunter sent Malcolm a pleading look.

"Hunter is no' a bairn." Malcolm arched a brow and shrugged.

"I'm almost eight winters, and I'm a page." Hunter shot a look of pride Erin's way. "Da, tell Ma I can stay."

"Nay." Malcolm set True on her feet and stood. "You will listen to your mother. Always. There will be time enough for you to hear the tale another time. I'll call Beth to take you both."

Robley pushed his empty bowl aside. "Erin, come finish your stew, and if your chamber is ready, 'twould be best if you also took your leave. Give me your phone, though, so I can share the pictures."

"See? Told you. Bossy." True snorted. "MacKintosh men are all controlling and arrogant, and mine is the worst of the lot." She kissed Malcolm's cheek and laughed at his disgruntled expression as he left the solar.

"I really am beat. Plus, I know Rob's story. I was there for the whole thing." Erin fished her iPhone out of her purse and handed it to him. "If there's a place ready for me, I'd like to call it a night." She glanced at True. "We can talk more tomorrow."

"Of course. I've been there. I know what the journey through time does to you." True lifted the leather Harley jacket from the bench and handed it to Erin before settling herself in the spot Malcolm had vacated.

Sky climbed over to snuggle against her mother. "Night-night," she muttered before sticking her thumb into her mouth.

"That's right, Sky." True kissed her daughter's forehead and ran her finger along her cheek. "Our guest is going to bed, and so are you."

"I'm sure your chamber is ready, my dear," Lydia added. "Beth will take you to it anon."

"Does anyone ken what a pensieve is?" Rob asked. "'Tis at the center of the tale I'm about to share, and I've no bloody idea what one might be." Content to bide his time until the children and his lady were gathered up and led to their rest, he didn't want to begin his tale with Erin present. He needed his family's help and guidance in more matters than one.

"A pensieve is an object infused with magic," True answered. "When you look into one, you can see the past, the future or spy on others in the present."

The laird shook his head and sighed. "I willna ask how you ken this, good daughter."

"Harry Potter movies?" Erin asked, glancing at True.

"Exactly." True laughed.

"You could have asked me, Rob." Erin shrugged. "I have all the movies on DVD. We could've watched them together."

Malcolm returned, trailed by Beth. Erin and the bairns were led off to their rest, and his cousin settled himself beside his wife. "I've dispatched a messenger to Meikle Geddes. I'm certain your parents will be here within a few days."

"My thanks." Rob raked his hand through his hair, unsure where to begin. "I was bespelled by Madame Giselle to take the journey to the future. I am sure of it now. I couldn't shake the compulsion from my mind, and she made it far too easy. That I landed in Erin's arms when I came through time's passage only convinces me even more she's meant to be here. We need her, but . . ." He shook his head.

"Start from the beginning, lad," his uncle admonished. "Erin mentioned drama with a faerie, and I gather you're in some difficulty. May as well make a clean breast of it so that we can put our heads together and find a solution."

"Och, aye, Uncle. You could say I've landed in quite a bog." Rob launched into the story, leaving nothing out, including the part about Connor McGladrey and the job he'd been doing for the older time traveler. He passed Erin's phone around so they could see the pictures for themselves. Finally, he shared what had transpired with the faerie who appeared in Erin's apartment. "I have thirty days to convince Madame Giselle to return the stolen pensieve—or my life is forfeit."

"Shite, Robley," Malcolm bit out. "Did we no' tell you to keep your distance from the fae? Do ye ne'er listen?"

"Malcolm, making him feel worse is not going to help." True rested her hand on her husband's forearm. "We need to focus on finding a way to help him. None of this is Robley's fault. I wondered if Giselle might have planted the compulsion within him, and now I know she did. I've no doubt she wanted Erin here. Maybe she's just looking out for me and our twins. To her, Rob is nothing more than a pawn. She managed to find a way to kill two birds with one stone. Erin is here, and Giselle has the pensieve." She turned to Rob. "You and Malcolm must travel to Inverness to confront her."

"Me!" Malcolm's brow shot up. "What have I tae do with this tangle? You ken how I feel about the fae. I dinna wish to be within a league of her."

"Giselle knows you're my husband." True placed her hands on her belly. "Obviously, I can't travel, or I'd talk to her myself. If she knows how much we care for Rob, maybe she'll find a way to fix all of this."

"'Tis unlikely," Rob muttered. "I will no' ask any of you to embroil yourselves further in this mess. Malcolm is needed here, and we canna put his safety at risk. What I seek from you are thoughts and ideas. Any notions of how to extricate myself are most welcome."

He scrubbed his face with both hands, weariness pressing upon him like a millstone. "And I must have your promise that Erin will be protected and given a place of honor within our clan should I fail. 'Twill ease my mind knowing she'll be taken care of no matter what becomes of me." A lump formed in his throat, and he tried to clear it away. "If I somehow survive, I plan to marry Erin. She's . . . I . . ." He blinked against the burn in his eyes, his jaw clenching.

"Of course. You need no' even ask. 'Tis done." His uncle pinned him with a look filled with concern. "However we might aid you in this, we will. Mayhap your ties to True and Hunter will be of some help. Mayhap we can gather together enough coin to buy the pensieve back."

Rob grunted. "I doubt silver and gold hold much value to the fae. 'Tis unlikely I will see Candlemas this year, Uncle." He raised his eyes to each member of his beloved family. "I leave for Inverness at dawn." He stood and stretched. "Take care of Erin in my absence. Tell my parents I love them, and pray for me. If all goes well, I will be back within a se'nnight."

CHAPTER TEN

After they handed the children off to Sky's nursemaid, Erin tried to memorize what landmarks she could while following Beth down the corridor. Without a guide she'd be lost. Her palms grew damp, and her heart pounded. Already she missed Rob's steadying presence. More than anything, she longed to have him beside her, with her hand safely clasped in his.

Beth stopped at a heavy wooden door and opened it for her, "Here we are, milady."

The fire burning in the small fireplace cast a warm glow over the sparse furnishings, calming her frayed nerves. A single chair sat by the fire. Several pegs protruded from the thick stone walls, and a wooden trunk sat on the plank floor beneath. Beth turned down the blankets on the narrow bed. "Do ye need aught before ye turn in, milady?"

Yes! I need Robley. "Where is Robley's chamber in relation to this one?" She hung her Harley jacket on a peg and wiped her sweaty palms on her jeans before turning to Beth.

Beth's brow rose slightly, and she wouldn't meet her eyes. "He's no' married, milady. He'll stay with the garrison or mayhap make use of his parents' chamber since they're no' in residence."

Great. Not like she could walk into the garrison's barracks to look for him, and judging by Beth's body language, seeking him out in his parents' chamber was a definite no-no. Her stomach plummeted. Maybe he'd stop by to check on her.

Beth lifted something lying across the end of the bed. "I've a night rail for ye, milady." Glancing at Erin's clothing, she handed her the linen garment. "And there's water in the ewer by the hearth should ye wish tae wash." Her head canted in the direction of the earthenware pitcher. A few squares of material had been laid next to it, and a small piece of soap rested on the edge of the stone fireplace. "I put a few willow twigs on the mantel if ye should wish tae clean your teeth. I'll leave ye now if that be all."

Biting her lip, Erin stifled the urge to have Beth ask Robley to come to her. "Thank you. You've thought of everything."

"Sleep well, milady." Beth curtsied and left, shutting the door behind her.

Feeling utterly lost, she stood in the middle of the room with the nightgown in her hands. What was she doing in this time? Would she ever return to her own? School, her family, friends—she might never see them again. Fighting tears, she laid the nightgown on the bed and began to undress. Her jeans and shirt she placed in the trunk, and thinking better of leaving the twenty-first-century leather jacket on the peg, she took it down and hugged it to her chest. Memories of her day with Robley washed through her. He'd been so happy with the jacket and looking at all the motorcycles.

"Will I ever again see him that happy?" She swallowed against the tightness in her throat, washed and put on the garment Beth had given her. She crawled into bed, surprised to find how comfortable it was, and burrowed into the down mattress. With a sigh, she let sleep take her far from her worries.

Erin awoke to the sound of tapping. Disoriented, she opened her eyes a crack and surveyed her surroundings. A shuttered window let sunlight slip in through the cracks, lighting an unfamiliar room with walls of stone. A small hearth held the ashes from the fire that had kept her warm through the night, and the borrowed nightgown she wore had twisted up around her legs.

It all came back to her in a rush of misery. She groaned, dropped her head back on the pillow and covered her eyes. Another tap sounded against the door. *Robley?* "Yes?" she called.

The door opened, and Beth strolled in with a pile of clothing draped over her arm. "Good morn, milady. I've brought ye something to wear." She opened the shutter to reveal a greenish, rippling pane of glass set in a hinged leaden frame. Light flooded in through the narrow window.

"I'm tae take care of you, just as I did our Lady True when first she arrived. I'm still her maid, but for the time being, I'm tae look after ye as well."

This part was said with a great deal of pride, bringing a smile to Erin's face, despite her disappointment that Rob hadn't come for her. "I'm grateful. I'd like to bathe if possible." And she'd also have to visit the garderobe, but she already knew where to find that particular room from the night before.

"Aye, we have a bathing room, milady." Beth hung the gown and undergarments on one of the pegs. "Come. Lady True awaits. I'm tae take ye down to the great hall tae break yer fast once yer ready."

Beth held a robe for her, and Erin threw back the covers and rose to slip her arms into the soft blue velvet. She tied the cord around her waist. "What time is it?"

"'Tis almost Terce."

She'd heard the hours of the day were measured by the church during this era, but she had no idea what Terce meant. It could be well into the afternoon for all she knew. She followed Beth down the corridor and waited while she checked to make sure the room was free.

A young boy around nine or ten years old shot out, flashing her a curious look. "There's plenty of hot water, mum," he said, bobbing his head before rushing off with buckets in each hand.

"Come, milady," Beth called from within.

The room had a steamy dampness to it and smelled of scented soap. Two narrow windows, also holding glass panes, lit the room. Beth filled one of the two copper tubs from a spigot on the bottom of a tank. The tank had been set into a hearth-like structure with a fire ring underneath. Ingenious. An early version of a water heater. Several buckets were stacked against the wall, along with a folded wooden screen. Benches were set around the room, and on one of them, several earthenware jars sat next to plates holding chunks of soap.

"Our Lady True has the best recipes for soaps and shampoos. Her concoctions are every bit as good as the milled soaps from France." She set one of the dishes of soap on a stool next to the tub she'd filled.

Erin picked it up and took a sniff. It had a floral smell and held bits of whatever plant went into making it. "Thanks." She unbraided her hair. "Shampoo you said?"

Beth lifted one of the earthenware jars from the bench and set it next to the soap. "Och, aye. The chandlers make the soaps and shampoos now. They're two elderly widows in the village. They offer them for sale along with the candles they make, adding quite a bit tae their coffers. 'Tis a good thing. Our Lady True always looks for ways tae improve the lives of those less fortunate. 'Tis one of the reasons we call her *nas fíor*, true of heart."

She poured the last bucketful of water into the tub. "Do ye need help? I've set clean cloths right here so ye can dry off." She gestured to the squares of linen folded on a bench next to her robe and nightgown. "And here's one tae wash with." She draped a smaller piece over the edge of the tub.

"This is great. Thanks." Erin smiled. Beth was a talker, and she was already fond of the vivacious maid.

"I'll go and get things ready for ye in yer chamber then." Beth crossed the room to the door. "Leave the water and the linens. The lad will take care of them once he returns." She curtsied and left.

Thoughts cluttered her mind as she slipped out of the nightgown and stepped into the hot bath. She hated the possibility that she might never hold that midwife certification in her hands. To her, that piece of paper represented so much more than the right to practice. She couldn't put her finger on what exactly, but the feeling was there anyway.

A lump formed in her throat as thoughts of her family filled her. Sure, they were a dysfunctional jar of mixed nuts, but they were *her* mixed nuts—steps, halves, shirttail cousins and her mom, even her dad whom she rarely saw. Boy, did she have a few questions for him. Did he know he had faerie blood? Did he have the same kind of abilities she had? What if she never got home?

Worse, what if Robley couldn't find a way to return the pensieve? The thought of him dying caused an ache so deep she could hardly breathe. She needed to see him, needed him to take her into his arms and tell her everything would be all right. Between the two of them, somehow they'd get the pensieve back in time. They had to. Did having a strand or two of faerie DNA carry any weight with those beings? There had to be a way to use her ties with the fae to their advantage.

She ducked her head under the water, letting the sudden flow of tears merge with the bathwater. There was nothing she could do about anything, and thinking about her own powerlessness would drive her crazy if she let it. She reached for the shampoo, washed and rinsed her hair, and then she finished the rest of her bath quickly.

True had been through this whole time travel thing, and if ever Erin needed anyone's friendship and advice, it was now.

As she dried off, she made a mental list of things to do. Once she asked True where he was, she'd find Robley. They needed to talk. More than that, she needed to ground herself in the familiarity of his presence. She slipped into the robe and put the soap and shampoo back where they belonged. On the way to the door, she gathered up her borrowed nightgown and headed back to the guest chamber.

The fire had been stirred back to life, and Beth sat her on a chair next to the radiating heat. She used the linen Erin had wrapped around her head to squeeze out the excess water from her hair, and then she began to comb through the tangles for her. "That feels good," Erin said, closing her eyes.

"Och, best leave it down till it dries," Beth said. "Ye have lovely hair, milady."

"So do you." Erin glanced at her over her shoulder. Beth's golden hair shone with good health. She had a sweet look about her, and her blue eyes sparkled. Erin imagined how her reenactment club would take to her. "I wish you'd call me Erin."

"Mayhap in your chamber, Erin, but 'twould no' be proper anywhere else in the keep. You're the young lord's lady."

I am? She swallowed against the sudden constriction in her throat. The need to lay eyes on Rob and assure herself that he was OK overwhelmed her. "I'd really like to get dressed and go downstairs now."

"As you wish." Beth quickly finished combing her hair and fetched the chemise from the peg. She slipped it over Erin's head. "I'll personally see tae washing the clothes ye wore last night. Once they're dry, ye'll find them back in yon trunk." Next came the long, sage-green velvet tunic and finally a darker green surcot with gold trim. "'Tis a lovely color for ye, Erin. The gown brings out the green in yer eyes."

"Thank you." What would people think when they saw her leather lace-up hiking boots underneath? She'd be glad she had them once the snow started falling. They were warm and sturdy. "Elaine's clothes fit well."

"Aye, ye are near the same height as Lady Elaine, though a bit thinner," she said, giving the laces at the sides a final tug before tying them off. "There. Off to the great hall now. Lady True awaits. I ken she had Cook save ye a bit of porridge to break yer fast. Ye must be famished by now."

Erin followed her into the passageway. "I don't suppose there's coffee?"

"Coffee?" Beth's face clouded. "I dinna believe so. I've no' heard of coffee. Is it a kind of grain ye eat where ye come from?"

"No. It's a drink made from ground-up roasted coffee beans and boiling water." Lord, she'd miss her morning caffeine fix, among other things.

They took the narrow stairs down to the great hall. True sat in a chair next to the fireplace. She had a lap full of baby clothes, and a basket holding sewing gear sat on the ground beside her. She started to get up when she saw Erin.

"Stay where you are." Erin waved her back down before turning back to Beth. "Thank you, Beth."

"Milady." She curtsied and took her leave.

"I saved you some breakfast," True said, pointing with her chin to a covered bowl on the trestle table.

"Coffee?" Erin asked hopefully.

"Afraid not." True laughed. "I can have Cook bring you rosehip or chamomile tea if you'd like. I never was a coffee drinker, but I can imagine it's going to be a few weeks before you stop missing the caffeine."

Erin took a seat at the table and uncovered the bowl. The smell of honey wafted up from the oatmeal. Picking up the wooden spoon, she glanced at True. "Coming here must've been quite an adjustment for you. I have so many questions." Her stomach rumbled in protest, and she took a few bites of the oatmeal. To her surprise, it was very tasty, though much more coarse than store-bought Quaker Oats.

"I grew up on my father's reservation in northern Minnesota near the Canadian border. I'm half Anishinaabe. Growing up in the bush, I was used to roughing it, hunting, trapping and tanning hides with my uncles and aunties. I came here with a skill set that helped a lot." True put her sewing down. "I imagine the adjustment is going to be more difficult for you. But as far as keeps go, Moigh Hall is as modern as they come. I'm so grateful for the bathing room and glass window panes, you can't even imagine. We're slowly putting glass in all of the windows. You're staying in the same room I did when I first arrived." True shot her a wry grin. "Only, I mostly hid out there for the first month."

"Oh?" Erin's curiosity was piqued. "If you're willing to tell me, I really want to hear your story. Rob said you were sent here to save Hunter's life."

"This evening after dinner we'll talk, but this morning I thought I'd show you around the castle and grounds. I'll answer any questions you might have. I've taken over Hunter's grandmother's cottage. It's located just outside the bailey wall. It's now my stillroom, and it would be an excellent place for you to work. Rob told us you're interested in setting up a clinic of sorts."

"I am." She ate a few more bites. "Speaking of Rob, I really need to see him. Can we do the looking around later? He and I need to talk about what we're going to do. We have to come up with a plan to get the pensieve back from Giselle before that awful faerie returns for him."

True pushed herself out of the chair and came to her, placing a hand on Erin's shoulder. "Erin . . ."

"What?" In a flash, she knew what True was about to tell her. Disbelief and anger sent adrenaline pulsing through her. Her heart rate took off, and her palms began to sweat.

"Robley and seven men from our garrison left at dawn. He's on his way to Inverness to confront Giselle."

"Without me?" she cried. "How do I get there?" Her lungs seized. She shot up from the bench, her breakfast forgotten. "How could he leave without letting me know? We have to make a plan *together*. I'm a part of this mess. What was he thinking?"

"Welcome to life in 1426." True grunted. "Your safety comes first, and consideration for your feelings in the matter doesn't even make it onto the list. Having you along would've slowed them down, and worrying about you would've distracted Robley. We have criminals in this age just like in the twenty-first century, especially along well-traveled roads like the one to Inverness."

"But . . . why didn't he tell me?" Stricken with this new development, Erin was stung by the betrayal.

"You would've insisted on going with him. He asked us to look after you in his absence." She gently pushed Erin back to sitting. "We would have done so even if he hadn't asked, of course."

"Any idea when he's coming back?" She twisted her fingers in her damp hair. "If he comes back at all, that is. What if Giselle does away with him to eliminate being caught red-handed with that stupid pensieve? I should've gone with him."

"Could you prevent Giselle from harming him if you were there?"

"Yes!" Her gut twisted. "No." She recalled the epic fail her last attempt with the pepper spray had been. "I don't know. I thought maybe my faerie DNA might help." Once again, reality bit into her with savage force. "There's really nothing I can do, is there?"

"No. There really isn't. I've been where you are. We'll keep busy, and that will help keep your mind off your troubles."

Erin's mouth had gone completely dry. "I need a glass of water." She rose again. "Point me toward the kitchen."

"Unless it's straight from an underground spring, don't drink water unless it's been boiled. We drink mostly tea, ale or watered wine. I've made sure the villagers know to boil their water first. It's really cut down on the cases of dysentery. Finish your breakfast, Erin. I'll go get some tea. No need to shock the kitchen staff with your presence in their midst, though they've been informed we have a guest." She waddled toward a corridor at the back of the great hall. "You'll be formally introduced this evening. We're having a feast to celebrate."

Formally introduced? Yikes. Her breath hitched, and once again her heart raced. Erin had never enjoyed being the center of attention, and she avoided it whenever she could. True was right though. Dwelling on her troubles wouldn't affect the outcome. Distracting herself, she took the time to study her surroundings while she dutifully finished her cereal. The room looked like something out of a book on medieval castle life.

Colorful tapestries adorned the walls, along with an impressive array of weaponry and shields bearing two distinct crests. She sat at a rough-hewn trestle table with benches on either side, and another similar table took up the dais, only that one had chairs with backs rather than benches. A minstrels' balcony overlooked the room, and a huge hearth dominated each end. She kept getting smacked between the eyes with reality. This was the fifteenth century. Lord help her, was this century before or after the plague wiped out a third of Europe's population?

True reappeared with two earthenware mugs in her hands. She set one in front of Erin and eased herself down on the opposite bench at the table. "Another change I've made is the switch to pottery for drinking and serving food. Pewter isn't safe. The lead leaches into whatever is being consumed."

"Do you worry about changing history at all? We're both bringing knowledge from another time to these people. Are we changing things that shouldn't be changed?"

"Frankly, I don't care." True shrugged. "It's not like either of us chose to be here, and caring about my people supersedes any concerns some anthropologist or archaeologist I'll never meet might have. If I can help my clan in any way, I'm going to do it. History and the time continuum be damned." She snorted. "I often wonder what will happen when my twenty-first-century cell phone, laptop and iPod are discovered in these castle ruins in the distant future. What will the scientists make of that?"

"Good point. I won't worry about it either then. Rob said you have some knowledge about healing plants. I have nursing and midwifery skills. Between the two of us, we can have quite an impact."

"I do have some knowledge about healing herbs. My grandparents were healers for my tribe, and a lot of what they knew has been passed down to me, and my grandmother gave me a book of herbology. Keep in mind these people are very superstitious. A lot of what I've accomplished is because I'm married to the earl's heir. If I say they must wash after using the privy and bathe regularly, Malcolm backs me up. They do it because he says to, not because I do." One side of her mouth quirked up.

"Remember to put things in terms they can relate to, like boiling water steams out the bad humors that cause the bloody flux. You start talking about *E. coli*, *Salmonella* and other microbes, and they'll do the sign of the cross and back away."

Erin scraped her bowl clean and forced a grin. "I get it. Since there's nothing I can do about Rob or the fae, I may as well check out the cottage you spoke of." She rose from her place. "Is it all right if I bring the tea with me?"

"Sure. I will too. One of the scullery maids will come fetch your bowl." She labored to rise from the bench. "I don't even remember what my feet look like anymore or what it feels like to bend at the waist." Placing her hands at the small of her back, she stretched and rubbed. "Let's go."

"Where are the children?"

"Sky's with her nursemaid, and Hunter is with the men in the lists. He's now a page, the first step toward knighthood. He follows my husband around all day, trains and does whatever Malcolm tells him to do." True led her to the tall wooden doors leading outside. "It's a good thing I have help, especially with twins coming. There are definite benefits to marrying into the nobility."

A pang of longing shot through Erin, and Rob's image filled her mind. She bit her lip and fought the sudden sting at the back of her eyes. "Can I ask you something?"

"Of course. Do you have any idea how great it is to have someone from my time to talk to? I'm hoping we'll become great friends. Elaine and I are very close, but I hardly ever get to see her. She and her family will be here around Christmas. You'll love her." She giggled. "Sorry. What was it you wanted to ask?"

"Your in-laws, are they really as happy together as they seem?" Too revealing? It didn't matter. She wanted to know.

"They are. William tore Scotland apart to get Lydia back from a rival who kidnapped her. Their story is very romantic. Another tale I'll share later." True glanced at her, a speculative glint filling her eyes. "Why do you ask?"

"Rob told me that once a MacKintosh man gives his heart, it's given for good." She averted her gaze. "I'm just trying to get the lay of the land." Judging by True's knowing grin, she hadn't fooled her.

True became distracted by the numerous greetings fluttering through the air like sparrows around her. Erin smiled and followed as they made their way to the portcullis. True was wrong. The MacKintosh clan did what she asked because they loved their mistress. She belonged.

They followed a path close to the massive stone wall, and as they continued on, Erin thought about her life. She suddenly realized she'd joined the historical reenactment club because she wanted to feel as if she belonged somewhere, but it was all make-believe. Just like the roles they all played. She had acquaintances, but not close friends. Whenever anyone attempted to get closer, especially men, she'd close up tighter than an oyster about to be shucked. Did she even know how to open up?

True stopped at a cottage made of timber beams and filled with something similar to plaster or stucco. "This is it." She opened the door and waved Erin through.

The rafters and walls were crowded with drying plants and herbs. A counter-height table had been set in the center of the one room, and a narrow rope bed with a straw mattress took up the space against the wall. A ladder led to a sleeping loft, and a small hearth held two hinged iron hooks for cooking. A variety of baskets, clay pots, utensils and iron cauldrons were neatly arranged in a crude cabinet set into the corner.

"What do you think?" True took a single book down from the mantel over the fireplace. "This is where I developed the recipes for soaps and shampoos."

"It's wonderful. I don't know a lot about homeopathic medicine. Can I see the book?"

"Sure. Take it with you when we return to the keep. You can read through it. It'll help."

"Do you know a good source of folic acid? It's important for expectant mothers."

"Of course. It's all in the book, but I make sure we get a lot of leafy greens and peas in our diet, and dried beans."

"Is it possible to have a frame built for women to hold on to while they're squatting to push? Gravity is the best thing for labor and delivery. Or maybe a thick rope hanging from the rafters would do." She studied the pitched timbers above her. "Lying flat in a bed isn't really the best position to give birth."

"Consider it done, but most of our women give birth in their homes. You're going to be busy. I can name about seven women in our village who are in various stages of pregnancy." She moved to the door. "I'll take you to the mainland tomorrow, and I'll introduce you to everyone. Let me show you the rest of the grounds so you can learn your way around."

For the time being, Erin would force herself to stop worrying about Robley. She had no idea how long she'd be in the fifteenth century or if she'd ever get back home. In the interim, she looked forward to working with the MacKintosh women, and she was grateful for True's friendship.

CHAPTER ELEVEN

Low gray clouds scudded across the sky, and a fine drizzle added to the chill permeating Robley's bones. He placed his palm on the hilt of the dagger at his waist and took comfort in the familiar weight of a claymore against his back. Both were useless against the fae, but they gave him a sense of security nonetheless. He'd been too long without his weapons.

Glancing skyward, he guessed the hour to be midmorning. They had indeed made good time. Still, every day he spent traveling was one fewer day he had to avert the disaster ahead. He and the seven men he'd chosen from the MacKintosh garrison had ridden hard to reach Inverness, barely stopping to rest. For certes, they'd even eaten their oatcakes and jerky while in the saddle. He ran his hand over two and a half days' worth of stubble, relieved that they hadn't encountered any trouble on the road as he'd expected. The castle was finally within their sights.

"Do ye want me tae go with you tae the old crone's cottage, Rob?" Angus brought his mount up to ride beside him.

Giselle was no more a crone than Angus was fae, no matter how much his companion wished to pretend otherwise. Superstitious to the core, the older warrior refused to refer to Giselle as anything other than human, as if doing so might precipitate more trouble. "Nay. I appreciate the offer, but I must do this alone." Rob shook his head. "I dinna want to risk anyone else's involvement."

He'd told Angus and Galen the entire tale. They were men he trusted with his life, as they could trust him with theirs. "Let the castellan know of our arrival, and make sure the men are fed. Have Galen see our horses are well cared for. I dinna plan to linger any longer than necessary."

Angus's obvious relief that he didn't have to face the ancient one brought a wry grin to Rob's face. If only he had possessed the same reluctance to begin with, he wouldn't be facing death in a month's time. Och, but he also would not have met Erin.

Never far from his thoughts, Erin's image filled his mind, and he wondered what she might be doing at this very moment. More than likely she'd already sought out all the women in their clan who were breeding. He imagined her growing large with their bairn, and the longing for her, for a family of his own, nearly knocked him off his horse. If just once he'd have the luxury of holding her in his arms and making love to her all through the night, he'd be content. He spurred his gelding into a canter. The sooner he confronted Giselle, the sooner he could return to Erin.

At least his love was safely ensconced within the bosom of his family. His uncle and cousin would not let any harm come to her, and his parents would soon arrive. True had welcomed Erin with open arms, and he had a feeling the two would become close. Having another lass from the twenty-first century in the keep, especially a midwife, would be a boon to True. They reached the portcullis, and Robley dismounted, handing his reins to Galen. "Angus has command."

"Are ye sure ye dinna want us to accompany ye?" Galen dismounted and faced him, his stance wide. "I'm willing, Rob."

"Nay." He let his glance rest on each of the seven men in his company. "Spend some time in the lists, if you've a mind to. No dallying this eve, though. You need your rest, for we'll ride home at first light." He straightened his shoulders. "I'll return to the keep anon. I've no reason to fear Giselle. All I mean to do is talk to her. I'll see you for the evening meal at the very latest."

He nodded his farewell and started out on the road through the village. What could he say to Giselle that would not raise her ire? Best approach the matter with the utmost humility. Be honest and tell her exactly what had transpired since last he saw her. Ask, nay, beg for her help rather than demand it. Aye, 'twould be wise to humble himself.

The chill, damp day was best spent indoors, and he encountered few villagers. Working through what he would say, he soon found himself on the same path he'd taken a mere four months past.

Damp leaves and fallen pine needles muffled his footsteps. A crow cawed from the branch of a rowan, taking off for the next tree as if leading him on his way. *Or mayhap to issue a warning.* Rob inhaled deeply, taking in the calming tang of pine and yew laced with the loamy smell of autumn's decaying vegetation.

He scanned the area when he came to the edge of the clearing. Everything was as it should be, yet somehow desolate. Giselle's cottage stood neatly in the center of the toft, only this time, no fowl foraged. The shutters were tightly closed, and not even a wisp of smoke escaped from the chimney. Dread settled in his chest like a stone at the bottom of a scullery maid's pail.

Mayhap Giselle had gone visiting, or tended the sick somewhere in the outlying vicinity. He'd acted the thief once before—or the fool, as it were—mayhap he should again. Aye, a fool and a thief, he'd sneak in, find the pensieve and be on his way home to Loch Moigh before Giselle returned. Determination coursed through him. He meant to take back the thing that had caused him so much grief.

Nay. 'Twas not the thing itself but becoming embroiled with the fae that was causing him grief, and he had none but himself to blame.

The closer he got to the cottage, the heavier the dread within him grew. His very limbs wore the weight like a mantle of lead. By the time he reached her door, he could scarce move his hand. He labored just to breathe, and lifting his feet took all his strength. A chill wracked him to the very marrow of his bones. Trembling, he struggled to swipe away the sweat running into his eyes, causing them to sting. "By the saints, 'tis unnatural," he muttered, and blinked. No doubt Giselle had laid some sort of warding magic over the place, and the spell assailed him from within and without.

More crows gathered in the boughs of the trees bordering the clearing. Cawing, several took flight, circling above his head. A few dove at him. He swung his arms and ducked. "Bloody hell!"

His life depended upon returning the silver platter. If the faerie warrior didn't kill him, the spell Giselle had laid over the grounds might. Either way, he had no choice but to try and force his way through whatever this was. Mustering all the will he could, he lifted the latch to her door. It opened easily enough, but crossing the threshold was nearly impossible. No matter how hard he tried, his legs would not carry him forward. He gripped the inside lintel with both hands and strained with all his might to drag himself across the threshold. 'Twas like passing through partially dried mud, but finally he broke through.

Gasping for breath, he pressed himself against the wall, leaned his head back and scrubbed his face with both hands. His lungs worked like a bellows, and his heart hammered so hard that his ears rang, competing with the cacophony of the crows. He blinked the sting from his eyes and surveyed the dim interior. His spirits plummeted even further.

Empty. Naught but the old scarred furniture stood before him. Gone were the vegetables and plants hanging from the rafters, the dishes upon the shelf, the wooden box she'd placed upon the table. Even the hearth had been cleared. Not a single ash remained to give testimony to Giselle's presence. No baskets or personal belongings of any kind were to be found anywhere. It was as if she'd never lived there at all, yet 'twas still eerily clean of dust and cobwebs.

Despair swallowed him whole as he faced the unwelcome truth: Giselle had left, and she'd taken the pensieve with her. What now? How was he supposed to find Giselle when she could jump through time, return to the faerie realm where no mortal could follow, or travel anywhere in the world her fancy took her?

Hopelessness tugged him down the wall until he landed on the wood-plank floor. He brought his knees up, propped his elbows upon them and buried his face in his arms. Anguish and regret—the most fearful of all enemies—drew him closer and closer to the black abyss waiting to drag him into its depths.

Tears and sweat filled his eyes. How would he face Erin? She would know the truth. Aye, he would reek of it. He could not protect her, nor could he save himself. How could he expect her to give her heart to such a fool as he? He blew out a shuddering breath. An entire se'nnight wasted, and for naught.

The raucous cawing from without roused him from the well of misery into which he'd fallen. On hands and knees he crawled out of the cottage. The door slammed behind him, raising the flesh on his arms and the back of his neck. Forcing himself to stand, he placed one foot before the other, heading for the path toward the keep—the chorus of scolding crows urging him onward. Were they wards as well, doing Giselle's bidding? One swooped down from its perch, aiming for his face. Rob ducked, covering his head with his arms as the foul bird pecked at him.

Another swooped, and another. Soon the entire murder circled him, driving him down the path and away from their mistress's dwelling. He offered no resistance and hurried toward the village. As suddenly as the attack began, it ended. Still, the harsh scolding continued until he was well away. He stopped and rested his hands upon his knees, sucking in several cleansing breaths. Each time his lungs filled, a portion of the heaviness and despair lifted from his soul. His limbs lightened.

Surely the hopelessness had been part of Giselle's spell. 'Twas not in him to concede to defeat. He had not an inkling what to do next or where to turn, but as long as he drew breath, he had no intention of giving up.

Once he returned to the keep, he found the four men he trusted most. They sat at the table eating their midday meal. Gareth and his brother Galen, Angus and Ian were all seasoned, blooded warriors who had been with their garrison since the day Rob had earned his spurs. Angus even further back, for he remembered training with the older man when he was but a lad. Rob took a seat and poured himself a goblet of ale. Angus cut him a generous slice of cold fowl, placed it on a slice of bread and handed it to him. Rob's stomach rumbled in anticipation. "My thanks." He needed a new plan, a new direction and action. After a few bites of his meal, he said, "She was no' there. Giselle's cottage was completely empty."

Gareth wiped his mouth on his sleeve. "What now?"

"On the morrow, we split into groups of two or three. Each group will take a different direction, and we'll search the surrounding villages for her whereabouts." She could be anywhere and in any century. Their search may be futile, but he needed to do something or he'd go mad.

"Humph." Angus shook his head. "Nay, lad. *Ye* must return to Moigh Hall."

"Nay, I—"

"What if one of the lads uncovers news of the old crone's whereabouts? If ye are scouring the countryside as well, how will they find ye tae let ye know?"

"Aye, Rob." Galen sent him a pointed stare. "Best return home where we can send word. Besides, yer parents will want to lay eyes upon ye, aye? They thought ye dead."

As much as he needed to act, what they said made sense. "All right," he capitulated. "Pair up, and decide amongst yourselves which villages you'll search. Angus, go with the least experienced pair."

"Nay, lad." The older man crossed his arms in front of him and shook his head. "Ye ken 'tis folly tae travel the roads alone. I'll stick close to ye." Angus arched a brow. "Malcolm will have my ballocks if I let aught befall ye."

Robley snorted. "'Tis a comforting thought, Angus." He rose from his place. "I'm going to find a bath and a bed. Wake me for the evening meal." There was naught else he could do, and exhaustion dragged at his limbs and muddled his thoughts. Mayhap he'd come up with a better plan once he was rested.

Heavyhearted, Rob crested the hill overlooking Loch Moigh. Angus drew his mount up beside him. Late afternoon and already the sun had begun its descent. His gut twisted. Each day nearer to the winter solstice brought him closer to the end of his life. He shook off his morose thoughts. Mayhap something would come of their search after all, and he'd find Giselle before the fae warrior's return.

"Your parents will have arrived, lad." Angus shifted in his saddle, placing a gnarled hand on Rob's shoulder. "Take heart. A solution will be found, and all will be well."

"Humph." Robley started his horse down the hill, a mixture of anticipation and reticence chasing through him. Erin would be upset with him for leaving her without word, yet he could hardly wait to lay eyes upon her. He wanted her in his arms more than he wanted food or rest.

He wasn't eager to face his parents. His uncle would've told them the tale. His father's disappointment would be difficult to bear, and his mother would wring her hands with worry. He rubbed at the ache in his chest as they entered the village. They turned their horses over to the stable master, and Rob ordered the guard not to sound the horn signaling their return. He couldn't face a crowd gathering to witness his homecoming.

He and Angus made their way to the ferry. Days of travel in the damp November chill had taken its toll—that and his failure had brought him to the edge of total exhaustion.

"Welcome back, milord," Arlen greeted, bobbing his head. "I took yer da and ma tae the island just yesterday. I ken they be eager tae see thee."

"My thanks, Arlen. How does your family fare?"

"Och, couldn't be better." Arlen gave him a gap-toothed grin. "My lass and her man couldn't be any happier tae ha' a midwife sae close, since she's breeding."

Rob's Adam's apple bobbed at the mention of his lass. "Erin has been to see her?"

"Och, aye. Lady True brought her tae the village but her second day here. Went 'round tae all the houses she did, and met with each and every family. Me own wife says she spoke of naught but 'wellness checks' and the importance of 'prenatal care,' whatever that might be." He chuckled as he untied the ferry from its moors. "Seems a dedicated lass, and comely too. The entire village is talking 'bout her. We're grateful tae ye for wresting her away from the Sutherlands, milord."

So the story they'd come up with had stuck. "I'm glad she was amenable to making Loch Moigh her home." As if she'd had a choice in the matter. He and Angus boarded the ferry, and Rob's gaze fixed on the island. He wished with all his heart for a happy resolution to his troubles. One where he and Erin had a lifetime to share, rather than a scant handful of days and nights. He swallowed against the sudden constriction in his throat and decided to seek her out first before greeting his parents.

Rob took a coin from his sporran and handed it to Arlen as they grew close to the island. "My thanks. I look forward to meeting your first grandchild, Arlen. Give my regards to your family."

"Och, I'll do that, milord." Arlen tugged at his cap and set about slipping the ferry into its landing.

Robley didn't wait for him to secure the vessel. Arlen would be shoving off for the mainland soon enough. "Angus, my thanks for your company. Greet your wife for me, aye?"

"Will do, lad. See ye in the lists on the morrow."

"Aye." Rob headed toward the keep, anticipation filling him. He caught a glimpse of the cottage True used as her stillroom, noticed the curl of smoke drifting out of the chimney. Mayhap True worked inside. At this hour she should be in the keep with her feet up, and he meant to tell her so. Erin had said carrying twins brought more risk. Shouldn't True be confined above stairs? He strode to the door, rapped his knuckles against it and waited.

"Yes?" The door swung open.

He came face-to-face with Erin. His heart leaped for his throat, and he lost his ability to think, much less speak. She wore garments suitable for work, with an apron tied around her waist and a cloth covering her hair. Her cheeks were rosy, as if she'd been exerting herself. He'd never seen such a beautiful sight. The need to reach for her nearly overrode his good sense.

Her eyes widened, then narrowed. "You left without telling me first."

"Aye. I thought it best." The smell of vinegar wafted out. "Do ye mean to pickle the place, babe?" His heart raced at the spark his words ignited in her eyes. No matter what the future held, in this moment he was with the woman he loved with all his heart. For right now, 'twas more than enough, and far more than he deserved.

"Don't call me *babe*." She swung the door open wider to let him in. "I'm pissed at you."

"Humph." He entered, taking note of the pail, scrub brush and rags. "Does that mean I can call you *babe* when you are more favorably inclined toward me?"

She glared at him and crossed her arms in front of her.

He placed his hands on her shoulders. "*Mo cridhe*, then," he teased, hoping for a smile. "I shall revert to fifteenth-century terms of endearment if it pleases you."

"Conking you on the head with that iron cauldron over there would please me right now." She backed out of his hold, blinking rapidly against the sudden brightness filling her pretty green eyes. Her chest rose and fell rapidly, and she kept her arms crossed tightly. "What were you thinking?" She raised her chin and glared at him.

"I was *thinking* to keep you safe whilst I sought an easy solution to a complicated problem."

"And how'd that work out for you?" She tapped her foot, her glare still fixed his way.

"No' so well, *mo cridhe*. Madame Giselle is no longer in Inverness, and I have no idea where she might be or how I might find her. I have men out searching as we speak."

"Oh, Rob . . ."

He glanced about the interior of the wee cottage. "What do you here? Why does this cottage smell so strongly of vinegar?"

"This is my clinic." She followed his gaze around the room. "Vinegar kills germs because it's a natural disinfectant. I'm cleaning and getting ready to see patients."

"Germs, disinfectant and patients." He grunted again. "I dinna ken the meaning of most of what you just said." Yearning to make things right between them, he kicked the door shut, giving them some privacy against prying eyes. He wanted her in his arms with her luscious lips pressed against his. "If I had told you what I intended, you would have insisted on coming with me."

"Of course I would have!" She threw up her hands. "This involves me. I should be there with you when you confront Giselle. Who knows? Maybe I can help find a solution. I have faerie DNA, Rob. That might carry some weight with the fae." She canted her head for a second. "Now that I think about it, did you notice how that faerie's expression turned to surprise when he looked at me?"

"Nay. My mind was on other things." He unbuckled the belt holding his scabbard and placed his claymore on the table. "When we travel to Inverness for the fair each autumn, the journey takes us five days." He flashed her a pointed stare. "Five there and five back would've left me with but a score of days. You're no' used to hardship, lass. Do ye even ken how to ride a horse?" he asked, raising an eyebrow.

She worried her bottom lip between her teeth and shook her head.

His heart wrenched at the sight. "I made the entire trip in less than a se'nnight. Had you been with us, 'twould have taken far longer, and every distress, every tiny hurt you suffered along the way would have preyed upon me. I had enough to worry about as it was." He took a step closer. "I kent you would be safe and well cared for here with my clan and family, lass."

"We should have had this conversation *before* you abandoned me without so much as a 'see you later.'" She huffed. "It would've saved me a lot of grief."

Ah, she thinks I left her! No wonder she was so angry. If she didn't care, she wouldn't be nearly so upset. "Nay, lass. We could no' have had this discussion before I left. Do ye no' ken I have no willpower where you're concerned? I canna say ye nay, and worrying about ye would have been my undoing."

"And what?" She lifted her chin again. "You don't think I suffer the same when it comes to you?" A single tear trickled down her cheek. "Don't you *ever* do that to me again."

He traced the trail of her tear with hungry eyes. "Suffer? You see caring for me as suffering?"

"Caring *is* suffering, Rob. Didn't I make that clear when we talked about my family?" Another tear fell from her other eye, and she swiped at it. "It's exactly why I don't want to get involved."

"I missed you, Erin," he whispered, taking another step closer. "You were on my mind every waking moment of every single day. Never before have I suffered so sweetly or with such a willing heart."

"Oh, Rob," she sobbed and threw herself into his arms. "I was so afraid Giselle would kill you. I haven't slept since you left. Don't you get it? You're the only link between her, the damned pensieve and the faerie searching for it. She knows you can rat her out!"

He drew her close and held her fast, his insides melting. "Rat her out?" He chuckled, happy for the first time in days. "What does that mean, sweetling?"

"It means telling on her. Tattling." She sighed, resting her cheek over his pounding heart.

"Erin?"

"What?" She lifted her head to peer up at him.

"If it pleases you, I mean to kiss you now."

"Yeah?" She blinked.

Her lovely green eyes roamed over his face, pausing at his lips and coming back to meet his gaze. Her expression filled with such tenderness and longing his lungs lost the will to draw breath. Lord help him, he could drown in the depths of her eyes. His heart strained toward hers as if to merge into one beating organ sustaining them both for all time.

She frowned. "Well, what's keeping you?"

"I've been days on the trail. I've no' bathed or shaved since—"

She tangled her fingers in his hair, drew his face down and kissed him. Surprise rendered him senseless, but soon the amazing sensation of kissing her overtook him. He tightened his arms around her slender waist, nearly lifting her off her feet, and plunged his tongue into the welcoming warmth of her scintillating mouth. She tasted of chamomile and honey—delectable. Her answering moan set his blood aflame.

Their heavy breathing filled the cottage. The sound was so erotic and inciting that he ached with wanting her. Backing her toward the small bed, thoughts of her bare, velvety skin next to his excited his senses till he thought he might burst. She was his, and he wanted to brand her skin with his possession, his scent.

The backs of her knees hit the straw mattress, and her legs buckled. He scooped her up in his arms and laid her out, easing down to cover her. "Och, love. You have no idea what you do to me." He covered her face in a spate of tiny kisses, over her eyelids, cheeks, the intriguing corners of her luscious mouth. "I've longed to hold you like this since first I laid eyes upon you."

She gave a breathless chuckle. "Seems to me we were pretty much in this same position when we met."

"Aye, and we should remain thus for days and nights on end." He rolled to his side to untie the apron knot at the small of her back. His fingers shook at the prospect of seeing her bare. He tugged the apron free and tossed it to the ground. Cradling her beloved face between his callused palms, he kissed her deeply, moving across her cheek to nuzzle one side of her neck and then the other. He found the laces to her surcot and freed her of the outer garment, exposing the linen chemise beneath. "I wish to take down your hair, lass. May I?"

A dazed expression suffused her face, and her lips were swollen from his kisses. "OK," she murmured, sitting up. She brought her heavy braid over her shoulder and took the binding from the end, unraveling the braid with her fingers.

The intimacy of seeing her in naught but her undergarment while unbraiding her hair sent his heart tumbling end-over-end. His groin tightened, and he grew even harder. He covered her hands and stopped her. "Let me." His words came out a gruff rasp. Running his fingers through the silken tresses, he savored the texture, longing to feel the softness all over his skin. Once it was free, he tangled his fingers in it and brought the handful of spun gold to his face, inhaling deeply. "You smell like wildflowers on a sunny summer day, lass." He grunted. "And slightly of vinegar."

"You smell like rain-washed air, leather and campfires." She pressed her hands against his chest. "I've always loved your scent, Robley."

He untied the front of her chemise and slipped it down her shoulders. Her breasts were perfect, fair, lush, with the nipples forming hard little buds just for him. "You are so beautiful, you steal my reason, lass." Running his hands through her hair again, he leaned in to kiss her, taking them both down to lie on the bed. It almost seemed a sacrilege, running his roughened hands over the perfection of her smooth, warm skin, but he could not help himself. He burned for her with a need that would not abate.

From the first he'd made up his mind to wed her. So what if they consummated their union before the banns were posted? They'd hardly be the first couple to do so, and none would know of it but the two of them—unless his seed took root.

"I want you, Erin of clan Durie." He cupped both of her perfect breasts in his hands and ran his thumbs over her hardened nipples, pleased beyond measure when she gasped and arched into him. He took one delicate bud into his mouth and suckled.

"Erin," a voice called, and the door to the cottage burst open. "It's almost time for supper. Enough work for one day. Come to the keep."

True barged into the cottage just as he pulled Erin's chemise back up over her breasts. Erin hid her flaming face with her arms and groaned. Rob remained where he was, covering her with his body, keeping his raging erection from his cousin's view. He avoided eye contact with True and dropped his forehead to Erin's. "We'll be there anon."

True gasped and slapped her hands over her eyes. "Oh crap, oh crap, oh crap! I'm so sorry. I didn't know you were back, Rob. I didn't hear the village horn announce your return. I didn't know anyone else was in here." She backed out of the cottage in a rush and slammed the door, calling as she went, "You could've latched this shut, you know."

He listened for a moment before rising to stand beside the bed. "I wish now I *had* latched the door. 'Twould have spared you this embarrassment. My apologies, Erin. It seems I canna do anything right."

"Don't say that. We're both consenting adults here. If anyone is embarrassed, it's True." She pulled her lovely hair over her shoulder and began to braid it. "She's not going to say anything to anyone about this."

"Humph." He straightened his plaid and tucked in his shirt, recalling the feel of Erin's soft hands roaming over the bare skin of his back. "I'll wager she tells Malcolm before the night is out. I'll hear about it on the morrow when we meet in the lists. See if I don't. Still," he said, winking at her, his grin unrepentant, "next time I'll be sure to latch the door."

She huffed out a breath. "I don't think we should do this again. We were probably both reacting to the stress of our situation. That's all. I was worried sick, and—"

"Is that what you believe this was, love?" He scowled at her. "A reaction to stress?"

"Sure." Her face turned a becoming shade of dusky rose, and she wouldn't meet his eyes. "What do you think it was?"

"I believe what happened between us has far more to do with all the *suffering* we feel for one another, lass. I expect I'll *suffer* for you all the rest of my days."

"All twenty-three of them?" she bit out, her voice quavering.

CHAPTER TWELVE

Erin rose from the bed she and Rob had just shared. Struggling to keep her emotions under control, she slipped back into her gown and laced up the sides. She'd been immersed in an ocean of his-and-her sensations. Robley's intense feelings for her, along with his arousal merging with hers, had saturated her until she felt as if she'd levitate off the bed. Or burst. What had she been thinking?

Oh yeah. You were thinking you'd never see him again, and there he was at the door, all alive, male and gorgeously sexy. She couldn't help herself; the relief of seeing him had been an overpowering aphrodisiac.

What would it be like to just let go, make love with him until she shattered into a million shimmering pieces? Hadn't she been about to find out? She forced her thoughts on other things. "What are you planning to do now? I mean we. What are *we* going to do now?"

"*We*, meaning you, will remain here where I ken you are safe. Six men from our garrison are out scouring the countryside for news of Giselle's whereabouts. There is naught that can be done until she is found." Rob picked up the sword he'd laid on the worktable. "She might ha' returned to the faerie realm. Though the more I think upon the matter, the more I wonder. She's no' likely to return to

Avalon if she truly is guilty of stealing the pensieve from their high king. Do ye think?" Flashing her a questioning look, he crossed the room, lifted her cloak from its peg and slipped it over her shoulders, gesturing for her to precede him through the door.

"Probably not, unless she's sure it can't be traced to her," she said. "But I don't know anything about faeries, so I can't really say."

"Her cottage was completely empty, as if she'd never lived there at all, but the villagers say 'tis Giselle's way to come and go like that." He took her elbow and guided her through the portcullis into the bailey. "For the time being, let us forget our troubles and fill our bellies in the good company of our kin."

"*Our* kin?"

"Aye." He drew her close to his side. "Our kin."

His sexy smile sent her pulse racing again. A needy, achy heat coiled inside her, and an answering flush engulfed her. One way or the other, she was going to be devastated. Either she'd be sent back to her own century without him, or he'd be incinerated by that faerie's blue fire. And if by some miracle they managed to return the pensieve, Robley would likely move on to some noble woman with a fat dowry. He might be forced to do so by his uncle. She knew that much about these times. Men of noble birth married women of noble birth—women who came with valuable political ties, land, titles and wealth. The thought of him with someone else was like a wrecking ball to the heart.

Damn. For all her bluster, for all her talk about not getting involved, she'd gone and done it anyway. She'd fallen for Robley of clan MacKintosh. Her breathing grew shallow, and tightness gripped her throat. She blinked against the sudden sting of tears.

He turned her by the shoulders. "Och, love. Dinna fash. I'll fix this. I swear it." He ran his hands up and down her arms.

She blinked harder, but it didn't help. The tears she'd been holding slipped out. Treacherous things, tears, revealing way more than a person wanted. Clamping her mouth shut, she looked everywhere but into Robley's brilliant blue eyes. Her heart was already breaking, and she didn't want to have a total meltdown in the middle of the bailey. Thank heavens only a few people were around to witness her emotional breakdown. Thank heavens it was too dark for those few to see her crying.

"Here's what I have in mind, *mo anam*." He drew her into his arms and rocked her back and forth, resting his chin on top of her head. "Once this is behind us, we'll post the banns."

She swallowed against the lump in her throat. "What does that mean?"

"*Mo anam?*" He leaned back to peer into her eyes. "'Tis a term of endearment."

"No, I meant the 'posting banns' part. What does that mean?"

"For three Sundays before a couple is to wed, they announce their intent to do so by posting the banns of marriage publicly." He winked at her. "We'll wed in the spring when our priest arrives."

No asking. Just telling? Stunned, her heart pounded so hard she was afraid one of her ribs might break. She couldn't breathe, much less speak. Her mind reeling, all she could do was follow along as he took her hand and led her into the keep. How did she feel about his proposal, if that's what you'd call it? She didn't even know. It would take her some time to process this new twist before she could respond. There were so many things to consider, like where she was and how things were done in these times. And what about her feelings for Robley, which were all jumbled up with her unfortunate past? Her baggage. They entered the great hall to find preparations for supper well underway.

"I must go clean up and change before we eat," Rob said. "You'll want to change as well, aye?"

She glanced down at the brownish wool gown she'd borrowed and nodded. They'd known each other for such a short time. How could he be thinking of marriage? If only she could straighten out all of the mess going on inside her brain, she might be able to make some sense of her thoughts and sort through her feelings.

"There ye are, milady," Beth called from the stairs. "I've been looking for ye. If ye please, come to yer chamber. There's no' much time."

Robley gave her a little push. "Go, love. I've much to do before greeting my parents."

His parents. Right. What would they think when he shared his grand plan? What did it matter? They only had about three weeks before the faerie warrior came back for Robley. Her heart slid to the pit of her stomach. Her life had been so simple, her goals clear, and then everything had gone all *Twilight Zone* on her. Erin hurried up the stairs and followed Beth down the corridor to her chamber.

"I've taken the liberty o' bringin' a ewer o' hot water so ye can wash up a bit." Beth hustled her through the door. "Then I'll do your hair and help ye into a fresh gown."

"Thanks." Obediently, Erin removed her work clothes and washed. Her mind on other things, she allowed Beth to dress her in another of Elaine's left-behind gowns, this one a lovely shade of gold. Beth led her to the chair beside the hearth, sat her down and brushed her hair, arranging it into a French braid. She was going to have to face True in a few minutes. Embarrassment heated her face again, and she blew out a long breath. Best get it over with.

"Something troubles you, Erin." Not a question, but a statement.

Well, that was an understatement. She'd been caught up in Rob's wake as he'd been returned to his own time. Life as she knew it had been ripped from her, and she'd just been informed that should Robley survive past his allotted thirty days, he'd post the banns for their wedding. "Are you married, Beth? I didn't think to ask you before."

"Aye, I'm wed to the weaver's oldest son. He tends the sheep along with his da and brother. We've a small cottage on the island." She helped Erin to stand. "Best be going."

"Are you happily married? Robley said a MacKintosh man gives his heart only once, and then it's given forever."

"Aye, 'tis true." Beth grinned dreamily. "Verra happy. We want a bairn sae badly though, and none ha' taken root thus far. Mayhap you have some herbs or a concoction?" Sadness flashed through her eyes, chasing the dreamy look away.

"How long have you been trying?"

"Since midsummer."

"I wouldn't worry yet. If you'd like, I can show you how to tell when you're ovulating. In fact, I've been thinking about teaching a natural family planning class for any of the women who might be interested. Do you think that would go over well?" Thoughts of the villagers doing the sign of the cross and backing away from her flitted through her mind.

"Ovulating?" Beth's brow creased. "I dinna ken what that means."

"When you're most likely to get pregnant." Put it in terms they understand, that's what True had told her. "The time in your cycle when your husband's seed is most likely to take root."

"Och, aye?" Her face lit up. "I'm certain many of the women would be grateful for any help you wish tae share, milady."

"Good." Excitement for the project gave her a reprieve from the worries crowding her brain, if only temporarily. Planning the curriculum for her class filled her mind. Where would she hold the sessions? The clinic was tiny. Maybe she'd start with small groups, or perhaps True could arrange for her to have the classes in the great hall while the men were all doing their testosterony type things in the lists. How would birth control go over with the men, she wondered. They made their way back to the great hall, and Beth left her.

True crossed the room, smirking all the way. "Sorry about bursting in on you two like that," she whispered. "I had no idea Robley was back."

She shrugged, feigning nonchalance. "No biggie." Her eyes slid to True. "You *will* keep it to yourself, right?"

The sound of True's laughter drew Malcolm's gaze—along with the attention of Rob's parents, uncle and aunt. Great. Erin could feel the color rising up her neck again. Robley's mother and aunt left their husbands' sides to join them.

"Good eve to you, my dear," Rosemary greeted her warmly.

"Good evening." Erin curtsied, encompassing Lydia in her greeting.

"How are things coming along with your *clinic*?" Lydia asked.

"They're going well. I've assembled the things I need to attend births, and I've cleaned the cottage from top to bottom. It's nice to have a central place where I can organize." She smiled. The clinic was a definite bright spot in the dome of doom she was living under.

"Come." Lydia gestured toward the dais. "Let us sup. You must be famished after all your efforts this day, aye? And I see the servants are eager to begin serving."

Robley appeared at the top of the stairs, and her breath caught. His hair still damp, he wore a clean white shirt with billowing sleeves under a crimson plaid. Her pulse went wild at the sight of him. He hadn't shaved. She liked the beard. A lot. Her mouth must've dropped open, or she was drooling, because True nudged her, smirking again.

"Busted," True whispered into her ear.

Rob's mother and aunt exchanged an inscrutable look before Rosemary made a beeline for her son. Flustered, Erin stood awkwardly aside as Rob's parents converged on him.

"My lad," Rosemary cried, wrapping her arms around him. "We thought we'd lost you."

Robert clasped his son's shoulder. "Good to have you home," he croaked. "You gave us quite a scare."

"'Tis good to be home." Rob hugged his mother and turned toward his father. "I'm sorry I caused you such worry."

"We'll discuss it later," his dad said, ushering them toward the dais. "Now that your mother kens you're safe and sound, she can eat again."

Erin felt Rob's internal flinch of regret and guilt at his father's words, and she suffered an echoing internal cringe of her own.

"You OK?" True asked her.

"Not really," Erin muttered. "Robley—" The doors to the great hall swung open, and the ferry master burst through.

He removed the cap from his head, twisted it in his hands and shifted his weight back and forth. "Begging your pardon." He bobbed his head. "I've come tae fetch the midwife." His Adam's apple bobbed this time. "My daughter . . . 'tis too soon, but . . ."

Instinct kicked in, and years of training wiped away any thought of her own problems. She had a job to do. "I'll go change, and I have to stop at the cottage for my bag. I'll meet you at the ferry."

"My thanks, milady." Arlen turned and left just as suddenly as he'd arrived.

"Do you need help?" True asked.

"No." She stared pointedly at her friend's belly. "*You* need to take care of yourself. Rest. I know what I'm doing."

"I'll see you safely to the mainland." Rob came to her, placing his hands on her shoulders.

"I'm only going to the village. Stay. Have supper with your parents." She reached out to touch his cheek, thought better of it and dropped her hand to her side. "They've missed you, and I know how worried they've been."

He gripped the hilt of the dagger at his waist, his brow furrowed. His glance went back and forth between his family and her, clearly torn.

"It's all right, Rob. I'll be fine. Arlen will be with me, and anyway, it's not like I'm going to be with strangers."

He snatched her up in his arms, kissed her soundly on the lips and let her go just as suddenly. "Should you need aught, send someone to the island for me."

"I will." His inner conflict and desire washed over her, and she responded in a rush of breathlessness and want—as she always did with him. She headed for the stairs, keeping her eyes focused in front of her. His family had witnessed their kiss. What must they think?

She undid her gown along the way, tugging it off as she crossed her room to the peg where her work clothes hung. She changed quickly, drew her cloak around her shoulders and raced down the back stairway to the shortcut leading to the postern gate. Rushing through the kitchen gardens, she glanced at the dry stalks, all that remained of the vegetables and herbs from the summer.

This was the woman's first baby, and it was coming early. Arlen was worried. She had fears of her own, but if her presence helped ease the ferry master's fears, the sooner she reached him the better. She stopped at the cottage she and True shared, grabbed the sack containing everything she'd put together and rushed down the path to the ferry. Arlen paced in front of the mooring.

"Let's go," she told him as she jumped onto the wooden planks. "Did your wife start water boiling like I instructed?"

"Aye, lass." He threw off the ropes and pushed out onto the lake.

"What's your daughter's name again? I've forgotten. I've met so many people in the past week."

"Alma, and me wife's name is Etan."

"Right. Got it." She placed her hand on the old man's forearm. "Everything's going to be fine, Arlen."

His Adam's apple bobbed again, and he nodded. "'Tis grateful I am tae ha' you here, lass. This being her first and it coming sae soon and all—me and the missus is a bit fashed."

"I understand." Her touch soothed him, and he visibly relaxed.

They made record time to the opposite shore, where a younger man waited. Arlen left him to secure the ferry, and he led her to his daughter's home a short distance away.

"Who is the young man you left with the ferry? Is that Alma's husband?"

"Nay. 'Tis my son. Monroe will man the ferry this eve. Though 'tis unlikely any will want tae cross at this hour. Alma's husband will be at home with her by now, I expect."

First order of business would be to send the men away. She was all for husbands being labor coaches, but not without prior training, and not without making sure they had bathed and changed into clean clothes beforehand. She didn't want the risk of infection, and a new mother didn't need her husband's anxiety adding to her own, especially in the case of a preemie. When she'd visited Alma, she'd guessed her to be around thirty-two weeks. She hoped her guess was accurate. A baby had a good chance of surviving at that point, especially if it was a girl.

They came to a small cottage with a loft, and Arlen knocked on the door. A young man answered, his face tight with tension, he sucked in a huge breath when he caught sight of her and launched into rapid-fire Gaelic. All she could do was shake her head.

"Speak the words of the *Sassenach*, lad," Arlen admonished. "Lady True has said more than once the lady was no' raised amongst her kin."

"Och, begging your pardon," the young man said, bowing his head to her. "Welcome to our home. We're verra grateful to ye."

"I'm glad to help." Erin's brow rose. What story had been circulated regarding her upbringing? "Please, call me Erin." She pushed her way past the men and surveyed the interior. The scent of mint permeated the place, and everything appeared to be clean and tidy. Alma and her mother stood by the hearth. The young woman's eyes were huge with fright, and a sheen of perspiration made her forehead glow in the light of the fire.

"If it's all right with you"—Erin turned to Arlen and the father-to-be—"I'd like to send you both on your way. Is there somewhere you can go?"

"Aye." Arlen put his hand on his son-in-law's shoulder. "To the inn for a pint, and then we'll await news at me and me wife's cottage." He shot Etan a look as if asking her permission.

"'Tis a good idea, Arlen. We'll send for ye." Etan shooed them toward the door. "Be off now, and let us do what needs tae be done."

Erin rolled up her sleeves and took out the soap from the bag she'd brought with her. "You've boiled water?"

"Aye, mum. There's some cooling on the table there and more a boilin', just as ye said tae." Etan pointed to the table.

"Let's wash our hands and arms, and then we're going to give you a quick bath as well, Alma. It'll help you to feel more comfortable." She started washing, and Etan joined her. They stripped Alma down, washed her and put a short linen gown over her head, just as a contraction hit her.

"It's too soon," Alma wailed through her pains. "The bairn is comin' far too soon."

"There's not a lot we can do about that." A narrow cot had been set up in one corner, and Erin noticed the ticking was wool rather than straw. Hopefully that meant fewer vermin, and from what True had told her, mint was used as a repellent. After the contraction passed, she had Alma lie back and lift her knees so she could check to see how dilated and effaced she was. "You're at four centimeters." She frowned. Something wasn't right. She didn't get anything from the baby—no signs of life emanated from the fetus. *Oh God.*

After she washed her hands again, she rested her palms on Alma's belly once more, hoping against hope she'd been wrong. What she would give for a stethoscope and fetal monitor about now. "When was the last time you felt movement, like the baby kicking?"

Alma's expression shifted into alarm. "Why do ye ask. Ah!" Another contraction began.

"Breathe, Alma. Pant like a hound. It'll help you get through it." Erin kept her hands on her patient to ease some of the discomfort as she strained. Alma rode the crest, blowing out a long breath once the pain subsided. Should she tell her?

"Etan, in my bag you'll find a smaller bag with some herbal tea inside. Can you make up a nice mug for Alma? It'll help her labor progress and ease some of the pain."

"Aye, mum."

"Please, call me Erin."

"Aye, mum." The older woman gathered what she needed to brew the herbs Erin and True had blended for the purpose. "What else can I do? I've got the drying cloths folded and ready tae go right there, and we boiled them clean like ye said tae." She jutted her chin toward the neat pile of linens set on end of the cot. "The water is boilin'. Shall I move it awa' from the fire?"

"That would be good." Erin turned to Alma. If it were her, she'd want to know. "Alma, I'm afraid for your baby. I don't detect any signs of life. That's why I asked about the last time you might have felt any movement."

"Nay. You're wrong," she cried. "It can't be. I felt the bairn kick earlier this day. I swear it."

"I hope so." She knew better, but upsetting Alma further would not change anything.

Time went by, and Alma made steady progress in textbook fashion. Sometime around midnight, the urge to push came over her. "Etan, can you prop her up from behind?" Erin got into position to catch the baby. One more push and the tiny body slid from its mother, perfectly formed, but stillborn. "I'm so sorry, Alma.

I'm so sorry." She remained where she was to ensure the placenta delivered as well.

"Oh, sweet girl," Etan muttered. "Oh, my dear."

Alma wept and held out her arms. "Let me see him. Let me hold my bairn," she wept.

"I'll go get her man." Etan rushed out of the cottage.

Erin cut the umbilical cord and wiped the tiny baby clean. She wrapped him in a blanket and placed his still form into his mother's arms. "I'm so sorry." Her eyes stung, and helplessness to give any kind of meaningful comfort broke her heart. There were no words that could assuage the kind of loss and grief Alma was suffering. She hadn't been prepared for this side of being a midwife. While Alma held her son, Erin cleaned up.

The door opened, and Alma's husband strode through, rage contorting his features. "What did you do?" he growled at her.

"What did I do?" Erin blinked. "These things happen. Nothing I did caused your son to be stillborn, and there isn't anything I could have done to prevent it."

"Humph. Mayhap you're bad luck, and that's why the Sutherlands let ye go sae easily." He strode over to his wife's side.

"Roderick, dinna blame the midwife. She had naught—"

"Go. All of ye. Leave us," he shouted. "Now." The bereaved father turned stricken eyes to them. "I dinna want ye here."

This time his gaze fixed on her, and the suspicion and rage she glimpsed behind his grief stole her breath.

Etan tugged at her arm. "Come, lass."

They walked silently toward the ferry landing, and Erin felt as if all the eyes of the villagers were peering at her. She even caught movement from one of the windows, though when she turned to look, all she saw was the dim light of a candle coming from inside. Her tears fell freely down her cheeks, and she racked her brain for something to say that would ease Etan's grief. Nothing came to her.

What a way to begin her career in her new home as a midwife. How could Alma's husband possibly blame her for the death of their baby? Arlen arrived at the ferry just as she and Etan did. "I'm so sorry about the loss of your grandchild, Etan, Arlen, but nothing I did caused the baby's death. I believe he was already gone before Alma's labor started." She sniffed and wiped at her eyes.

"Of course ye are no' to blame." Etan patted Erin's arm. "These things happen. Take Erin back tae the island, Arlen. Good eve to ye, lass. Our thanks for coming." She turned and hurried back to the village.

"Off you go, lad." Arlen gestured for his son to return home. He helped her onto the wooden planks and shoved off without a word. It was the longest trip she'd ever made. The older man's grief pressed painfully against her. The fifteenth century was a scary place to be, and right now all she wanted was to find Robley. She needed him. Too bad it was well past midnight, and she had no idea how or where to find him.

She jumped off the ferry before it landed, and strode to the keep. Straining to open one of the heavy double doors to the great hall, she was surprised to find a fire still burning brightly in one of the hearths. A form moved from the shadows. "Rob," she sobbed, all the grief and fear rising to choke her. In an instant, she found herself caught up in his arms.

"What is it, love? Why do you cry?"

"The baby . . . Alma's baby was stillborn. There wasn't anything I could do about it, but . . . but Alma's husband blames me." She burrowed her face against his shoulder, and her tears came in such a flood, they dampened his shirt. Her heart ached for the young couple, and at the same time, the suspicion and rage aimed her way still spooked her.

"Och, love. 'Twas his grief that caused him to lash out as he did." He ran his hands up and down her back. "He'll come to his senses ere long. Dinna fash."

"You waited up for me." She leaned back to swipe at her eyes. "Thank you. I . . ." She sniffed. "I was going to try to find you."

"Come. Sit with me awhile until you've calmed." He led her across the great hall toward the hearth.

She sank down onto the bench and leaned back against the edge of the table. Staring into the flames dancing in the fireplace, she sucked in a huge breath and let it out slowly. "Not a very auspicious way to begin my career as the MacKintosh midwife, was it?" Torn, she wondered what the future held.

She loved Rob, but she wasn't sure she could withstand the mentality of the era. They didn't even really understand how pregnancy worked. They still thought a "man's seed" planted itself inside the woman's womb. How could she function surrounded by such ignorance?

Another happy thought knotted her gut. If Alma's husband went around to everyone in the village with his accusations, who would want her to attend them during their births? No one, that's who. Starting a clinic had seemed like such a good idea, but what business did she have doing such a thing? Given the superstitious mentality she faced in the fifteenth century, she'd surely fail. Besides, more than likely, she'd be hurled back to her own time before she could make any difference in the lives of the villagers. That thought sent another pang ricocheting through her. Robley. She'd lose the best friend she'd ever had.

"What are you thinking about, love?"

She shrugged. "Just that it might be a huge mistake for me to practice midwifery in your century."

"Dinna give up just yet. 'Tis unfortunate, but no' all that uncommon for bairns to be stillborn. It happens with the livestock as well." Robley sat beside her and put his arm around her shoulders. "There will be other births to attend to."

"What if no one wants me to be there after this? Alma's husband said the Sutherlands let me go because I'm bad luck."

"Ridiculous. You were never with the Sutherlands."

"You and I know that, but the rest of the villagers don't. That man is going to bad-mouth me all over town."

Robley frowned in confusion. "Bad-mouth?"

"He's going to gossip about me in the very worst way."

"Humph. I'll speak to Arlen."

"Thanks, but I don't think that's going to make a lot of difference." She leaned against him, exhaustion and defeat dragging at the edges of her soul. "Your century certainly is a minefield." He grunted beside her, and she knew he didn't have a clue what a minefield was. Still, his presence filled her with warmth, and she was overwhelmed with gratitude. Never before had she experienced the kind of support and loyalty Robley provided for her on a daily basis. Lord help her, she had to find a way to save him from the faerie coming to take him away, or die trying.

CHAPTER THIRTEEN

Another se'nnight gone, and still no word of Giselle's whereabouts. Robley took his place upon the dais, his mood surly. Even though he expected his men's journey would come to naught, every day that he waited for news grated upon his nerves until he was edgy and raw. He had but a fortnight left to live and no resolution in his sights.

He caught movement from the top of the stairs. Erin. His poor heart strained at the sight of her, and frustration brought him even lower. He wanted her with an intensity that stole his breath and weakened his knees, yet with his future so uncertain, the strong mix of emotions—love, desire and despair for a future he might never have with her—did naught but churn his insides to mash.

What would become of her? How could he secure her future? Swallowing the tightness in his throat, he stood to pull her chair out for her. "You look lovely this eve, *mo cridhe.*" She did indeed steal his breath away with her beauty, despite the lines of worry etched around her eyes and mouth. He'd heard the whispers amongst the villagers and servants. Since the ferry master's daughter gave birth to a stillborn son, they feared her, and he kent she'd heard the whispers as well. None of the women who were breeding had sought her help. Yet another reason to secure her future before his demise.

Her small smile in answer to his compliment smote him on the spot. Was love always this unsettling? Did all men suffer this same shaky weakness? Nay. Most men believed they'd have a lifetime with their beloved. He kent well he did not.

At least his immediate family understood the truth where Alma's bairn was concerned, and True still relied upon Erin as her time drew near. In that he took comfort. Gently, he pushed her chair in and took his place beside her, just as his parents, uncle and aunt began to filter into the great hall for supper.

Erin's expression clouded. "Have you heard anything from the men looking for Giselle?"

"Nay." He took her hand and kissed her knuckles. "'Tis as if my neck were already on the block, and I'm just waiting for the blade to fall. I've no notion what to do. Walk to the loch with me after supper? 'Twould do me good to have your company for a bit. Mayhap we'll think of aught we've overlooked."

"I'd like that." Erin squeezed his hand before turning to greet his family. Tieren, Hunter's closest friend and Malcolm's page, began filling their goblets with watered wine.

Malcolm and Hunter were the last to arrive, and Hunter took up the mantle of page, eager to serve them. Malcolm sat in his customary place. "True is no' happy to be confined above." He flashed a wry grin to Erin. "She's used to being the *boss*."

"'Tis for the best," Rosemary said, nodding to Erin.

"We'll keep True company anon." Lydia smiled. "I ken her time is near, for she's quite restless. I had to stop her from scrubbing the walls of our solar this morn."

Platters of food came from the kitchen, filling the hall with savory smells. Rob's mouth salivated in anticipation. He helped himself to two large portions of meat, placing them on the trencher he shared with Erin. "Turnips?" he asked, his dagger hovering above the root vegetables.

"Yes, please. Carrots and cabbage too." She glanced his way, lifting the small dagger he'd given her. "I still miss my fork."

"You'll become accustomed to the wee dagger, lass," his uncle William said, rubbing his hands together. "I do enjoy freshly roasted pork."

Robley's father sneezed and sneezed again. Slumping forward, his head fell to the table.

"Robert!" his mother shook him by the shoulders. "Robert, what is it? What ails you, my love?"

"Father," Rob cried. Leaping to his feet, he hurried to his side. Rob's lungs seized with alarm at the sight of his father's limp form. He'd always been so strong, invincible in Rob's eyes.

"Oh God." Erin pushed him aside and pulled his father upright. She placed her hands on either side of his head, and a look of intense concentration suffused her face. "A stroke. He's had an ischemic stroke. I can sense the blockage." She kept her hands on him as he leaned precariously.

Rob reached out to support his father where he teetered in the chair. He would not let him fall. His heart in his throat, fear and grief pierced him through. He held his father by the shoulders, and all the while childhood memories played through his mind. He'd never had a moment's doubt that his da loved him. Despite the many hours of worry he'd caused his parents, they'd always been there for him, offering encouragement and direction. "What can be done, Erin?" he asked.

"Keep supporting him, Rob." Her gaze shot to Hunter. "You know the trunk in my room?"

"Aye." He nodded, wide-eyed.

"Inside you'll find a leather bag. Bring it quickly." She returned her attention to Robert. "Once I get some aspirin down his throat, we need to transfer him to his bed."

His mother wailed, and his aunt went to comfort her. William came to stand on his da's other side. Rob looked to Erin. "What is a stroke?" he asked, his voice breaking.

"Um, I think you'd call it apoplexy. He has a clot in one of the blood vessels in his brain, and it's blocking the flow of blood." Erin pressed two fingers upon his father's neck, just below his jaw. "His pulse is strong and steady. His respiration is good."

"What can I do?" Malcolm stepped forward.

"Have someone make sure there's a good fire in his chamber, and have the bed ready," Erin directed.

Hunter returned and handed Erin her purse. She riffled through it, bringing out a small vial. Her hands shaking, she untwisted the lid and poured a few white disks into her palm. Using the flat side of a dagger, she crushed the things into powder atop the table linen, poured out most of the wine from his father's goblet and brushed the powder into what remained in his cup. "Help me get this down his throat." She turned to him. "Ready?"

"Aye." Robley pried his father's jaw open and tilted his head back, his heart breaking at the sight of his father's slackened features and ghostlike pallor. Erin poured the contents down his throat and massaged his neck until his Adam's apple gave indication that he swallowed the concoction.

"Will he live?" his mother asked in a tremulous voice. "Speak plainly, lass. Will my husband live?"

"The next few hours are critical." Erin spared her a glance. "I don't know. I hope so. He's a strong, healthy man. If he doesn't have another episode, the odds are in his favor."

His father made a gurgling sound and opened his eyes. One side of his face drooped slightly. He reached for his wife, and she moved to his side, clasping his hand to her chest.

"We need to get him to bed." Rob sought his cousin, who had sent servants scurrying to make ready his parents' chamber. "Help me get him upstairs. I'll take his shoulders." Between his uncle, Malcolm and himself, they managed to wrest his father up the narrow staircase and to his bed. The women followed, and Lydia continued on down the corridor. For certes she meant to inform True of what had happened.

"How is he?" True soon appeared in the doorway, breathless and flushed, followed by Lydia. She clutched a small pouch in her hand and hurried to Erin's side. "What needs to be done?"

Rob moved out of the way, guilt and helplessness reducing him to near tears. Was this his fault? He'd always been the one to cause them worry, what with his recklessness and constant desire for adventure. They'd thought him dead these past few months, and he still might die if he didn't succeed in accomplishing what the faerie warrior had asked of him. Scrubbing his hands over his face, he stayed out of the way as the women tended his father.

Erin fussed with making Robert more comfortable. She removed his boots and smoothed the blankets beneath him. "I've given him aspirin to thin his blood. Hopefully that should help." She straightened. "Wish we had a hospital down the road." Her face was drawn, and concern formed creases across her delicate brow. "And physical therapists nearby." Her eyes caught and held True's.

"I have red willow tea. It's made from the inner bark." True placed the pouch in Erin's hands.

Erin shot her a stern look. "Tell me you didn't go all the way to the cottage for this. We don't need another emergency tonight."

"No. I keep some on hand in our chamber. Aspirin is made from red willow, right? Will this have the same effect?"

"Probably."

"My . . . Rose . . ." Robert croaked, trying to rise. "Rosemary."

"I'm here, *mo céile*." Rosemary rushed to Robert's side. Perching on the edge of the bed, she put her arms around her husband's shoulders. He sighed, calmed by her presence, and relaxed back onto the mattress.

"That's a good sign." Erin caught his eye. "He's able to talk, and we got the blood thinner into him immediately. Hopefully the damage is minimal." She began herding everyone toward the door. "I'll stay and monitor his progress, but all we can do now is wait and see. He needs to rest. Go. I'll let you know if anything happens." Erin turned to Rob. "I left my purse in the great hall. After Hunter has something to eat, will you send him up with my bag and some boiled water for the tea? I'll keep dosing Robert with aspirin or willow bark tea through the night."

Robley studied his mother and found he was reluctant to leave. Grief and fear suffused her features, and her eyes were overly bright with unshed tears. His own helplessness to do anything to help pained him. Another crisis he couldn't control. Frustration at his own inadequacies burned through him. Worse was the niggling suspicion and corrosive guilt that his foolhardy actions may have precipitated his father's ailment. He strode to his mother's side and rested a hand on her shoulder. "Would you rather have me stay?"

"Aye. If you please," she said, her voice quavering. "'Twould give me comfort, and if Erin needs to move him, she'll need your help."

"I'll send Hunter with the things you need," Malcolm said. "Have the lad pass the night here. If you need aught, send him in your stead." He placed his hands on his wife's shoulders and guided her toward the door. "Back to our chamber, True. Like Erin says, we dinna need another crisis this eve."

"But—"

"Please. I don't want to worry about you right now. I have enough on my hands as it is," Erin pleaded. "You should be off your feet and in bed."

"All right." Reluctantly, True let Malcolm guide her out of the chamber.

Erin's eyes met Rob's, and in an instant, she was in his arms, soothing him with her touch.

"It's going to be all right. I can feel it. He might need some help, but he's going to recover."

Resting her cheek over his heart as was her habit, she tightened her arms around his waist. His throat worked, and his eyes stung. Unable to speak, he did the only thing he could. He held her, taking the comfort she so generously offered. Would she ever ken how much having her with him mattered? Did she not realize how much they already leaned upon one another during their trials? In her heart she trusted him. 'Twas in her head where the problems lay, keeping them apart. If he did naught else, he meant to convince her they were meant to be together.

The night passed slowly. With Rob's help, Erin and his mother undressed his father and made him more comfortable. Rob tended the hearth and did what he could to comfort his mother, while Erin tended his da, waking him oft to drink tea or to take more of the white powder. Each time she roused him, she laid her hands on his temples to ease his pain, or to heal him. She only hoped it helped.

Erin stretched and rubbed her back. "He's stable and sleeping well. I'm not worried that he'll worsen or have another episode."

"Go to your rest, lass." Rosemary clasped Erin's hands in hers. "I am so grateful to have you with us. I've no idea how we would have managed were you no' here." Rosemary reached out a hand to Robley, and he took it. She drew him into their circle. "See Erin to her chamber. I'll stay up with your da, and if there's any change, I'll send Hunter for you."

Rob looked at Hunter where he slept on a pile of blankets by the hearth. "Are you certain? If it would give you ease, I'll keep the vigil with you."

"Nay." She rubbed her eyes. "We all need rest. Erin says he's stable, and I can see it is so with mine own eyes. I will need your strength on the morrow. Go to your rest now."

"She's right." Erin sighed. "We won't be good for anything if we're both exhausted." She laid a hand on Rosemary's arm. "Just before dawn, see if you can get more of the tea into him. I'll be back in the morning."

"I will. Now off with you both." Rosemary shooed them out the door, shutting it behind them.

His heart faltering, he stood in the dimly lit corridor and tunneled both hands through his hair. His eyes stung with weariness and grief. "Erin . . ."

"I know. I'm sorry." She ran her hand down his arm.

"Do you ken if . . ." His throat closed up, and he had to swallow a few times before continuing. "Did I cause my father's stroke?" He stared down the hall, his jaw clenching. "My parents thought me dead. I . . . I gave them such grief and worry. Is it because of me that he—"

"No. You didn't cause the clot. Conditions leading to a stroke take years to develop." She placed her hands on his cheeks and turned his face so that their eyes met. "Nothing you did caused this, and there is nothing you could've done to prevent the stroke from happening."

He turned toward her hand and kissed the center of her palm. Relief and gratitude left him weak, and he took her hand in his. "I'll walk with you to your chamber. We never did take our stroll to the loch."

"Another time." She leaned into him as they made their way down the hall, and her warmth and presence calmed him immeasurably. Normally by this hour the halls would be pitch-dark, but someone had lit a number of torches to guide their way.

"He's going to live. That much I know for sure, but as far as how much damage was done to his brain, it's too soon to say. I tried to do some healing. I don't know." She shrugged. "Maybe it helped." Again she stroked his arm. "He spoke, and that's encouraging."

"Still, I'll have to take over his duties as seneschal, and only a fortnight remains until the faerie returns for me." They reached her door. Facing the rest of the night without her in his arms was more than he could bear. "Lass, what am I tae do? My responsibilities to our clan weigh heavy, and if I dinna return the pensieve . . ." Guilt for the foolishness that had led him to this desperate place swamped him. He blew out a long breath and shook his head, staring mutely into her lovely eyes.

The longing to lose himself in her arms, if only for the remainder of this one night, overwhelmed him. He couldn't tear himself away if he tried. "You ken how I feel about you, aye?"

She nodded and worried her lower lip between her teeth.

His heart pounded, and he could scarce draw breath. He railed at fate, at himself, and regret for what they might never have ate at him from the inside out. "Though you dinna trust your own heart, I ken you care for me as well. What if all we have is the fortnight left to us?" He brushed his lips across her forehead. "One night in your arms, and I'll die content, for you are and always will be the keeper of my heart, whether I die tomorrow or live another sixty years. You've captivated me from the start, Erin. I love you with all that I am."

"Oh, Rob," she cried.

"Without you beside me, I canna face what remains of this night." He ran his hands up and down her back, drawing her closer. "Say you're mine, *mo anam*. Say the words I long to hear so that I might possess some small portion of joy to sustain me."

"I love you. I didn't want to, but I do." She sniffed. "What are we going to do?"

"Love each other." His spirits soared to the heavens, and need ignited his blood. She loved him, and for the moment, naught else mattered. He opened her door and lifted her through. "And this time, I'll no' forget the latch." He pushed the iron bar through its frame. Embers still glowed in the hearth, and someone had thought to bring food to her chamber. A covered tray and a goblet sat atop the small trunk. "Come, my love. See what there is to eat while I stir the fire back to life. I'm famished."

Erin uncovered the platter. "It's the roasted pork and vegetables from earlier, plus some kind of berry tart."

"Sounds wonderful." He moved the single chair so that it rested by the trunk. Taking a seat, he drew her down to his lap. "What shall you have first, my lady?" He drew his dagger from its sheath and speared a piece of meat. "Would you like a morsel of this fine roast Molly prepared for us?"

She nodded and opened her mouth. He fed her. "It should always be thus, sweetling. Would that I be granted the honor of providing for you for the rest of a very long life together."

"I love the way you talk." She sighed.

"How I talk? Humph. I dinna take your meaning."

"Everything you say sounds like a love sonnet. Shakespeare has nothing on you."

"I dinna ken whom this Shakespeare fellow might be, but when it comes to you, my very breath is a testament to the love I bear you, lass. How is it you are no' aware my heart beats solely for you?"

"See?" She smiled, her eyes bright, and took the dagger from his hand. "Here, let me." She cut a piece of the roast and fed it to him with her fingers, following the morsel with her own sweet lips.

They fed each other and shared kisses until every bit of their meal had been consumed. Rob imagined this was their wedding night. They might not get another, unless . . . Thoughts crowded into his mind, and a way to at least ensure her future dawned. "What would you say to a handfasting between us?" He rubbed his thumbs over her palms.

"I've heard the term, but I'm not clear on what it means. Is handfasting like getting engaged or betrothed?"

"No' exactly. We have no priest in residence, and with winter soon upon us, 'tis unlikely we'll see one ere spring. The church has decreed handfasting to be as valid as the sacrament of marriage due to the remoteness of so many of our clans, because they dinna want couples living together in sin. A couple speaks their vows before God and witnesses, and the priest blesses the union come spring. 'Tis a wedding."

She tensed in his arms, and her parents' unsavory past clouded her lovely green eyes. "Think, lass. You may never be able to return to your time. 'Twould be far better for you to be my widow than no'. Your place within my family would always be assured—until such time as you may choose to remarry."

His heart wrenched painfully. The thought of her with another man had him wishing for his claymore. He couldn't stomach the notion of another man's hands on his woman.

"Rob, you know how I feel about marriage." Her expression troubled, she rose from his lap and paced. "I—"

"Think upon it. 'Tis all I ask." He swallowed the lump in his throat. "Faith, lass, do ye no' ken how already we turn to each other in times of trouble? Let me be your strength, as you are mine."

She sniffed and wiped the tears from her cheeks. Staring into the flames leaping in the small hearth, she frowned. "Your parents adore each other. Anyone can see that, especially after tonight. So do William and Lydia, but—"

"Aye, as do Malcolm and True. 'Tis the way it should be. Did I no' tell you so over and over?" The need to haul her into his arms nearly undid him, but he forced himself to remain seated. She needed to work through things on her own. "I'll grant you this; no' all marriages are happy within the nobility. Most are arranged for political or material gain. But because of William's experience with first an arranged marriage, and then his second, he's more amenable to let his kin make their own choices. Let me love you. For whatever time remains, let me be your husband."

"I'm not a virgin," she said, shrugging slightly. "Does that bother you?"

"Nay. I ken well enough virginity is no' as highly regarded in your time as it is in mine. And besides, it's ne'er seemed just that it should be thus for women and no' for men." His mouth quirked up. How long had she worried over this? "I'm no' a virgin either. Does that bother you?"

"Yes." She flashed him a pointed look over her shoulder. "You know my history. Infidelity is a deal breaker."

His heart took flight at the fierce look of possessiveness on her beloved face. "Had I kent you existed, *mo anam*, I would have waited, and gladly so. But I despaired of ever finding you. 'Tis true, I sought comfort where I could." He rose from his place and crossed the short distance to stand before her. "But I am a faithful man. There will never be another for me. I pledge my troth to you and you alone. Will you no' do the same? Whatever may come, let us join our hearts together so that we face our fate united."

"OK," she squeaked out, tears filling her eyes again. "I don't want to lose you. Not ever. There has to be something we can do, right?"

"Aye, but no' this minute. This night let us consummate our bond." He brushed the tears from her cheeks. "Let this be our wedding night, and on the morrow we'll arrange to say our vows before our clan." Tipping her chin up, he kissed her with every ounce of love he held for her in his battered heart.

CHAPTER FOURTEEN

Awash in the tender adoration emanating from Robley, Erin melted into his kiss. A delicious shiver of need sluiced through her, heat following in its wake. Her wedding night. Never in a million years would she have believed she'd agree to marry anyone. But the man creating such havoc within her wasn't just anyone. This was Robley of clan MacKintosh, the fifteenth-century knight who had stolen his way into her life and lodged himself deeply inside her heart and soul.

For once she intended to let go of her fears, give herself completely and keep nothing back. She might not get another chance. These next two weeks might be all they *ever* had. Her chest ached. She raged against the circumstances threatening their happily-ever-after.

Forcing it from her mind, she focused on the present. Tonight she'd love Robley like they had forever. She'd love him without regret or sadness.

He nibbled his way down her neck to her collarbone. "Och, love, have you any idea how desperately I've longed to hold you in my arms like this?" He managed to untie the laces of her gown and help her out of the yards of wool. "From the very first moment I laid eyes upon you, I prayed you were meant for me." His fingers trembled as he undid the ties holding her chemise. A look of awe filled his eyes as the garment slipped down her shoulders to the floor in a billowing puddle of linen at her booted feet. Except for the footgear, she stood naked before him, her nerves stretched taut. He sucked in a breath. His eyes darkened with approval as they roamed over her. She basked in it. "Turn around, lass," he commanded in a husky voice that sent fresh shivers running through her.

"What for?"

"I want your hair free and flowing about your shoulders." A grin broke free when his gaze met with her twenty-first-century footwear. "And then I'll remove those boots."

She did as she was told, and flutters tripped through her each time his fingers brushed against her skin. Once her hair was free, he moved close and wrapped her in his arms. His erection pressed against her backside through his plaid, causing a throbbing ache in her core. She leaned into him, her knees going weak as he caressed her sensitive breasts. His breathing grew heavier, brushing against her skin, arousing her even more than she ever thought possible. It was all she could do to remain standing. One hand continued to stroke her breasts, while the other stole down to the junction of her thighs.

"Open for me." He pressed her into his groin and rocked his hips into her.

Her own breaths came fast and shallow. She widened her stance, giving him access.

"Och, lass." Sliding his fingers into her, he found her clit with his thumb, rubbing it while making love to her with his fingers. "You're so soft here, so hot and slick for me." His movements became more frantic, and she moaned with pleasure.

"Too fast." Grunting, he took his hand away and turned her. "'Tis happening too fast, when what I want is to take my time with you."

"I don't mind." She ran her hands over his chest, working her way lower. "Really. But it's not fair that I'm naked and you aren't."

She unfastened the belt around his waist. His plaid, sporran and belt joined her chemise on the wooden planks. He was gloriously naked from the waist down. Her heart bounced to her fluttering stomach and back to her throat. With his help, she tugged his shirt off over his head.

Ah. There they are. Those six-pack abs she'd always known were hidden beneath the sexy T-shirts he'd worn. Scars crossed his powerful shoulders and biceps, one made a diagonal ridge across his chest—from past battles?—and not an ounce of flab marred the perfect male landscape. Lean and muscled, Rob could've been a sculpture. He was a study in prime masculinity.

Magnificent. No other word described him better, and she couldn't keep her hands off of him to save her life. His skin was so hot and soft to her touch, except the wiry patch of hair on his chest. Caressing his pecs, she traced the scar there and stroked her way down to his abdomen, gratified when his muscles rippled and jumped under her fingertips. His shaft jerked, and a tiny droplet appeared at the tip. "We don't *have* to take our time." She raised her eyes to his, pleading.

He let out a chuckle and held her at arm's length. She scowled at him, too far gone in lust to wait much longer. What she wanted was to explore the rest of him, and he'd stopped her mid-quest.

"Sit, love. I'll remove those boots."

"Oh, all right," she grumbled, doing as he asked. She held out one foot, then the other. Once the shoes were gone, he rose to tower above her, his expression turning fierce. Wave after wave of possessiveness and desire flowed from him to the very center of her being.

"I claim you as my own. Before God, I am your husband; you are my wife." He tilted her chin up so that he had her full attention. His blue eyes scorched her as they bored into hers. "Say it, Erin. Say the words. Make your vow to me now."

Her heart pounded so hard the sound echoed in her head. Blinking up at him, she parted her lips to speak, and couldn't. She cleared her throat and sucked in a breath, steadying her nerves. "Before God, I am your wife," she vowed in a quavering voice. "You are my husband."

All the air left her lungs, and she was left gasping for breath. *Finally I find a man worth taking a chance on, and more than likely I'll lose him in two weeks.* If only this could last. She'd give anything to make it last, even the possibility of finishing her midwife certification. Had she been born under an unlucky-at-love star or something? Tears filled her eyes.

"Dinna think on it, *mo céile*," he gritted out. "I ken where your thoughts are taking you. Dinna fash about the future. This night is for naught but consummating our vows. 'Tis a precious gift indeed."

She nodded, pushing her grief to the far recesses of her mind. "You're right. Sorry."

His eyes softened and then smoldered. He lifted her into his arms and laid her down on the narrow bed. Covering her with his heat and hardness, his bare skin against hers stole her ability to think at all. The sheer force of his physical reactions to her, the intensity of his feelings dizzied her senses. Arousal, love, possessiveness and passion swirled around and between them like a dust devil.

"Mine," he growled, before taking her mouth with a kiss so hungry and hot her heart forgot to beat. He raised himself on his elbows, and his eyes roamed over her. "I want to taste every inch of you, wife." He nibbled her neck, working his way to her jaw. A rumbled purr vibrated from low in his chest.

Breathless and needy, she pulled him close for a kiss. He plunged his tongue into her mouth, circling and sliding it against hers. He nudged her thighs apart with his knees and rocked there, teasing her with his erection. His hands and mouth left a trail of flame wherever they touched. She groaned, arching into him as he took a hardened nipple into his mouth and sucked. His callused palms ran down her sides, caressing, worshipping. He moved to her side, giving his hands better access to where she needed his touch the most.

Oh, he had such talented fingers, and they drove her to the edge. She lifted her pelvis, seeking more pressure, desperate for release. "Don't make me wait, Robley. Please . . ." She reached for him, stroking his length and absorbing his heat. He shuddered at her touch. Encouraged, she reached lower to cup him, caressing and loving him with her hands.

"You are so beautiful, lass. The way you respond to my touch drives me mad with wanting you." He groaned, trembling in her arms. Positioning himself between her thighs, he used one hand to guide himself in and filled her completely.

Exquisite pleasure rolled through her, merging with his and increasing the sensations tenfold. She tightened around him, bereft when he pulled back, only to crest higher with his return. He took his time, and she rode the slow build toward ecstasy. "More. Faster," she demanded.

He answered her with a kiss, his tongue mating with hers, and his moan sluiced through her. She ran her hands over his perfect butt, savoring the tautness of every well-formed muscle. She continued to stroke up his back, over his shoulders and along his biceps. Surrounded by his scent and heat, consumed by his passion, she lost herself in the glory of their lovemaking. All worry for the future, all the fears rooted in her past dissipated like so much mist before the brightness of the burning sun.

His thrusts came faster, harder, and she met them, rising to the pinnacle of pleasure. She hovered for a second before her release sent wave after wave of glorious ecstasy rushing through her. Rob soon followed. Throwing his head back, he called her name just as his pulsing heat filled her. She took his full weight as he collapsed on top of her. Running her hands up and down his back, she soaked in the sated contentment flowing between them.

"You were made for me, Erin of clan Durie. I felt it in my heart the moment I fell through time right into your arms." Robley rolled to his side and drew her close. He ran his hands over her and nuzzled her temple. His satisfied sigh tickled her ear. "Dawn approaches, and we've much to do on the morrow. Sleep, my love."

Snuggling closer, she laid her head on his shoulder and yawned. Pleasurable aftershocks still pulsed through her veins. Rob's love and his tender embrace cocooned her, and the heat radiating from his body lulled her into satiated drowsiness. "I love you, Robley," she whispered.

"And I love you," he whispered back, and hugged her close. "We'll find a way, Erin. We'll find a way to defeat our foe."

Lord, she hoped so, because she didn't think she'd survive the alternative.

Erin awoke to the sound of frantic rapping on her door. Robley shifted beside her, his soft snores taking up where they'd left off once he settled again. "What is it?" she called softly. Her room was bathed in the soft light of early morning and tinged with pinks and golds.

"Milady, True needs ye," Beth called through the door. "Her water broke, and she labors."

Adrenaline chased the remnants of sleep from her brain. *Oh God.* What if things went badly, like they had with Alma? Twins came with double the risk. *No, don't think like that!* True needed her. Erin threw her covers off and swung her bare feet to the floor. The chill air sent goose bumps skittering up her arms, and she could see her breath. Rob woke up and rubbed his face before winking at her. She shook her head and placed her finger against her lips, begging him to be quiet.

"Have a bath prepared for me, Beth," she called, "and send someone to the clinic for my satchel. I'll go to the bathing room right away."

"Aye, milady." Beth's footsteps faded down the hall.

"I have to go. True is in labor." She frowned. "You know, the villagers are probably going to blame me for your father's stroke now too. I hope everything goes according to the textbooks with True. I'll be tied up for hours, and—"

"My father's ailment has naught to do with you. 'Tis more likely they'll blame me." He scowled. "I'm certain my mother has already informed the servants of your role in saving his life. The villagers will soon learn the truth of it."

"I suppose it's too much to hope that they'll realize no one is to blame." She grabbed her brush and a twig to clean her teeth. "Will you make sure your father's breakfast is something light and easy to digest? Watered down oatmeal or broth would be best. Then give him more of the willow bark tea. I'll look in on him when I can."

"Aye, *mo céile*." Robley stood up and stretched.

"It would be nice if someone brought a bowl of oatmeal to True's chamber for me too. I'm starving, but I don't want to take the time to eat until after I've checked on my patient."

He reached for his clothes where they lay on the floor. "You *are* a managing female."

"Is that a bad thing?" She scowled at him as she gathered her clothes.

He drew her into his arms. "Nay. I love that about you, but I've been thinking. 'Twould be wise for you to take on an apprentice. Once our clan realizes you are no' bad luck, you will need help. You canna be everywhere at once." He kissed her forehead and let her go. "Hopefully, I'll see you for the evening meal. I've things to do as well." He pulled his shirt on and began pleating the wool around his waist. "Give my regards to True. I'll see to everything you've asked of me before I visit the lists." Another quick kiss and they left the chamber together.

She found a tub ready for her and linens folded nearby. Not wanting to take the time to wash her hair, she brushed it out and braided it before stepping into her bath. She washed quickly, dried and cleaned her teeth in record time. True would be anxious, and this was not her first. More than likely, her labor would take half the time it did when she had Sky. Erin dressed and gathered her things, bringing them back to her chamber. Beth would forgive her for leaving everything in a heap on the middle of the bed. She turned to leave just as Hunter reached her door.

"Here." He thrust her satchel at her. "Is this what ye wanted from the cottage?"

"It is. Thanks."

"Take care of my ma." His chin trembled a bit before he firmed it up and stood a little straighter. "I ken you're from the future, so you know more about these things than we do. You'll see that . . . that she—"

"Do you know something I don't?" Erin frowned. "Have you had a vision or some kind of premonition that I should worry about?"

"Nay, but I dinna need a vision to ken birthing is dangerous." He shrugged his narrow shoulders and studied the floor.

Even though boys in the fifteenth century grew up much faster, right now Hunter looked like the eight-year-old child he was—vulnerable and scared that he might lose his mother. Her heart went out to him. "I'll do my very best, Hunter. Would you take me to her chamber? I don't think I can find it on my own."

He nodded once and turned down the corridor. She followed. "How's Robert? Have you seen him this morning?"

"Aye. I brought him broth and toasted bread to break his fast. He was no' pleased with the meal and asked for more." He shot her a grin over his shoulder. "His words come slowly, but they do come clearly."

"Good. Has he gotten out of bed, walked around a little?"

He nodded. "My da and Robley helped him to the garderobe. One foot drags a bit, but he seemed to fare well enough."

"They know True is in labor?"

Hunter stopped at a door and knocked. "They ken where you'll be, my lady. Should they need you, they'll send me." At this his chest puffed out a little.

The door opened, and Lydia peeked out. "Oh good." She took her arm to pull her into the room. "Thank you for bringing her, lad."

"I'll be back anon with food to break her fast." A slight grin tugged at his mouth. "Robley's orders."

"Thanks, buddy." Erin grinned and tousled his hair, eliciting a manly look of disgust. She scanned the room for True and found her in a linen shift, pacing in front of the hearth.

"This is it. Your big day." Erin set her bag on the table in the corner. A pile of baby clothes and blankets were stacked on top, along with squares of clean linens. A basket holding the silky insides of cattails sat nearby. True had told her she used them for diapering material, and for other things. "How are you feeling? How close are your contractions?"

"Not close, but they started shortly after midnight." True's brow furrowed. "They don't seem to be too regular. They get closer, and then a half hour goes by with nothing happening."

"Hmm. That's not so unusual." Erin rolled up her sleeves and washed her hands and arms in the bowl by the hearth that had been set up for her. "Let's take a look." She nodded toward the bed. True crossed the room and took her place, and Erin did a quick pelvic exam. "You're at three centimeters."

"Shall I take some of the tea?" True asked.

"No. Let's try acupressure to stimulate your labor. Cohosh can cause an increase in bleeding, and with twins coming, I don't want to take any additional chances."

"Acupressure?" True's brow creased.

Lydia joined them. "What is that, lass?

"You put pressure on certain sensitive spots on the body, and it encourages cervical dilation and labor."

"Oh my." Lydia's eyes widened. "For certes? This acupressure works?"

"Yes, it does. Let's get True up, and I'll stimulate the pressure points on her lower back first." She and Lydia helped True to her feet, and Erin guided her to a wall. "Place your hands against the stones and brace yourself. It's more forceful than you think it's going to be." She lifted True's shift. "Ready?"

True nodded, and Erin placed her thumbs where the dimples formed above her friend's bottom and placed her fingers slightly below the spots. She applied steady pressure and held it.

"Ah, that feels kind of good," True murmured.

Erin kept the pressure firm. "There are two other places I need to address. Turn around and hold out your hands." True did as she was told, and Erin worked the pressure points between her thumb and index fingers. Next she crouched to the floor to press the spots on her ankles. "Walk now," she said, coming back to her feet and flexing her hands to relieve the muscle ache.

True circled the chamber and pressed her hands against her back. After a few moments, a contraction began. She leaned over and held on to a bedpost.

"Pant," Erin told her while massaging True's back.

"That one was stronger," True said, blowing out a cleansing breath. She pushed off the post and continued her pacing.

Throughout the morning they repeated the process: acupressure, walking and contraction. By noon, Erin's concern had grown. True hadn't progressed nearly as much as she should have. She'd gotten stuck at four centimeters. The twins weren't engaging in a way that promoted dilation. She wished she had modern-day drugs to stimulate hard labor, not to mention equipment and a hospital staff of experts.

"I want another read on the babies." Erin's heart raced, and memories of Alma's stillborn infant filled her mind. She placed her hands on True's belly and focused all of her energy on the tiny twins. Relief flooded through her. Neither was stressed at this point, but they weren't in position to be born, either. Both were determined to be out of the chute first, and both were anterior. At least they weren't breach. She heaved a sigh for that small bit of good news.

"They're facing your belly button, which is why you aren't progressing more rapidly. Being anterior prevents them from dropping into the pelvic floor in a way that causes dilation." Alarm flashed across the faces of the other two women.

"What can we do?" Lydia asked.

"Keep walking. Babies often work themselves around to where they need to be. Even if they don't, they won't be the first to be delivered sunny-side up." She smiled encouragement, but a peach pit of dread lodged in her gut. Too soon to tell if they were headed into troubled waters. She forced the worry back. "Stay the course."

Two hours later, the peach pit turned to full-fledged dread. True had been laboring for more than twelve hours, and she was tiring fast. Worse, the babies were beginning to show signs of distress. "Rest," she ordered, leading her back to bed. "Try to get some rest between contractions." Once True was on her back, Erin did another pelvic. She was discouraged by the results. "You're at five centimeters. I want you to shift to your left side for a bit."

"This is why you're here, Erin." True's gaze met hers. "Giselle knew I was going to be in trouble, and she sent you to us." She shifted to her left side and stared out the window. "No matter what, I want you to save the babies. Even if it means . . . even if I don't . . ."

"Don't think like that." An oppressive weight settled on her shoulders, and tension gripped her so hard it hurt. So far, delivering babies in the fifteenth century had been disastrous. She couldn't face another failure, and this was Malcolm's wife and her good friend. She didn't know what to do.

No, that wasn't entirely true. It wasn't that she didn't know what to do; it was more that she lacked the experience and confidence she needed to feel in control of a bad situation. Courage. She lacked courage.

"Poor Rob," True said, her voice breaking. "He got caught up in the middle of something that never really had anything to do with him." Tears traced down her cheeks. "He's going to . . ."

"Stop, True. Don't say it, much less think it. Everything is going to be fine." She turned to Lydia, mouthing for her to get Malcolm. The older woman slipped out of the room without a sound.

"It's all my fault," True croaked out between sobs. "I don't want Rob to die because of me. I don't want to die. I don't want my sons to die."

Oh shit. She went and said it all anyway. "Stop it." Erin's hands fisted in helpless frustration. "You need some rest, that's all." Her heart split wide open, and the pain nearly unhinged her. She sucked in a breath, and then another. "And anyway, you're wrong. Everything is Giselle's fault, and if she were here right now, I'd let her have it with a good right hook to the chin."

Panic began a slow override, eroding what little confidence she still clung to. Scared out of her wits, Erin rubbed True's back as another contraction took her.

Once the contraction passed, True grabbed her forearm. "Save my babies. Don't let them die."

The door flew open so hard it bounced against the stones. Malcolm strode to his wife's side, lifted her from the bed and settled himself on the mattress with her in his lap. "What is it, my heart? My mother sent for me but would say naught." He cast an accusing glance at his mother, who followed him into the chamber. Worry etched lines around his eyes, and his mouth formed a straight line. "What is she no' telling me?"

"I'm not getting anywhere. I have contraction after contraction, but the twins aren't any closer to being born." True threw her arms around her husband's neck and cried against his chest. "I'm afraid and . . . so exhausted. I don't think I can do this for much longer. I'm afraid I'm going to—"

"Wheesht now, lass." He rocked her in his arms and ran his hand over her hair. "All will be well." He threw Erin a questioning look, his Adam's apple working up and down. "Is there no' something you can do?"

Her heart dropped to the floor. How had she ended up with all this responsibility? She was just a twenty-first-century student! Three pairs of eyes fixed her to the spot, pinning all their hopes squarely on her. She couldn't breathe.

She met Malcolm's eyes first, then True's and finally Lydia's. "Things aren't that desperate." *Yet.* "She just needs to rest. True, you told me about a concoction you've made that puts people to sleep. Do you have any of it here, or do I need to make a trip to the cottage stillroom?" She bit her lip, and sweat beaded her brow and upper lip.

"The herbs are strong, and I don't know how they'll affect the babies," True whispered. "You said you were an OB-GYN surgical nurse, right?"

"I wouldn't worry about how the herbs will affect the twins. We use a lot stronger stuff in the twenty-first century, and right now it's you I'm concerned about. And yes." She nodded, not liking where this was going. "I am a surgical nurse. Not a surgeon." All three of them continued to stare at her, only this time their gazes held desperation.

"But you must've seen hundreds of cesareans performed. You know how to do one."

All the air left the room, and black spots danced in front of her. She inhaled through her nose and exhaled through her mouth. "True . . . I can't . . . I don't have the right tools or a sterile operating room. No blood bank in case something goes wrong—or IV paraphernalia, for that matter, and certainly no anesthetics."

True gripped Malcolm's forearm as another contraction wracked her. "Please, Erin. Take my babies before it's too late."

"Is there a possibility that doing such a thing will save my wife?" Malcolm laid his cheek on the crown of True's head. He closed his eyes and clung to his wife. "Please. Tell me there's a chance . . ."

Erin couldn't answer. Thoughts of infection, accidental blood loss or some other disaster clogged her throat.

"Could it?" Malcolm's voice boomed. "Answer me, Erin. Could what my wife suggests save her? Could you save our bairns?" He stopped, his throat working furiously. "Can you save my family?" His eyes filled with tears.

"It's possible," she muttered.

"What do you need?" Lydia rushed to her side. "I'll aid you however I can."

She stared mutely back at them, gathered her resources and bled inside for how it all might come out in the end. What she needed they had no possibility of getting for her. Scalpels, cauterizing tools, clamps, suction, staples, dissolvable suturing thread, heparin, antibiotics, painkillers . . . the list was endless.

Blowing out her breath, she rubbed her face with both hands, dropping them to meet their expectant stares. "I'll need the sharpest dagger you can find, embroidery silk and a couple of good needles, more boiled water and plenty of clean cloth, lots of light and someone to hold her still."

"Thank you, Erin." True collapsed against her husband, her voice quavering. "Thank you."

"I won't do this if you won't take the sleeping potion. I won't be able to handle it."

"I will take it, but I'll probably pass out before it takes hold."

Lydia gathered the items she'd asked for. Malcolm set his wife back on the bed and moved to a chair. There he began sharpening the edge of a dagger he'd taken from the sheath at his waist.

"Where are the herbs for the sleeping draught?" Erin asked True.

"Once we get them into you, I'm going to bathe the area where I'll make the incision. It's the best I can do to ensure against infection."

True nodded. "The tea for sleeping is in the basket on the mantel. It's in the red bundle. There's also a salve to put on the wound. You'll find it in a small clay pot with a cork. It should be next to the bundles of herbal teas."

"Lydia, did you hear all that?" Erin asked.

"I did, lass. I'll make the tea and get the salve."

A flurry of activity went on around her, and Erin let her mind drift back to the many cesareans she'd assisted. She did know how they were done, though she'd never been the one holding the scalpel. She could do this. She *had* to do this. Her friend's life and the lives of her unborn sons depended upon her.

She forced the trepidation from her mind and scrubbed her arms and hands. Next she washed True's belly, and her patient downed the sleeping draught Lydia had made. Erin insisted Lydia and Malcolm wash up as well. Of course there was no autoclave to sterilize the dagger, thread and needles, so she attached the embroidery thread to the hilt of the dagger and threaded the needles before immersing them in the water boiling over the fire. All the while she prayed fervently for courage and a miraculous absence of infection-causing microbes.

Malcolm gathered all the candles in the room and set them on the trunk he'd moved near the bed and upended so that it stood taller. Erin instructed Lydia what her part would be, and then she gathered the now-sterile implements. All was ready. Was she? Not by a long shot. "Hold her, Malcolm. I'm going to lose it if she moves or screams."

"Don't worry about me, Erin." True's eyes saucered when she caught sight of the blade coming toward her.

"I've got her," he said gruffly. He placed his hands on his wife's shoulders, and Lydia held True's ankles.

Erin's hands shook, and she took a long, steadying breath while flexing them. *I can do this. I can do this. I can do this.* The second she touched blade to skin, True groaned, then went silent. Her heart in her throat and her stomach in rebellion, Erin made the first incision. Once she was through the layers of skin, she cut into the muscle. Finally she reached the uterus. Slippery. Everything was slippery and wet. "Wipe please, Lydia."

Her assistant mopped up the area, and Erin placed her hands on True, pouring all the painkilling vibes she could muster into her friend. "How's she doing, Malcolm?"

"She swooned with the first touch of the blade, as I kent she would." He grunted. "She's breathing. Her sleeping draught is strong. 'Tis best she remain . . . unaware."

Relief nearly felled her. Lydia moved away, and Erin went in for the next incision. Immediately a head crowned through the surgical opening. She guided the infant out into the world and cleared his mouth and nose, and he began to cry. Lydia took the squalling newborn and laid him across True's chest. Baby boy number two appeared just as quickly, and the process was repeated. Both of the boys were in great shape considering the circumstances, and soon their skin turned rosy.

"Thank God," Malcolm cried. "They're both hale, and my wife . . ." He stifled a sob. "She lives, and I have you to thank, lass."

"I still have a lot to do," she said. Her patient wasn't out of the woods yet. Infection was Erin's biggest worry. The actual surgery had been fairly simple, but opening her up was only part of the risk. "You two are going to have to cut the umbilical cords and clean them up. I need to close her incisions and wash her before I put some of her salve on the wound."

"I'll take care of my grandsons," Lydia said. "You keep holding your wife, lad, lest she awake and thrash about."

While Erin's focus went back to True, Lydia worked quickly and soundlessly, cutting the cords and tying them off, bathing one boy and then the next. She swaddled them and tucked the two next to their mother.

"Put those babies to her breasts. Nursing will help True." Erin never took her eyes from her work. She delivered the placentas, making sure both were intact, and began suturing the edges of True's womb back together. Next came the layer of muscle, and finally she closed the wound across her lower abdomen and washed her patient with the cloth, soap and ewer of fresh water Lydia had brought over to her.

A little dazed, sweating and fatigued, Erin leaned back. "She didn't bleed much, which means I did it right. Thank God for that." On shaky legs, she headed for the pail of water and washed her arms and hands again. "Everything went better than I thought it would." Drying herself with another square of linen, she returned to her patient's side and checked her pulse. "Heartbeat's strong. Respiration is good."

Malcolm's shoulders shook, and he struggled to hold it in, but sobs erupted from him, and his profound relief filled the room like a living thing. He held one of his sons tenderly to his wife's breast, and the little bugger sucked greedily. Lydia held the other. Like his brother, he too had latched on with gusto.

"As long as we can keep her wounds clean and free of infection, she should be fine." She took True's jar of salve from the upended trunk and sniffed it. Honey? Applying a liberal amount to the freshly stitched incision, she continued to babble. "No more babies for at least two years though, you hear me?" All the control she'd exerted over herself during the surgery leached out of her, and she careened toward the edge of hysteria.

A strangled laugh erupted from Malcolm. "I hear you, lass. You have my word. No bairns for the next two years—mayhap five."

"Normally we use thread that dissolves over time when we close internal incisions, and we staple the skin together," she muttered. Her head throbbed, and her mouth was plaster-dust dry. Everything was catching up to her, the stress, the fear, the crushing weight of accountability on top of the regret she suffered over the loss of Alma's baby. "That embroidery thread is in her for good. I sure hope she likes the color."

She couldn't stop herself, as if talking would somehow keep her grounded. It didn't. "Well, we should clean up here and . . . and get something to eat. I'm hungry. Aren't you hungry, Lydia? I haven't had a thing since this morning's oatmeal, and it's got to be around five now." She pinched the bridge of her nose. "Man, I'd love a Diet Coke with lots of ice and a large combo pizza with thin crust. I really do miss pizza." Was she hyperventilating? "I miss coffee, chocolate, ice cream and . . . and . . ."

"Bacon cheeseburgers and extra-crispy fries," True murmured.

Erin gasped. "Is she awake? Oh God. Tell me she's not awake. I don't have any morphine, oxycodone or . . . or . . . even extra-strength Tylenol to give her."

"Humph." Malcolm brushed his wife's forehead with his knuckles. "Nay, she's no' awake. She does that sometimes. True has a way of taking herself far from us, yet she remains aware of what is being said and oft responds." He shrugged a big shoulder. "She sleeps still."

"Oh. Good." Erin frowned, leaned over and placed her hands on her knees, trying to suck more air into her depleted lungs. "That worries me a little, you know? The thread being in there forever, I mean. But I think our bodies are pretty miraculous, and new tissue will just . . . just . . . grow around it." She glanced at Lydia. "Don't you think?"

"Mayhap it will." Lydia shot her a concerned look, her hands full of drowsy, burping baby. "Sit down before you fall down, lass. You've gone as pale as the linens on yon bed."

"God, what did I just do?" she mumbled and made the mistake of straightening. "I . . . I don't have any business doing any kind of surgery on anyone." Her limbs went wobbly. The room spun, and spots danced before her eyes again. She sucked in a gulp of air. "What the hell was I thinking? A C-section by candlelight in the fifteenth century! That's . . . that's insane."

"Mother . . ."

"Aye. Go, lad. I'll stay and look after things here."

Malcolm and Lydia's voices sounded as if they came through a storm drain from a great distance away. Erin lifted her hands and stared at them, vaguely aware that Malcolm had left the room. *Where is he off to in such a big hurry?*

"Jeez. Look at the way my hands are shaking. Maybe I *should* sit down." She crumpled to the floor in a sloppy heap, and then everything went black.

CHAPTER FIFTEEN

Robley sat across from his uncle as they went through the ledgers and planned for the hard winter months ahead. Erin was never far from his thoughts, and once they finished tallying the bushels of wheat, oats, barley and rye, he broached the subject most pressing to his heart. "Uncle William, Erin and I would like to handfast before the clan ere long." Before his thirty days were spent, to be more specific. "What say you to that?"

"Hmm." His uncle leaned back in his chair and steepled his fingers. "She's a fine lass, Rob, and a welcome addition to our family. I've no objections, but do you rush into this because of what may befall you? Or are you rushing because of the way the gossips are perpetuating the rumor that she's bad luck to the breeding women of our clan? Mayhap 'twould be best to resolve both matters first, aye? Post the banns, and we'll have the wedding come spring."

"Nay. If I die, I want Erin's status assured within our clan." He stared blankly at the figures in the ledger. "We've already pledged our troth to one another . . . and she may already carry my bairn."

"Och. I see." His uncle's brow rose, and he sat forward. "If that be the case, we'll see it done within the se'nnight. We've a feast to plan in honor of the birth of my grandsons. We'll have the handfasting then, since the clan will already be gathered."

"Good."

The door to his uncle's solar burst open, and Malcolm strode through. "You're needed, Rob." His glance went between Rob and the earl. "We've two fine, strong lads, but the birthing was difficult." Malcolm's eyes were bloodshot and his features tight. "Erin . . . She saved True's life and the lives of our sons. She had to open my wife's belly with a dagger to take the bairns from True's womb. My wife and sons live only because you brought Erin to us, Rob." He fixed his stare on Robley. "You ken what that means?"

"It means I was right all along." Rob rose from his place. "She was meant to be here." He resisted turning his mind to the implications, yet they pressed in upon him nonetheless. Erin's role in Giselle's scheme had been fulfilled. Now what? Cold premonition snaked its way down his spine. With Erin's purpose fulfilled, Giselle had no reason to intervene on his behalf. "I'm needed, you say?"

"Aye. The day has been long, and it's taken a toll on your lass. She's in need of your strength and comfort right now."

"Where is she?"

"In my chamber."

"I'll announce the births and that we have Erin to thank for the fact that Robert, True and your bairns live. Mayhap 'twill put to rest the rumors she's somehow responsible for Roderick and Alma's sorrow." William pushed back his chair. "You two see to your women, and to your mother, if you please, Malcolm. What with Robert's ailment, and True's difficulties, she must be beside herself. She's insisted upon being in the thick of it for two evenings past with little sleep, and I canna go to her just yet."

"I will, Father." Malcolm reached for the door. "Our wee midwife looked to be on the verge of collapse as I left. Mother is more than likely looking after her as well by now. I'll see that she goes to her rest."

Rob followed his cousin out of the solar. "Sky will want to see her new brothers, aye? Have you sent word to her nursemaid?"

"I dinna want my daughter to see True just yet, no' until she wakes. No sense in frightening my lass. Hunter has already been to our chamber, and his fear upon seeing True so pale and still gave me cause enough to wait."

They'd reached the chamber, and Malcolm knocked, waiting for permission before entering. Rob followed close upon his heels, his heart wrenching at the sight of Erin stretched out on the rug with Lydia pressing a cloth to her forehead.

"I fainted, but I'm fine now. I did a cesarean." Erin's eyes rose to his. "I guess it freaked me out a little," she muttered.

"You were very braw to do what you did," Lydia said, smiling. "We are all grateful to you for the lives you saved this day." Lydia glanced at him. "Best help her to her chamber."

"And you must go to yours, Mother." Malcolm held his hand out to help her stand. "Father's orders. Food will be sent to you there. Eat and rest."

"I will." She took his proffered help. "Once I've checked in on Rosemary and Robert."

"Oh." Erin pushed herself up to sitting. "I should check in on him too, and True should have liquids as soon as possible. Broth and something light to eat. She's nursing and needs the fluids. When she wakes, we need to get her up on her feet for a little while, and—"

"Enough, *mo céile*." Rob helped her to her feet and scooped her up in his arms. "You've done enough for one day. Off to a meal and bed with you."

"She's your wife now?" Malcolm frowned. "What did we miss, Rob?"

"She is." Rob jutted out his chin. "We've made our vows to each other, and we'll hand-fast during the feast to celebrate the birth of your heirs." He carried her to the door. "I've already discussed this with the earl." He turned back. "We'll be needing a larger chamber, Aunt."

"Humph." Malcolm scowled.

"I'll send a chambermaid to make ready the east turret chamber on the morrow," Lydia said, patting him on the shoulder. "Until the handfasting, 'twould be best if she kept to her chamber and you to yours." Her face lit up. "These are glad tidings indeed, Rob. Welcome to the family, Erin."

"Thank you." Erin smiled back. She yawned and wrapped her arms around his neck, settling her head on his shoulder.

A rush of love and warmth filled him to bursting. "I'll no' leave her alone. Best get our chamber ready yet this eve." He sent Malcolm a look he hoped his cousin and best friend would understand. But a handful of days remained to them before the faerie's return. He had no intention of wasting a single second. "We'll go to her chamber for now and await word that it's ready."

"Mother, they—"

"Och, aye." Lydia's eyes filled with consternation. "I had forgotten the . . . circumstances."

"So be it." Malcolm nodded. "I'll see that it's done with all haste."

"Erin already feels like part of the family, and the rest simply fled my mind." Lydia sighed. "I am tired and hungry." She headed for the door. "We'll talk more on the morrow. Dinna fash about Robert, Erin. He's in good hands."

"Thank you for your help, Lydia. You were the best assisting nurse ever." Erin turned her gaze to him. "I can walk."

"And I can carry." He brushed his lips over her forehead. "My will in this matter is greater than yours, for I take great pleasure in the feel of you in my arms."

Malcolm grunted behind them. "'Tis a good thing you'll be handfasted ere long."

He shot his cousin a grin. "Congratulations on the birth of your lads. I look forward to hearing what you and True name them." He hoisted Erin higher in his arms and strode with her toward the door. "See you in the lists on the morrow?"

"Of course." Malcolm cleared his throat. "I wish you both much happiness, and if there's aught I can do—"

"My thanks." Rob didn't want to hear the rest. He didn't want the reminder of his troubles while he held his future securely in his arms.

Erin snuggled closer. "Giselle owes us a favor now."

"How do you reckon thus?" His brow furrowed.

"I saved three lives today. True said she's sure that's why I ended up here in your time. Giselle wanted me to help her with the birth of her twins. Plus, I have fae blood, and I'm gifted. I figure since I was ripped from my life to perform this feat for Giselle, she has to be grateful. She obviously has some attachment to True and her family. Maybe I've become part of that group by virtue of my faerie ancestry."

'Twould be nice, but he didn't see it that way. More than likely he and Erin were but chess pieces to be sacrificed on the board of Giselle's grand game. "Humph."

"Sir Grunts-a-Lot." Erin nuzzled his neck. "Thank you for carrying me to my little room."

"*Our* wee chamber, but no' for much longer." He set her down before the open door, just as Tieren came out.

"I've brought supper for the both of ye. My lord, my lady, good eve to you both." The lad bobbed his head and took off down the corridor toward the back stairs, not even waiting for their thanks.

"Let us eat, and then you'll rest. Once our chamber is ready, I'll move you there as you sleep."

"Sounds like a plan. I'm famished." She crossed the chamber to the tray that had been set upon the trunk. "We have cold pork, cheese, dark bread and butter." She glanced at him over her shoulder.

"And another one of those wonderful berry tarts." She broke a piece off and popped it into her mouth. "I had no idea you all ate so well in this century. Yum."

Robley saw to it that his wife ate her fill and took enough tea to satisfy her thirst before he tucked her into bed. Within seconds her breathing took on the deep, rhythmic cadence of well-deserved slumber. He sat in the single chair by the hearth, propped his feet up on the stones and rested his chin upon his fist. Turning over in his mind what Erin had said earlier, he considered the possibilities. Would Giselle be grateful? Would it be enough to secure her favor and mayhap her help with the faerie who meant to kill him if he didn't return the pensieve? With all his heart he prayed Erin was right. Indeed, he'd cling to the notion, for he had no alternative.

Robley surveyed the great hall. Five days had passed since Malcolm's heirs had been born, and their clan had gathered this eve to celebrate the births of Bizhiw and Migizi—Lynx, the eldest, and Eagle, the younger of the two—as True called them. Of course they had Scottish names as befitted their rank, but to the clan and family, their sobriquets had taken well enough. His clan had also gathered for his handfasting, including his father, who had walked down to the great hall with the aid of a walking stick and his wife's support at his side. He glanced at his parents, who smiled back at him with bright eyes. True had also come for the feast, already looking much stronger and well on the way toward healing.

Excitement and anticipation chased through him in equal measure, weakening his knees. "I can scarce believe it. This is my wedding day," Rob said, grinning at his cousin, who stood beside him.

"Aye." Malcolm clasped Rob's shoulder. "And here comes your lovely bride."

Robley's gaze shot to the stairs, and he promptly lost his breath. Erin wore a lovely green velvet gown. A wreath of dried flowers adorned her hair, which fell loose around her shoulders in a golden veil. *Mine.* His heart leaped inside his chest, and he couldn't take his eyes from her. Everything and everyone else faded, disappeared from his awareness until only he and she existed. He memorized everything about her, from how the gown caressed her figure, to the brightness of her emerald-green eyes.

His uncle William led her to his side. "With your right hand, clasp your man's right wrist, lass."

Erin's face shone with love and joy. She clasped his wrist, and he held hers. His uncle bound them together with a strip of MacKintosh plaid, stepping back once the task had been completed. The earl turned to their assembled clan. "Before God and your clan, what say you, Robley, son of Robert of clan MacKintosh?"

Robley lost himself in his love's beauty. His heart full to over-flowing, he said his vows, his voice sure and loud enough for all to hear.

"I, Robley Alexander, son of Robert Douglas of clan MacK-intosh, and fourth in line as earl of Fife, pledge my troth to thee, Erin Margaret of clan Durie. With my hands, I shall provide for thee. With my body, I pledge to protect thee. With my heart, I shall cherish thee, and only thee, all the days of my life. As God is my witness and before my clan, from this day forward, we are husband and wife."

William turned to Erin. "Before God and our clan, what say you, Erin of clan Durie?"

"I, Erin Margaret of clan Durie, daughter of Aaron Durie and Jane Anderson, pledge my troth to thee, Robley Alexander of clan MacKintosh. With my hands, I shall provide for thee. With my body, I shall succor thee. With my heart, I shall cherish thee, and only thee, all the days of my life. As God is my witness, and before this clan, from this day forward, we are husband and wife."

Erin blinked, and her voice quavered as she spoke the words, but the love flowing from her nearly stopped his heart, and her sincerity rang through every word. Could he be any happier than he was at this very moment? It didn't seem possible. She loved him. His good nature and natural optimism had been restored, and with all his heart he believed they would live a long and happy life together.

"Before God and your clan, you have made your vows. 'Tis with great gladness that we welcome you into our keeping, Erin." William raised a goblet. "A toast to the new couple. May you find joy and strength in this union." A cheer erupted, and goblets were lifted in their honor. Once the first round of good wishes settled, William lifted his cup again. "And another toast in celebration of the birth of my grandsons and Malcolm's heirs, David James, whom we call Migizi to honor his mother's people, and Owain William, whom we call Bizhiw." Another hearty cheer filled the hall. "Let us bow our heads and give thanks, for we have been blessed many times over." The earl's voice reverberated through the great hall.

His uncle led them in prayer, and the moment the last amen had been said, pages and servants brought forth the roasted beef, stuffed swan and platters laden with vegetables, fruit and sweets. Rob took the plaid binding their wrists and tucked it in his sporran for safekeeping. Taking Erin's hand, he led her to her place upon the dais. "Are you hungry, babe?"

She shot him an incredulous look. "Now that I'm your wife, we're back to *babe*?"

He laughed. "Aye, as a reminder of how far we've come. For if you'll recall, you did no' wish to *get involved*." He lifted their clasped hands and kissed her knuckles. "And here you are, my wife." He placed her palm over his chest. "You are my heart, *mo anam,* which means my breath. You are the very air I breathe, Erin of clan MacKintosh."

She swallowed, and a shadow of doubt flashed in her eyes. "What if I can't make it last?" she asked in a shaky voice. "I haven't exactly had the best role models."

"When you feel yourself falter, look to me, lass. With God's help, I'll carry you through whatever trials we might face."

"Our thirty days are up in a little over a week," she whispered. "How do you plan to carry us through that?"

"I've given it a great deal of thought, and I agree with you." He pulled her chair out and settled her at the table. "Giselle owes us a debt of gratitude. I dinna believe she meant for us to end before we've barely had the chance to begin. If she saw True's future need of your skills, it stands to reason she's also aware of what will befall us if she does no' intervene." Whether or not she cared was another matter altogether, but this was their wedding night. No sense in dampening both their spirits with things out of their control.

He took his place and heaped their trencher full with generous portions of meat and vegetables. "If you're correct, I expect we'll hear of her whereabouts very soon." Skewering a succulent piece of beef, he fed his beloved. "Faith, *mo céile*. We must have a little faith that all will be well." He took a bite for himself. "In the meantime, let us no' tarry too long at table. We've important matters to attend to above stairs."

Her expression turned to puzzlement. "We do?"

"Och, aye." He winked at her. "We must christen our marriage bed."

Her lashes lowered, and a smile graced her luscious mouth. "I'm pretty sure we've already done that. Several times in fact."

"Tonight is different, for we've handfasted before our kin. For certes this warrants another christening." He raised an eyebrow, and his gaze roamed her beautiful face. "Does it no'?"

Her laughter washed over him, and a flood of tenderness and love turned his insides to melted wax. "I love you, wife."

"I love you, husband." She reached for his hand. "How soon can we slip away?"

Robley caught Hunter's eye and gestured for his attendance. "Hunter, can you fill a tray and bring it to our chamber along with a flagon of wine?"

"Aye," Hunter answered, grinning from ear to ear.

"Let us go to our chamber, my dear." He rose and offered her his hand. She took it, and he led her off the dais to the stairs amid the calls and jeers of the revelers who had noticed. Rob turned and bowed, eliciting bawdy shouts. Erin's eyes widened, and color flooded her cheeks.

"Pay them no heed, love. 'Tis always thus on a couple's wedding night."

"Great," she muttered, lifting her hem and taking the first step.

The ferry master's daughter, her husband in tow, hurried toward them. Rob's protective instincts kicked in, and he positioned himself between his wife and the couple.

"Beggin' yer pardon, milord, milady," Alma said, gripping her husband's arm. "We wish tae speak with ye. It will take but a moment." She sent her husband a forceful look. "Roderick has somethin' tae say."

Rob's jaw tightened. "Aye?"

Roderick cleared his throat and shuffled his feet. "I owe ye an apology, Lady Erin. I ken my son's . . ." His hands fisted at his sides. "'Twas no' yer fault. Me and Alma . . . this is no' the first bairn we've lost, and the others happened long afore ye arrived." His eyes pleading, he glanced at Erin. "We dinna ken why, but . . ."

"How many miscarriages have you had, Alma?" Erin stepped around him and took Alma's hands in hers.

"Thrice, including this last. But this one, I was so sure . . . He was almost tae term, and the others were lost early on."

"Hmm." Erin frowned. "I'm so sorry."

"Is there aught you can do tae help us?" Alma asked.

"I don't know." Erin bit her lip. "Let me think about it. Perhaps between Lady True and myself, we can think of something."

A look of gratitude and hope passed between the couple. "I'm sorry for blaming ye. Can ye forgive me, milady?" Roderick asked.

"Of course. I understand your grief and frustration. Please, enjoy the feast, and we'll talk again soon."

"Thank ye." He bowed his head. "We both wish ye much happiness."

The couple rejoined the festivities, and Erin's expression turned pensive.

"What are you thinking, love?" He took her hand again and guided her up the steps toward their chamber. Two wedding nights! He was a lucky man indeed.

"Early on in my midwife program, I met a couple who had a similar history to Alma and Roderick's. An autopsy was done on the baby they lost at twenty-seven weeks. Turns out the husband and wife were passing a *Streptococcus* bacteria back and forth that was infecting the fetuses. We treated them both with antibiotics, and last I heard, they had a healthy daughter." She shrugged. "I don't have any antibiotics. I don't know how to help them."

"Humph."

She grinned at him. "You don't understand half of what I just said. Right?"

"Aye, but it matters no'. I ken the gist of it." He opened their door and ushered her through. A fire burned in their hearth, and the bedcovers had been turned down. "Come here to me, sweet wife. Your husband desires some of the succoring you vowed to provide."

Her smile bright enough to light the day, Erin walked into his arms. "Hunter will be here in a few minutes with our supper. The succoring will have to wait."

"Och, aye? A kiss then to tide me over." Cradling her face between his palms, he kissed her deeply. Already he kent how to please her, how she liked to be touched and where. Anticipation sent a rush of heat to his groin. The kind of heat that felt less frantic and much deeper. The bond between them grew stronger every day, as did his contentment. "My forever love," he whispered into her ear before nuzzling her throat, eliciting a shiver from her. "Shall we eat first, or should we make love before we feast?"

A knock on the door interrupted him, but he kept his wife in his arms. "Enter."

Hunter walked through the door with a heavy tray balanced upon his right hand. His eyes widened when he beheld the two of them embracing. "Your supper," he stammered.

"Our thanks, lad." Robley nodded toward the table set before the hearth. "Put it there, if you please." He gazed into his wife's eyes. "Hungry?"

"Not really."

"Then it's a feast of the flesh first, and then—"

"Hush." Her eyes alight, she glanced toward Hunter.

"Begone, lad. I wish to make love to my wife."

Hunter made a sound of disgust and hurried out of the room, slamming the door behind him.

"You are incorrigible." Erin laughed.

"Nay." He worked at undoing the laces of her gown. "I'm blissfully, ecstatically in love with you, and once I get you naked, I intend to show you just how much I hunger. But no' for food." Drawing her close, he kissed her, welcoming the need igniting his blood and filling him with the familiar ache in his groin. She was his, and they had all night to satisfy their carnal desires.

He did just that. Twice. He'd never before known such joy and contentment as he found in his love's arms, and he meant to keep her close until they both grew old and wizened with their grandchildren romping about them. *I will not let the faerie take me.* His warrior's mind went to ways he could defeat his foe, for he would defeat him. He had to.

CHAPTER SIXTEEN

Erin perched on the edge of True's bed with a drowsy Migizi snuggled warmly against her shoulder. True nursed Bizhiw, while Sky played contentedly with wooden blocks set on a thick Belgian rug. Erin glanced around at True and Malcolm's chamber. The couple's personalities showed clearly in the decor. True had woven baskets out of rushes and some out of strips of wood, and they held a lot of her things. A large one was filled with Sky's toys. A few of Malcolm's weapons hung out of the children's reach on one wall, along with True's bow and a quiver full of arrows.

A lovely harp took up another corner, and everywhere there were piles of baby things and the books True had made for Hunter and Sky. Malcolm had carved the wooden blocks and other toys for his children. The two of them were outstanding parents.

The room Erin and Robley shared was just beginning to reflect their personalities. He'd been teaching her how to play chess, and their board and pieces were set up on their table. Smiling at the memory, she thought about how Rob's clothing generally fell to the floor at the end of the day, despite the numerous pegs where he could hang them. He often draped his scabbard over the corner of a chair back. A spare pair of his boots stood next to their hearth, and his hand drums leaned against the wall on one side. *Bodhran*, he called them. She was thankful they were his instrument of choice and not the bagpipes. Smiling at the thought, she savored the intimacy their lives had taken on. She'd never thought it possible.

Since the birth of True's twins and Erin's handfasting with Rob, the MacKintosh women had begun to trickle back to Erin for help. She kept a number of items on hand in their room in case she had to assist in a birth during the night. Soon the blacksmith's son's wife would be due, and Erin prayed for a safe, ordinary delivery. No surgeries or tragedies, thank you very much. She was due for a simple, straightforward midwifery experience.

That thought had her reviewing the eventful weeks she'd already spent in the fifteenth century. November had quietly slipped into December, and Robley's thirty days had passed without incident. Nothing had happened. He tried to convince her that the faerie crisis was behind them. The warrior who had sworn to come after him was a no-show, and Rob believed Giselle had intervened on their behalf. She wasn't so sure.

"You need to have new gowns made," True said, interrupting her thoughts. "And we'll have a wardrobe built for your chamber."

"I suppose. I have a few bolts of wool from the pile of wedding gifts we received, but I have no idea how to sew any kind of clothing. If I had my way, I'd hang out in my jeans all day."

"I hear you. I still wear my jeans when I hunt, which hasn't happened for quite some time. You did well enough sewing me back together," True said, rubbing the spot of her incision. "Believe me, sewing a gown is far easier. I have patterns we can use, and between me, Lydia and Rosemary, we'll teach you."

"Thanks. Speaking of making things, I really want to learn how to make the salve you used to prevent your wound from becoming infected. That interests me a lot more than making dresses."

"It's a combination of lanolin, honey, royal bee jelly and a variety of roots and herbs known to have antiseptic and antibiotic properties." True moved the now satisfied Bizhiw to her shoulder to burp him. "Did you know that bacteria won't grow in honey?"

"No, I didn't." She turned to face her. "That reminds me, do you have anything in your arsenal of herbal remedies that might eradicate a strep infection?"

"Hmm. I can make antibacterial teas, but nothing like the antibiotics from our century. I suppose if a person kept drinking the concoction over a long period of time, it might work. Why?"

Erin explained what she suspected was the cause of Alma's stillborn son. "If strep is the cause, and we can find some way to treat them both, they could go on to have healthy children."

"Once the nursemaids come to take the children to their nursery for the afternoon, let's walk to the clinic. I need to stretch my legs, and we can put something together for them. If we give them a month's worth, maybe it'll do the trick." True shot her a pointed look. "Only we aren't going to talk to them about bacteria or strep. We'll just say it's a potion that we hope will help them."

"Sure." Erin grinned. "Keep it fifteenth century. Do you have any idea what a relief it is to have someone to talk to without guarding what I say?"

True laughed. "Ditto." She rose from the chair and put a sleeping Bizhiw in his cradle, gesturing that Erin should do the same with Migizi.

She missed the little bundle of warmth once she set the tiny boy next to his brother.

True kept her voice low and pointed to Sky, who had fallen asleep in the middle of her toys. "We've received word that my sister-in-law

Elaine and her husband are on their way here. They'll remain until after the New Year. Liam and his wife will also join us for Christmas. They don't normally, but because of the birth of Malcolm's heirs, they're coming to meet their nephews. They're only about a day away." She smiled happily. "We'll have a full house for the holidays."

Erin picked up the little girl from the floor and set her on the bed. Thoughts of her own family flooded her mind, and a lump formed in her throat. More than ever it seemed she'd never see them again. Her parents would never meet their grandchildren. Would they even care? A hollow ache spread through her chest. She'd never been that close to her mom, and she couldn't imagine what kind of grandmother she'd be anyway.

What if she were pregnant right now? From the very first time she'd fallen into bed with Robley, she'd been heedless that they'd done nothing to prevent pregnancy. It wasn't like her to be so careless, but then she'd never fallen in love before either. She tried to remember when her last period had been.

"It looks like we're going to have snow soon," True said, interrupting Erin's calendar count.

Erin walked toward the window to peer out at the gray day. "Does it get as cold here as it does in Minnesota?"

"No, but it does get cold enough to snow, and the snow stays." A light rapping on the door drew her friend's attention. An older woman entered, followed by a much younger servant.

"We've come for the bairns, milady." The grandmotherly woman grinned broadly at the sight of the sleeping children. "Och, look at them. Wee angels, they are, all three."

"Thank you, Ellen. I hope you still think so when the twins are running in opposite directions and getting into all kinds of mischief." True helped the two women gather up the sleeping children. "I'm going to my stillroom if you should need me."

"They're fed and content, milady. We shan't need ye for a while yet," Ellen said, her tone confident. "I'll send a lad for ye when the bairns wake."

"I should be back before then." True fetched her cloak from its peg. "Come, Erin. We'll stop at your chamber on the way."

Erin led the way to her chamber. Opening the door, she gestured to True to precede her.

"Are you satisfied with your new room?" True sent her a sly look. "And your new husband?"

"I'm very happy with both." Again the nagging worry reared its serpent-like head. Their problems weren't really behind them. "I just hope—" Just then, two tones from some kind of horn echoed from the mainland. She frowned. "What's that?"

"One tone means someone of importance has arrived, two means clan members have returned, and three means danger. When there is danger, the villagers come to the island." True hurried toward the door. "I don't know who it could be. It's too soon for Mairen and Liam to arrive, and I don't believe we'll see Elaine for another week or so."

Erin threw her cloak around her shoulders and followed. It could also be any of the men who had been out looking for Giselle. Rob's search party must have realized the thirty days had passed. They didn't have a reason to continue searching any longer. With winter approaching, of course they'd return to the safety and warmth of Moigh Hall.

"Are we still going to the clinic?" They left the great hall and crossed the bailey. Erin's words created puffs of steam in the damp, cold air. She wrapped her hands in the thick fabric of her cloak.

"Let's head to the ferry landing first." True glanced at her. "Don't you want to see who's here?"

She blew out a steamy breath. "I have a feeling it might be one of the pairs of men Rob sent out in search of Giselle. The thirty days have come and gone."

"The fae don't measure time like we do."

"So you don't think the danger has passed?" Her eyes widened. "I don't think so either, but Robley is convinced that it's all been somehow resolved without his involvement."

"Wouldn't that be nice?" True snorted.

"Yeah, it would," she muttered under her breath. They'd arrived at the ferry landing, along with Malcolm, William and Rob. She scanned the ferry as it made its way toward shore. Two men stood on the deck.

Robley came to her side. "It's Galen and Gareth. I expect the others will return soon as well."

She nodded mutely. Perhaps he was right, and they'd have nothing to tell. Perhaps thirty days to a faerie lasted an entire lifetime for humans, even though the faerie had made a point to mention that he meant thirty human days. She kept her eyes focused on the two men on the ferry. Their expressions gave nothing away.

The ferry landed, and the two men disembarked, heading straight for Robley. A flurry of welcomes ensued, and the attention of the crowd centered around the two returning MacKintosh clansmen. She and True had been relegated to the outer circle, but at least they were close enough to hear what was being said.

"She's returned to Inverness, Robley," Galen huffed out. "We returned there to rest and restock our supplies before the trip home. Giselle is back in residence in her cottage."

"Did you speak to her?" Rob asked.

Gareth shook his head. "Nay, my lord. We did no' wish to alert her to the fact that you sought her whereabouts."

"Good. My thanks." Robley clasped each one by the forearm for a moment. "Welcome home."

"Get something to eat and then rejoin the garrison roster," Malcolm commanded the two clansmen. "'Tis good to have you both back safe and sound."

"The others were just arriving at Inverness as we took our leave." Galen started for the keep. "They'll soon follow."

"What do you mean to do?" William asked, turning to Rob once Galen and Gareth left.

"Naught. I've seen no sign of the faerie sworn to return for me." Her husband shrugged nonchalantly, but he couldn't hide the underlying tension pulsing from him—at least not from her. "The only reason he has no' come for me that I can think of is that the matter has been resolved amongst their own kind. He's no longer interested in my role in their affairs."

A look passed between Malcolm and his father. Malcolm turned to Rob. "Mayhap, but 'twould be prudent to make certain before—"

"I plan to," Rob snapped. "In the spring when traveling is more convenient."

Brows raised, and another look passed between the group. This time True was included, but no one looked Erin's way. Unease arced her nerves—and Rob's.

"We can discuss this more at length after supper." True hooked her arm through Erin's. "Come on. Let's continue to the stillroom so we can fill the prescription for Alma and Roderick."

"Prescription?" Malcolm frowned.

"I'll explain later." True glanced at her husband and turned Erin toward the cottage.

"Will you play your wee harp for us this eve, good daughter?" William called after her. "It soothes my brother to hear your music."

"Of course I will." True stopped. "I'm so relieved Robert is recovering so well. I know we all are. Shall I play in the great hall for everyone, or just for family?"

William glanced at Rob before answering. "In the solar, if you please. This eve is just for family. Soon our keep will be filled to overflowing, and we'll no' have the chance to speak intimately again until after the New Year."

True nodded, and they continued on their way toward the cottage. "Are you OK with waiting until spring to talk with Giselle?"

"No, but I wasn't going to bring it up in front of everyone." Once again the unease skittered through her. "I'm afraid the faerie will appear sometime between now and then, and we won't have any defense against him."

"My thoughts exactly." True opened the door to their shared space.

The green, earthy scent of all the plants hanging in the rafters wafted over her as she entered the cozy cottage, settling the unease just a little.

"I'll start a fire. It's chilly in here." True walked to the hearth and took the flint and steel from the mantel. "Open the herbology book to antibiotics and antiseptics. If memory serves, we'll need blue and yellow ginseng for the most part, referred to by my people as 'papoose root.' I have the herbs drying in alphabetical order, for lack of a better system. The pictures will help identify them."

"Couldn't we have someone build shelves to cover one wall?" Erin opened the book to the index and ran her finger down the print in search of the antibiotic plants they needed. "We could commission a bunch of earthenware jars with lids and label them."

"Great idea." True struck flint and steel together, blowing on the spark that landed in the wood shavings and dried grass. "I'll talk to Malcolm about it. I'm sure he'll put the castle carpenters to work on them right away. You and I can talk to a few of the women who make pottery. It'll be a great winter project."

"If I'm still here . . ."

"Right." True's expression darkened. "I hope you are. I know it's selfish, but . . . I can't help hoping you'll stay here with us."

Her throat tightened. True was the first truly close friend she'd had for a very long time, and she didn't want to lose her either, but what could she say? She had absolutely no control, especially if she and Rob put off confronting Giselle until the spring. "What do you

know about the fae? Are they . . . killable?" Her heart thumped painfully at the thought of Rob doing battle against the faerie warrior,
but she knew he would attempt it if he had to.

"I only have the stories I've been told since I came here, but as
I understand it, they can only die by their own weapons. They're
pretty much immune to ours."

"Of course. Makes sense." They had to talk to Giselle now. The
sooner the better, and definitely before the faerie showed up for her
husband. Blinking back the sudden sting in her eyes, she focused
on the rafters, matching the pictures to the plants. "It's the roots we
need from the ginseng. Right?"

"Yes, that's right."

"I have it."

Next she searched the book for antiseptics. "Barberry and mountain cranberry. Hmm, do cranberries grow here? They'd be great to
have on hand for bladder infections."

"Not that I've been able to find. Mountain cranberry is an evergreen bush that grows in sandy soil."

"Do you have any of the berries?"

"I do. They're in a basket along the wall near the rosehips."

"You're really something, True." Appreciation for her friend
swelled in her chest. "Amazing."

"Not really. I'm just doing what my grandfather, grandmother
and my relatives have always done, only on a larger scale. I spent
many a summer and fall out in the bush, gathering medicinal plants
with my family, so it comes naturally."

"Did you gather all of this on your own?"

"No. I have lots of help here with the gathering part. Our clan is
not without knowledge of the healing properties of the plants around
here. They've taught me a lot. According to them, the thistle plant
will cure just about anything."

"Will it?"

"I have no idea. It's not in Gran's book, but the locals say it's used for tumors, all kinds of joint complaints and illnesses."

"I hope I get the chance to gather with you." She kept her eyes on what they needed. "We make a good team."

"We do." True came up next to her and nudged her shoulder. "Have I thanked you today for saving me and my sons?"

Erin shot her a wry grin. "You don't have to keep thanking me. I'm glad it all worked out, and I'm even kind of glad I had the experience." She toyed with the plants in front of her. "I'm not going to be nearly as apprehensive about cesareans now, and you know yours won't be the last. I've already begun stocking my bag with embroidery silk, needles and a sharp dagger. That's one of the reasons I want to learn how to make your salve."

"I'll teach you."

They continued to work side by side, gathering, cutting and mixing the herbs and roots they needed for the tea until they had a good-sized batch for the afflicted couple. Erin couldn't remember a time when such contentment filled her. Maybe it was because she and True shared so much in common that their friendship had blossomed so easily. She'd never met anyone else with abilities similar to hers, and it was a relief.

"I hope this works." Erin went for an empty basket to carry their remedy. "Do you have some kind of cheesecloth or linen to line the basket?"

"Yep. In the trunk at the end of the cot."

She rummaged through the trunk full of strips of cloth for bandages and squares for bundles until she found the right size. Placing the square inside the rush basket she'd chosen, she brought it back to their pile of the loose tea on the worktable.

"Do you want to take this to them, or do you think it would be better if we went together?" True asked.

"You have to get back to your babies. They'll want to nurse soon. Besides, it's important that I be the one to bring them the tea. They need to know I'm invested in finding a solution."

"Arlen might still be here," True said. "He often spends time visiting his sister's family while on the island."

"Good. If you'll take me to him, I'll ask him to take me to the mainland. I'm procrastinating an argument I know I'm going to have with Robley. I need a little time to formulate my thoughts. We need to head to Inverness to confront Giselle together, and we need to do it soon."

The evening had been long, and Erin's eyelids drooped. Still, she was determined to have it out with Robley before they slept. His family had tried and failed to reason with him earlier in the evening, and now it was her turn. Erin followed the family procession out of the solar and again formulated the argument she needed to have with her stubborn husband. Once they were within the privacy of their own chamber, she turned to him. Her palms grew moist, and her heart crept up her throat.

"I can't live with this threat constantly hanging over our heads, Rob. I know you believe everything has been resolved, but I don't agree. I want to go to Inverness as soon as possible. If we leave in the next few days, we can be back before Christmas." She doubted their visit with Giselle would be that simple, but for Rob's sake she had to put it out there as if she believed it would be.

"Nay." He sat on the chair and removed his boots. "There's no need. 'Tis done."

"No, Rob. It's not, and judging from the emotionally tangled vibes you're giving off right now, you don't really believe it's over either. What's going on in your mind?"

He rose from the chair and strode toward her. "What is really going on in my mind is the thought of you naked and in my arms." He drew her close. "I dinna wish to discuss this any further, babe. We are no' going anywhere but to bed, where I plan to make love to you until we both fall asleep."

"Nope." She disentangled herself from his arms. "We need to resolve this. Giselle is back, and the faerie warrior could make an appearance at any moment. Making love leads to babies. With the prospect of your death riding herd on us, I don't want to get pregnant." She crossed the room to the pegs on the wall and began to undress. "If you won't come with me, I'll arrange to travel to Inverness on my own."

"Nay. You will do no such thing. I am your husband," he snapped. "I make the decisions for the both of us now, and I say this can wait 'til spring."

"Huh. I don't recall that being a part of the vows we took. I've always made my own decisions, and I'm not about to stop just because I'm living in your century." Her insides knotted. "Don't you get it? I can't bear the thought of losing you. I can't live with that fear every single day while waiting for the other shoe to drop. The stress is too much. I can't sit idly by knowing Giselle is in Inverness. How can you?"

"Och, woman." He plowed his hands through his hair. "I canna bear the thought that this fragile peace might be upset if we *do* confront her. Leave it be."

"I can't." She bit her lip, wondering just how far she could push him. Dammit. What choice did she have? "Ignoring the problem isn't going to make it go away."

He tugged his shirt off and dropped it on the floor. "Stirring the pot might bring the faerie to us."

"He's going to come for you one way or the other." She shot him an incredulous look. "Having Giselle on our side is the only hope we have."

"Ignoring the entire affair may make it disappear. The fae are a capricious lot." He unbelted his plaid and let it fall where he stood. "I am certain they've been distracted by other more pressing intrigues."

He drew her into his arms again and nuzzled her neck, trailing kisses to her jaw. His warmth, bare skin and obvious arousal wreaked havoc on her resolve, and at the same time she wanted to shake him so hard the stubborn fell right out of him. "I doubt it. The pensieve belonged to their king. They're not going to let it go."

"Humph." He yanked at the tie to her chemise, and it soon fell to the floor to join his pile of wool and linen.

"Robley." She pushed against his chest. "I mean it. We have to travel to Inverness, or I'm moving back to the room I started out in, and the door will be barred on a nightly basis." She reached for her chemise and brought it to the pegs, ignoring his pile of garments.

The muscles in his jaw twitched, and anger pulsed from him in waves. He strode toward the hearth and gave her his back. "You think to issue ultimatums to me, wife?"

"I guess so," she whispered, her heart aching. She'd never meant to issue any kind of threat. It just sort of slipped out, but she had to follow through, or they would continue to be at an impasse.

"I will no' allow it."

"Robley," she pleaded. "Please be reasonable. You can't just stick your head in the sand and hope that everything will pass us by. Life doesn't work like that, and I'm pretty sure you know that."

He swallowed hard and shook his head. "You dinna understand."

"Explain it then. Help me to understand. I can feel your stress and unhappiness, but I don't know what you're thinking."

"My da's health. You. Responsibility to my clan and kin." His shoulders slumped. "What does no' weigh upon me at present? The faerie has left us alone. I dinna want to risk drawing his attention by being anywhere near Giselle. He tracked me through centuries, lass. Surely he can track me from Moigh Hall to Inverness."

He glanced at her, his expression determined and stony. "He kens I dinna have the pensieve. I'm naught but a mortal who was ill used by one of their own. What use am I to him when I dinna ken Giselle's true identity? He's had time to think upon the matter, and I'm certain he's come to the same conclusion. I'm of no further use to him."

Fear and despair. The emotions filled her husband and flowed straight to her. A rush of empathy and understanding surged through her. He feared losing his father to another stroke, and he feared losing her to the future—more than he feared losing his life. Never had her insights and impressions from another been so clear. Her soul wept for what he was going through, for what they both must face.

"Oh, Rob." She wrapped her arms around him, pressing herself against his stiff back and absorbing his tension. "I get it. I really do. Let's do what we can to put all of this faerie drama behind us once and for all. I have your father on a daily dose of True's willow bark tea. He's getting stronger every day. You're not going to lose him anytime soon."

"Aye? And what about you? Can you guarantee I willna lose you should we confront Giselle?" He turned in her arms, crushing her to him. His mouth found hers in a hungry kiss, and his hands roamed over her as if he meant to memorize her by touch. She caved. So much for her ultimatum. He needed her right now, needed her loving touch to soothe the fears and lessen the weight of all that rode upon his broad shoulders.

He backed her to their bed, and she let him. They fell onto the mattress in a tangle of limbs, heat, need and love, losing themselves in each other. Their lovemaking was frenzied and intense. She welcomed the respite from the grim reality they faced. Immersing herself in the sensations of their joining, she gave herself up to the love they shared, trusting in the strength their bond had woven. He'd voiced his worst fears, and she knew he'd soon come to see things her way.

Sated and spent, he wrapped himself around her and settled, as he did every night. She smiled into the darkness. He loved to spoon, and the sense of peace and security it gave her evoked a resonating hum within her. She wanted forever with him. Didn't she deserve to be happy? Hadn't she paid her dues with an unstable childhood and a lonely adulthood?

"I'll travel to Inverness to speak with Giselle, lass," he mumbled into her ear, "if it will put you at ease."

"I'm coming with you."

"Nay. You'll stay here where I ken you are safe."

"Nope. I'm coming with you to bargain with her. I did what she wanted me to do, and now she owes me a favor."

"Humph. Do you mean to take me from one argument to the next, woman?" He smacked her bare bottom. "You are a wee, managing termagant."

"OK. Whatever." She snuggled closer. "So long as I get to be by your side while I'm a *wee termagant*, whatever that is."

CHAPTER SEVENTEEN

Robley turned his mount from the lead of their party and cantered back to where Erin rode in the wagon with the supplies. "Are you well, love? Warm enough? Comfortable?"

"I'm fine," she grumbled. "You don't have to ask me every half hour. I have my jeans on under my woolen gown, my Harley jacket, the shearling wrap and the mittens True loaned me." She scowled at him, eliciting a grin from the soldier driving the ox cart. "It's not even that cold."

"Mayhap you'd like to ride in my lap for a time. You can join me at the head of the line." True's gentle mare was tied to the back of the cart. He'd secured the horse for their journey in the hopes Erin would learn to ride along the way. They'd been on the road toward Inverness for days, and still she'd opted to sit in the back of the wagon to be jostled about with their tents, gear and food.

"I'm good. Thanks."

"Do you fear the horses?" He couldn't understand why anyone would chose bumping along in a wooden cart over riding.

She shrugged. "Maybe. I've never been on one."

"Ride with me for a bit, lass. I desire your company." Her brow rose at his suggestion, and heat crept up his neck. Memories of last night's lovemaking in the privacy of their tent flooded his mind. His desire for her was insatiable, and he thanked the powers that be that her passion equaled his in every way.

"Remember how you reacted to riding in my car"—she glanced at the men accompanying them on their journey—"er, wagon? I didn't give you a hard time."

"Aye, I do remember. My *reaction* did no' stop me from continuing to ride with you, did it? Come, lass. Having you in my lap will keep me warm."

He wore soft, fur-lined boots, trews and a tunic for the journey, along with a parka designed by True. He was comfortable and warm enough, but aroused. He wanted his wife. He always wanted her.

She glanced up at him. "Oh, I don't know."

He brought his gelding up beside the wagon, leaned over and scooped her up into his arms.

"Hey!"

"Wheesht, ye wee termagant. We'll see Inverness ere long. Surely you can indulge me for a short while." He drew her close and settled her on his lap. "'Tis no' so bad, is it?" Truth be told, he needed the physical contact to assuage his mounting anxiety. Nothing good would come of their meeting with Giselle; he was certain. Erin's expression grew pensive, and she focused upon him in that way she did when trying to gain some idea of his physical well-being.

Slipping her arms around his waist, she snuggled against his chest. "It'll be all right, Rob. I don't believe Giselle is evil, and keeping us around is good for True, Hunter and the rest of our clan."

"Humph. 'Tis against my better judgment that we travel here. Betwixt you, my parents, uncle, aunt and cousin, what choice did

I have in the matter? With all of you haranguing me daily, I could find no peace."

"You'll thank us once all of this is behind us."

He rested his chin on top of her head, hoping with everything within him that she was right. They rode on in companionable silence, and by twilight, she'd fallen asleep. His arms ached from supporting her, yet he had no will to place her elsewhere. She belonged in his embrace, sheltered and protected by his strength. His chest ached, and the backs of his eyes stung. He did not want to face a life without her. Mayhap he'd lock her up in one of the dungeon cells in the keep when he went to Giselle's cottage. Erin would be furious, but she'd still be there when he returned—if he returned.

The castle came into view as he continued to ponder his options. If he did lock his wife up, he'd have to let someone know where he'd put her in case he didn't return. Mayhap one of the turret chambers would suffice. He grunted. What was he thinking? If he met his end, surely she'd want to be returned to her life in the twenty-first century. 'Twas selfish to think of locking her away. Doing so would not alter his fate or hers. His heart heavy, he shook her gently. "Wake, love. We've arrived."

She stirred, rubbing the sleep from her eyes. "It's dark."

"Aye, but look you there." He pointed. "The lights ahead will guide us." Torches burned upon the ramparts, and candlelight shone from several narrow windows of the keep. "We will sleep in a bed this night."

"A bath too? Can I have a bath?" She straightened.

"Aye, and a hot meal before a warm fire."

Sighing, she began to fuss with her gown and then her hair. He chuckled. "No need to fash about your appearance, lass. They'll ken we've been on the road for days." A snowflake drifted down to land on her shoulder. He brushed it off. Another landed in her hair, and soon fat white flakes began to fall in earnest. "It appears we've arrived just in time." He squeezed her shoulders. "What do you think of riding horseback?"

"It's OK, as long as you're holding me. Horses are so big, and we never had any kind of pets when I was growing up. I guess I'm just not used to being around animals." She shrugged. "I never had a puppy or a kitten—no sleepovers or birthday parties either." Regret laced her tone. "If we ever have children, we're going to make sure they know with absolute certainty that they are loved."

"For certes our bairns will know we love them." She glanced at him, her expression vulnerable, and his heart tumbled. She was so beautiful, and more than anything he desired to have a family with her. Any son or daughter of theirs would surely be adorable. If they had a daughter, he hoped she'd have her mother's eyes, and if by chance any of their bairns should inherit her fae gifts, he'd be sure they would ken those gifts were cause for celebration.

"For certes, love." Robley hugged her close. "But since you never had a pet of your own and are uncomfortable around horses, I'd like to teach you to ride. I believe you'd come to enjoy it, and I'll secure a gentle palfrey for your very own. Your first pet."

She bit her lip, and even without special abilities he sensed her anxiety. They'd just been talking about bairns of their own, and what had happened with True and the ferry master's daughter must be fresh on her mind, as it was on his. Mayhap 'twas the thought of childbirth in the fifteenth century worrying her. Or mayhap thoughts of what might happen once they confronted Giselle vexed her. "First thing on the morrow we'll set out to see Giselle. Let us no' dwell on our worries this eve. This is your first visit to Inverness." He nodded toward the keep. "What think you of the castle?"

Against the starry sky, the darker outline of the imposing structure stood out. Situated on the banks of the river as it was, Inverness was the hub of commerce for the entire region, and that his clan had the keeping of it for their king filled him with pride. As seneschal, 'twould be within his power to make Inverness even more profitable—for the good of the clan and their people.

"It's hard to say in the dark, but it looks huge."

"It is quite imposing." He kicked his horse into a canter, leaving the rest of their group behind with the wagon. Erin clung to him, giving a little cry of alarm at their pace. "I've got you, Erin." They were close enough to the keep now that he had no worries for their safety upon the road. He approached the portcullis and greeted the guards. He and Erin passed through to the bailey, and he instructed the guards to keep the gate up for the rest of their men. An hour later, he and Erin were awaiting a hot bath and food to be brought to them in the chamber usually reserved for his parents.

"It's nice to be inside again," Erin said while hanging her jacket on a peg. "Not that I have anything against camping out. All things considered, I was never terribly uncomfortable."

She sent him a beguiling smile just as a line of servants entered the chamber, two bearing the tub and the rest carrying buckets of hot water, soap and linens. Yet another started a fire in the hearth, and a groom from the stable set their trunk against the wall.

The head housekeeper came in last and greeted them with a tray in her hands. Her curious gaze fixed upon Erin. "Welcome tae Castle Inverness, milady. We all wish ye happy. 'Tis good tae see our lad wed at last." She set the tray on the table. "I've hot stew, bread, cheese and mulled wine for ye tae sup. Is there aught else ye'll be needing before retiring?"

"Nay. Our thanks, Margaret. That will be all." Truth be told, he wanted them all gone so he could have his wife to himself. Thoughts of a meal consisting of more than jerky and oatcakes elicited a rumble from his empty belly. He poured two goblets of the spiced wine and brought one to Erin.

She cupped her hands around the warmth of the goblet and took a sip. "Mmm. This is good."

A flurry of activity went on around them, and once again his mind wandered to thoughts of locking Erin away while he pled with Giselle. Finally, the last of the servants departed, closing the chamber door behind them. "Come eat, Erin. The bath will stay warm enough by the hearth." He pulled out a chair for her.

"Just a minute. I can't believe I'm going to say this, but I've grown used to wearing gowns every day, and these jeans gotta go." She lifted her skirts and unbuttoned the denim, sliding the trews down her hips and legs. She kicked her jeans up and snatched them from the air with one hand. "Ah, that's better," she said, folding the garment and setting it on the trunk.

His breath quickened at the glimpse he'd caught of her bare legs, and his blood rushed to his groin. Soon. He'd have her in his arms soon, but first a meal and a bath for them both. To distract himself, he tore the bread in two and placed one of the pieces beside Erin's bowl. Then he took the dagger from his waist and cut slices of cheese. "Erin, if aught happens to me—"

"Nothing is going to happen to you." She scowled. "I won't let it."

"Och, aye?" He grinned at the ferocity in her tone. "Have you brought the pepper spray with you? Think you we'll have better luck with the stuff this time 'round?"

"I have it. It's in my purse. Maybe I'll bring it tomorrow just in case." She took her seat. "I plan to stage a sit-in on Giselle's doorstep until she agrees to protect us both."

"Humph." He sat across from her. "Back to my question. If aught happens to me, would you want to return to your own time or remain here with my family?"

"Don't ask me that. It's not like I'd have a choice either way." Her eyes glistened with the moisture filling them.

"I need to know." His heart thudded against his ribs. If she wished to stay, mayhap locking her away was not such a foolish notion after all.

"I don't know." She blew out a breath and leaned back in her chair. "Life is precarious in your time. One unfortunate infectious disease and it's all over. We have hospitals and antibiotics in my century. We have vaccinations against most of the diseases that kill people in your era. Plus, I'm not a noble, Rob. I have nothing to offer to anyone other than my skill as a midwife, and I don't know that I'd enjoy being a burden to your family forever. Without you, my future here would be pretty bleak." She averted her gaze. "Besides, I did have a life before you traveled through your time to fall into mine. I guess I'd want to finish my education. Like I told you before, getting that midwife certification has always been very important to me."

"What if you're already breeding?"

"If I am, the argument for returning is even stronger." She sent him a pleading look. "Can we talk about something else?"

"Of course." He dipped his bread into the savory stew and took a bite. "Mmm." He gestured toward her steaming bowl. "'Tis good. Eat, and then I'll wash your hair for you." He'd lost his appetite, but he didn't want her to see how her words affected him. He'd brought her back in time against her will, turned her life upside down and all on a whim—or mayhap a fae-induced compulsion. Forcing his thoughts away from the path they'd taken, he focused upon more pleasant pursuits, like bathing Erin.

Washing her hair had become one of his favorite intimacies, and he did so as frequently as she'd allow. The groans of pleasure his ministrations elicited, the sensuous feel of her silken locks tangled in his fingers and the erotic picture she presented while relaxing in a tub all acted to heighten his desire for her to a fever pitch. Anticipation had him growing hard, and he too found his trews restrictive. Her face flushed, and she graced him with a knowing smile.

"I forget sometimes that you sense how you affect me physically."

"I do pick up on your reactions, but it's OK." She took a mouthful of her stew. "This is good."

Their meal finished, he refilled their goblets and set them on the mantel. "I packed some of True's shampoo and soap. I ken how much you favor them." He rummaged through their trunk until he found the ceramic jar and the wrapped bar of fragrant soap. "Come, love. Let me help you out of your travel-encrusted clothing."

"If you insist." Grinning, she unbraided her hair and moved to stand before him.

Her eyes smoldered with the same anticipation stirring within him. "Do you ken 'twas first your emerald eyes that enticed me? There I was, entangled in your arms and legs, fresh through time, and all I could do was stare into them. You are an enchantress, *mo céile*."

"Your baby blues had the same effect on me."

"Truly? I had no idea." His fingers skimmed her bare shoulders as he undressed her, eliciting a swift intake of her breath. An echoing ripple of excitement sluiced through him.

"What could I have said?" she asked. "I knew nothing about you, and the way I reacted frightened me. People are not supposed to get turned on by strangers who pop out of thin air to land on top of them. Are they?"

He chuckled. "I dinna ken. Mayhap, if fate has more in store for those who find themselves in such straits, 'tis only natural to react as we both did." Divested of her gown and chemise, she stood gloriously naked and within his reach. How could he refuse such an enticement? He drew her close and kissed her deeply. "You smell of the outdoors and wood smoke," he murmured against her throat.

"I need a bath." She backed out of his arms and stepped into the tub. "Ah, the water is still hot." Lowering herself into the large copper tub, she sighed. "This feels good after days on the road."

"And the view is also quite grand." Rob grabbed the shampoo and soap. "I'd like to bathe all of you, Erin. May I?"

"Oh yeah." She tipped her head back and sent him an enticing look before ducking her head under the water to wet her hair.

Rob tore off his clothing and studied the tub. "Do you think we'd both fit?"

"We can give it a try, but maybe take some of the water out first." Erin pointed to a bucket that had been left behind.

He snatched it up and scooped its fill from the tub. "Lean forward." He filled his palms with shampoo and stepped into the water, settling behind her. She rested her arms on his knees and leaned back against his chest.

"This is wonderful," she whispered as he massaged the shampoo into her scalp and worked it down to the ends of her tresses.

"After your emerald eyes, 'twas your tawny golden hair that caught my attention."

"Oh?" She wiggled closer. "I drooled over your broad shoulders and muscled everything."

He laughed. "Muscled everything?"

"That's right. You're way too sexy for your own good, Robley. You have no idea."

He reached for the wooden bowl provided with the tub and rinsed her hair. "Aye, and I find your curves enticingly soft and sexy as well." He took up the bar of soap. "Up, babe."

She straightened, and he soaped her back, coming around to run his sudsy palms over her breasts, his groin tightening at her gasp. "Mine," he rasped, moving his hands lower. "You are mine, and I love you, Erin. Dinna ever forget that you mean more to me than life itself."

She moaned as he parted the folds of her feminine flesh to find the nub of pleasure there. Opening for him, she rested her head on his shoulder. Her lids half closed, and her mouth opened slightly. Throbbing to the point of pain with his need to be inside her, he plied her the way he kent would send her into the throes of ecstasy, watching intently as she came closer and closer to release. His breathing grew heavy, and his hips lifted and thrust against her bottom. With one hand he continued to pleasure her, with the other he turned her head to kiss her deeply, plunging his tongue into her mouth to mate with hers. Her taste, the feel of her wet, soapy skin against him brought him as close to heaven as he ever hoped to be.

She shuddered and writhed in his arms, taken by her climax. Lifting her by the hips, he positioned her above him. "Support yourself on your knees and place your hands against the foot of the tub." Gently he helped her into the position he desired. "Lean forward," he commanded, sliding down slightly into the water. Using one hand to guide him, he brought her down, entering her slick heat. "Och, lass, ye do me in." He moved against her, and water splashed out over the sides. "Damnation, we'll soak the floorboards."

She laughed and lowered herself to meet his next thrust. "It's just water. We'll clean it up later. Don't stop."

He grasped her by the waist and moved in a circular fashion inside her. "Ah, lass. Stay still." She held herself firmly against him. "Aye. Right there. Dinna move." The water lapped gently around them as he continued to find his pleasure within her, coming nearer to losing control. He reached around to fondle her luscious breasts, tweaking her erect nipples until she moaned and arched into his touch. She tightened around his shaft, spasms wracking through her, drawing him up in their wake. His climax sent spirals of sensation pulsing through him. One more thrust, and he lost his seed inside her. Settling back against the copper back, he drew her in, sighing with contentment. They rested together, replete.

Erin stirred, twisting around to kiss him briefly. "Water's getting cold. Let's finish washing and do that again, only in the bed this time."

"Have I mentioned how much I truly appreciate the way you think, *mo céile?*" He did as he was told, and helped her dry off as well, lingering over his favorite dips and swells. He followed the linen towel with kisses. He scooped her into his arms and carried her to the bed, loving her all over again until she cried out his name. Wrapping himself around her, he pulled her close. A small sigh, a slight adjustment to her position, and she fell asleep.

Sleep did not come so easily for him. He held the center of his world in his arms. She nestled against him, her warmth seeping into his heart and soul. Worry for the coming dawn plagued him, kept him wakeful and restless with apprehension. So much to lose. Never before had the stakes been so high. Tightening his arms around her, he placed a kiss on her bare shoulder, stroked her side where her waist flared to her hip. His eyes stung, and his throat tightened. Everything in him screamed to turn around and head home for the safety of Moigh Hall, with Erin thrown over his shoulder if need be. Folly. 'Twas folly to consort with the fae, and he'd stepped willingly into the trap. The price of his bargain was far too high. All he wanted was a way out that dinna cost him his wife—or his life.

Rob clasped Erin's hand in his. The path to Giselle's cottage lay covered in snow. Their footprints the only thing marring the sparkling white purity, they made their way toward whatever fate held in store.

A strangling band of tension squeezed his chest, and he gripped the hilt of the dagger at his waist.

Erin puffed out a steamy breath. "Slow down. I can't keep up with your strides."

"Och, I'm sorry." He slowed his pace. "I was no' aware."

"Phew." She grinned. "That's better. It's really pretty through here. I always love the first snowfall, but by February I'd be happy never to see another white flake again as long as I live."

How could she be so carefree? He frowned at her. "Humph." Searching the tree limbs, he noted the absence of the menacing crows. No cawing warnings this morn. The sun rested low on the eastern horizon, just beginning its journey through the domed heavens above. He glanced at his wife. The physical exertion and the chill air had put roses on her cheeks. True to her word, she'd brought her satchel containing the wicked pepper spray. He shook his head.

"What?" She met his gaze, her eyes glinting with challenge. "Why'd you shake your head like that?"

"'Tis the notion that somehow your pepper spray will be of any use to us that caused me to shake my head, lass." He raised an eyebrow. "Did ye no' learn anything from our last encounter with the fae?"

"Sure, but I also have the diamonds in here." She patted the leather bag hanging from her shoulder. "I thought we could give them back. They're worth a lot. Maybe it'll make a difference."

He shook his head again. "I doubt it."

"Look," she said, throwing her arm out in an expansive gesture at their surroundings. "It's a gorgeous morning. These woods are so peaceful and pretty," she said while squeezing his hand. "I just have to believe that everything is going to go in our favor."

In the absence of the black-winged sentinels, he could almost believe it himself. He stopped, turned Erin toward him, and gripped her shoulders. "I pray it is so, lass." Drawing her close enough that the steam from their breaths mingled, he kissed her. Passion flared, along with hope. Mayhap having her by his side would make all the difference.

"Come," he huffed out. "Let us get this over with." Once again he grasped her hand and led her along the path.

"We're jogging again, eh?" She trotted along beside him.

"Aye." They came to the edge of the clearing, and he halted, scanning the area for immediate danger.

Erin hugged his arm. "Nice little place."

He eyed the cottage, wariness raising the fine hairs on the back of his neck. A curl of smoke rose from the chimney, and the chickens were back. The early morning sun cast a mellow glow over the glittering snow. "Erin . . ."

"I love you, Robley." She placed her palm on his face and brought his gaze to hers. "It's going to be all right. I know it is."

Placing his hand over hers, her turned toward her hand to kiss her palm. He took a fortifying breath and stared at the cottage. The door opened, and Giselle peered out at them. Mayhap she'd spied their approach through one of the windows, but more than likely she'd been expecting them. Robley looped Erin's arm through his and brought her toward the faerie awaiting them. "Good morn to you, Madame Giselle."

"And to you." The old crone's eyes narrowed. "What brings you to my doorstep, young Robley?" She opened the door wider and bade them enter. "I would have thought you'd be content to spend the winter at Moigh Hall with your new bride."

They passed through the same threshold he'd forced himself through but a few weeks past. Erin gasped. "Then it's true. You did send him to me on purpose."

Giselle's cackled response sent shivers down Robley's spine. All of his protective instincts surging, he put his arm around Erin's shoulders and tucked her against his side. The urge to get his wife away from this place and away from this being nearly unhinged him.

"Of course," Giselle said, closing the door behind them.

"Then do you also know what has happened since then?" Erin shot her an expectant look.

The interior once again held all the vestiges of long habitation. Rob surveyed the room, surreptitiously searching for the stolen pensieve.

"Much has happened since then." Giselle went to the cauldron hanging over the glowing coals of her hearth. "To which happening do you refer?" She glanced at them over her shoulder. "Sit. Have some tea, and we'll talk." Pointing to a crude wooden bench set against the wall, she said, "Bring that over, lad, so that we might all have a place at my table."

Giselle poured boiling water into her teapot and set it on the table next to three mugs. She brought over a bowl of fragrant honey and a board holding fresh bread and placed them beside the mugs.

The ordinary fare set him at ease. He placed the bench by the table and pulled out the chairs for the women. Only when they'd been seated did he take his place on the bench. "I assumed you sent me to Erin specifically. She saved True's life and the lives of her twins. I believe that is one of the happenings my wife speaks of."

"I knew what was to be, and I took advantage of your desire to visit the future." Giselle canted her head. "I placed no compulsion on you, though I know full well you believe I did. Your thirst for adventure leant itself well to my purposes, and I acted accordingly." She raised her brow. "Are you displeased with the end result? You are newly wedded, as was your truest desire, though I doubt you saw it so clearly. And my wish to provide help to Hunter's guardian has been fulfilled." She busied herself with pouring their tea. "All in all, I believe our bargain was fair. Do you not agree?"

"Then you don't know about the faerie warrior who followed Robley to my apartment?" Erin's eyes widened. "The faerie accused him of stealing a pensieve from your high king, the same silver platter you had Robley retrieve for you. He gave my husband thirty days to get it back. If Robley doesn't return the pensieve to him, the faerie said he's going to kill him." She raised her chin. "That's why we're here. We need your help."

Giselle laughed. "Your man and I struck a bargain, and I held up my end. I owe him nothing."

"Here," Erin said, riffling through the purse hanging from her shoulder. "I brought the diamonds back that you gave him. Surely they're worth something to you. We can trade them for the silver platter."

"You brought the crystals here?" Giselle shot up from her place. "Foolish mortal!"

"Why? They don't work anymore." Erin frowned. "We tried them both when the faerie warrior sent us back to this century."

The temperature took a sudden drop, and the scent of impending rain filled Rob's senses. "Shite." He grabbed Erin's hand and dragged her toward the door. "Make haste. We need to be away from here." A blasting force slammed against them, pinning them both against the wall beside the door, their hands still clasped.

"I can't move." Erin's panicked tone matched his own.

"Nor can I, lass. Be quiet."

"Áine!" A voice boomed, causing the shutters covering the windows to shake. Two beings appeared, crowding the small room with their magic and the sheer force of their presence.

Robley tried to free himself from whatever held him. His arms and legs were frozen in place, and fear gripped him by the throat. One of the beings was the warrior he'd hoped against hope never to see again. The other could only be the high king himself. He radiated such power and majesty there could be no doubt.

"You will return to me what you took." The high king floated above the wooden planks of the floor. Blue fire danced along the surface of his skin, and he glared at Giselle.

"It's mine, Father."

Father? God's blood, Giselle was the king's daughter? What the bloody hell had he embroiled himself—and his love—in. The warrior's brow lowered as he fixed his sights on Erin.

"It *was* yours, and I took it from you because you abused the pensieve and defied my laws." The king glided toward Giselle.

Rob's lungs seized. The old crone's appearance shifted, turning ethereal before his very eyes. She was no longer the stooped, wrinkled old hag. Her skin smoothed to perfection, and hair the color of moonbeams cascaded down her back. Her eyes glowed an impossible blue. A halo of the same blue light emanating from her eyes gilded her entire form.

"I only use it to watch over my progeny. You forbade me to visit them through time. What choice did I have?" Giselle—no—Áine declared.

"And yet you do so regardless." The king glanced their way.

"Of course I do. You would too if you had halflings to watch over." She turned to the warrior. "How could you, Haldor," she snapped, her tone dripping with disdain. "You were there when the pensieve was given to me. How dare you accuse me of stealing what was mine from the start."

"I serve my king, Princess." Haldor's gaze slid to Áine and then once again focused upon Erin. "She does not belong here, and the human male—"

"Don't you dare hurt him," Erin gritted out between clenched teeth. "I belong with my husband."

"Och, lass. Wheesht." Robley's heart pummeled against his rib cage, and tears blurred his vision. "Wheesht now, my love," he begged, hoping against hope the warrior's attention would stray from Erin and once again turn to the argument between the king and his daughter.

The air beside Erin rippled and pulsed with pale greens and pinks. Her hand was torn from his. "Rob!"

"Nay! Dinna take my wife from me," he shouted. "Please, I beg of you . . ." She disappeared from his sight. "If you must send her back, send me with her, but dinna separate me from her," he implored. "I canna bear the loss." A rending grief stole the breath from his lungs and the beat from his heart. His soul ripped asunder, and yet he remained fixed to the wall, unable to move or to act.

Erin was gone, taking his reason for living with her. "Please, send me to her," Rob rasped out.

"You have trespassed where you ought not to have tread, mortal." Haldor stared at him, his features inscrutable. "But you have led us to the orchestrator of your crime against my king. With my liege's permission, I will spare your life." He glanced at the faerie king, who nodded slightly in agreement.

His limbs were once again his to command. "I canna bear to live without my wife by my side." Robley gripped his dagger and lunged for Haldor.

"Foolish human." The faerie warrior raised his hands.

The air rippled and shimmered before Robley, and joy exploded within him, replacing his sorrow. He would be with Erin, and it mattered not whether it be in his time or hers. Fixing her in his mind, along with her apartment and the year, he dove for the portal with all his strength.

Pressure assaulted him from all sides, hurling him through time and space. Blackness edged in around him, clouding his vision. He struggled to remain conscious. He had to remain fixed upon his love's image, had to keep his mind focused upon the time and place he wished to be. Still, the darkness encroached, robbing him of his ability to focus, swamping him with misery until he could no longer hold on to his thoughts—or awareness. Unable to hold on, the darkness took him where it would, and his last thought was that he must surely be dying after all.

CHAPTER EIGHTEEN

Erin fell through time's portal to land with a thud—facedown in the middle of her living room floor. Her head throbbed and her joints ached, but those hurts were nothing compared to the pain in her heart. *My God! What just happened?* She rolled to her back as tears flooded her eyes. What had become of Robley? Had the faerie warrior killed him? *No!* She covered her face with her hands and forced her mind away from the unthinkable.

Somehow she'd managed to hold on to her purse while being hurled through time. She fished around inside for her cell phone. Once she had it, she drew it out, turned it on and checked the date and time. A sob erupted just before the battery died and the screen went black. How could it be? Today was the very same date and time she and Rob had been sent to the past.

How was it possible she hadn't lost a single day of her life, yet at the same time she'd lost *everything* that mattered?

She'd been the one to insist they go to Giselle. Robley had known better from the start, and she hadn't listened. None of them had listened. *Oh, Robley, what have I done?* She curled up into a fetal position.

The damned diamonds! That's how the faerie had tracked them, and he'd waited to appear until *she* led him straight to Giselle—and to Robley, the only man she'd ever given her heart to completely. She might very well have been the cause of his death. Grief and anger tore her apart. She put her arms around her middle and sobbed until she had no more tears left to cry.

She must have fallen asleep, because she awoke to find her apartment dark. Drawing in a ragged breath, she prayed Giselle had spoken up on Rob's behalf. He might still be alive. Right? After all, he'd only done the faerie's bidding, and by the sounds of the argument, the pensieve really had belonged to Giselle. She grasped at that straw with both hands, wrapped her mind firmly around the hope and built a solid wall of denial to keep out the alternative. *Sure. He might be alive, but we're separated by centuries, by an ocean and continents.*

It might as well be a universe. She had no way to cross the divide.

Obviously the faeries used the crystals for a number of purposes. Maybe Giselle had manipulated the power so Erin couldn't travel through time to return home before helping True. Maybe . . . She rose from the floor and turned on the lights before reaching into her purse for the leather pouch holding the two gems. Her hands shook as she opened the drawstring and dumped the crystals into her palm. Picking up the larger of the two, she closed her eyes and sent up a prayer. With Rob's image firmly in her mind, along with the keep in Inverness and the date, she crouched down and sent the diamond spinning.

Nothing happened.

Her hopes shattered. She threw the second diamond across the room. It hit the back of the couch and came to rest in the place Rob always sat when they watched movies together. She blinked against the tears blurring her vision and imagined him sitting there with his sexy, dimpled smile aimed her way. The memory of his warm gaze stole the air from her lungs and turned her into a mess of blubbering misery. What gave the *Tuatha Dé Danann* the right to interfere with her life? Damn them.

Erin pushed herself off the floor and wandered down the hall to Robley's room. She turned on the light and stared at his claymore leaning against the wall. He'd regretted losing the weapon. Hadn't he said the sword had been made especially for him? Now it was hers. A rumpled T-shirt lay at the end of his unmade bed. Snatching it up, she brought it to her face and inhaled deeply. His scent brought a fresh wave of pain. Still, she breathed it in over and over. How long would the cotton hold his smell? Desperation clawed at her. Would his scent last longer if she kept the T-shirt in a ziplock plastic bag? She'd do it if that's what it took to keep this reminder of him with her.

Hugging the cotton shirt to her chest, she crossed the room to his dresser and pulled open one of the drawers. It held his plaid. *Oh, God!* Memories of the day he'd fallen through time engulfed her. Every day they'd spent together played through her mind. His endearing gestures and mannerisms, his cocky, easygoing nature, his optimism, his fifteenth-century chivalry—she'd lost her perfect match. Everything about him made her a better person. Because of him, she'd made friends at Loch Moigh and finally felt like she belonged somewhere. How weird was it that the only time in her life when she'd had *a place*, or felt as if she belonged, existed long before she'd even been born?

Erin had to talk to someone, or she'd go nuts. Connor needed to know Rob wouldn't show up to work for his next shift, or ever again for that matter. She headed back to the kitchen, still clutching Rob's T-shirt, and used her landline to make the call.

"McGladreys' residence, Meghan speaking."

"Hey, Meghan, this is Erin Durie. Is your dad around?"

"Sure. Hold on."

What would she say? How would Connor feel if she revealed how Rob had come to be in this century in the first place?

"Hello, Erin. What's up?"

"Robley is gone." Her chin quivered. "I thought you should know."

"Gone?" A few seconds of silence passed before he continued. "When will he be back?"

A lump formed in her throat, and try as she might, she couldn't speak around it. Her eyes brimmed with tears again. She should've waited until tomorrow to make this call. Everything was still too fresh. Too raw.

"Can ye drive, lassie?"

Had she left her car keys in the pocket of her Harley jacket? If so, the jacket was still in the chamber she'd shared with Rob. Another sob threatened to spill out of her. She'd slept in his arms just last night. Had she known it would be their last, she wouldn't have slept at all. Swallowing hard, she shook her head. "No," she whispered.

"I'll come for you. Look for me out your front door."

"OK," she squeaked before hanging up. Her limbs heavy, she forced herself to her room and changed into jeans and a sweatshirt. She hadn't even missed a day of school. At least she had obtaining her midwife certification to keep her going. She'd need a reason to get out of bed in the morning. She searched for her keys in her purse. They were there. Good thing. She grabbed a jacket out of her front closet and left her apartment to wait for Connor.

It didn't take him long to reach her apartment building. Erin's eyes widened as Mark Pilon hopped out of the car and held the door open for her. Great. She wanted to bare her soul, and now she couldn't. She slid into the front seat, and Mark moved to the back. Disappointment coursed through her, and it must have come through in the expression she shot Connor. "Thanks for coming for me, but—"

"It's all right, Erin." Connor pulled his car away from the curb. "Mark knows everything."

"He does?" She twisted around to glance at him. "You do? How?"

"I do teach high school physics, you know. I'm not stupid." Mark raised an eyebrow. "Once I saw Connor and Robley sparring with their broadswords, I began to put a few things together—like the way Robley is always in medieval mode with his speech. And he did say he'd fought for real before. The way he reacted to my motorcycle was a big tell too. I confronted Connor, and he told me his story, but not Rob's, though he did admit your *cousin* came here from the fifteenth century."

"I've never thought of you as stupid, Mark." She couldn't help the defensive tone infusing her voice. "I only said Robley was my cousin because I didn't know how else to explain him. He'd just landed in our time the day you met him."

"Sure. I get that." He shrugged. "I was hanging out with Connor when you called. Don't worry. He's dropping me off at my place on the way back to his."

Mark's hurt feelings and his interest in her surged toward her. She cringed, shutting out the unwanted emotions. "I'm sorry. I'm just not in the best of moods right now. It's been a really rough few weeks. Day. I mean day."

"It's OK. Time isn't linear. The past and the present coexist simultaneously, or so theorists believe." Mark leaned forward and placed his hand on her shoulder. "I hope someday you'll share your story with me." He patted her shoulder before turning to Connor. "It's the next corner, man. I'll get out here so you don't have to turn."

Connor pulled over, and Mark climbed out of the car. He leaned down to peer at her, motioning for her to lower the window. She did.

"You ever need someone to talk to, my number's in the club directory." He nodded to Connor. "Later."

"Later," Connor said, returning the nod. Mark straightened and shoved his hands into his pockets, and Connor drove back into traffic.

Erin closed the window. She heaved a huge sigh and stared out the windshield. "I've been gone for about six weeks," she said. "A faerie appeared in my apartment on this very date, only six weeks ago, and tossed me and Robley back to the fifteenth century."

"You were sent back as well? Why do ye suppose?"

"The faerie didn't intend to send me back with Rob. I just got caught up in the whole thing when I tried to douse the faerie with pepper spray."

"Pepper spray on the fae? Hmm. This is a tale I wish to hear in full, but let's wait until we're at my house. Katherine will want to hear it as well." He glanced at her. "Relax, lassie. You look as if you've been through quite a lot for one day."

"You could say that." She leaned back against the leather seat of his sedan and closed her eyes. "I married him, Connor. Robley and I said our vows before his clan, and now he's lost to me forever." She rubbed at the empty, aching place in her chest.

"Ah. I thought there might be something between the two of you."

She swiped at the tears on her face. "I just needed to talk to someone who understands the whole time travel thing—someone who's been through it." She bit her lip, struggling to keep it together. "I need to be with people in this century who knew Rob."

"Of course." Connor turned into his driveway, parked the car and shut it off. "Come. I can offer you wine and sympathy. My wife and I are here for you."

Gratitude sent a fresh spate of tears flowing. She really did need to get herself under control. Maybe talking about the whole thing would help. Connor led her to the door to their kitchen.

Kathy met them there, her expression filled with concern. "Oh, sweetie." She drew Erin into a brief hug. "I've opened a bottle of wine, and we have all night. Tell us what happened." Katherine walked to the counter, took a few paper towels from the roll and handed them to her.

A bottle of wine and three glasses awaited them at the kitchen table. Erin settled herself there and buried her face in the soft wad of paper towels. "Where do you want me to start?"

"Start at the beginning, lassie." Connor's deep voice washed over her, along with his concern. "Robley told me he fell into you at the Renaissance festival. Start there."

"He planned his trip. He was going to stay here for a month and then return to his own century." She leaned back and met their curious stares. "He made a bargain with a faerie named Áine. She lives among humans and calls herself Madame Giselle. I guess she's a faerie princess or something."

Connor's shocked expression made her turn away. "Rob didn't want you to know he had a way back. He thought it would upset you. And besides, things didn't turn out as he planned anyway."

"Things rarely turn out as we hope when it comes to the fae. Rob shouldn't have worried about us. I would not go back even if I could. My life and family are here." Connor reached for Kathy's hand. "Tell us about this bargain Rob entered into."

Erin accepted a glass of wine and launched into the tale, sharing all that had happened since the day Robley had fallen into her. By the time she was done, she'd consumed two glasses of the Merlot and felt the mellowing effects. "I even tried to use one of the diamonds to get back to him." She sighed. "It's pretty clear the entire thing was orchestrated by the damn faerie princess."

"Humph." Connor nodded.

Kathy leaned forward and placed her elbows on the table. "What do you intend to do now?"

"I'll go to school on Monday." Erin expelled a shaky sigh. "What else can I do but pick up the shreds of my life and continue on? There's no way to go back, and I don't even know if Rob is . . . if he's still . . ." She blinked against the sting in her eyes and tried to swallow the tightness clogging her throat. All she could do was shake her head. "I just needed to talk to someone. Thanks for letting me purge, but there's nothing to be done. I have a life to get back to, and that's all there is to this heartbreak."

"We're here for you." Kathy reached across the table and placed her hand over Erin's. "Connor and I understand, and whenever you need to talk, give us a call." She glanced at her husband. "In fact, I don't think you should be alone tonight. Why don't you stay in our guest room, and Connor will take you home after breakfast tomorrow morning? Sunday is waffle day around here." She rose from her place and picked up the empty wineglasses.

"Thank you for the offer, but I really want to go home." She had a Robley-scented T-shirt to snuggle with. She stood. "I hate to put you out. Are you OK to drive me home?"

"I am." Connor pushed his chair back. "I had but one glass of wine, and it takes far more than that to affect me. If home is where you wish to be, I'll take you there now."

Erin glanced at their kitchen clock. It was nearly midnight, and she was drained. "Thanks for listening, and for coming to get me. I really appreciate it." She slipped her jacket back on and followed Connor to his car. Settling herself in the front seat, she yawned. Time travel did take a toll, and she was exhausted and aching all over. All the emotions churning through her wore her out even more. "I'm sorry Robley didn't tell you about the deal he made and that he had a way back."

"Think nothing of it. Do you want the documents being made for him? I should be getting them in the next week or so."

"Sure. They're souvenirs of my brief marriage to a fifteenth-century Scottish Highlander." Her one and only marriage, that was certain. For the rest of the trip home, she stared out the car window at nothing. She'd throw herself into school, pick up as many nursing shifts as possible and keep herself busy until the pain of her broken heart dulled. What else could she do?

Erin shifted her school backpack to her left shoulder and stuck her key into the lock. Her first week back to her routine had been brutal, beginning with this morning's proof that she wasn't pregnant—another loss to grieve. A small part of her had wished for that forever link to Rob, and it sucked to find out she'd been denied even that comfort. The rational part of her knew it was for the best, but love wasn't rational.

She had just enough time to make herself something to eat before showering and changing into scrubs for the nursing shift she'd picked up for tonight. *Keep busy.* Her new mantra. Sighing, she dumped her stuff on the kitchen counter. She opened the freezer in search of something to tempt her nonexistent appetite. The phone began to ring just as she popped a frozen dinner into the microwave and pushed the start button. She snatched up the phone. "Hello?"

"Erin, it's Mom." Her mother's voice sounded shaky. "You got a minute?"

"Only a minute." Her heart wrenched. She knew what was coming. "Thirty seconds, actually. I'm working tonight." She had no sympathy to offer. Her own heartbreak still smarted.

"I'm leaving George," she said with a watery sniff.

"I'm sorry to hear it."

"Can I come stay with you until I get myself on my feet again?"

Erin stifled the rising groan. Her mother getting herself on her feet again meant finding stepdad number five. "Sure. You have a key."

She'd moved Robley's stuff to her bedroom. It made her feel more married, or like he was still in her life. Crazy, she knew, but it helped ease the grief. The microwave dinged. "I've got to go. We'll talk later."

"Thank you, baby. Don't know what I'd do without you."

"You'd manage, Mom. Give yourself some credit." Maybe this time she could talk some sense into her mother, get her to consider a few alternatives. "You know where everything is."

They said their good-byes, and Erin ate, got ready for work and left for the hospital. Funny. Her heart was broken, and instead of turning to her mother for comfort, she'd called Connor and Katherine. *OK. Not so funny. Mostly tragic.*

Her shift at the hospital had been an easy one, and it was still early enough for Erin to get a decent night's sleep. For that she was grateful. She pulled her car into her parking space, glancing at her mom's car in one of the guest spots. Hopefully Jane was already in bed. Erin was too tired to listen to her go on and on about how her soon-to-be ex-husband was the one at fault for yet another failed relationship.

She climbed the stairs to her apartment, thoughts of Robley filling her mind. How long would it take before the memories began to fade? Maybe she'd write it all down just so she could look back and remember. *A scrapbook!* Yes, she'd create a scrapbook. Thank goodness they had taken pictures with her iPhone. Unlocking her door, she heard the muffled sound of the TV from inside. "Drat," she muttered as she opened the door to the smell of cigarette smoke. "Hi, Mom. You can't smoke in here. This is a smoke-free building. It's in my lease."

"Oh. I thought that was just when you were here. Sorry." Her mom stubbed out her cigarette on a coffee saucer set on the table. "How was work?"

Erin surveyed her apartment, taking note of the dirty dishes filling the sink and her mother's clothing and shoes strewn about. Robley's bedroom might've been a mess, but when it came to the rest of the apartment, he'd always been thoughtful about cleaning up after himself. "Work was fine."

That's all the invitation her mom needed. She launched into her diatribe about all the wrongs done to her by her loser husband. Erin listened awhile before anger stiffened her spine. She had her own losses to deal with.

She studied her mom. Bleached-blond hair and puffy around the eyes, Jane looked older than her forty-four years, but she still dressed like she was in her twenties. Life hadn't been easy for her mother. Mostly due to her own bad decisions, but still, Erin could see that she'd been crying. She softened, and her anger dissolved. "Any chance you and George might reconcile?"

"I don't think so."

"Have you tried marriage counseling? You never know; it might help."

Jane gasped. "That's what I said, but he won't go. We never do anything together anymore. All he does is go to work, come home and sit in front of the TV, drinking beer." She swiped at a single tear making its way down her cheek. "He doesn't love me anymore."

"Did he say that?"

"No, but I can tell."

She wondered what George's side of this argument might sound like. She'd always liked the guy. "Why don't you go to school, Mom? Get some kind of training so you can make a decent living on your own. Stay single for a few years."

"What?" Jane reached for her pack of cigarettes. Glancing at Erin, she put them back down. "I can't afford to go to school, and besides, I'm too old for that now."

"No you're not. Lots of people who lost their jobs in this recession are back in school and starting over. Get into a program that only lasts for eighteen months, something in the medical field." She had the two diamonds to sell, plus she still had True's debit card. "I can loan you the money, and once you have a job, you can pay me back."

Her mother shrugged her shoulders as if disinterested and turned back to the TV, but Erin saw another tear follow the first. "Mom, you've been married and divorced five times. I've had four stepfathers. You can't keep looking for men to take care of you. At some point you have to start being responsible for yourself."

"What do you know about it?" her mother snapped. "You've never been in love. It's not like I set out to wreck my life because of some man. It just happens. Besides, I have a job. I'm a receptionist at—"

"I know plenty," Erin snapped back. "I just had my heart broken. I lost the only man I will ever love," she muttered under her breath.

"Really?" Her mother blinked at her. "Well, you'll get over it. I always do."

How like her mother to dismiss Erin's pain. Her hands fisted at her side, and her chest tightened.

Jane rose from her huddled place on the sofa. "I'll clean up here before I go to bed. I do appreciate your letting me stay with you, sweetie, and I promise—no more smoking in the building."

"Thanks."

"You know," she said, her voice hesitant, "your daddy was the love of my life. My biggest regret is that he and I didn't make it stick. We were just so young, only nineteen when you were born. All that responsibility was just too much for a couple of kids."

Erin's eyes widened. "Did Dad have any special abilities that you know of?"

"Hell yes." Her mother chuckled. "That man was the best lover I ever had. He knew what I wanted and how I wanted it without my ever having to say a word."

"Ew. TMI." Erin shot her mother a shocked look. Did that mean her dad had the ability to pick up on the physical reactions of others? "I'm beat." Erin stretched. "Will you at least think about school?"

"Sure, baby. I'll think about it." Her mom crossed the room and gave her a hug. "I'm proud of you. I'm so glad you're doing something with your life, and you aren't making the same mistakes I did."

"You are?" Her eyes filled. "This is the first time you've ever said that to me."

Her mom let go of her. "Maybe getting older is making me a little wiser."

"Things are going to work out," Erin told her. "I don't believe George has fallen out of love with you. Maybe he's going through something that has nothing to do with how he feels about you. Did you ever think about that?"

"Maybe. Whatever it is, he won't talk about it."

"Give it some time." She started down the hall. "Good night."

Sadness pressed painfully against Erin's heart for what she'd lost and for what she'd never have—a family of her own. Too much. It had all been too much. She thought about calling the McGladreys or Mark, just to talk to someone who'd known Robley. But she didn't want to encourage Mark. She was a MacKintosh, and MacKintosh women gave their hearts only once and for all time. Besides, she had a more pressing call to make.

She closed her bedroom door behind her and took her cell phone out of her purse. She had to search in her contacts for her dad's number. Her calls to him were so seldom she didn't have his number memorized. She touched the numbers and brought the phone to her ear.

"Hello?"

"Hi, Dad. It's Erin."

"Oh, hey. How're you doing, kiddo? It's kind of late. Is everything OK?"

"Yeah, everything is fine. I'm almost done with school, and I'm still picking up nursing shifts when I can. How are you and your family?"

"Good. Good." There was a long pause. "What is it, Erin? Something's bothering you."

"I have a few really weird questions." She bit her lip. "Genetic, family history type questions."

"Fire away. I'll answer if I can."

"Well, here goes. I've always had this ability to pick up on people's physical reactions to things. I can tell where my patients hurt and what they need in order to feel better. I can also ease their pain with my touch." She sucked in a breath and forged on. "Do you have any special abilities, or did you ever hear of anyone else on your side of the family tree who had . . . gifts like that?" Another long pause ensued. "You still there, Dad?"

"Yep. Just chewing on my answer before I spit it out." He sighed into the phone. "Yeah, I guess you could say I have what I've always called 'an edge.' I know what people want from me, and when I want to, I can use that to my advantage. It's why I'm so good at sales. Your great-granny, now . . . she was downright spooky. If anything happened to any of her children, she'd know about it long before word came to her. She'd get these spells where she'd know what was going to happen before it happened. Not that it did any of us any good, though. There weren't any lotteries back then." He chuckled.

"Any idea where it comes from?" she asked, and then held her breath.

"Granny always said it came with being Scottish. I don't think it comes from anywhere, kiddo. I think some of us are just born that way."

"I'm glad it's not just me."

"Me too, I guess. Granny told a few stories about the other odd apples on our family tree who had the gifts."

"Thanks. At least I know where I got it from now." Of course, he'd made no mention of faeries on that family tree, and neither would she. More than likely her dad had no idea faeries even existed. Until a certain fifteenth-century knight had plowed into her life, she'd had no idea either. They spent another few minutes getting caught up, and she listened to her dad tell her what all her half siblings were up to, making appropriate sounds of interest when necessary. "Are you interested in attending my graduation in December, Dad?"

"I'll try. Send me the info, kiddo, but you know what my schedule is like, especially around the holidays."

"Well, let me know and I'll reserve chairs for you and Cheryl."

"Will do. Good talking to you, Erin."

"You too." They hung up, and she held her phone in her lap for a while and stared at it. At least she could say for certain which side of the family tree her abilities had come from—not that it changed anything or did her any good. Her dad hadn't brought up faeries and neither had she. Probably not likely that her great-granny had brought up the subject either. If they did have fae genes, it would've happened so long ago that they'd have no way of knowing.

With a sigh, she set her cell on the end table. She got ready for bed, her mind drifting back to Robley. Her future had been all figured out before her fifteenth-century knight had charmed his way into her heart. No entanglements, focus on her career and help others—that had been the plan. Robley had turned everything topsy-turvy, and as a result, she'd become the walking wounded.

Erin stared at Rob's claymore, then at his plaid draped over the end of her bed. The wool also held his scent, and she planned to hold it to her face all night long. She picked up the swath of cloth, wadded it up in her arms and climbed under the covers. *Life sucks.*

Tomorrow she'd look into selling the diamonds. It had been her intention all along, but she hadn't given it much thought. Too much of her energy had been needed to deal with other things—like mourning. Selling them would solve her financial problems. All she had to do was figure out how to deal with the rest of her life.

Blinking against the sting in her eyes, she flipped off the lamp and let exhaustion take her away from the pain. Sleep sent dreams of Robley and brought her back to her happy place.

Erin walked across the auditorium stage to receive her diploma. The McGladrey family along with Mark and a few of her reenactment friends cheered for her. Even her mom had made it to her graduation. Warmth filled her heart. It had been a grueling couple of months, but she'd done it, finished her masters degree and reached her goal. She had her midwife certification and a job.

Funny. It didn't feel nearly as satisfying as she'd hoped it would. The piece of paper she'd been coveting so badly had been nothing but a filler for the things in her life that she lacked: loving and being loved by one man and a family of her own. Her career, though satisfying, was a poor substitute. She swallowed the lump rising in her throat and made her way across the stage. She returned to her seat with her diploma clutched to her chest and thoughts of Robley filling her mind.

Turning to happier thoughts, she glanced at her mom. Jane gave her a small wave, her face shining with pride. Erin smiled back. They had their differences, but they were both trying. She'd managed to sell the diamonds, and her mom had decided to give school a try, and that made Erin happy. Her mom and George were talking too, and things were way more hopeful on that front. Stepdad number four had been shaken out of his stupor by his wife's absence. He'd agreed to see his doctor for a complete physical and to begin couples' therapy. He also promised to stop drinking so much beer.

Once the graduation ceremony was over, she joined her friends, and they headed to the restaurant where she'd reserved a back room for the party she'd planned, including some of her fellow graduates, women she'd done clinicals with and knew well enough to invite—especially those whose families were out of town and couldn't make it. Everyone deserved to celebrate when they graduated, and she made sure they had the opportunity tonight.

Mark approached her, drinks in hand. "I got you a glass of wine," he said, smiling as he handed it to her. "Congratulations. I guess this means a lot of sleepless nights for you."

"Thanks." She accepted the glass and took a sip. "Lots of babies are born in the early morning hours, but I don't mind." She scanned the room. It was filling up fast, and servers were placing chafing dishes over flaming canisters. Plates, silverware and cloth napkins were set up at the end of the long buffet table. Linen-covered tables filled the room, and the open bar had been set up in a corner.

"Have you given any more thought to my offer?" Mark's face reddened. "You know how I feel about you."

He'd asked her out several times, and she'd even agreed to a couple dates, mostly when she needed to talk about Rob. They went to dinner once and out for coffee another time. He'd told her he really wanted to start something with her. She'd tried to muster up some enthusiasm, but it just wasn't there. "I think you are such a great guy. I wish circumstances were different, but—"

"It's OK. I don't want there to be any awkwardness between us." His warm brown eyes gazed into her hers. "Friends?"

"Always." Disappointment pulsed from him, and she searched the room. "You're going to meet someone special. I know you are. In fact, let me introduce you to a few single women right now." Taking his elbow, she led him to two of her acquaintances from school who stood chatting together. They were both attractive, really nice women, and she sensed Mark's heart rate ramp up. His interest surged. Smiling, she made the introductions and stayed long enough to ensure a conversation started. She left them just as the McGladreys entered the room. Her mom greeted them at the door, and Erin joined them.

Connor engulfed her in a bear hug. "Congratulations! We're so proud of you, lassie."

Gratitude filled her, and her eyes stung. "Thank you so much for being here tonight." Erin smiled at Katherine. "It means a lot to me that you came to my graduation. You've been so great these past few months, and I just want you to know how much I appreciate it."

"We wouldn't have missed your big night for anything," Katherine said, grinning back.

By the time Erin freed herself from Connor's hug, Meghan had already joined the line for the food. Erin pointed to the table with the "Reserved" placard in the center. "Mom, Katherine, that's our table. Go get something to eat and drink, and I'll join you as soon as I've greeted a few more people."

For the rest of the evening, she pasted a smile on her face and pretended to enjoy herself. Missing Robley hadn't lessened, and the hurt hadn't dulled. Her future stretched out before her like a deserted road. Her mom and the McGladreys said to give it time, that her grief would heal, but she didn't believe them. Something had been torn from her, the half that made her whole, and that kind of tear could *not* be mended. So she put on her "everything's OK" face and chatted, ate and drank.

Finally, the last guests left, and Erin settled the bill. "Are you ready to go, Mom?"

"I am now." Jane held several containers of leftovers from the buffet in two large bags. "I can't believe you were just going to leave all that good food to go to waste."

Her mouth quirked up. "I'm glad you thought to have them pack it up for us. We won't have to cook for a month."

"Never waste," Jane said, shaking her head. "You paid good money for that spread."

"My party turned out pretty well, don't you think?" Erin opened the door to the parking lot and held it for her mom.

"Oh, it was perfect. I like those McGladreys. They're good people." She sent her a sidelong glance. "That Mark fellow's not bad either. It's obvious he has a thing for you."

"I don't have any interest in him." She longed to blurt out that Connor McGladrey was from medieval Ireland. How would her mother take it if she told her that she'd married a fifteenth-century knight? What would Jane think if Erin told her she had no idea whether or not Robley had lived through their last encounter with the faeries?

Keeping everything to herself while living with her mother grew more and more difficult, but no way was she going to reveal how she'd been sent back in time to the Middle Ages where she'd married a man her mother would surely never meet. Even to her own ears that sounded crazy. Why rock the boat when she and her mother were finally growing close? No matter how much she wanted to pour out her heart to her mom, she couldn't bring herself to do it. Not yet anyway. Maybe someday she'd tell Jane that for a brief moment in time, she'd had an amazing son-in-law. Did she still? The familiar tightening rose to the back of her throat.

Not knowing whether Rob had lived or died twisted like a knife through her heart. The pain was as sharp and fresh as the day she'd been taken from his side. She blinked back the sting in her eyes and unlocked her car door. Her mom kept up a constant stream of chatter the rest of their drive home. Erin responded just enough to keep the one-sided conversation going. She couldn't face silence right now.

Once they'd packed the leftover meatballs, miniature quiches and the other goodies away in baggies and plastic containers, Erin started rearranging the freezer for room to stow the new stuff. The memory of Rob's first encounter with a bag of frozen peas came to her in a rush, and tears sprang to her eyes. "I gotta go to bed. Can you put the rest of this stuff away?"

"Sure, baby. You go on." Her mom put her arm around Erin's shoulders and gave her a brief hug. "It's been a big day. I'm sure you're exhausted."

She nodded. *Heartbroken too.* She made quick work of getting ready for bed and slid under the covers, Rob's plaid clutched to her chest. Once she turned off her bedside lamp, she let the tears fall until she fell into a dreamless sleep.

Erin woke with a start. The fine hairs on the back of her neck stood on end. Goose bumps skittered over her, and a shiver traced down her spine. Her pitch-dark room was cold enough to set her teeth chattering, and the smell of impending rain was so strong she could taste it on her tongue. Her heart beat out a staccato warning, and she could hardly breathe. She pushed herself up to sitting and turned her lamp back on, fully expecting to see one of the fae in her room.

No one was there. She bit her lip. Were the faeries spying on her now, making sure she stayed put? Already the temperature in her bedroom had risen a notch, and the scent of rain had begun to fade. She looked around her room. Nothing was out of place or missing. Glancing at her dresser, she gasped. An uncut diamond sat on top at the very edge—impossible to miss or ignore.

What did it mean? She leaped out of bed and raced to her dresser. Fear stayed her hand as she reached for the gem. Was this a message from Madame Giselle or Haldor? Were the faeries offering her a way back? It had to mean Robley had lived through the ordeal. Didn't it? Maybe not.

Her heart soared and plummeted almost as quickly, leaving her dizzy.

If Giselle had been in her room, it could be that the faerie princess simply felt she owed Erin and wanted to reward her for saving True's life. Maybe guilt had motivated the gift. If Haldor left it . . . Wait. Why would Haldor give a gnat's ass? He'd been the one to separate her from her husband in the first place. More than once he'd said time travel was against their laws. Yet there was something about his expression the first time he'd laid eyes on her that made her wonder. She frowned and stared at the crystal, trying like hell to decipher whatever message it might hold.

Did this new crystal possess the magic needed to send her back through time to Loch Moigh? Did she have the faith or the courage to take that journey not knowing whether or not Robley still lived? Life in the fifteenth century was filled with peril. Could she give up modern-day medicine, technology and creature comforts, knowing full well a single illness could snuff her life out in an instant—or Rob's? If he still lived, that is.

What if she went back and found Robley had lived, only to have him die an early death from tetanus, the plague or influenza? She'd go through this rending grief all over again without a way back to the comforts of her own time. *I don't know if I can face this kind of pain all over again.*

She had a career, friends, and what about her mother? For the first time in Erin's life, she felt as if the two of them were becoming close. Her insides quaked, and she twisted her fingers together, quelling the impulse to reach out and pick up the diamond. She was faced with one big fat unknown after another, and she had no clue what to do. She'd always been a survivor, a loner, goal-driven and focused on her career. Could she change that about herself, throw it all away for the sake of her love for Robley? Not without some kind of assurance he would be waiting for her on the other side, she couldn't.

"Damn those enigmatic, game-playing, manipulative faeries! Why not at least leave a note? Is a little bit of clarification just too damned much to ask?"

CHAPTER NINETEEN

Five months had passed since Erin had been taken from him, and still the wound in his heart bled like it had just happened. Five months since the faerie warrior had sent him back to Loch Moigh, when what he'd really wanted was to follow his wife—wherever she might go. The injustice burned through Robley from the inside out, and his only salvation was to throw himself into his role of seneschal for the clan. Constant physical and mental engagement were all that kept him from raging and tearing out his hair.

Robley shook off his morose thoughts as he stood in his uncle's solar and pointed to the crude map he'd drawn. "If we create a drainage ditch here, we can turn this hectare into productive land. Once that's done, we can settle another crofter or two into the area. Here"—he placed his finger on the map—"there is forest for swine to forage, and the hills to support sheep and kine." He glanced at his father and then at his uncle. "Do I have your permission?"

"Hmm." His father nodded.

Thanks to Erin, his father had recovered well. Speech took some effort and full concentration, but that was improving. His father now spoke with a slight slur, and he walked with a barely noticeable limp. Still, he worked daily, and though he tired more quickly than he once had, his input was still valuable. His father had much to teach him yet, and Robley was grateful for the guidance.

"There are men in the village wanting work," his uncle interjected. "We can begin the ditch anon and till the land yet this spring."

"Aye, 'tis what I'd hoped you'd say. I've workers ready to begin at a moment's notice." Rob took a seat at the table. "Once the fields are planted, we can build a cottage or two for the new crofters to set up housekeeping. The land will support two families at least. Our clan is growing, and we must think of their future needs."

"You've done well, but I fear you spend too much time working and no' enough time living." William sent him a pointed look. "Mayhap 'tis time you turn your mind toward finding a suitable bride and marrying once again. You'll want bairns of your own, a son to carry on in your stead, aye?"

"Nay." His chest tight, Rob plowed his fingers through his hair. "Betwixt Malcolm and Liam there are nephews enough to take my place. I'll be a doting uncle. 'Twill be enough, for I willna wed another."

"You're young yet." His father's expression clouded. "The pain in your heart will lessen with time, lad. Your mother and I canna bear the thought that you'll spend the rest of your days alone without the comfort of a wife by your side and bairns of your own."

"I have a wife." His throat closed, and his eyes stung. "She is no' dead, only far from me."

"Think you she will return?" William frowned at him.

"Nay. I willna have further dealings with the fae. They took what they wanted from us. 'Twas no fair bargain after all, and I willna seek them out for redress lest the result be even worse." Anger welled within him, and he fisted his hands by his sides. "I told Erin that once a MacKintosh gives his heart, 'tis given for life. I canna betray her. I willna betray my vows."

William rose from his place. "Mayhap you'll see things differently one day. In the meantime, you have my permission to see this project completed."

"My thanks." Once again he forced his thoughts from the pain eating away at him and broached another subject. "There is one more thing I wish to discuss before you take your leave, Uncle. Malcolm, Liam and I have been talking. We feel between the three keeps, we can support a priest in residence year round. I'd like to begin building a small kirk in the village with living quarters nearby. The priest can travel between Loch Moigh, Meikle Geddes and Rait, but his primary residence will be here." He glanced at his uncle.

"With your approval, I'll send our request yet this day. If all goes well, before the summer is through, we'll have our own parish, and the construction of our kirk will be well underway. Think of it, Uncle. Our clan will be able to attend mass, receive the sacraments and marry when they wish. We can have our bairns baptized in a timely manner. "

"See it done, Rob." William smiled. "If that is all, I'll take my leave. Malcolm awaits me in the great hall. We've a number of disputes to settle in the village."

"I'm finished." Rob rolled up the map as he rose from the table. "I'll head to the village with you. I wish to get the ditch begun while the weather holds."

"Stay a moment, Robley," his father said, gesturing to the chair. "I've something I wish to discuss with you."

A look passed between Rob's father and his uncle. William gave a slight nod before leaving. More puzzled than alarmed, Rob sat back down. "What is it you wish to discuss?"

His father shifted in his chair. "'Twill soon be May."

"Aye?" He nodded.

"You're doing a fine job, my lad. Our clan is in good hands, and William is well pleased."

"My thanks. I find the work suits me after all." Rob rose from his place again, impatient to begin his new project.

"Your mother and I intend to travel to France. We leave within a fortnight."

"Och, aye?" He sat back down, his brow raised. "Are ye certain 'tis wise?"

His father's mouth, the good side, quirked up. "If there's aught this malady has taught me, 'tis that life is fleeting. Your mother yearns to see her sister. We will stay a month at the marquis's keep near Flanders, visiting with her family. Then we'll travel to Paris and mayhap continue on to Spain."

"You've ne'er left for so long before." Rob frowned. "When do you intend to return?"

"Within the year. I'm retiring as seneschal and plan to pursue my own interests once your mother and I return."

Rob's eyes widened. "You have . . . interests?"

"Aye." His father chuckled. "I wish to oversee the breeding and training of horses and hunting dogs. 'Twould be another source of income, and I've always been interested in improving the lines of both. Erin said exercise and involvement are both important to my continued recovery and good health."

Rob's heart wrenched at the mention of her name. "She did, and you've proved her right."

"Go. Begin your project, lad. We'll talk more this eve."

"Where will you undertake this new venture, Father?"

"Meikle Geddes, of course. 'Tis our home, and the land is well suited to raising horses."

"I'll help however I'm able." Rob headed for the door, his mind spinning with this new twist.

"You'll have your hands full enough, I trow." His father chuckled again. "Overseeing the management of the entire earldom will take up all of your time, my lad. I speak from experience."

"'Tis my hope and my salvation," he muttered.

"Your lass is sorely missed by all." His father sighed. "Your mother and I grieve for your loss."

A lump formed in his throat. He nodded to his father and left for his chamber to change into garments more suitable for labor. He planned to lift a pick and shovel along with the villagers. Exhaustion gave him a small portion of relief. He'd tried drinking himself into a stupor when first he'd been sent back to Loch Moigh. Too much wine only added to his misery. Besides, the pounding head and sour stomach the day after made it difficult for him to do his job well. Nay, physical and mental endeavors were his only respite. As long as he was able, he intended to throw himself into the betterment of their holdings, and with his parents leaving for the continent, Rob would be needed even more.

As a youth, he and his brother had always traveled with their father as he oversaw the management of Inverness, Meikle Geddes and Loch Moigh. Rob would be the one making the rounds. The thought of journeying to Inverness sent a shudder of dread through him. Last he'd heard, the faerie's cottage was still deserted. Mayhap Giselle had left for good after her confrontation with her father. Rob could only hope, for he had no wish to ever see another faerie for as long as he lived.

He entered his chamber, and his eyes lit upon Erin's Harley jacket where it hung next to his on the pegs. Her satchel rested atop the small trunk where she kept her clothing. He had no heart for the task of disposing of her things. Having them near gave him comfort. Crossing the room to his trunk, he considered how he'd dig the ditch and what he and his men would need in the way of tools. He took out an old plaid and a shirt that was more rag than garment, rope for a belt and a worn-out pair of boots. He made quick work of changing, and then he headed to the great hall to break his fast.

Malcolm and William were already gone by the time Rob made his way to the table. True sat by herself before a bowl of porridge. "Good morn to you." Rob settled himself beside her and tore off a piece of dark bread. He placed a thick slab of ham atop it and took a bite. "Where are the bairns?"

"In the solar with their nursemaids, Lydia and your mother." She smiled. "They ordered me to have my morning meal unencumbered. It feels weird not to have one twin or the other in my arms, with Sky climbing onto my lap. How are you?" She glanced askance at his rough plaid.

"Well enough." He took another bite and waved toward the door. "I'm off to the village to assemble men for my latest project. We're digging a ditch this day."

Her gaze pierced him. "How are you really?"

He averted his gaze, and his heart wrenched. "No' a day goes by that I dinna miss my wife. Everyone says time will lessen the pain, but I dinna believe it is so," he answered, shrugging.

"I'm sorry. I feel as if I'm partly to blame. I should have stopped you from traveling to the future."

"Nay, lass. Your two lads are hale and hearty. We have Erin and the fae to thank for that, and for my father's recovery. As much as I detest the fae, I canna find it in me to regret the journey or the outcome." He wolfed down the rest of his meal and stood. "Give my niece and nephews a hug for me. I'll see you at the evening meal."

"Rob—"

"I do well enough and dinna wish to speak any more on the subject." God's blood, he needed to remove himself from all the pity aimed his way inside this keep. Once the ditch was completed, he'd travel to Meikle Geddes to stay for a month. "I've work to do."

He had no intention of waiting for the ferry to return from the mainland and took one of the many skiffs upturned along the shore.

Morning was fast waning, and he'd already wasted too much time. Setting a rapid pace, he rowed across the loch to the village and thought only of what needed to be done in the immediate future.

Once he'd secured the small boat, he set out for the stable to have a wagon hitched. Next he visited the inn and arranged for a meal to be brought out to the field, and finally he gathered the lads.

By midmorning, Rob was knee-deep in mud and positioned at the head of the line of men wielding pickaxes and shovels. His muscles strained with each load of earth he heaved, and he welcomed the fatigue sure to follow. Sweat covered his brow and chest from the exertion. Behind the lead, others arranged rocks along the sides of the newly formed ditch. He and the men aimed for the burn that ran at the bottom of a slight decline. The waterlogged fields would empty into the burn, and the land would be dry enough to plow by planting time.

Lads brought them ladles filled with water from a nearby spring, while others too young to dig gathered stones for the sides. Rob drove the edge of his shovel into the dirt and straightened. He stretched and surveyed the activity going on all around him. "Water," he called. The miller's son hurried over and offered him a wooden ladle filled to the rim. "My thanks." Rob took it and slaked his thirst.

"We're making good progress, milord," Kenneth, the strapping brother to their blacksmith, remarked.

"Aye, that we are." Mayhap after a full day's labor, he'd be able to sleep this night. He handed the ladle back and lifted his shovel, just as two tones sounded from the village horn.

"Who'd be coming home?" Kenneth wondered aloud. "Do ye know aught of any who be gone of late, milord?"

"Nay, but I expect we'll learn of it once the innkeeper's wife brings our midday meal. Until then, let us be about our task." He sank the edge of his shovel into the heavy, rocky soil and put his muscle into lifting the pile up and over the rim of their ditch. "If the rain holds, we'll be able to put in a full day." He glanced at the gathering clouds above. "Put your backs into it, lads, and hope for naught but mist," he called. To those nearest he said, "We'll dig only to yon pine. Then we'll help with the lining of what is done thus far. It will no' do to have our efforts washed away in a single rainfall."

A chorus of agreement echoed around him, and Rob set himself to his work. Mayhap someone from Meikle Geddes had arrived, or his brother Liam from Rait. Liam's visits had become more frequent once winter was behind them. He, Liam and Malcolm oft planned for their villages and clan late into the night when his brother came for a visit. Liam would depart the next day, eager to get home to his wife and their wee lad. Would Liam venture forth when Mairen was so close to birthing their second bairn? "Mayhap my brother sends word that Mairen gave birth. Last he was here, he did say it could happen any day."

"'Tis certain you are right, milord." Kenneth nodded, wiping the sweat from his eyes.

His muscles ached by the time the clatter of the approaching oxcart reached him, and hunger set his stomach rumbling. "Cease your labors," Rob shouted. "Our meal is come."

Friendly banter filled the air as the men climbed out of the ditch and laid down their tools. Rob did the same and followed the crowd to the burn to wash the mud from his arms and face. By the time he returned, the innkeeper's wife was handing out slices of beef, bread, cheese and dried apples.

"Yer wanted at the keep, milord," she said as he reached the front of the line.

"Do you ken who has come?"

"Nay. I've heard naught. I'd already set out when the horn sounded. A stable lad rode out to me and bade me deliver the message. That is all I ken." She shook her head and handed him his food.

"Humph." He frowned. Most likely word had arrived from Liam regarding the birth of Rob's newest niece or nephew. "My thanks." He filled his belly first, then gave instructions to the men before departing. The sky had darkened considerably, and he wanted the ditch lined with well-secured stone before the rain began. Robley wended his way through the groups of men resting and taking their meal. He informed his men he'd return by None if he could. If he didn't return, they were to put in a full day if the weather permitted.

Mounting his horse, he turned toward home, his curiosity piqued. The village was quiet, and the ferry gone. Whoever had arrived must have been delivered to the island, and the villagers must also be taking their noonday meal. Rob didn't wait for the ferry master's return. He brought his mount to the stable and handed the gelding off to a stable lad. His curiosity grew as he retraced his steps to the skiff he'd borrowed earlier, and he set off for the island.

Things were fairly quiet on the island as well, but that was not unusual. He strode from the ferry landing to the portcullis. Glancing up to the guards, he called to one of them, "Geoffrey, who is come?"

"I canna say." He shrugged. "The earl and Malcolm bundled someone through with great haste, but I caught nary a glance."

"No danger?"

"Nay, milord. None that we've heard of."

Rob made his way to the doors of the keep. If the arrival had not been important, why had he been called from his task? Irritated by the interruption, he scowled as he swung the doors open. The great hall was empty, and his mood darkened. Beth came around the corner from the back stairway. Her eyes went wide when his scowl turned her way.

"I was told my presence was required," he snapped. "Where is everyone?"

"Above stairs in your mother's solar, milord. You'll want to change first, aye?" She looked pointedly at the mud clinging to his plaid and his boots.

"Humph." He turned toward the stairs, taking them two at a time. It couldn't be one of their own if he was required to dress properly to receive them, could it? He froze outside his door. Someone was inside. The muffled sound of movement, of things being shuffled around came to him. His scowl deepened. Had someone sent a servant to clean—at the very time he was expected to make himself presentable? What the devil was going on?

Robley swung the door open wide and stomped inside, ready to dismiss whoever it was who'd meet his wrath. He lost his breath. His knees went weak, and he had to lean against the wall. Two large packs rested on his bed, and his wife busied herself with unpacking. She wore the same gown she'd had on the day he fell into her arms. "Tell me you are no' an apparition. Am I going mad with missing you?"

"Oh, Robley!" Her eyes filled.

The apparition threw herself into his arms. He crushed her to him, inhaling her beloved scent and drinking in the feel of her solid warmth against him. The pieces of his heart knit back together, and his insides filled with indescribable joy and relief. "How is this possible?" His hands shook as he framed her face between his palms and gazed into her eyes. He took inventory, comparing memory to reality. Aye, she hadn't changed one whit. "How are you here?"

"Can we discuss that later?" She blinked against the tears streaming down her face. "Would you just hold me for a few minutes? Being hurled through time with luggage is tough."

He glanced at the packs on their bed, and laughter seized him. "What have you brought with you, my love? Your entire apartment's contents?" Again he crushed her to him, seeking her mouth with his before she could answer. His body reacted immediately, as if finally home after a long and lonely journey. "I need you, lass. I need to feel your body against mine before I know this is real and not a dream." He let her go and raced across the chamber to remove the packs from their bed.

She frowned and pointed to his garments. "Have you taken a vow of poverty or something? Why are you dressed in rags and covered in mud?"

"I've been digging a ditch." He tore out of the filthy plaid and tossed it on the floor. Leaning over with his bare buttocks against their bed, he tugged off his muddy boots. Feminine laughter filled the room, sending his heart tumbling over itself. God's blood he'd missed the sound of his wife's laughter. He took it in, letting the sound fill his heart and soul. Tears sprang to his eyes, and he grinned so hard his cheeks ached with the force of his happiness. "Come here to me, *mo céile.*"

"Impatient much?" She stepped closer and began to undo the laces of her gown.

Robley straightened, shaking his head. The tears spilled from his eyes, and he did naught to stop them. "My sweet wife, 'tis no' impatience that drives me but the need to prove that you are real." His voice broke, and he cleared his throat. "I have need of you—I must have you in my arms, or I fear I will wake, and this will all have been but a dream. I will no' survive your loss yet again. I willna."

Her gown dropped to the floor just before she launched herself into his arms. He kissed her, tangling his fingers in her glorious hair. With fumbling fingers he helped her out of the rest of her garments. Tenderly he scooped her into his arms and laid her upon the mattress. Feasting upon the sight of her, his eyes roamed over every precious dimple and curve. His hands still shook, but he could not keep from touching her. "Your skin is warm and silken. Is this a memory, or are you real?" He took a moment to pull off his ragged shirt before lying down beside her.

"I'm real." Erin reached for him, drawing him into her embrace. "I'm here for good, and I need you too. You have no idea how much I've missed you. It never entered my mind that I'd be able to return. I didn't even know whether or not you were still alive." She planted kisses all over his face. "I love you. For as long as I live, I will always love you."

"As I love you. I would hear how this all came about, but no' now."

Robley made love to his wife, reacquainting himself with every delectable inch of her in the process. Long after they were both spent, he held her close. Stroking her back, over the swell of her hips and the roundness of her sweet derriere, he sighed with contentment. Her hands did the same, running over his chest, his shoulders and down his arms.

"It's good to be home," she whispered against his chest.

"Never leave me again." He pulled her into his arms and held her tight.

"I won't. I promise."

"How did you find your way back?"

She blew out a long breath. "It's an interesting story and a mystery. I want to tell it to our whole family at once."

He squeezed her again. Without thought she'd referred to his family as hers. 'Twas final proof that she belonged here with him, and his faith in the future was finally restored. "Let's start a family of our own."

"OK." She sat up, her eyes glowing with love. "But can we gather the forces first, so I can explain everything just once? Then I want to start the inoculations."

"The what?" He frowned, taking in her love-tousled appearance. By the Virgin, he'd sorely missed the sight. Her lips were swollen from his kisses, her hair mussed and her skin rosy from their lovemaking. She enchanted him.

"I intend to vaccinate you all against the most common illnesses that are killers in your time, like tetanus, diphtheria, measles and mumps, especially the children. Katherine McGladrey helped me put together everything I needed. It's all there in my packs." Erin climbed over him to get out of bed, and he got an enticing eyeful of her breasts.

"Get dressed, Rob. We'll have the rest of the evening to ourselves, but right now I'm eager to see everyone. I've missed you all so much."

"As usual, I understood but a small portion of what you just said." Grinning, he too left the warm cocoon of their marriage bed. "But if you wish it, we'll spend the rest of the afternoon with our kin."

A half hour later, he and Erin were ensconced within the bosom of his family in his aunt's solar, sans the children. Rob couldn't keep from touching Erin, and he held her hand in his as she told the tale of the diamond's appearance on her dresser.

"I didn't know what it meant, but I suspected that if it could be used to get me back here, it had to mean Robley had lived through our confrontation with the fae. Before I decided to see if the diamond held power, I had a long talk with my mom." Erin's eyes clouded. "I told her how Robley had come to the future and how I went to the past." She leaned closer to him. "I told her she had a son-in-law, and that if I could, I'd go back to him. She didn't believe a word I said." Her mouth drew down. "Mom had been living with me for a while, because she and her husband were going through some difficulties."

Puzzled looks passed across his family's faces. They didn't handle troubles by separating. The very concept made no sense to them. He put his arm around Erin's shoulders and drew her close. "Go on, love."

"Well, I sold the other diamonds, which gave me enough money to see that my mom would be OK. She started school to become a medical assistant, and she and her husband are in counseling together. I believe they're going to be fine." She glanced at him as if needing reassurance.

"For certes." He gave her a squeeze. "Who do you think left the third diamond in your room?"

"I don't know."

"Giselle, most likely," True offered. "She may have intended for you to stay all along, but when her father and Haldor appeared, there really wasn't much she could do."

"Maybe, but I can't shake the feeling that there's more to Haldor than meets the eye. I keep flashing back to the way he seemed so surprised when he saw me." Erin nudged him. "And he didn't kill you."

"We'll never ken for sure where the gift came from." Malcolm shrugged. "Suffice it to say we are all relieved and overjoyed to have you back, Erin."

"Aye." His uncle William nodded. "Let us have no more dealings with the fae, if you please."

"I'm more than happy to comply with that request." Erin huffed out a breath. "Here's to no more faerie drama."

"What of these inoculations you spoke of?" Rob asked.

"Oh, right." Erin glanced at True. "I brought vaccinations."

"You did?" True's eyes lit up. "Oh my God, thank you. Do you have any idea how much I worry about my babies catching something fatal?"

"I also brought a plethora of antibiotics, though they will eventually expire. The time continuum be damned. We'll do whatever we can to protect our clan, right?" Erin's chin lifted. "Tomorrow morning I want all of you here. I even managed to get the smallpox vaccine, even though the disease has pretty much been wiped out in the United States. Also, I now have proper surgical tools." She smiled at Rob. "And a dowry. I bought gold ingots with some of the money I got for the diamonds."

He rubbed her back. "You've been busy preparing for your journey home, lass. We're all grateful."

"Yes, I have been busy. I finished school too. I'm now a certified midwife."

He chuckled low in his throat. "I'm proud of you, love, and so very glad to have you home." He stood and pulled her up with him.

"I hope you will all understand, I wish to have time alone with my wife."

"Of course," his uncle William said. "We'll see you in the morn for our . . . Humph. I dinna ken what you spoke of, but we'll be here for it nonetheless."

Robley and Erin took their leave and walked arm-in-arm back to their chamber. Peace and a bone-deep happiness filled him to the brim.

"Did you notice I brought your claymore back?"

"Did you? Nay, I did no' notice, being so taken with everything else. My thanks. I'm quite partial to that weapon." They reached their chamber, and he opened the door for her to precede him.

"I also brought you a gift." Her tone turned shy.

His brow furrowed. "You've no need for a dowry, or to bring me gifts, *mo anam*. You have my undying love and fidelity without such."

She sighed. "I know, but this was important to me." She crossed the room to her trunk and opened it.

Curious, he followed, crossing his arms in front of him.

She drew out a wee box and handed it to him. Robley opened it. Inside, encased in velvet, rested two matching gold bands decorated with Celtic knots.

"I know it's silly, but I wanted wedding rings." She looked up at him through her lashes. "What do you think?"

"They're grand." His heart melted, and a wave of tenderness nearly brought him to his knees. He took the rings out and studied them. Tossing the box back into the trunk, he turned his full attention to his one and only love. "Let me put this wedding ring on you, lass." He slid the smaller band onto her left ring finger. It fit perfectly.

"Give me yours." She held out her hand. "I had to guess on the size. I hope it fits."

"If it does no', the blacksmith can adjust it. He's a fair hand at such things."

"Hold out your left hand, Robley," she commanded.

He did as she bid him.

"With this ring, I thee wed," she whispered and slid the ring onto his finger. She sucked in a breath. "It fits!"

"Of course it does. 'Twas meant to be, lass." He put his arms around her and drew her close. "After all is said and done, it seems I made the best bargain after all."

EPILOGUE

"Congratulations! You have a beautiful baby boy." Erin placed the squalling newborn on Alma's stomach. Tears of joy filled her patient's eyes, and her own. "He's healthy, and he has a good set of lungs."

"He's perfect." Alma stared lovingly at her son. "We owe you a great debt, milady."

"You don't owe me anything. I'm happy for you and Roderick. Hopefully this little man is the first of many bairns to come." Erin turned to her young apprentice. "Mabel, I want you to cut the umbilical cord and deliver the afterbirth. Then you must bathe the newborn and swaddle him."

Mabel's eyes lit with excitement. She moved close and accepted the scalpel from Erin. "My thanks, milady."

Erin stood and stretched, placing her hands at the small of her back. Her own growing baby bump added strain to the positions she took while delivering. Once she found out for sure that she and Robley were expecting, she finally agreed to take on an apprentice. Mabel, one of the miller's many daughters, proved to be very adept and eager to learn. "You don't mind if Mabel takes care of things, do you, Etan?" She turned to the older woman who sat at the head of the bed, admiring her new grandson. Erin nodded toward the door. "I figured you'd want to go get the new father and grandfather. While you're at the inn, please let my husband know I'm ready to head home whenever he is."

Robley always accompanied her on the late-night births. She suspected he feared a faerie would snatch her away from him again if he wasn't nearby. He insisted it was only because he couldn't sleep without her anyway, so he may as well see to her safety himself.

"Och, aye! I'll go fetch the menfolk anon." Etan leaped up from her stool and clasped Erin's hands in hers. "Thank ye, milady. If it weren't for ye, we'd ne'er ha' seen this joyous day."

"I'm just glad I could help." Erin grinned.

Etan hurried out the door and headed across the street to the inn where the men awaited news. Once Erin had returned to Loch Moigh and the fifteenth century, she'd given Alma and Roderick a course of antibiotics known to be effective against *Streptococcus*. Maybe True's tea had worked, or maybe it was the twenty-first-century medicine. It didn't really matter, so long as this happy day was the outcome.

She gathered her things. "I'll stop by tomorrow to check on you and the baby." Alma already had the newborn to her breast. "You'll be all right without me, Mabel?"

"Aye. I ken what tae look for."

She'd already cut the cord, and Erin handed her the embroidery silk to tie it off.

"Push once more, Alma. We've yet tae see the afterbirth," Mabel instructed. Her apprentice did her job efficiently, and began cleaning.

Mabel spared her a glance. "Go to yer rest, milady. I'll take care of everything here. On the morrow, I'll bring yer wee satchel back tae the clinic."

"I know you'll take care of everything. You're doing a wonderful job." She grinned and pulled her warm cloak around her shoulders just as the men burst through the door. Robley stood outside, patiently waiting as Roderick and Thomas thanked her.

Erin stepped out into the crisp autumn evening and drew in a deep breath. "I'm beat. Should we stay at the inn, or do you want to return to the island?"

"The moon is full to light our way, love. Let's go home." He took her hand and led her toward the shore. "After an evening spent with an anxious father-to-be, I long for the peace and comfort of our own chamber."

"Roderick had reasons enough for his anxiety. Do you remember what happened the last time?"

"I do, and 'tis surely a blessing that we have you to care for us all." He raised her hand and kissed the back of it. "Though I'd prefer no' to be inoculated ever again."

She laughed. "Who knew such a brave and worthy knight would swoon at the sight of a few tiny needles?"

"Humph." He helped her into the skiff and pushed it into the water before jumping in and settling himself at the oars. "They were no' *tiny.*"

She yawned and gazed over the lake reflecting the full moon's light. "Beautiful."

"Aye, you are."

"I was speaking about the view."

He winked at her. "As was I."

Grinning, she drew her cloak tighter. Soon Robley was dragging the dinghy onto the sandy beach on the island. He helped her disembark, and then he turned the boat over. They made their way to the keep in companionable silence. She couldn't wait to fall into bed. "Don't wake me when you get up. I want to sleep in."

"If it pleases you." He led her to the postern gate, which had been left unlocked for their return.

She climbed the back stairs with a single candle held high to light their way and reached their door with her husband right behind her. The moment she opened the door, Erin was assaulted by a wave of cold air and the scent of rain. "Oh, crap." She stepped back, and the candle she held went out. Her heart thundered, and she was instantly on full alert, all her fatigue forgotten. A shiver of dread wracked her. "Do you smell that?"

"Och, aye." Rob scowled and drew his claymore. "What now?"

"I don't know, but I don't want to go in there." She clutched his arm. "Let's go sleep in the room where I used to stay."

"Nay, lass." He shoved her behind him. "Stay here until I call for you."

"Don't go in there!" She grabbed his arm again.

He leaned his sword against the wall and reached for one of the unlit torches from the hall sconces. He thrust the torch at her, forcing her to let go of him. "Hold this while I light it."

Groaning, she took it and held the oil-soaked end out to him as he struck the flint and steel together. The torch burst into flame, and Rob took it from her hand and lit the candle she still held.

"Stay," he commanded, putting his flint and steel back in his sporran. He took up his sword and moved silently into their chamber.

Her heart in her throat, she bit her lip and waited as he disappeared inside. Torchlight from inside the room sent shadows flickering into the hall, and she strained to hear what was going on inside. Seconds turned to an eternity before he called her name. Relief swamped her, and on trembling legs she entered their chamber.

Rob crouched by the hearth and lit the fire that had been laid for them. Candles burned where they stood on the mantel and on the table, and he'd set the torch in a bracket on the wall. "You've a letter, *mo céile*, and a scroll."

"Gah!" She wrung her hands together. "What do the fae want now?"

"I canna say. 'Tis addressed to you." He pointed. "You'll find both there on the table."

The sound of her racing heart buzzed in her ears, and her palms began to sweat. She wiped them on her gown and inched her way over to the table. Maybe she should throw the letter and rolled parchment into the flames Robley had just lit. She stared at the table. Both items that had been left for her had been sealed with wax imprinted with a crest, and her name was written in a flourishing scrawl on the letter. "What should I do?" Her gaze flew to her husband.

"Open it, I suspect. Bring it here and sit in my lap. We'll read it together." He reached out for her. "It willna bite, lass. If the sender meant you harm, the harm would already have befallen us."

"You're right." She relaxed a fraction. "Of course you're right," she repeated, reassuring herself. Carefully she lifted the letter and crossed the floor to the safety of her husband's waiting arms. She handed the message to him. "You open it."

"I canna. I tried, lass." He shot her a wry grin. "'Tis warded."

"Bummer." She glared at the letter still in her hands. "Well, here goes." She held her breath, lifted the sealing wax and opened the folded parchment.

Robley peered over her shoulder. "I see naught but a blank page."

"Really? Hmm. I'll read it out loud then."

My Dear Erin:
First and foremost, we are not "enigmatic, game-playing, manipulative faeries." We are Tuatha Dé Danann, *children of the goddess Danu, and you, child, are of my line. We are demigods, and were once revered as such by mortals throughout Eire, Scotia and Northumbria. Many eons ago, I took a mortal to wife. She was a Durie, and I recognized you as my kin from the very start. I regret the circumstances under which I found you, but I cannot regret that you are found. You look so very much like her. Lo, I have missed my love for so long! I could not reveal you to my king, nor could I send you back to*

your mate. The best I could do for you both was to give you the means to return and place the decision in your hands. Know that I will look after you and yours. Should you need my help, call to me and I will come to your aid. Kin is everything, my dear girl. I wish you happiness, and I am well pleased by the choice you have made.

    Yours,
    Haldor

"Wow. I suspected the diamond came from Haldor. I felt the link when he looked at me in my apartment, but I didn't know what it meant." She folded the letter. "You couldn't see any of that?"

"Nay. 'Twas meant for your eyes alone." Rob hugged her close. "Do you wish to look at the scroll?"

"Do you think I should? Didn't we swear off the"—she glanced around the room—"children of the goddess Danu?"

"He's your kin and will keep you safe. That puts my heart at ease."

"OK." She rose from her place on his lap and crossed to the table. She set down the letter and opened the scroll. Laying it flat on the table, she gasped. Ornately illustrated with deep reds, greens and golds, it was a family tree. "Come see if this is visible to you, Rob."

He came up behind her and put his arm around her waist. "Och, lass. That I can see. 'Tis your lineage, your patents."

Erin traced her finger from the top, where the goddess Danu's name presided over all. She followed Haldor's line all the way to her own father, and then to her. "Why is our clan so tangled up with the children of Danu? Did it start with True?"

"Nay. The tie began with Hunter, and as to why, I believe the link to our clan began by chance."

She sighed. "I don't want to think about this now. All I want is to go to bed with my husband's arms around me. I always feel safe when I'm in your arms."

"As you wish, my lady." He bowed. "I believe that scroll proves you are above me in rank. After all, you are descended from Danu."

"Other than the circumstances of my birth somehow leading me to you, the tie doesn't mean a whole lot to me." She brushed a kiss against his mouth.

"Aye, and for that alone I am eternally grateful." He helped her out of her clothes and tucked her under the blankets before snuffing out the candles. "Dinna forget that because of your ancestry, you are gifted in ways that will help our clan." Robley undressed and slid under the covers to draw her into his arms.

"True. I'm glad for that." Just then her baby turned, and she sensed their growing link. Somehow, she knew her son was smiling. The sound of Haldor's laughter echoed through their chamber, and the slight scent of rain haunted her senses. "Did you hear that?" Erin propped herself up on her elbows.

"Aye, but I'd prefer to pretend otherwise." Robley drew her back down. "In-laws," he huffed. "I would prefer those of a mortal bent, but as long as I ken Haldor will see to your safety, I can tolerate his presence." He wrapped his arms around her. "From a distance, that is," he called out into the darkness.

Once again the sound of laughter resounded, fading as if her ancestor were moving away from them. "So be it." Erin sighed, stretched and snuggled up against Robley's warmth, content to be home for good.

Read on for a sneak peek of Barbara Longley's next novel of Loch Moigh.

Available 2015 on Amazon.com

THE HIGHLANDER'S FOLLY

"Hunter! How fortuitous that our paths should meet thus. Long have I yearned to lay eyes upon you." The old crone's dark eyes gleamed, and a cunning smile lit her wrinkled face.

Hunter's blood rushed through his veins. His ears rang, and sweat beaded his brow. "Madame Giselle." He made her a slight bow. "I suspect luck had no part in our meeting this day." She cackled as he dismounted, and trepidation sluiced through him. Hunter tied Doireann's reins to a low-hanging pine bough and turned to face her. Masking his expression, he did his best to hide the fear and revulsion her presence elicited.

He wanted no part of the unnatural association he had with the fae. Gladly would he give up the gifts bestowed upon him if it meant severing the ties of kinship that bound them.

"You have naught to fear from me, grandson."

Was that hurt he spied flashing through her eyes? He'd gotten his abilities to read others from her. Surely she'd be aware of everything he felt and thought.

"Come in." She beckoned with a gesture and preceded him into the tent. "I wish only to spend a bit of time with you." She cast him

a glance over her shoulder. "Mayhap I'll tell your fortune whilst you're here."

"Nay." He ducked to enter, his glance darting around the interior. A trunk sat to one side, and rushes covered the hard-packed ground. In the center, a roughly hewn table and two chairs had been set. A teapot and two mugs next to a deck of cards drew his attention. "I dinna need you to tell my fortune or my future, Madame Giselle. By my will alone do I forge my future, and by my sweat and blood do I earn my fortune." She cackled again, and his muscles tensed for flight.

"By whose blood? Thanks to me, none can touch you with mere weapons of steel." She took a seat at the table. "Are you so certain of what the future holds for you, my lad?"

"Aye."

"Mayhap the path you've laid for yourself leads you astray." She shrugged. "'Tis possible fate has other plans in store for you."

"I am a knight, and I have made a vow which I intend to keep. Indeed, everything that I have worked toward these five years past has to do with keeping that promise." In fact, he'd spent the whole of his life attempting to live up to the faith and expectations placed upon him by his foster family and clan. Their approval and high esteem meant everything to him. He owed them his life and his loyalty.

"I ken your true identity and what you are." He remained standing, his posture rigid. "I suspect you are aware of the intentions I made clear the day Sky Elizabeth was born. Think you to alter my path or to induce me to renege?" He raised an eyebrow and sent her a pointed look. "I willna. What is it you want from me this day?"

"Aye. I'm well aware of the vow you made as a mere lad of five years. Sit." She gestured to the chair across from hers. "Have some tea. You are my kin." She canted her head and studied him. "Is it so beyond the realm of possibility that I wish only to spend a bit of time in your company? I have not seen you for far too long . . .

in the flesh, anyway. The *Tuatha* have hearts not unlike those of mortals. We too bear affection for our progeny, whether they accept it or not."

His eyes widened, and a sliver of guilt wedged its way into his heart. He had intended to thank her for saving his life, and he'd done naught but posture defensively. "My apologies if I have offended you. For certes I have you to thank for my life, and I am grateful." He bowed to her again and sat down.

"Hmm." Her eyes filled with a triumphant glint, and her face creased with amusement. "Then you will not be averse to doing me a small favor in return?"

"Och!" He plowed his fingers through his hair, his position suddenly untenable. "I am no match for you, Madame Giselle. What is it you wish of me?" Apprehension sent his heart racing again.

"Restore balance." She shrugged. "Make right a wrong of old."

"Is that all," he bit out in a dry tone.

She laughed, only this time the sound was less a cackle and more melodious. Tiny bumps raised upon his flesh. "If you please, dinna shift your appearance. I canna abide your true mien. I will admit I fear you in your fae form. 'Tis no' of this world." Hunter said.

"As you wish, my lad." Her smile softened. "I do not want you to fear me. I wish only the best for you, and I hope one day you will see the veracity of that for yourself." Her expression turned inward as she scrutinized him. "You are so like him—so much like the mortal man I wed. It does my heart good to look upon you."

He squirmed in his chair and gripped his mug with both hands. "The favor?"

"Ah, yes." Her gaze sharpened. "'Tis a small thing, really."

Frustration overwhelmed him. For certes this favor would delay his homecoming or inconvenience him greatly in some unforeseen way. God's blood, he hoped it did not involve time travel! Too well he kent the havoc 'twould wreak upon his well-laid plans. His entire being rebelled at the thought, and mortification burned a path through his very soul. He had been so easily manipulated, and now he was truly caught up in her machinations. "What must I do to make right this wrong that in no way involved myself in its inception?"

"Ha!" She shook with mirth. "Trust your instincts, Hunter, and leave the rest to me."

"I dinna wish to leave my time, madam. Do I have your assurance that this *favor* involves the present, and no' some distant future or past?"

"Grandson, you must learn to give up your false sense of control. Your fate, no matter how you will it otherwise, is already written in the stars by another's hand." She rose from her place and pointed toward the rear flap of her tent. "Go now, and have faith. You are my kin. You will always hold my deepest affection."

May the saints preserve me! He didn't want her *affection.* Hadn't he learned long ago the trouble such affection had caused his kin— both MacKintosh and MacConnell? He clung to the notion, no matter how false Giselle deemed it, that he did indeed control the course of his life. Hadn't he proved it these five years past? He rose, and a sickening dizziness overtook him. Pressure assaulted him from all sides, pulling and pushing all at the same time. "Nay! Dinna send me—"

"This way."

Giselle shoved him through the rear door of her tent into a rending vortex so powerful he feared he would not survive. For certes he would be torn to bits! God's blood, the pain was enough to make him weep. Trapped in the center of the forces hurtling him forward, all he could do was grit his teeth and pray.

Just when he thought he could not bear another second, whatever held him spat him out, and he landed with a thud. Prostrate on the ground with the tent still at his back, Hunter shook his head in an attempt to free himself of the disorienting dizziness that held him in its grip.

The sound of steel upon steel fell upon him where he lay. *God's blood!* He'd landed in the midst of a battle! He raised his head, shock and the will to survive restoring his wits in a rush. Spectators ringed the combatants, booing and cheering them on. Some were dressed like he was, and others wore garments not unlike those Lady True wore when hunting. As he regained his feet, Hunter glanced toward the combatants. His vision went red with rage.

A large knight attacked a younger knight half his size and less than half his weight. Still, the lad acquitted himself well against the brute. He must have just earned his spurs, because he could not be more than ten and seven or eight years. Hunter straightened just as the youth tripped over an exposed tree root and fell flat on his back. The larger knight gave a shout of glee and moved in for the kill.

"Nay," Hunter shouted as instinct took over. With a battle cry, he drew his claymore and lunged forward, blocking the blow meant for the lad. Straddling the youth where he lay on the ground, Hunter engaged the blackguard. "Coward! Knave!" In a flurry of strikes, he beat the man back. "If you wish for a fight, let me accommodate you."

"Who are you?" The knight parried his blows with ease. "What the hell do you think you're doing?"

"Upholding my vow to protect those weaker than myself, as you ought." The familiar sense of anticipation flowed between the knight and him, and he blocked the blows coming at him.

"Wait!" The youth clambered back and leaped to his feet. "Stop!"

But it was too late. He was in the throes of battle lust, and he had no cause to cease that he could see. Hunter attacked, slicing through the knight's chain mail to draw first blood, leaving a gash across the man's shoulder. His opponent hissed in pain and faltered. Hunter took advantage, sending the man's sword flying out of reach.

Screams erupted from the crowd. Men bearing arms surged forward. Hunter gripped the lad's wrist and dashed toward Giselle's tent. He tossed his charge through the entrance first and dove in after him.

Giselle stood by the tent's opposite exit. "Hurry! Through here." She held the flap aside.

The young knight struggled to get past him. Once again Hunter gripped his wrist. "That way is no' safe, ye wee fool."

He struggled to free himself from Hunter's grip. "You don't understand. Let me go!"

"Be off," Giselle commanded. "Go before they come through after you."

Hunter's gaze went between the panicked face of the lad and Giselle's imploring look. Indecision seized him. "Call 911!" The roaring shouts grew closer. "Stop him! Get him!"

The sounds of pursuit spurred him to act. Grabbing the lad around his waist, he dashed through the tent's front opening. Once again the debilitating force took hold, hurling them both through a bone-crushing tunnel that tore at his limbs and propelled them forward. The ground rushed up to meet them, and the lad let out a cry as they came to a sudden and painful halt.

"We must be away," he shouted, pushing himself to his feet. He helped the youth up and lifted him atop his mount. Hunter snatched Doireann's reins from the tree and swung up behind his ward. Spurring his destrier into a full gallop, he wended his way through the wagons, booths and tables, heading toward the hills as if chased by the devil himself.

He topped the first rise and urged his horse onward to the bridge across the Esk. They raced over the cobbles, Doireann's steel-shod hooves raising a thunderous clatter. Finally they were upon the slope of the hill where his men awaited him on the other side.

"You moron!" The lad wriggled as if he meant to leap from the horse's back in mid-gallop.

"Moron?" He encircled the fool's waist, lest he injure himself trying to get free. "I just saved your life."

"No you didn't." He tried to pry free of Hunter's hold. "I didn't need saving."

About the same time the swell of breasts atop his forearm registered, along with the slender curve of a feminine waist where it met the slight flare of hips, the cap upon his captive's head blew off in the wind. A wealth of silken auburn tresses cascaded down across his chest and arms, and a sweet floral scent filled his nose.

He was a she.

"Bloody hell!" That made the attack against her even more foul. He checked over his shoulder for any signs of pursuit and saw none. Hunter reined his horse to a stop.

She turned to glare daggers at him. "Take me back."

Now that he got a closer look at *her*, he wondered how he could have mistaken those comely features for that of a lad. She had wide-set dark-brown eyes, framed in thick lashes. A sprinkle of freckles covered the bridge of her finely wrought nose and cheeks. Her mouth—wide with full, ripe lips—drew into a straight line of displeasure at his perusal.

He stared, disconcerted. "I saved your life. You wish to be returned to the cur who attacked you?" He scowled, taking his arm from around her waist. "Why are you dressed as a knight? You've no business wearing chain mail or spurs. None. What manner of lass are you to wield a broadsword thus?" He dismounted, reaching up to help her down.

She batted his hands away, swung her leg over his mount's back and slid free to land lightly upon her feet. "How is anything about me your business?" She widened her stance and crossed her arms in front of her. "Take me back where you found me right now, or you *will* regret it."

He already regretted it. "Think you to threaten me?" He grunted and pointed at his chest. "I am a blooded knight and undefeated in battle. What harm can a wee lass do to me? You've no right to carry a broadsword, much less to wield it. No. Right. Do ye no' ken 'tis a crime to impersonate a knight of the realm? You should be—"

She let out a growl of frustration and whipped around so fast she became a blur. Her booted foot connected with the center of his chest, sending him reeling back. Before he could regain his balance, she crouched low and swung her leg behind his heels to trip him. He went sprawling.

Bloody hell! Somehow she'd managed to wrest the dirk from his belt in the process. With her boot once again planted firmly upon his chest, she pressed the point of *his* dagger against his throat. He seethed. Humiliation and anger fought for dominance within him.

"No *mere* woman can defeat a big, strong knight such as yourself, eh?" Her brown eyes flashed. "Well, score one for the wee lassie."

ACKNOWLEDGMENTS

I want to thank the wonderful folks at Montlake Romance for giving this trilogy a home, and especially JoVon Sotak and Jessica Poore for their support and enthusiasm. I also want to thank Nalini Akolekar, my wonderful agent. I so appreciate having you in my corner. I want to give a nod to Midwest Fiction Writers and Romance Writers of America. If it had not been for these organizations, I wouldn't have had the opportunities I've had. Nothing compares to being in the company of other writers!

ABOUT THE AUTHOR

As a child, Barbara Longley moved frequently, learning early on how to entertain herself with stories. Adulthood didn't tame her peripatetic ways: she has lived on an Appalachian commune, taught on an Indian reservation, and traveled the country from coast to coast. After having children of her own, she decided to try staying put, choosing Minnesota as her home. By day, she puts her masters degree in special education to use while teaching elementary school. By night, she explores all things mythical, paranormal and newsworthy, channeling what she learns into her writing.

Ms. Longley loves to hear from readers and can be reached through her website, www.barbaralongley.com, Twitter @barbaralongley or on Facebook, www.facebook.com/barlongley.